SWEEPER

A SPORTS ROMANCE NOVEL

AMY DAWS

Published by: Amy Daws, LLC
ISBN 13 paperback: 978-1-944565-40-4

Proofing: Julia Griffis & Lydia Rella
Editing: Jenny Sims with Editing4Indies
Formatting: Champagne Book Design
Cover Design: Amy Daws

SWEEPER

PROLOGUE

Football Over Bullshit

Zander

"Zander!" my teammate Jude McAllister's British accent barks from somewhere in the locker room. "Where are you, mate?"

"Back here!" I yell from my cubby while stuffing muddy socks and shin guards into the club hamper. Fuck, that set needs to be washed. Or better yet, incinerated. Playing soccer in Seattle is always wet and muddy, but today's game was next-level soaked.

And sadly, the stench of my gear is affecting the enjoyment of my mom's oatmeal raisin cookie. Before game days, my mom mails me an oatmeal raisin cookie. And I only eat it if we win. If we lose, it goes in the trash. And nothing devastates me more than throwing away my mom's oatmeal raisin.

It's a tradition that started when I was playing soccer for Boston College, and the one time my mom forgot to give me a cookie before the game, I got red-carded for arguing with the ref. It was the cookie's fault, naturally. Or the absence of the cookie. So now, if I don't have one in my locker waiting for me after a game, I'm convinced that we're doomed no matter how well we play.

I know it's a cliché athlete superstition, but it's a hell of a lot better than wearing rank socks over and over like several of my other teammates do when we're on a winning streak.

Cookies smell good, win or lose.

Jude appears around the corner and tosses a muddy soccer ball at me, his tattooed arms caked in mud. His eyes are wide and alert, still riding a high from today. The old man played a hell of a game. I catch the ball in one hand and shove the rest of the cookie in my mouth as he approaches.

"That recruiter friend of mine from London is here, and he wants to see you in Coach's office." Jude waggles his eyebrows at me, and my heart plummets to the floor along with the filthy ball.

"Fuck," I mumble around a mouthful.

Jude's brows furrow. "This is a good thing, kid!"

I swallow, nearly choking on the giant bite going down my throat like a brick. "How can this be a good thing?" I wipe my mouth off and shake my arms out nervously.

"We've talked about this. Bethnal Green Football Club in London would be a *massive* step up for your career." Jude moves to stand in front of me, projecting that fatherly vibe on me he's developed ever since he had his son, Gabriel. "They're Premier League. This was all a part of our plan for you."

"This was a stupid plan." I shake my head adamantly. "I never should have let you talk me into this. That recruiter is going to know something is up." The cookie turns to lead in my stomach. What if this guy sees I have other motives to join Bethnal Green?

"He knows nothing, Zander," Jude snaps, shooting me a grumpy look. "Shawn's here because I told him months ago to keep his eye out for you. If I had to guess, he sees what I've been seeing since I came to this club, and they're calling you into the office to begin negotiations."

"Fucking fuck." That oatmeal raisin threatens to make a reappearance. "This escalated way too quickly."

Jude's hands rest heavily on my shoulders. "Forget the personal connection to Bethnal Green, okay? Focus on the fact that you might be getting a shot to play in the UK. Do you know how many footballers in this changing room would kill for that chance?"

I glance around at my teammates scattered throughout the locker room. Many have been playing professional soccer a lot longer than me, and for Americans, playing in the Premier League is a dream very few ever achieve. I know I can't walk away from this opportunity. I just wish it wasn't happening with *this* particular club.

I shudder as the memory of finding that envelope hits me full force. That damn piece of paper is what set this wild plan in motion. If I hadn't found that letter, I wouldn't have told Jude about it. Then Jude wouldn't have been inspired to talk to his recruiter friend for me, and I'd still be in my safe, oblivious bubble.

I miss that fucking bubble.

Six months ago, I was living a charmed life as a professional soccer player. I'd finally earned my stripes as a center-back for the Seattle Sounders, and they'd upgraded my contract and salary in a big way. I'd just purchased my first apartment with a killer view. I bought a new car. I was hitting nightclubs with the team, and girls were on constant rotation. I had the world by the soccer balls.

Then my mom called.

Told me my dad was in a horrible car accident.

Killed instantly.

Didn't suffer.

Life had done a one-eighty on me.

The next day, I was on a plane back to Boston and peeling my mom off the bathroom floor. I'd never seen her so distraught. So here I was, twenty-four years old and helping her into the shower while talking to the funeral home to decide what kind of urn I should put my cremated dad in. How the fuck does life prepare you for that?

Then the funeral director asked me to gather some old pictures for the wake. My mom was in no position to help, so as I was digging through old boxes, I stumbled upon an aged envelope addressed to a man named Vaughn Harris in England. Knowing my mom went to college in England and worked there for many years after, I had a bad feeling. I opened it up, and the hits just kept on coming.

Dear Vaughn,

An old-school letter feels so formal, but every time I try to pick up the phone to call you, I can't seem to find the nerve. I think I'm too scared to hear your voice. So I'm hoping I'll have the courage to send this, and you'll know I'm pregnant with your son. It doesn't get much more dramatic than that, does it?

Except it does because I'm back in the US now, and you're still in London. Another complication is the fact that you're already raising five children on your own. I came to tell you about the baby before I left for my new job in Boston, but you were in the middle of a massive fight with your eldest son, and there was so much pain in both your voices, so much hurt and loss. I couldn't stomach the idea of adding more to your plate, so I left without telling you.

And that's wrong. I know that's wrong. I've spent the past eight months watching this baby grow inside my belly and hating myself for not telling you. However, I can't get over the fact that it's been six years since Vilma died, and there's still so much agony in your eyes, in your home, and with your children. Vilma was my best friend, but she was the love of your life and a mother that five children lost much too young. You do not need this complication in your lives.

And maybe that's okay because I've met someone. His name is Jerry, and he's in accounting at my new job. He's wonderful, and kind, and sweet, and safe. But most especially, he's not still madly in love with his wife that died years ago. I'm sorry if that comes across as harsh, but it's the truth. You and Vilma were soul mates. I knew that the night I saw you two meet in that London pub, and if I'm being honest, I knew it the night you and I slept together. You were in pain, and I feel awful that I took advantage of that.

Which is why I think it's best if we go our separate ways. Jerry and I are getting married. He loves me so much, and I love him. And he's excited for the baby. He's always wanted to be a father, and I know he'll be a great one. And I want my baby to grow up with two parents. That's important to me after losing my own father much too young. I know that might not be fair to you, but you have your own children to focus on, and I hope you can respect my decision on this.

So please, don't call, don't write. Just try to understand that with you in the UK and me in the US, this is what's best for everyone. I truly do want the best for you, Vaughn. And all your children. I hope eventually you can heal with your family and begin a new life with a love like I have been blessed with.

All the Best,

Jane

The letter was dated one month before my birthday, so I knew without a shadow of a doubt that my mother was talking about me. And I knew my mom had gone to college and worked in London for many years before I was born. She never spoke of it much, but I was aware of her time there. A lot of fucking shit matched up, and I did not like the feel of it.

I wanted to confront my mother from the jump and demand to know the whole story, but she was so depressed over losing my dad, I had to drag her to the funeral. Then I had to get back to Seattle for the season, and dropping this bomb on her right before I left seemed cruel...even if she may have lied to me my whole life.

And my dad...did he know? Had he lied to me too? Or did my mom lie to him? That thought has fucked with my head every single day. So much so, it still hasn't fully sunk in that he's gone.

His funeral feels like a shitty dream, and he's still back home in Boston sitting at his nerdy home office with double computer monitors where he edits my match highlights together like always. I could come home next week, walk into his office, and he'd whirl around in his giant swivel chair and say, "That was a killer stop last week, buddy boy. Check out this highlight I captured of it!"

My hand runs over the inside of my bicep where his nickname for me is etched into my skin. *Buddy boy.* I got this tattoo the night my mom called to tell me Dad was gone and before I got on a plane to see her. After hearing such horrific news, I had to do something to mask the pain that tore through me when I realized he wasn't going to be at the airport to pick me up in his stupid minivan. He was fucking gone.

The ink felt right at the moment. Honorable. Now, it serves as a constant reminder of a lie I've possibly been living my whole life.

Did I even give a shit about who Vaughn Harris was? It's kind of fucked up to be curious about him when my dad's ashes are barely cold in the ground, right? And maybe my mom got it wrong. Maybe she slept around back then and just assumed Vaughn Harris was the father. Maybe it's some other random dude?

The problem is, (well, one of the problems, because there are many) Vaughn Harris isn't just some rando in England who might be my birth father. Vaughn Harris is a legend in the world of soccer. Not only did he used to play professionally for Manchester United, but sometime after I was born, he began managing a club in London that catapulted its way up from the Championship League to Premier League along with his four sons, who all play professionally as well. They are infamously known as the Harris Brothers, and a quick Google search shows pages and pages of these players and their careers. The four of them won the World fucking Cup for England…you'd have to live in a damn hole not to have at least heard of the Harris Brothers. The entire Harris family is a legend in professional soccer, and here I am, an American kid playing professional soccer, so I can't help but wonder if there's some truth to that fucking letter.

Could I be related to those people?

Fuck, every time I think of that thought, my entire body starts shaking. I seriously need more therapy. Coach made me talk to the team counselor when I returned after the funeral, but I didn't even get a chance to mention the letter. The doctor was more focused on the fact that I still hadn't shed a tear over the loss of my dad. Apparently, not crying like a baby when one of your parents dies is concerning or some shit.

I tried to cry. I'd stare at myself in the mirror and remember my mom sobbing into my arms and how I wish I could do anything to take her pain away. I'd remember standing at the gravesite where my dad's urn was buried. I reminded myself we couldn't have an open casket because his body was too messed up from the accident. Surely, that should trigger something inside me to break.

Nothing worked. My mind was stuck on that letter.

When my soccer game started to suffer, I decided to open up to Jude about everything. I thought maybe telling a friend about the letter would help snap me out of it. Bring me some perspective. Bring me back to reality. His reaction wasn't what I expected.

"You're not crying because you don't know who you're grieving. And you won't until you sort out this Harris family situation."

And since talking to my mother was out of the question, Jude went completely rogue on me. He called his friend Shawn who was the recruiter for Bethnal Green F.C. in London. He thought that getting recruited to Vaughn Harris's club was the best way for me to find out who the Harrises really are and if I even gave a shit about being related to them. Apparently, one of the twin brothers is an assistant coach, and the youngest one is still the team keeper, so there are lots of opportunities for me to see what kind of people they are.

Jude said the primary goal would be that I'd get a giant leap up in my career and the secondary goal was to meet them while I was overseas to see what they're like.

I didn't think I had a shot in hell at Premier League, so I just rolled my eyes and let Jude spin his wheels. However, I will admit that having a goal to strive for helped my game a lot. It was a lot easier to kill it on the soccer field than to consider the fact that I may have been betrayed my whole damn life.

But now, if Bethnal Green really is here to make me an offer, shit just got really real.

"Jude, you gotta help me out here. What do I do if they make me an offer?" I ask, swallowing the lump in my throat. "Go there and play for Vaughn Harris's club and pray like fuck there's no family resemblance?"

Jude winces as his eyes rove over my face. "That's probably not going to work because you really do look just like the eldest brother, Gareth."

"Fuck you!" I growl, shoving my friend away from me. "God, I can't believe I let you talk me into this. How the hell did we make this happen? Seriously! Who just cherry-picks their fucking pro soccer club like this?"

"I'm kind of in shock over it too. Manifestation always seemed like utter bollocks to me." He laughs nervously and then steels himself to look calm and collected. "But just relax. No one will put two and two together. It's not like people see their doppelganger on the street and say... Oi! I think you might be my long-lost brother! Can I get a DNA sample?"

My teeth crack at his cavalier tone. "This is my life here, Jude."

Jude's face bends with sympathy. "I know, I know. Just focus on the facts, kid. Vaughn Harris doesn't know you could be his son. And your mum doesn't know you found that letter. That letter could be fake for all we know. This is your secret right now...and mine." He lifts his brows and gives my arm a playful punch. "And the opportunity to play in the UK is ten times bigger than any family drama. Go kill it for this club, and no one has to know your connection to the Harris family. That's up to you to decide once you're over there. Football over bullshit, right?"

"Football over bullshit," I repeat with a heavy sigh. Using the term football feels foreign, but I vow to get used to it if they offer me a deal. "I'm going to need you to remind me of that mantra if they actually fucking sign me, or my career will get a whole lot muddier than today's game."

1

I'll Have The Duck

Zander
Six Months Later

"**M**ORE FUCKING RAIN," I GROAN AS I TURN MY RED SOX BALL CAP forward and wheel my two heavy suitcases and a carry-on toward the cab line outside of Heathrow airport.

"Where to?" a cabbie asks as he wrestles my bags into the trunk, flinching against the cold January wind.

I hand him the slip of paper from my pocket. "I need to go to a pub called Old George in Bethnal Green."

"East London, got it," he replies with a thick British accent. "Sit on that side. You're a big bloke, and there's more legroom there."

I nod and fold myself into the back, adjusting to the feeling of riding on the wrong side of the road. I came to England for a camp once when I was twelve. My dad came with me, and I remember him telling me that England was here first, so America is actually the weird one.

I'd do anything to call my dad right now and talk to him about this big transfer. He was my biggest fan, and even though it's been a year since he passed, I still catch myself picking up the phone to call him. And the number of times I've replayed the voicemails I have on my phone from him is crazy unhealthy. But each time I do, I can hear the smile in his voice. It reminds me of the man I love, regardless of whether or not he lied to me.

It'd be nice if I could talk to my mom, but things between us aren't exactly copacetic. As we exit the airport, I pull out my phone to reply to the texts I've received from her since my phone connected to my international plan. After several flight delays, I'm here a good five hours later than I was supposed to be.

Me: Made it to London finally, and I'm in a cab.

Mom: Did all your luggage make it?

Me: Yeah.

Mom: Are you going to be on time to meet your landlord?

Me: Yeah, I texted him when we departed, and he said he could meet me later.

Mom: Did you sleep on the plane at all?

Me: Not really.

Mom: You have your endurance test tomorrow, right? Will you be rested enough for that?

Me: I'm good.

My jaw clenches as I see the bubbles on the text thread bounce and disappear, bounce and disappear. She doesn't know what to say. We had a huge fight when I told her about the offer from Bethnal Green. She said it was too soon for me to transfer clubs after Dad died, which shocked me because it had been six months at that point, and this offer could change the entire trajectory of my career. And I knew it wasn't the distance that bothered her because I was already thousands of miles away from her when I took a contract in Seattle.

The silent elephant in the room had to be that I was going to play for a club managed by a man she knew all too well, based on that letter. That fucking stupid piece of paper that I carry with me in my wallet like a psychopath. I waited for her to bring up the connection. I was patient because I knew she was still struggling with grief and depression. She was seeing a therapist for it and taking all these new meds. It took her months to go back to work, so I delayed my transfer from August to January, hoping she'd finally be honest with me.

At Christmas, it'd been a year since my dad passed, so I practically teed her up by asking all sorts of questions about the years she lived in London. I asked her advice on the area, the lingo, and sights I should see. I gave her a million chances to tell me that she might know Vaughn Harris from her time spent over there. Anything.

But she said nothing.

In fact, the day before I was supposed to leave, she told me that soccer was too cutthroat overseas, and I was better off being a star in America than a bench warmer in England.

It felt like a fucking knife through the heart. My own mother didn't believe in me.

Dad would have *never* said that shit. He would have put a damn sign up in the yard to tell all the neighbors that his son was signed to the Premier League. He would have written an editorial for the newspaper. He would have changed his career from accountant to "Father of a Premier League footballer" on his Facebook profile.

I realized then that I lost more than my dad last year. I lost my mom too.

On the flight, my mind swirled with doubt. Maybe the fact that she didn't say anything means that letter is bullshit? Maybe she had some DNA tests done on me when I was younger and realized she made a mistake, and Vaughn Harris wasn't my father. Maybe that's why she never sent the letter. Maybe I'll get to Tower Park Field, take one look at Vaughn Harris, and know he's not my father. Then I can get back to focusing on what I'm here for: Soccer over bullshit.

Or football over bullshit, as Jude says.

Either way, I deserved better parting words from her than "good luck being a bench warmer."

I stare out the cab window at the drizzling rain and pray like hell this miserable day isn't an omen for how my season will go. Bullshit or not, Premier League is a huge step, and I can't fuck up this opportunity.

After a long ride, the driver stops in front of a bar situated on the corner with a weathered green wraparound banner and gold letters that spell out The Old George. My stomach rumbles as I pay the man and lug my bags inside.

It's a dark, cozy bar with a long, heavily lacquered wooden bar off to the right and a mashup of quirky old furniture scattered throughout. Past the bar, I notice a corridor that leads to more seating and what looks like a patio outside.

The landlord of my flat is supposed to meet me here with a key, so I do a quick sweep of the empty space, looking for a guy who looks like he's waiting for someone. My phone pings with a notification, and I glance down to see he's texted me.

Hayden Clarke Landlord: Running about twenty minutes late.

Please order yourself some tea on me, and I'll get there as quick as possible.

"Tea?" I frown and turn my baseball cap backward. Surely, they have coffee in England. Plus, it's nearly five, and I could use a beer and some food. My phone pings again.

Hayden Clarke Landlord: Tea is British for dinner, by the way. Cheers.

Dinner I can handle. I type back my reply of two beers clinking just as a raspy feminine voice yells, "It's seat yourself so just pick anywhere you like. Except the garden. It's closed as it's brass monkeys out there."

"Brass monkeys?" I look up and do a double take as I lock eyes with the British blonde bombshell talking to me. "Um…hey." For fuck's sake, have I lost the ability to form sentences?

She pauses with a spray bottle and rag propped on her hips as her eyes zero in on me. "Hiya. I said seat yourself. You can put your luggage in the corner. It's dead in here, so no one should nick it."

"Nick it?" I repeat, my brows furrowed as I do my best not to ogle the girl in front of me and fail miserably following her every curve.

She frowns at me again. "Steal it. Are you the American footballer?" I nod.

"Okay then," she adds a bit slower like I'm hard of hearing. "Put your suitcases in the corner and sit wherever you like." She resumes her work, and I hear her murmur, "He doesn't speak British even though it's English."

I exhale a breath I didn't even realize I'd been holding and try to shake off my stupor. Jesus, it's not like I've never talked to a pretty girl before. I mean, I have had a bit of a dry spell this past year, but the last girl I hooked up with before that was a *Sports Illustrated* swimsuit model, so surely, I haven't completely lost that swagger. Must be the jet lag.

After dumping my suitcases, I take a seat and glance at the menu, gazing creepily over the top of it as the blonde sprays and wipes down ten tables at Mach speed. Though her shredded jeans and baggy black T-shirt hide her curves, she has me practically drooling. This girl isn't just pretty… she's a smokeshow. But in a chill, unassuming way. I wonder how fast I could get her number. Sex has always helped my soccer game.

Back in college, it was easy to pull girls. My school had loads of jersey chasers, and since I was one of their top players, I barely had to lift a finger. Then in Seattle, the Pacific Northwest girls fawned over my Boston accent even though it's not even that strong. I wonder if British chicks like a Boston tone?

The blonde abandons her rag and spray bottle on the table next to me. "Normally, you order at the counter, but you can let me know what you want since it's dead in here right now."

"What do you recommend?" I ask, drawn to her steel-blue eyes. They're super round and sparkle like they're reflecting off the water. It's highly distracting.

"The fish and chips are good," she responds, gazing at me with those magnetic eyes. "Or the smoky beef…the sticky wings. It's all good pub food, especially if you're a carnivore."

I nod and watch her chew her lower lip distractedly. They are obscenely plump, and my thoughts go dirty as I ask, "Can I get some fries?"

Her dark brows lift. "Chips are fries, crisps are chips."

"Why is that?" I frown up at her.

Amusement flickers over her cherubic facial features. "Because you're in England, mate."

"England was here first, right?" I shoot her a playful smile, my eyes drifting over her body as if they have a mind of their own.

She exhales heavily. "Can you just let me know what you want? I have things to do before the after-work rush starts coming in."

"What's your name?" I ask, ignoring her request as a noisy group comes in the pub door.

"Daphney," she replies, glancing at the new patrons.

"Did you say Daffy? Like the duck?" I ask with a laugh. "That is adorable."

"No…it's Daphney, like…*Bridgerton*." She rolls her eyes and says the last word through clenched teeth. "But it's spelled differently."

"I have no idea what Bridgerton is. Is it on the menu?" Or are you on the menu? I ask to myself, not even trying to hide my amusement at my own joke as she glares at me with annoyance.

"Oh my God, just order some food," she snaps as she blows away a strand of blonde hair that fell over her eye.

A lazy smile spreads across my face. She's cute when she's frazzled. "Sorry, Ducky. I'm new to the area and just trying to make a friend."

She props her left hand on her narrow hip. "You've known me all of four seconds, and you think you can give me a nickname? A word to the wise, the British aren't that matey."

"I'm a soccer player." I shrug and sit back, crossing my arms over my chest. "We give all our friends nicknames."

Her eyes narrow as she hunches over and splays her hands on the table, furrowing her thick, dark eyebrows. "Well, it's called football here, so maybe focus on your British-isms before nicknames, or you're going to get eaten alive."

Her nose wrinkles, and I lean closer to her as my eyes zero in on the dimple on her chin. "Maybe I could sample the duck if it's available?"

She blinks blankly at me before standing back upright. "Is that supposed to be a pickup line?"

I lick my lips knowingly. "Depends on if you like it."

Her nostrils flare as her voice shifts into a saccharinely sweet tone. "Do you actually want me to spit in your food?"

"I think I'd let you spit in a number of places." I shoot her my legendary boyish smirk that several magazines have remarked on in my media interviews. She sucks in her lips as her face contorts into a bizarre sort of expression, and it isn't until she topples over, clutching at her belly, that I realize…

She's laughing.

At me.

Hard.

It's a burst of strange, silent laughter, but the tears leaking out of the corners of her eyes and the occasional gasp for breath make it pretty clear she's laughing her ass off. She's close to rolling on the floor like the acronym. I didn't think anyone actually ever did that, but she's making me doubt that thought.

"He wants to sample the duck!" She turns on her heel to walk away from me as she throws over her shoulder, "I'm not even going to touch your spit remark. It's too easy. But the duck? That one will stick with me."

My brows furrow as a strange sensation sweeps over me. Is it…humiliation? I turn my hat forward and pull the bill down low, glancing awkwardly at the group nearby and hoping like fuck they didn't overhear any of that exchange. I've never been so firmly checked by a woman before. I've never asked to sample their *duck* before either.

Jesus Christ, it has to be the jet lag.

A few minutes later, a heavyweight, bearded man by the name of Hubert appears behind the bar, and I sigh with relief that the cute blonde might have left for the day. One mortification per hour is plenty for me, thank you very much. I order a beer and some fish and "chips" from him at the counter and head back to my table to wallow in my pathetic-ness. Maybe British girls won't like me? Maybe I'm not boyishly charming here?

Fuck, I miss home.

Just as I'm polishing off the last of my food, a voice calls out, "Is there a Zander Williams here?"

I turn toward the entrance and see a guy who looks to be in his late thirties with a little blonde girl clutching tightly to his hand. Beneath her puffy winter coat, it looks like she's dressed in a black leotard and pink tights with big fuzzy boots on her feet.

"I'm Zander," I reply, standing up and giving him a head nod.

He smiles and walks over with the girl in tow. "Sorry I'm late. My wife was supposed to be home to take Rocky here to ballet…but she had an emergency at work." He digs into his pocket and glances at his phone briefly. "Here are the keys to your flat. It's in that brownstone building just across the street." He points at the far windows that face the smaller side street. "This is the key to the building, and this is the key to your flat. You're in unit seven on the third floor. It's fully furnished as you requested."

I take the keys from him. "Great, thanks."

"Normally, I'd help you with your luggage and give you a tour to show you how things work, but Rocky can't miss ballet—"

"Or the instructor will make me be a tree in the recital," the little girl chimes in with a severely sour expression. "I will not be a tree again, Daddy."

"I know, darling. That's why Auntie is going to help out." Hayden looks up at me. "My sister will take you over and give you a rundown of everything. She lives in the building as well and is sort of the unofficial building manager." Hayden's eyes move past me and widen. "There she is now!"

I turn to follow his gaze and feel a sudden chill wash over me when I see the blonde from earlier striding toward us. Her eyes lower to the little girl as she moves past me and scoops the little ballerina up off the floor.

"How's my favorite rock star?" she asks as the girl's long legs dangle around her petite frame.

"Daphney, Daddy is going to be late again, and I'll have to be a tree." She scowls at her father, and I must admit, I feel bad for the guy. Rocky doesn't look like a girl who forgives easily.

"No, you won't." Hayden glances down at his phone again. "But we must leave now, or you could end up as a bush. Daphney, this is Zander. Zander, this is my sister, Daphney."

"Oh, we've met," Daphney says with a bright smile on me that shows a bit too many teeth. "We go way back. Isn't that right, Zander?"

My brows furrow as I attempt to find a suitable response.

"All the way back to the duck?" Daphney offers, and my eyes widen with horror.

"What duck?" Hayden asks, and all the spit in my mouth dries up when I realize she's going to call me out in front of her brother for hitting on her.

"I want a duck!" Rocky peals.

After clearing my throat, I open my mouth to come up with something, anything that can save my ass from this horribly awkward encounter without informing my landlord that I'm a fucking douchebag who hit on his sister by asking to sample her duck.

Daphney laughs and turns to her brother. "Just a little inside joke in regard to the menu. You know footballers and their weird diets."

Hayden frowns at me like I'm a headcase and then shakes it off. "Okay then. So, are you good, Daphney? You've got this all handled?"

Daphney nods. "All good. You two go on."

Hayden shoots me one more quizzical look as he swoops the little girl into his arms. "Santino Rossi, the football club lawyer, has your lease agreement, Zander, so he'll be popping by sometime."

"Okay," I reply, nervously gripping the back of my neck that's now covered in sweat.

Hayden turns to leave and then pauses to call back, "Welcome to Bethnal Green, and good luck this season!"

"Thank you." I force a smile and slowly turn to Daphney as my shoulders feel permanently stuck under my ears. She's pulling a large set of keys out of her back pocket as I state, "You're making me sweat over here."

"I noticed." She laughs, and it's wild that my body can shift from humiliated to horny in two seconds flat with that husky and sexy sound.

"Listen…about earlier," I start, going for broke.

"No need to mansplain." Daphney smirks as she walks over to my luggage. "Let's just get you to your flat, *Soccer Boy*."

"I wasn't going to mansplain." Was I?

I ponder that thought as we lug my suitcases across the side street toward the building. My head snaps up when it dawns on me that she called me Soccer Boy, which is obviously a nickname. It's a condescending one, to be sure, but a nickname nonetheless. That small fact gives me a tiny glimmer of hope that I haven't totally ruined my chances with this chick.

She pauses on the corner and points. "The Bethnal Green station is just a five-minute walk that way. You can get an Oyster card there."

"I can't do oysters. Too slimy."

She turns and blinks back at me. "It's the tube card."

"Oh." I swallow a knot in my throat. *I have a degree in mathematics. I'm not this stupid, I swear.*

"And bus stops are all along the main road here. There's a Tesco about a ten-minute walk that way."

I cringe as I look in the direction she's pointing. "Is Tesco like a grocery store?"

"It's a supermarket." She huffs out a laugh. "Did you do any research on the area before you moved here?"

"Just soccer...um...football research," I reply, turning my hat backward nervously. Jude and I did a crash course on European football, but I didn't think to ask him about basic British-isms. "But it's fine. I'll use cabs to get me around."

"Cabs are going to be a nightmare when you need to get a lot of groceries."

I cringe. "You don't have a car, do you?"

"I do." She eyes me cautiously.

"Well, maybe Soccer Boy can ride you sometime?" My eyes widen as her face turns hard. "Fuck, that came out wrong. Shit." *Jesus, I need sleep. Or medication. Maybe even an exorcism.*

Rolling her eyes, she turns to walk toward the large brownstone building, and I wonder if I should even bother following her or just throw myself in front of one of the red double-decker buses. She'd probably like to push me at this point.

When we reach the door, she replies, "You can go with me on my next trip. One time."

I exhale at that small sign of compassion while she opens the door and moves inside. I try not to stare at her ass as we lug the suitcases up three flights of stairs. I guess asking for a building with an elevator wasn't something I even thought about. I didn't consider a lot of things when I signed that contract...except maybe backing out altogether and pretending that stupid letter never existed.

Daphney rounds the landing and stops at the door with a seven on it. "This is you."

"My lucky number." I smile like a dope. "What's yours?"

A quizzical look mars her face. "Don't really have one."

Shut up, Zander. You sound like a fucking weirdo. I grimace and prop myself against the wall for support. "I swear I'm not usually like this."

She holds her hands out for my keys and uses them to unlock the door. "This building used to be a biscuit factory, so all the flats are sort of misshaped and studio-style. This is the corner unit with twenty-foot ceilings. It also has the best view, so I think you'll be pleased."

I shuffle the suitcases over to the side, and my eyes go wide as I take in the space that I did not at all envision. To be fair, I didn't envision much. It was Jude's idea for me to negotiate lodgings because my head was such a mess over whether I should even sign with Bethnal Green. I couldn't even imagine what my life would look like in London. But if it's anything like this, I think I'm going to be looking pretty good.

The apartment has large industrial windows that overlook the main road and the side road that goes alongside the Old George beer garden Daphney mentioned earlier. The warm, earthy décor has knotty pine flooring and exposed metal beams. It's completely different from my modern high-rise in Seattle. A bit smaller but very open so it feels spacious.

A king-sized bed sits in front of the windows on the left overlooking Old George. A couple of giant cream privacy curtains hang from the pipes above to close off the windows. It'll be nice not to feel like I'm living in a fishbowl twenty-four seven. The bedroom flows into the dining and living area. Off the living room is the kitchen, fashioned with white subway tile, stainless steel appliances, and a glossy wooden breakfast bar dividing the living room and the kitchen.

I point at the flat screen in front of the chocolate-colored sectional sofa. "Is that an Xbox?"

"Yes, it is." Daphney's eyes narrow. "Hopefully, you didn't prefer PlayStation. We tried to get more information about what you wanted, but you were so hard to reach."

I shake my head quickly. "Xbox is cool."

She exhales. "Okay, good. There are games in the console below. The club got access to next year's FIFA footy video game early, so you might want to check that out. The PR person told me they might hit you up for social media promotions."

"Okay." I nod and turn my hat around, my brows furrowing at her earlier remark. "It was hard to get ahold of me?"

She blinks curiously at me, her blue eyes still distracting. "Yes, well, you didn't have an agent for us to contact, and you were supposed to come six months ago, so we were rushing around like crazy to get this space furnished. Then all of a sudden, they said you weren't coming right away, so we had more time."

"Oh…right." I bite my tongue as I recall several contract revisions with the club lawyer, Santino. They were really frustrated that I represented myself because I had no clue what I was doing. And then when I asked to delay my transfer, I was worried it was all going to hell.

Signing with Seattle was so much easier because I had my dad's help. He took care of all my contract negotiations, my money, sponsorships, everything. Jerry Williams knew the business side of soccer inside and out, and what he didn't know, he researched fervently. To hire some random agent so soon after my dad passed felt like I was betraying him, so I just limped through it all on my own.

I clear my throat and grip the back of my neck, not wanting to explain how it was my first time negotiating a contract without my dad's help. "Sorry about the delay. Contract stuff is complicated."

"I can imagine," Daphney replies, that dimple under her lower lip re-appearing. "Anyway, the loo is through that door." She points at the closed door adjacent to the bed. "Since we had extra time, we were able to upgrade it, so it's fully situated with a shower/tub combo and a steamer. I'm told that's good for footballers. And…oh…if you stand right over here." She moves past me to stand beside the large, perfectly made bed with more throw pillows than I ever would have picked out. "You can see your pitch, Tower Park."

I leave the bags by the kitchen and join her to see the view of the place I'll be playing soccer at in a matter of hours. It feels surreal that I'm actually in London, getting ready to play for the Premier League. Dad would be so damn proud of me, even if Mom isn't. A deep pain niggles inside my gut.

Daphney nudges me with her elbow. "Pitch is British for a soccer field, in case you didn't know."

I smile gratefully at her joke. "Believe it or not, I actually knew you guys call it a pitch." I shoot her a wink, and her eyes glance at my lips, causing a damn near aggressive reaction to happen in my jeans.

She licks her lips and adds, "On match nights, when Tower Park is lit up, this is a great view." Her eyes narrow. "But I suppose you'll be out there when that's happening, so you'll have a much better view."

I watch her inquisitively. "Do you actually like…football?" I catch myself before saying soccer.

"I'm British. We're pretty much born loving football." She huffs knowingly as she runs a hand through her hair. "I can't say I'm a Bethnal Green fan, though. But I've been living in Bethnal for about a year now, and hearing the locals describe the FA Cup win you guys had a couple of years ago definitely warmed the team to me. Not just because I'm chasing wins but because Bethnal Green really plays with spirit. I'm excited to see if they can re-claim their title this season. Your club is the ultimate Cinderella story. Rags to riches without the pompous overpriced egos of a longtime Premier League club with the ridiculous player budgets. "They're the people's team, you know? They even made me consider cheating on my precious West Ham, but I'm not a fickle fan, so never repeat anything of what I just said to you, or I'll have you beaten and evicted. I know people."

She deadpans that last bit, and I can't fight the smile that spreads across my face. Ducky is no jersey chaser. She's a jersey-wearer…and those chicks are the holy grail of hot girls. I'm not mad at this realization. Not mad at all.

My mind begins to wander again, and I tell myself that she smells like beer and fryer oil, as if somehow that will lessen her appeal. It doesn't. I'd still easily fuck her. Especially now that I know she likes soccer. An image of her naked in nothing but my jersey invades my thoughts.

Daphney clears her throat, and I wince when it looks like she quite possibly read my dirty mind. "Anyway, there's a folder in the kitchen with where to take your rubbish, takeaway menus, a map with places of interest nearby, and a number for maintenance in case you need it."

I could use some naked maintenance right about now. It was a long damn flight, and it's been a beat since I've had a girl in my bed. I jam my hands into my pockets and try not to sound too obvious when I ask, "Where's your apartment?"

Her cheeks turn a rosy hue as she points at the wall holding the television. "My *flat* is on the other side of that wall."

My eyes widen when I think about how truly close we are to each other. "Well, howdy neighbor." I flinch at the creepy tone in my voice.

She fights back a laugh as she turns to walk away. "I'll let you get unpacked. Oh…the boxes you had sent are in the wardrobe on the other side of your bed. Wardrobe means closet in case you didn't know English." She shoots me a wink, and I smile in appreciation.

"Okay, thanks. For everything. Really. The apartment is awesome, and

I assume you had a hand in it, so I appreciate it." She has no idea what a relief this is to me.

She nods, seemingly pleased by my gratitude. "I'm glad you like it."

She begins to open the door, and I follow her, desperation blooming in my chest because I kind of wish she'd stay and keep me company while I unpacked. Not just because I want to fuck her…because clearly, I do. But because it's been a hell of a year. My dad died, I found a messed-up letter that turned my whole life upside down, I'm barely speaking to my mom, and I'm in a new country starting with a new team that I may or may not have a genetic connection to.

It's been a year.

And the past hour I've spent embarrassing myself in front of Daphney has been like a breath of fresh air that I don't want to end. It's not loneliness I'm feeling. I was an only child my whole life, so spending time on my own was a regular occurrence. It's just been so long since my brain has been able to focus on anything other than my messed-up life.

I lift my hat and run a nervous hand through my hair as I step out into the hallway and watch Daphney head to her own door. "I'm actually pretty likeable once you get to know me."

She shoots me a rueful smile. "Good for you."

"Seriously. And if you don't like me, I'm pretty much a golden retriever. Very trainable." I stick my tongue out and pant like a dog.

Her adorable nose wrinkles. "I'm more of a cat person."

My face distorts at that horrifying thought, but I quickly shift gears. "Well, maybe envision me like a nice fat cat who doesn't bother anybody… just likes to sit around and eat pu—" My voice cuts out as I realize that I was about to make a really disgusting joke about eating pussy. "Bad joke," I confess, hoping she didn't hear me.

Her eyes go wide as a smile ghosts her lips. "Get some rest, Soccer Boy. British football is no laughing matter."

When I'm back in my own apartment, I thump my forehead against the door. If this was a soccer match, it'd be Daphney: one, Zander: nil.

2

Premier Blood

Zander

STRUGGLE TO HEAR MY ALARM THE NEXT MORNING, HITTING THE snooze button more times than I'd like. My head is a foggy mess of exhaustion, confusion, and jet lag. The sun hasn't even risen yet as I stumble through my apartment, ripping open boxes in search of the workout gear I need for my first day at Tower Park. Today, they want to do a simple medical exam. It's a little weird because I'd already completed a full physical a few weeks ago with a doctor they sent over, but I guess Bethnal Green likes to complete one in person before the endurance training this afternoon. I better find the will to live because if I'm feeling this shitty, who knows what my test results might say?

Thankfully, the steamer shower helps me feel mildly more human, and by the time I'm dressed and stuffing soccer gear into my gym bag, I hear a firm knock on my door. I shuffle over to the foyer and open it, hoping to see my sexy neighbor with coffee and donuts because that'd be a great way to start my day, but instead, I come face-to-face with a tall, suited man who looks to be in his late thirties.

The guy's eyes zero in on my face, and his voice is a gruff whisper when he says, "Well fuck."

"Excuse me?" My hand itches to close the door in this weirdo's face.

The guy shakes his head, ruffling his black hair as he clears his throat. "Sorry, erm…I'm Santino Rossi, Bethnal Green football club's lawyer."

He reaches out his hand, and I shake it dubiously and then recall Hayden Clarke mentioning that he might stop by. "Oh yeah. You needed me to sign something?"

Santino nods, his brows furrowed as he gapes at me for longer than feels necessary. "Yes, that's right. Do you mind if I come in?"

I step back, gesturing for him to enter. "Sorry about the mess. I literally just arrived last night, and well…" I stare at the boxes strewn all over. "I clearly have some unpacking to do."

Santino nods again, his eyes not lingering on the mess but on me. "Sorry for staring…you just look like someone I know."

"Do I?" I grip the back of my neck and wonder if all British lawyers are this creepy.

Santino huffs out a laugh and then reaches into his satchel to pull out some paperwork. "I'll just get right to it." He lays out the paperwork on the dining room table and clicks a pen. "This is a standard lease agreement. It just says the club will cover the lease, but any damages or remodeling requests will be on your own dime."

I nod and walk over to where he's standing to pick up the pieces of paper and read through them. Santino watches me, so I ask, "It's okay if I read this, right?"

"Yes, of course." Santino snaps out of his stupor as he backs off to give me some space. "Take as long as you need."

I focus on the text, and after reading it thoroughly, I determine it all seems pretty standard. I sign the flagged areas, and when I turn, I find Santino staring pointedly at the pen in my hand. "Here." I hand it back to him because it's like he was expecting me to steal it or something.

"Thanks." He slides it and the papers back into his bag. He glances around the space and says, "Happy with your accommodations?"

My brows lift. "Yeah, they're great."

"Brilliant." He stares at me for a silent beat. "Any…issues you want to discuss?"

"With you?"

Santino shrugs. "I am the team counsel. You can feel free to come to me with anything that might be concerning you."

"Okaaay," I reply hesitantly, feeling like he's talking to me more like a shrink than a lawyer.

"I've gotten many players out of some really awkward situations," Santino offers, sliding his hands into the pockets of his pants. "Nothing shocks me."

"Well, considering I haven't even been in the country twenty-four hours, I think it's safe to say I haven't had any time to get into trouble." I shoot him a knowing wink, but he doesn't seem to find the humor in my reply.

Santino's lips thin. "Problems can follow you from anywhere."

Annoyance prickles in my veins. "Is there a problem I'm unaware of? 'Cause the only problem I see right now is a lawyer I just met asking me really bizarre questions."

Santino winces. "Sorry, mate. There's no problem. I just wanted you to know I'm here if you need anything. Completely confidential." He hands me his card.

"Message received." I huff out a laugh and set the card on the table. "Mind if I finish getting ready for work now?"

"Not at all." Santino reaches out to shake my hand again, gripping me firmly. "It was nice to finally meet you, Zander. I know what Vaughn Harris's plans are for you at the club, and I'm hopeful this all works out for everyone."

His odd choice of wording causes my brow to furrow, but I quickly school my features to hide my reaction. The truth is, just the mention of Vaughn Harris's name causes anxiety to bloom inside me. I've been trying to forget about the fact that I'll be meeting the man soon. A man who could be my father? No…he's not my father. I had a father. Jerry Williams. He was the fucking best.

Football over bullshit.

I pin Santino with a knowing look. "I fully intend on rising to the challenge."

"Welcome to Bethnal Green, gentlemen," Coach Zion says, walking in front of two other Americans who were recruited at the same time as me. "You're about to find out what real football is like." Coach stops and bends over so he's eye level with us. "I hope you're up for the challenge."

I glance to my right at Link Conlin, a striker from Arizona, and on my left is Knight Timmons, a midfielder from Florida. We all have the same expression of complete and total *Oh fuck, this is really happenin'* as we sit in our custom green and white Bethnal Green F.C. uniforms with our names on the back.

"First order of business," Coach says, gesturing for us to follow him. He stops at a door at the end of the hallway down a ways from the locker room we were just changing in. "Don't embarrass me."

He opens it to reveal a room packed with reporters, and my stomach roils as all eyes turn toward us. I've done press conferences before, but I guess I thought they'd prep us a bit. Jude told me that the British press is brutal, and as American soccer players in England…surely, there's some inside info that might be helpful right about now?

We walk into the lion's den in single file and sit behind the table with several microphones and recorders spread out as everyone in the room goes quiet. Coach gives us a quick introduction and then opens the floor for questions.

"Zander Williams!" a reporter in the back says. "You're the youngest recruit from America. Do you actually think you have what it takes to play in the Premier League?"

Link's and Knight's eyes both go wide as they stare at me with equal parts pity and relief that they didn't get asked the first question. It's a no-bullshit question, cutting straight to the point. I take a drink of the water bottle sitting in front of me, trying to bide my time because what the fuck do they expect me to say? Finally, I lean forward and reply honestly, "I guess we'll find out."

The room laughs even though I wasn't really making a joke.

"Why do you think they picked you?" a female reporter in the front adds.

I shrug. "I've been asking myself that for the past six months."

"Speaking of six months," another reporter adds. "Why did you delay your transfer from Seattle? Most blokes your age would jump at the opportunity to play in Europe."

I swallow the knot in my throat and hear Knight murmur, "Jesus Christ," under his breath.

I grimace before saying, "I had some family issues at home that I needed to deal with."

Murmurings from the crowd indicate they know the reasons behind my answer, and I pray like fuck no one asks me anything about my dad's death.

"He will be worth the wait, I assure you," a deep, gravelly voice echoes from the back of the room.

Everyone turns to see a man standing by the rear exit. As he makes his way past the reporters and the light illuminates his face, I instantly recognize Vaughn Harris.

He's tall and broad-shouldered, very clearly a former athlete. He has a head full of salt-and-pepper hair, more salt than pepper, and severe eyes that have zero bullshit in them. He locks his gaze on me, and I tense, knowing this moment was coming. During my health exam with the team doctor, I was on edge, just waiting for him to walk in to meet his new recruits. The female doctor examining me had to retake my blood pressure because it was way too high. She probably thought I was attracted to her—which I was—but that wasn't why I couldn't calm down.

I was freaking out because in the six months I waited for my transfer window, I did stalker-like research on the entire Harris family. Which meant the minute I saw the redheaded doctor with matching red-framed glasses, I knew she wasn't just a random team doctor. She was Dr. Indie Porter-Harris, wife of Camden Harris, one of the twin Harris Brothers who's currently a striker for Arsenal. They have two young daughters and live in Notting Hill, according to this website I found.

God, even just remembering the name of the site makes me recoil with humiliation. The site was called HarrisHoandProud.com. It's like the universe knew I'd come looking for intel on this family, so it spread out their entire goddamn family tree.

Naturally, I wasn't a branch on that tree because that letter I found was probably bullshit or read out of context, and none of this matters because I'm here to play soccer, not find a new damn family. Regardless, I knew after being a disaster with Dr. Indie that this moment right here, meeting Vaughn Harris, wasn't going to be easy.

Vaughn stops in front of the table we're seated at and turns to address the media. "Zander Williams was a recruit that my American scout has had his eye on for a while. We think he's the perfect player to bring back some old-school soccer techniques that we expect will elevate our club in the Premier standings. It's our goal to train him to be our sweeper. That's a position that's been long forgotten in the beautiful game of football, but back when I used to play for Man U, the keeper and the sweeper had serious potential to drive the pacing of the game…whether to keep a ball or send it. A sweeper can set up plays from the back, and I've long wanted to weaponize my defense for offense. Coach Zion and I think Zander Williams can make that dream of ours a reality."

Chills run down my spine as I realize I've been holding my breath far too long as Vaughn moves onto Link and Knight. Christ, I need to get my shit together. I just didn't realize how weird it would be to hear a man who could very well be my father speak highly of me and how I play the game. The pride is instantly snuffed out by guilt because I already have a father who spoke highly of me. And he's all that should matter in my head.

Fuck, this situation is going to be harder than I thought.

Football over bullshit, I repeat in my head. That letter was bullshit. It told me nothing concrete, and right now, Vaughn Harris is nothing more than my new club's manager. That's it. I'm here to play soccer and be all the things that he wants me to be. In order for me to do that, I need to focus on that.

The press conference wraps up, and Vaughn and Coach Zion escort us out of the room that feels about twenty degrees hotter than the hallway. When we stop in front of the locker room, Vaughn finally turns and reaches his hand out to me first.

"It's great to meet you, son. I've watched a lot of your match tapes, and I think you're incredibly talented."

He pins me with a genuine look of gratitude that I can barely register because the word "son" causes a flash of angst to shoot through my entire body.

Did he call me son like generically? Or does he know something I don't? There's no fucking way, right? Jesus, of course there's no way. If he knew something, the first time he mentions it wouldn't be standing in a fucking hallway outside of a locker room with a bunch of the press filing out noisily behind us.

This man isn't my father. I had a father.

Attempting to shake off the cold sweat breaking out over my face, I try to focus on images of my dad instead of the man in front of me. Images of his dirty blonde hair blowing in the wind as he blasted classic rock in his minivan. Images of his lanky frame in his dress slacks and button-downs as he struggled to kick a soccer ball with me in the backyard. Images of his hands that were always so delicate and narrow. Like a pianist.

My damp grip tightens nervously as I glance down at my hand in Vaughn's. Vaughn and I are much more similar in size and stature, and I notice his fingernails look a lot like mine.

Clearing my throat, I yank my hand out of his and cringe inwardly when his smile falters. I force myself to plaster on my own smile that feels plastic as I reply robotically, "I'm happy for the opportunity and excited to meet the team."

"That won't happen today," Coach says gruffly, slapping his hand on my shoulder. "I have a little tradition of personally running the endurance tests for all our new recruits. The team will be off with Vaughn watching game tape to prep for the first FA Cup match we're hosting tomorrow at

Tower Park. We don't need you newbies interfering with their focus. So today, it's just you three, me, and a seriously empty training pitch next door ready for some fresh blood."

"Blood?" I repeat his word with grave eyes.

"It's Premier blood if it makes you feel better." Coach Z waggles his eyebrows at me, and I don't like the glint in his eye.

Vaughn slaps him on the back. "Don't be too hard on the lads, Coach. They've not even adjusted to the time zone yet. We don't want them to think the Premier League is full of a bunch of sadists."

"Don't we?" Coach's returning smile doesn't reach his eyes.

3

Soccer Boy

Daphney

"**D**APHNEY, HI…IT'S DRAKE LAMBERT FROM COMMERCIAL NOTES."

"Oh yes…hello, Mr. Lambert." I hop out of my bed and quickly scrub my hands over my face to wake myself up. It's nearing two o'clock in the afternoon, and I was just about to take a nap before my shift at Old George tonight, but a call from Drake Lambert, the talent manager who buys music from me, is much more important.

"I'm calling with a bit of a request."

"Okay." I grip the phone tightly to my ear and move to stand by my piano like I've been working on it all day.

"First off, you've been submitting some great tracks for our royalty-free music library, so keep up the good work there."

A proud smile spreads across my face. I've been submitting tracks to Commercial Notes for a few years now, but the deals are always completed within the Commercial Notes freelancer portal, so getting a call from the man who signs my checks is really exciting.

"Well, thank you so much for saying that. I really enjoy the opportunity, and I'll be laying down a few more tracks later this week."

"Brilliant…but I was calling today to see if you wanted to try your hand at a proper jingle."

"A jingle?" I bite my lip as nerves tickle my spine.

"Have you ever seen any of the national adverts for Tire Depot?"

"Oh, the tire shop with the five-star waiting rooms? I have actually," I reply honestly. "I've been meaning to take my car to one of them for its next service. They all look crazy nice."

"Well, their creative team fancied one of your instrumental tracks called 'Driving to Nowhere' and are wondering if you could add some lyrics to it for a television spot they want to produce. You can sing, can't you? Your profile on Commercial Notes said you could, but nothing you've submitted to us thus far has featured any lyrics."

"Oh…um…yes, I can sing a bit," I confirm. A pit forms in my stomach as the image of having to stand on a stage hits me. "I won't have to perform it for them or anything, right?"

"No, not at all," Drake responds quickly. "This would just be for the advert. You can record it in your home studio."

"Okay, good." I sigh with relief. "I'm not keen on being in the spotlight."

"I understand. And just so you know, since this is a custom jingle request, we'd be paying out ten thousand pounds for a local run and more if the advert runs nationally."

"Did you say ten thousand pounds?" My jaw is permanently on the floor. I've been working for Commercial Notes for about five years now and have sold fifteen of my compositions to them. None of them paid anywhere close to ten thousand pounds. "Bloody hell."

Drake laughs into the line. "I thought you'd like the sound of that. Quite a wage increase from the royalty-free tracks, isn't it?"

"You could say that."

"They'd like a vocal submission in three weeks' time. Do you think you can manage that?"

I bite my lip as I silently laugh to myself. For ten thousand pounds, I'd consider selling him my firstborn. Clearing my throat, I attempt to sound calm and professional. "I believe I can make that work."

"Excellent. I'll send you the details of what they're looking for in terms of messaging, and you can let your creativity flourish. I look forward to hearing what you come up with."

We hang up, and I lower myself onto the sofa, my mind reeling from that surprising call. Ten thousand pounds is at least ten times what I normally make for my other tracks. I hadn't realized how much money was in jingle work. It always seemed a bit corny to me, but for that kind of money, I can be corny!

I used to write lyrics all the time, so I should be able to manage. And maybe if I succeed at this, I can finally pay my parents back for all the lawyer fees they covered for me last year.

I shudder as the memory of my ex and what he did floods through me. Rex Carmichael was a wanker. More than a wanker, he was a dodgy git. A lazy sod who thought he could make money off me and I'd be none the wiser. *God, I still hate him just as much as I did when I first discovered what he'd done.*

The whole ordeal was so awful, I wasn't sure I'd be able to write lyrics ever again. But this opportunity could be just the driving force I need to push that nightmare out of my mind for good.

Glancing around my tiny flat, I smile proudly to myself. This opportunity is exactly why I moved to London nearly a year ago now. I needed to get out from under my parents' roof, forget all about Rex the Hex, and find myself again.

And when you're a country girl who grew up in a small village in Essex, nothing says "finding yourself" more than moving to London.

Perhaps if I'm successful at this jingle, enough money would be left over so I can quit working at Old George. Not that I hate working there by any means. Hubert is a great boss. But between working at Old George and being the building manager for my brother's property to get a discount in rent, I'm often too exhausted to work on what I came here for—my music.

Glancing at the clock, I only have two hours before my shift at Old George starts, so I could still try to catch up on some sleep if I hurry. Then I can start fresh on the jingle tomorrow.

I settle back into my bed and am just about to drift off to sleep when a deep bass blares into my flat. I sit up, my heart rate spiking as I focus on my neighbor's television blaring through my flat wall. Sports announcers, it sounds like, at an alarmingly high level. I'd heard some movement in my neighbor's flat before Drake called, so I assume it's just Zander, but what I hear beyond the telly announcers is much more difficult to disregard.

It's a high-pitched cry that sounds like a screaming goat. Definitely not human. It's followed by several bouts of weeping and some awkward moaning and groaning. What the bloody hell is Soccer Boy doing over there? If he's shagging a girl, he's clearly doing it wrong.

Soccer Boy, aka Zander Williams from Boston with the accent to match, has barely been in the UK for twenty-four hours, and he's already driving me a bit mental. It's a new record for me with a bloke, and I've dealt with plenty of arseholes at the pub. Rex need not be mentioned.

But Soccer Boy is particularly irritating.

First was his horrifying attempt at flirting when we first met. At least I think that was flirting. It wasn't well done, I know that much. Then last night after I got back from working late at Old George, I noticed that he left his telly on *the entire night.* At a volume that projected right through the wall and into my room.

If that wasn't maddening enough, this morning, I was awakened at an ungodly hour by his alarm going off a dozen bloody times. From 5:55 a.m. until 6:55 a.m., I had to listen to the song "Baby Got Back" every five minutes. *I wanted to murder him.*

I gave him the benefit of the doubt for having jet lag this morning, but now I can't even nap because it sounds like he's performing a human sacrifice next door. We have got to find some common ground here, especially if I'll be working extra hours on this jingle project.

I throw back the covers and stride over to our adjoining wall to bang my fist on it. "Oi! Are you okay over there?"

The low murmuring of weeping is all I hear in reply, so I clench my teeth and try again a bit louder, hoping I don't strain my voice too much. When I still get no response, I grab my floral silk robe up off my sofa and throw it on over my silk pajamas to pad barefoot to his door. Being cute doesn't give Soccer Boy a pass for being a pain in the arse.

And the worst part is, Zander knows he's cute. He came strolling into the pub yesterday with his backward baseball cap looking all American and cocky and clueless, and I would have to be blind not to notice his adorable, crooked smirk. It kind of curls up on one side and not the other. It's strange but oddly comforting because if he had a perfect smile, it would truly be unfair to humanity for one man to look that good.

But there's one huge problem. Zander is my neighbor. As in, there's no escaping him. And thankfully, the second he opened his mouth at the pub, I knew without a shadow of a doubt he wasn't anyone I would give any lasting attention to. Been there. Done that. Exhibit A: Rex.

Zander is a manwhore. A cute, awkwardly charming, and ridiculously cocky manwhore who's also a footballer, which means he's the worst cocktail of a male specimen, and I need to stay far, far away.

Or at least…a wall away. Once he figures out I can hear absolutely everything he does over there.

I bang my fist on the thick wooden door original to the Victorian building and wait, my nerves feeling electrified at the prospect of seeing him again. But it doesn't matter. I'm just here to inform him of how thin the walls are. Open mic at Old George tonight means I'll be there until well after midnight, so listening to this man do whatever he's doing over there simply will not work.

After what feels like ages, his door finally swings open, and my body sways as the vision before me comes into full view. Soccer Boy stands before me, covering his groin with a very small, pale pink tea towel that I recall hand-selecting for his kitchen. The shocking sight forces me to reach out and grip the doorframe for balance as I weakly attempt to shield my eyes from the mounds of flesh only inches away from me.

But of course, I can't help but chance a quick look. It's quite impressive what the human eye can absorb in a matter of seconds because one glance tells my brain fervently that Soccer Boy is *fit*.

Not that that makes him special. Most footballers are fit. I'm sure if I had a job that paid me to work out for hours every day, I'd have muscles for miles as well. But that doesn't erase the fact that Zander's build is utter perfection. Like a work of art that needs to be memorialized in a sculpture, sans washcloth.

He isn't a bulky, live at the gym and survive on protein shakes type. He's lean and brawny like he could run for days without breaking a sweat. And his large, sculpted shoulders, tight pecs, and abs are a lovely olive tone like he spends a lot of time outside with his shirt off. Damn him. How can he be tan in bloody January? Winter turns me into the ghost of Christmas past while he's over there displaying bronze muscles that I didn't even know existed on the human body. It's quite upsetting. Even his nipples are tan.

Oh fuck, I just looked at his nipples.

Finally, I shake myself out of my stupor and hit him with a firm look. "Can I ask what on earth you're doing in there?"

He trembles before me as I notice the goose bumps erupting all over his arms. "I was t-t-taking a bath," he stammers.

"And you couldn't grab a proper towel to cover yourself?" I glance down at his abs that pop out with every exhale of breath. I wonder what they would feel like if I just reached out and poked them? "If this is some sort of ridiculous pickup move again, I'm going to raise your rent." Not that he pays it.

"This was all I could find. I looked everywhere." He curses and runs a hand through his damp, curly locks. His hazel eyes are red-rimmed.

"Why are you shaking so much? Is your hot water not working?"

He swallows, and it looks painful, his face almost haggard as he stares back at me. "Ice...bath," he chatters.

"Ice bath? Whatever for?" I look him up and down like he must have been in some sort of horrid accident to require such cruel and unusual punishment.

"My body hurts everywhere." His face scrunches in agony, and he looks like he wants to cry.

"Are you sick?" I reach out to touch his forehead. It's an instinctual move as I've had my nieces over enough to know when something is wrong. He's cold and damp but doesn't feel feverish. In fact, now that I'm standing this close to his glistening, naked body, I fear I might be feverish in places I should be very ashamed of. I daresay there's bloody steam rising between the two of us at this moment.

He shakes me off, and I'm snapped back to reality as his teeth chatter noisily. "I'm not sick. First training session today. Coach is trying to kill me. Which is actually fine by me because right now I want to die." He groans, hunching over, while maintaining a white-knuckled grip on his towel.

Shamelessly, I can't tear my eyes away from his shaking hands that look dangerously close to dropping the one scrap of pink material covering his manhood. A small tremor runs through his whole body, and I jerk my focus off his groin long enough to thank the heavens he hasn't noticed I've been silently praying for that pink fabric's demise.

"Step aside," I exclaim louder than I intended, placing my hand on his firm, albeit frozen body. God is he firm. He feels like rocks. I march into his flat and glance back. "I'll show you where the bath towels are."

I nearly choke on my own words when I catch sight of his very uncovered backside. It looks like two perfectly glazed biscuits that you could bounce a coin off. Positively inhuman.

My eyes jerk forward as I march into his loo to pull open the cubby located behind the large antique mirror that I had hinges put on. "All sorts of toiletries are in here as well." I grab a large fluffy white towel and turn around to find him standing in the doorway. I toss it at him.

"I didn't know that opened." He blinks back curiously.

I roll my eyes as he struggles to hold the tea towel over his willy and wrap the larger one around his waist. He's standing there freezing to death while my own body heats to an uncomfortable degree. This is going to be a problem. I turn my back to give him some privacy, trying my best to ignore how sculpted his thighs are too. Good God, footy players and thighs…it's better than cream and jelly, isn't it? I glance at the soaker tub. "My word, you must have emptied the entire building's ice machine."

"Didn't want the other recruits to see me doing an ice bath in the locker room." He exhales a heavy breath. "I gotta look tougher than the other newbies."

I let out a laugh and notice the sudoku puzzle book on the floor. "So this is an ego thing. Why am I not surprised?"

"It's a survival thing," he corrects, his voice firm. "Is using that much ice against the building rules?"

"It's not against the building rules but only because I never realized I needed to make that rule." I turn around to find him somewhat covered again, and my traitorous eyes zero in on his hip bones that protrude above the bath towel, giving me a visual that I will struggle to erase from my mind in the dark of night. "Do you want me to turn the heat up in your flat?" Hell, I might need an ice bath after this ordeal is over.

He shakes his head, looking a little sad as he tightens the towel around his waist. "I have to get back in."

"What does it even do for you? Physically?" I blink back in shock.

"It helps my muscles recover quicker. I can't be sore tomorrow when I meet the rest of the team for the first time. I can't." A look of desperation flits across his face, and I nearly feel sorry for the bloke.

"Well, you're fine to use all of the ice, but I have to ask, do you have to leave your telly on while you do this? You can't possibly hear it from in here, and that along with your inhumane screams as you torture yourself make it really difficult for anyone to sleep around here."

The color begins returning to Zander's cheeks as he glances at the clock beside his bed. "It's three o'clock in the afternoon. Why would any-one be sleeping?"

"Because some of us work evenings. And not all of us start our day at six a.m. after pressing snooze a million times." My cheeks heat in anger at the recent memory of not being able to sleep this morning.

"What?" he asks, a look of confusion sweeping across his boyish features.

"You snoozed your alarm at least ten times today." I pin him with an unamused glower.

"It couldn't have been ten times." He rolls his eyes, the muscle in his jaw shifting as he shakes his head.

I ignore his stupid bare torso as he crosses his arms to tell me I'm out of line. "You're right." I cross my arms back and quirk a challenging brow. "I may have slept through the first few times, so it was likely more than that. Though it was slightly hard to hear over the blaring of your telly that you left on all night. I'll do a poll with the other neighbors in the building and get back to you on the exact number."

Zander's brows furrow, his hazel eyes glittering with mirth in the warm bathroom lighting. "Am I being a bad neighbor, Ducky?"

"Your cheekiness isn't going to work with me." I hate how he seems to inspect every feature on my face every time I speak to him. It's unnerving. "Honestly, Zander, who snoozes their alarm that many times?"

He huffs out a laugh, looking a lot less pathetic than he did moments ago and a lot more irritating. "Well, I didn't know the walls here were so thin. Seems like a construction problem if you ask me."

"Is it that hard to wake up on the first alarm?" I prop my hands on my hips. "Or can you perhaps edit your alarm to the time you actually have to get up?"

"I need time to come to." His nostrils flare as he eyes me with blatant irritation. "Not all of us have the luxury of sleeping in."

Oh, the cheek of him! I take a step closer to him so he can feel the full effects of my annoyance. "I didn't get to sleep in today because I had to listen to my neighbor's alarm go off over and over. Which is why I was hoping to get a nap in before my shift tonight when you so keenly had to screw that up as well. You're two for two on mucking up my day, Soccer Boy. It's quite impressive."

It's then that I realize he's moved closer to me as well. I have to crane my neck up to look at him as he bows over me, his chest rising and falling as he breathes, making it really difficult for me not to inhale his damp scent. He smells of menthol sports cream and sweat. Not an attractive combination by any standards, but I still slightly wonder what it would be like to have a big man like him wrap himself around me and press me up against the glossy white tiled wall.

Bloody hell, if he could hear my thoughts, his ego would explode.

I force myself to maintain eye contact, but the problem is, his face isn't all that awful to look at either. The natural curl in his shaggy dark chestnut hair only adds to his boyish features and that crooked smirk. And his eyes are rimmed by dark, impossibly long lashes. Mine are blonde and only visible with the mascara that I have to apply every single day. Men really do have all the luck.

"Just please try to be considerate of others in the building, okay?" I state through clenched teeth, trying to de-escalate this little row we're currently having in the loo.

"You could work on keeping it down too," he grates, his full lips resting in a simmering glower that I can't help but notice is very kissable. "I heard some music drifting through the walls earlier, so you're no quiet church mouse."

I deflate slightly at that accusation. This flat Zander's occupying has sat empty for a year, so I hadn't even considered that if I can hear his telly in my flat, he can hear my music in his. I'll have to rework my process a bit. "I'll see what I can do."

"So will I." His eyes glance at my body, where a rush of goose bumps erupts over my skin.

"Cheers," I blurt out and move quickly to walk out, brushing shoulders with him in my haste.

"We're not even drinking," he replies with a confused puppy dog face.

"Cheers means *thanks*, Soccer Boy." I can't help but laugh at him from his bathroom doorway. I spread my arms out on the frame and add, "My God, you really need to read a British book or something. Try *Bridget Jones's Diary*, I beg of you."

He freezes as his eyes dip low, and every muscle visible above the towel flexes, popping the veins in his arms as I follow where his gaze has landed. To my horror, I realize when I grabbed the doorframe, my robe fell open, revealing my very thin satin cami where my very hard nipples are trying to cut through the fabric.

Quickly, I cover myself, my face flush with embarrassment. When I meet Zander's eyes, his jaw is clenched, and his nostrils quiver with a stuttered breath. A rush of tension builds between my legs at the look in his eye that gives me no doubt what he's thinking.

I open my mouth to say something but choke on the gasp that comes out when he looks like he too is about to speak. The air around us thickens as I struggle with a way to diffuse this tense moment.

I need to leave.

With firm determination, I nod briskly and turn on my heel to walk out of his flat as fast as my bare feet can take me. I'm quite certain that if I looked in the mirror, I'd see the same heated look in my eyes I just saw in his.

4

Part of the Family

Zander

"**D**O YOU GUYS THINK COACH SAW ME PUKE YESTERDAY?" KNIGHT grumbles quietly from the locker room bench beside me. He's kitted out in his green and white Bethnal Green F.C. uniform just like me, even though our cleats won't break a blade of grass today from the bench.

"If he didn't see it, he could smell it." Link chuckles with a disgusted look on his face. "What the fuck did you eat yesterday, bro?"

"Airplane food. Fucking delayed flight screwed everything up. I was lucky I made it in time for our health check." Knight combs his hand through his long brown hair as he ties it up into a messy bun on top of his head. He's redone that fucking ponytail eight times in thirty minutes. His anxiety is giving me anxiety.

"You need to chill out, dude," I state, leaning back into the cubby with my name engraved on it as I adjust my soccer socks and stare at the coach's closed office door.

"You struggled yesterday too, Williams." Link's blue eyes zero in on me. "Did you give a British cheerio to the porcelain gods yourself?" He tucks his shaggy blonde hair behind his ears, his eyes narrowing like he's a detective investigating a crime.

I wince as I attempt to forget how bad I looked yesterday at that endurance training. It wasn't the normal type of struggle that I expected as a new player in the UK. It was like I had two left feet. My focus was all over the place. Coach Z had to repeat my name several times when it was literally just the four of us out there. But I'll be damned if I clue these guys in on what was going through my mind the whole time.

Clearing my throat, I reply, "I just had more unpacking to do. I ended up going for another run late last night 'cause I couldn't sleep."

"What?" Knight and Link say in unison and blink horrified looks at me.

I feign that it was no big deal, but it was, in fact, a very big deal. Yesterday's training was awful. Coach Zion is truly a sadist, which must make me a masochist because instead of going to bed early to let my body recover, I went for a run to try to shake the bizarre thoughts swirling through my head.

Meeting Vaughn Harris yesterday rattled me more than I thought it would. It triggered thoughts of what it'll be like when I come face-to-face with his son, Booker Harris, the keeper. Or his other son, Tanner Harris, the assistant coach. Will I creepily inspect their fingers like I did Vaughn's? What if the other two brothers, Gareth and Camden, happen to be here to cheer on their brothers? They have a sister named Vilma that they call Vi, too. How do I know that? Why do I give a fuck? I need to get my shit together and try to forget about this entire Harris family. Football over bullshit.

Last night, to get control of my traitorous thoughts, I decided to direct my focus on my cute neighbor: Ducky.

Good grief, I'm low-key obsessed with winning her over. I went to a fucking bookstore and picked up *Bridget Jones's Diary*, for Christ's sake. I've never done something like that for a woman in my life. And I didn't do it for research on British lingo. In fact, I love nothing more than saying something wrong to make her angry. She gets this little dimple in her chin, and I like knowing that I get under her skin.

The truth is, I picked up that book to get her attention. It was a move. And I don't usually require moves with women I want to sleep with. Usually, my move is just asking them to fuck.

Daphney will be another story altogether.

And if I want to hook up with her, I probably need to stop riling her up so much. If only she didn't look so cute when she was mad.

Images of her on my doorstep in a tiny pair of silky shorts and a tank top with no fucking bra flash through my mind. She had a robe on but didn't even notice or didn't even care that it was wide open and showing off all her curves that were even more impressive than I had imagined. She's hot, to be sure, but her fiery spirit makes it impossible for me to take my eyes off her.

Even my ice bath couldn't damper the stiffness in my cock. I jerked off twice after our little argument just to try to find some relief and still, nothing. Something is ridiculously sexy about having a girl next door to you who you aren't banging and who seems to basically hate your guts.

That is a very specific kink I should probably talk to a therapist about.

Thoughts of Daphney are what really inspired the late-night run. It must have helped because I came home and slept like a rock afterward. Though, I'm pretty sure my alarm went off several times, despite trying to yank myself up out of bed on the first chime. But if making her angry means she knocks on my door again, I won't be upset about that.

Regardless, today is a big day, and I don't need to be thinking about an argument I got into with my sexy neighbor. I shake off thoughts of Daphney and refocus back on the space around me.

It's game day at Tower Park, and the locker room is full of focused, professional athletes who have been warming up and talking strategy for hours. Coach told us to come in later and lay low, and he'd introduce us before the game. However, I have a feeling most of these guys don't give two shits about the three newbies in the corner. They are all likely assuming we'll fail and be gone in a matter of months. Three Americans coming to play in the UK is a risk any way you look at it, but I've played against both Link and Knight Stateside throughout the years, and they are here for a reason.

Personality-wise, they couldn't be more different. Knight is the brooding, sensitive type who lets his emotions get the best of him. I remember playing against him when he got red-carded for chest-bumping the ref. It was a bullshit call, but fun to watch him blow up on the sports highlights.

Link, on the other hand, is the typical loud-mouthed offensive player who makes friends with everyone. A charmer with the refs and the opposing team. He totally would have been the asshole flicking towels in the locker room in high school and hyenic laughing the entire time he did it.

Nevertheless, I will say it's nice to have fellow Americans to commiserate this unusual situation with. Hopefully, I can get my shit together so I can keep playing with them and not be booted back to America and prove my mother right.

Link elbows me and points at a player in the corner we all know as Roan DeWalt. He's the South African striker who's been crushing it for Bethnal Green for several years now. He's a bit older than the three of us, and Link informed me that Roan's married with a kid, but his age doesn't show at all. He easily keeps up with the other striker, Billy Campbell, who's only twenty-three years old.

At twenty-two, I was one of the youngest on the Seattle soccer club, but in the UK, they're ready for pro at a much younger age. UK football is an institution. A beast in and of itself. Players who grow up here don't need college to hone their skills. They start training when they're still in fucking diapers. It's why my dad pushed so hard for me to do that youth soccer camp over here when I was younger. He said I needed to see what soccer is like when a country treats it like America treats American football.

He wasn't wrong.

I got my ass kicked at that UK camp, and I came back to Boston and trained harder and longer than ever before. I won't let my ass get kicked at Bethnal Green. I refuse.

"Okay, gentlemen, listen up!" Coach Zion says as he steps out of the coach's office. "Before I let our manager Vaughn Harris inspire the lot of you for our first FA Cup game, I thought I'd let you know we have a few new faces in the changing room today. They aren't on the roster yet but will start training with us next week. I'm hoping today you can all give them a glimpse of what they can expect when they play for a proper Premier League club." The players make noises of agreement as Coach continues, "All three from America, we have Knight Timmons, a midfielder, Link Conlin, offense, and Zander Williams, center-back. And please, for the love of Christ, don't fuck with these three like you fucked with Billy. We don't need another media photograph of a footballer in women's knickers."

Billy's face turns as red as his hair, and everyone laughs as Knight, Link, and I shoot nervous eyes to each other, trying to look tough but failing miserably.

All humor vanishes from the space, and I look around to see all eyes zeroed in on Vaughn Harris, who's just entered the room. "Are they ready, Coach?"

"As they'll ever be." Coach props his fists on his hips as Vaughn claps his hands for our attention.

"Alright, this is our first FA Cup game, and we have a lot to prove after going out so early last year. I'm not going to sit here and give you a big speech to inspire. That was clearly bollocks last year. I'm just going to remind you that this is your job. To play football. To put it all out there. To be the best you can be. So, get your arses out on that pitch and show our fans that Bethnal Green is where the FA Cup belongs!"

The team jumps to their feet and rushes to the middle of the locker room, cheering loudly and chanting Bethnal Green over and over. Roan

DeWalt sees the three of us lingering in the back, so he head nods us over to the pack as they put their hands in the middle. A player I can't see yells out, "I am thine!"

And the team roars back with, "Thou art mine!"

As everyone breaks apart and begins filing out, Roan turns and offers out his hand. "Welcome, guys. I'm Roan DeWalt, team captain."

"Yes, you fucking are." Link steps forward and grips his hand first. He looks like he wants to kiss the striker as he shakes a bit too aggressively. "An honor, man. For real."

Roan smiles, his teeth bright white against his light brown skin. "Ag no, it's all good, man. I just popped over to tell you about that saying we just chanted," he says in his South African accent. He turns and points at an area above the locker room door that features a part of the wall never covered with drywall like the rest of the room. An exposed oak plank board has the words the team just yelled burned into it, and every player slaps his hand on it as they depart the locker room. Roan hits us with a serious look. "I am thine, thou art mine is our team mantra…it means we belong to football and football belongs to us. It might seem corny, but if you're looking for inspiration, you touch that shit every time you leave this locker room. Got it?"

We nod seriously because it wasn't a request. It was a command. We follow him out, grateful for the opportunity to press our hands on the holy grail of Bethnal Green F.C.

As I stand in the long concrete tunnel, the crowd noise becomes deafening as they chant their team's song loud and proud, waiting for the players to make their entrance. I inch myself up to the front to take in the view as the other team makes their appearance. The stadium is packed, the bright Saturday sun glistening off the electric green grass. The entire vibe is a fucking rush.

Soccer in America isn't like this. This right here feels like a religious experience. Daphney's words from a couple of days ago about Bethnal Green being the people's team feels truer than ever before. A once lower-level soccer club who fought their way to the Premier League and recent FA Cup champions coming out to grab that title back: *I am thine, thou art mine* in-fucking-deed.

"Gets you right in the trouser snake, doesn't it?" a husky voice says from behind me, blowing wet, hot air into my ear and causing me to nearly jump out of my skin.

I whirl around to find a blonde, manbun, bearded guy decked out in tan slacks and a white Bethnal Green polo and standing much closer to me than I expected.

He reaches his hand out to me. "Tanner Harris, assistant coach... didn't mean to scare you, bruv."

I take his hand and nod, recalling from that Harris Ho website that Tanner is the Harris Brother who retired not too long ago and is now the assistant coach for his dad's club. I try not to look at his fingernails to see if they're like mine. Instead, I wipe my damp ear and elbow him playfully. "Got my ear a little wet with that close talking you did there."

"No wetter than your dreams will be tonight after experiencing this from sniffer's row," he deadpans and then wraps his arm around my shoulders to turn us toward the field. "It's a beautiful fucking view, mate, and I appreciate the fact that you took a moment to drink it in. It's better than sex, some would say...then again, they haven't had sex with my wife. She's a doctor, by the way. You'll see her in the front row behind our team. It's where our family all sit."

I nod and force a smile, hating the fact that I knew his wife was a doctor already because I'm a fucking creepy stalker who subscribed to the Harris Ho and Proud newsletter months ago. Tanner's wife is Dr. Belle Ryan, and she is best friend's with the team doctor, Indie, because they went to med school together. Twin brothers marrying best friends...how fucking weird is that?

"Belle's got beauty and brains. She saves little babies before they're even born. Way out of my fucking league but we have two kids together, so I've properly trapped her, and she's doomed to stay with me forever now. I feel bad about that sometimes, but our kids are the fucking best. They—"

"Tanner, stop oversharing with the new recruits," another voice echoes from the other side of me. I turn and lock eyes with a player I instantly recognize. He reaches out his gloved hand to me, and I shake it, feeling a strange zing shoot up my arm at the contact.

"You're Booker Harris," I state knowingly as images from that website flash through my mind of him, his wife, and their twin boys.

"And you're Zander Williams," he says with a kind smile as he stands nearly two inches taller than me.

Fucking keepers. They're all giants. And glancing over at Tanner, even though I know they're brothers, the two of them look completely different. Both are athletically built, but where Tanner is blonde-haired and blue-eyed, Booker has a darker complexion and hazel eyes like mine, even if we do have different facial features.

"I hear my dad wants to make you my new best friend." Booker laughs.

"What?" I ask, feeling a strange sensation sweep over me as I stand here, flanked by two guys who I may or may not have a genetic connection to.

"Don't scare the lad, Book," Vaughn Harris's voice booms down the hallway behind us. The three of us turn to see him approaching. "I haven't had a chance to tell him all my plans yet."

"Plans?" I suddenly feel like I have a mouth full of cotton balls.

Vaughn rolls his eyes and places his hand on my shoulder. "You got the scope of it at the press conference with my ideas for the keeper and the sweeper to run the game. But what I haven't told you yet is that I want you and Booker to get together outside of training sessions. Really develop a connection and chemistry."

"A bromance," Tanner offers with a dirty smirk.

Booker laughs and shakes his head at his brother while directing his attention to me. "With you as the potential future sweeper and playing directly in front of me, Dad just wants us to be in sync."

"Like me and Camden were when we were strikers for this club," Tanner says, elbowing me like I know the entire history of Bethnal Green F.C.

Which I kind of do. The Harris Ho site is more geared toward the Harris family's personal business, but I did my own game tape research on the club. The highlights I found of Tanner and Camden Harris, twin brothers playing as co-strikers for their father's club, one with a strong left foot, and the other with a strong right foot, were incredible to watch. I actually wouldn't be able to tell who was who if it wasn't for Tanner's heavily inked arms and long blonde hair and beard. They practically ran in unison. It was like synchronized fucking swimming but on a soccer field. Bethnal Green fans were devastated when Camden left to play for his current team of Arsenal, but I can't blame the guy…back when Cam and Tan played for Bethnal Green, they were a mid-level team. They've come a long way since then.

Now Tanner is retired along with the eldest Harris brother, Gareth. Booker and Camden are the last two still commanding the pitch for different clubs.

"You don't have to go so far as a bromance," Vaughn states, pointing his finger at me. "I just want you and Booker to play…" He pauses as he attempts to think up a word. "Well, like brothers. Camden and Tanner had the sharing a womb thing going for them, but I think if you and Booker get to know each other, you can find a rhythm and be an unstoppable force. Maybe bromance is the right word after all."

I inhale sharply when I realize I stopped breathing for a second there. Here I stand, ensconced by three Harrises. Three men who…well…fuck, I could be related to. And it feels like the universe is laughing at me with this entire conversation right now. Does Vaughn Harris know something I don't?

Jesus Christ, that sounds nuts. It sounds nuts because it is nuts. These guys don't know shit about me. And I don't care if we do share a blood relation. *Football over bullshit, Zander.*

I clear my throat and reply with something I can't even believe I had the balls to say. "Well, consider me a part of the family then."

They all laugh and clap me on the back animatedly as we turn to make our way out onto the field and into a world I would have never expected for myself.

5

Color Commentary

Daphney

"**B**OOP, BOOP, BOOP," A DEEP VOICE ECHOES MUCH TOO CLOSE TO my face, and my eyes fly open in terror as I catch sight of Zander Williams's finger by my nose.

"What are you doing?" I exclaim, scrambling up off my sofa and standing behind the arm of it to put some space between us. I hold my chunky blanket out in front of me like it's somehow going to protect me from the psychopath currently standing in my flat.

Zander holds his hands up defensively, his eyes wide. "I didn't mean to scare you!"

I blink back at him as my sleep-fogged mind clears, and I take in the surroundings of my flat. I reach up and touch my nose. "Did you just touch my nose?"

"I booped it." An awkward smile spreads across his face as he grips the back of his neck. "You were sleeping so cutely. I thought it'd be a funny way to wake you up."

"Funny?" I repeat, forking my fingers into my messy bun and glancing down to make sure I wasn't having another wardrobe malfunction in front of him. "You thought it would be funny to break into my flat and touch me?"

His face falls. "Well, when you put it like that, it sounds creepy."

"Because it is!" I toss the blanket down onto the sofa. "What are you doing here?"

"It's one fifteen," he says like that should mean something to me. "I texted you about getting groceries. You said to come get you at one. And I didn't break into your apartment. The door was cracked open. I thought you were waiting for me because I'm fifteen minutes late. I didn't expect to find you sleeping so soundly." His eyes move down my body, and I find myself wishing I had that blanket back.

I glance at the clock by my bed, stunned that fifteen minutes have passed so quickly. I remember gently closing my eyes only seconds ago as I waited for him, and I must have dozed off.

Regardless, that doesn't ever give anyone an excuse to…boop another human. I hit him with a firm glower. "Please don't ever boop me again."

"Noted that the Duckmeister is anti-boop," he replies, rocking back on his feet, looking ridiculously cute. After a moment's pause, he adds, "So can we still go get groceries, or are you too mad at me?"

"We can go," I say, trying to shake away my initial annoyance. God, who boops people they barely know? Soccer Boy. Soccer Boy is a total booper. And why does he have to be so cute while being so annoying? It's an odd juxtaposition I do not like.

I walk over to my kitchen counter to grab my handbag and keys before heading toward the door. I pause when I see Zander isn't following me.

"So, this is your place?" he asks, looking at my tiny flat curiously.

"Yes." I take in my space to try to discern what sort of impression he'd be taking away. It's a great deal smaller than his, for sure. My unmade bed is pressed up against the wall on the right, and my black sofa sits at the foot of it smack dab in the middle of the entire studio space. I don't have the twenty-foot ceilings like he does because of the misshapen building, so it's much cozier, made even more so by the warm twinkle lights strung up along the walls. Zander could probably cross my flat in six large steps if he wanted to, but I still love my little flat.

My voice is teasing when I add, "I realize my entire studio is about the size of your sleeping area next door, but unfortunately, I didn't land a great football contract."

Zander shoots me his crooked smile as he walks over to my small piano keyboard that sits in front of the window. He hits a couple of notes and fills the room with dissonance. His gaze shifts to the corner.

"So you weren't just playing music on a speaker yesterday." He points at the giant structure that takes up a large portion of my limited floor space. "What is that?"

"It's a sound booth," I reply, my nerves prickling over him touching all my stuff.

"I take it you're a big-time musician?" Zander walks over to where my guitar rests in its stand. He strums it mindlessly, and I cringe at how out of tune it sounds.

"Not big time," I tut because I hate talking about what I do. People tend to glamorize the fact that I make music. They instantly think of me performing on a stage or going viral as an artist on TikTok. What I do is like the fast food of the music industry, so I'd just prefer not to talk about it.

"I see a sound booth, a keyboard, and a guitar. Plus, loads of recording equipment in that booth that look way too high tech for you not to be big time."

"Perhaps I'm a musical hoarder." I push my hands into my pockets, hating how awkward I feel being the center of attention.

"Bullshit," he replies with a laugh. "Are you famous or something?" His eyes are fixed on me with genuine curiosity. "Is there a Ducky playlist out there on Spotify I should be downloading right now?"

"If there was, it's doubtful I'd be working at the pub across the street," I respond firmly, my tummy swirling at the unpleasant memory incited by the word "Spotify." I tuck those dark thoughts away and pin Zander with a serious expression. "And if there was, I assure you that it wouldn't be under the name Ducky." I roll my eyes at the nickname, grateful that just the sound of it lightens my mood. "I record commercial tracks. Boring promo video-type music. Stuff you hear on adverts, documentaries, training videos. It's really no big deal."

Zander nods as he steps inside my booth and glances around. "This booth looks like a very big deal. Did you build it yourself?"

"My brother Theo made it for me. He designs custom furniture in a shop nearby, so he's quite handy. Can we please go? I have a dinner later that I don't want to be late for." I move to stand by my open door, feeling strangely unnerved by Soccer Boy being all tall and big in my flat.

"Have a hot date?" Zander walks toward me, his brows lifted with genuine interest.

I narrow my eyes on him. "Why would that be any of your business?"

"Just trying to be neighborly." A wounded look crosses his face as we walk into the hallway, and I feel slightly guilty for being such a bitch.

"It's just a family thing." I pause in front of his door when I see his rubbish bag sitting there, looking…well…like rubbish. I point at it, a sheepish look crossing my face. "I really hate being a nag, but you can't leave your rubbish in the hallway. A mouse got in the building a few months ago and nearly gave Miss Kitchems a heart attack. We had a pest problem for ages after that."

Zander exhales and shakes his head as he picks up his bag. "The bad neighbor strikes again."

I grimace as I follow him down the stairs. I really hate being such a bitch, but maybe it's better this way. If I'm bitchy, he'll be too irritated to flirt with me, and I won't have to try so hard to resist his annoying charm.

"Congrats on the win yesterday, by the way," I say, bumping my trolley into Zander's as I find him in the produce section. We've been shopping for over thirty minutes, and every time I spot him in an aisle, I swear, it's like he's reading all the food labels as if they're in a foreign language.

He returns a turnip to the display case and lifts his brows. "Did you watch the match?"

"It was on at the pub while I was working, so I caught bits and pieces."

He falls into step beside me and nods. "I can't take much credit for the W. I was too busy riding the pine pony."

"Sorry?" I frown at him in confusion.

"It means sitting on the bench. Read a book or something, Ducky." The flirtatious wink he shoots me sends a zing of electricity right through my body.

"We're still in England last I checked," I smart back and then realize I'm smiling stupidly up at him in a supermarket, and I should *not* be doing that.

I turn my attention back to my groceries as Zander adds, "We start training with the team tomorrow, so that's when we have to start proving ourselves, I guess." A nervous look flits across his face, but he tries to hide it with a forced smile.

"Knight and Link are the two other American recruits, right?" I ask, watching him curiously.

"Yeah, they're good guys," he replies, grabbing a bag of kale and tossing it into his trolley. "I knew them back in the States, so it feels like having a piece of home with me."

"You know all of Bethnal Green thinks Vaughn Harris is mental for recruiting three Americans, right?"

Zander winces. "I got that impression at the press conference I had to do. The team wasn't overly warm to us at the match yesterday either, but I fully intend on winning them over."

"I bet you do." I smile as my eyes dip down to his groceries. "God, what are you putting in your trolley?"

"Trolley?" Zander frowns in confusion.

"This," I reply, grabbing the metal trolley he's been pushing around. "What do Americans call this?"

"A grocery cart, which makes way more sense."

"God, that is so obvious. Americans call things so literal over there."

"Well, at least then we know what we're getting. Like this." He pauses as he picks up a bag of greens from the cooler he's standing next to. "What the hell is rocket? In the US, this is called arugula, so you know you're not getting a spaceship."

I bark out a laugh. "We were here first, remember?" I repeat the words he said to me at the pub when we first met, and a peculiar look flashes across his face.

He shakes it off quickly and yanks my trolley over to him. "Look at what you have in your cart...all sugar."

"I like my sweets!" I defend, staring down at a trolley full of biscuits and baking items I was running low on. "And I watch my two nieces a lot, and they love to make my chocolate chip cookies."

"And you actually eat all that junk?"

"Yes."

"Where does it all go?" His eyes wander down my body as a slow smirk forms on his lips. My body heats the longer he stares, and I hate how much he affects me.

Clearing my throat to break the moment, I reply brazenly, "In my mouth."

Mirth dances across his features. "Do you even work out?"

"I have a gym membership that I remember to use once in a while." I wince knowingly.

He presses his lips together and nods. "Well, I'll forgive your bad eating habits if you know how to make oatmeal raisin cookies."

"What is so special about oatmeal raisin?"

"It's my thing," he shrugs casually. "Nearly every athlete I know has a thing. For example, Knight said he eats a blade of grass from every field he plays on before the match starts. Link does this weird hopping on his left foot three times before he walks onto the pitch. He swears it makes his left foot stronger for the match. So stupid."

"And oatmeal raisin is smart?" I ask, shooting him a cheeky look.

"I only eat one after a win. That's my superstition because oatmeal raisin is a delicious and nutritious reward for a job well done. It has oats and fruit in it…chocolate chip cookies are pure sugar."

"My God, you have an answer for everything," I state, shaking my head. "Are you always like this?"

"Yes," he laughs to himself. "My dad used to tell me once my soccer career is over, I should go into sports broadcasting because I can color commentate my way through a funeral."

"He sounds like a smart man, maybe a bit dark," I reply with a laugh and expect Zander to laugh with me, but he doesn't. In fact, his mood has visibly shifted in the blink of an eye. "Did I say something?"

He shakes his head quickly. "No. You're good. You ready to check out?"

"Sure, I can be ready." I frown curiously at him. We make our way to the checkout counters, and that light-hearted boy who was here only seconds ago has been replaced by a pensive, brooding, distracted man.

"Penny for your thoughts?" I ask as we load our items onto the conveyor.

"They aren't worth a penny," he replies softly.

I chew my lip and nod thoughtfully. Perhaps it's better not to pry. The less I know about Zander Williams, the better.

6

Brothers From Another Mother

Zander

THIS WAS A BAD IDEA, I THINK AS I FIND MYSELF AT A PUB WITH KNIGHT, Link, and three other guys from the team. The bar is located down the street from Tower Park training facility, but I didn't even get a look at the name of it when we walked in. Although, saying I "walked in" is a bit of a stretch. We were pretty much pushed in by our teammates who play the same positions we do on the field. So, it's safe to say I'm a little uncomfortable by the crowd I'm surrounded by.

First, we have Scottish midfielder, affectionately nicknamed, Macky Junior in honor of the former Scottish midfielder, Maclay Logan, who retired a couple of years ago. His actual name is Banner Macleod, so the nickname suits him for a couple of different reasons. Banner has dark black hair and narrow blue eyes that sort of say, "you can fuck right off." Then there's Billy Campbell, the twenty-three-year-old striker from Wales. We were warned in no uncertain terms not to ask him about the women's knicker incident and that's about all we know about quiet Billy.

And finally, there's Lance Finnegan, aka Finney. He's a thirty-one-year-old center-back from Ireland. He has short blonde hair, a long face, and a permanent scowl that seems constantly directed at me.

"One more shot," Finney says, slapping the sticky bar with his hand. It's nearing eight o'clock and we've been here since practice ended at four. I have no food in my belly and I'm pretty sure I'm going to yack like Knight did last week.

"I can't drink anymore." I shoot Finney a pleading look. "I need food. I'm fucking wasted, man."

"You're pissed," Finney states firmly.

"I'm not pissed! I'm happy to be here," I lie through my teeth. I'm not happy to be here, but I need Finney to like me because I need a mentor more than a rival.

"Pissed means drunk. Saying you're wasted sounds American. Tell me you're having savage craic and we'll be mates for life."

My eyes go wide. "You do hard drugs? Doesn't the club test us for that shit?"

Finney's face bends in disgust. "The craic is Irish for a good time, you idiot! Savage craic is a mighty fine night."

He shakes his head like I'm a moron as he orders two more shots from the bartender. Dread washes over me as Finney pushes a glass of clear liquid to me. "If you don't drink this, then I will tell the entire team you're a wanker."

"I think that ship has sailed," I slur, my eyes slow blinking back at him. I've heard wanker dropped a few times throughout the locker room.

I pause as I recall how fucking hard the past four days have been. I knew training here would be difficult, but annoyingly, it seems worse for me than it does for Knight and Link. They seem to be keeping up while I'm looking like this is my first time at soccer camp.

Coming from America, I was always the quickest player on the field. But here, the speed and rate of attacking these guys all possess is a serious culture shock. I'm killing myself so much I've needed to do ice baths daily, and I'm damn near crying myself to sleep every night. Today, I literally considered asking for a wheelchair escort to heave my dead ass off the training field. I'm floundering big time.

"What does wanker mean exactly?" I ask Finney, even though I'm pretty sure I know the answer.

He makes a lewd gesture with his hand and I groan, scrubbing my hand over my face. "Pretty much what I thought. Hey, how are you going to be able to train tomorrow after this many drinks?"

"I'm Irish." Finney throws back his shot and with a heavy sigh, I do the same. He nods his approval at me and says, "Grand."

Nothing about the past few hours has felt "grand." Finney hasn't spoken a single word to me all week during training. He just glowered and took every chance he could to make me look like a rookie.

"Do you honestly think you have what it takes to be a leader, Williams?" Finney asks, shoving yet another shot in front of me.

"A leader?" I stare ominously at the liquid.

He nods and gazes forward. "A center-back...or sweeper if that's what

Vaughn Harris wants to call you…we see the field like no one else. We have to make decisions for the team on how we're going to move the ball away from our net and set up the next play. Do you truly expect me to believe you can come over from America where you're a big fish in a small pond and play closely with Booker Harris and lead a team of European footballers who were playing football while you were still shitting green in your nappies?"

"Not all of us are European," Link says, holding up a neon appletini that he and Billy have been drinking the whole time. The martini glass looks like a tiny child-sized cup in his large hand. Finney cuts Link a punishing glower so he redirects his attention back to his green liquid.

"I'll tell you what I think." I straighten my posture and do my best to focus on one of the Finneys sitting beside me, not the other two swirling around him. This asshole brought me here to fuck with my head, not to bond, and seeing how I'm fucking with my own head *plenty* enough this week, I refuse to let him pile on.

I lean forward and do my best to sound sober when I say, "I think that you've been nursing a bum knee for over three years and big pond or small pond, a guy your age will eventually drown with an injury like that." I lift my brows knowingly. "And deep down, you know that's why Vaughn Harris recruited me. And if you think one bad week of practice and trying to get me wasted is going to sabotage my potential with the club, I promise you're going to be sorely disappointed."

Finney's nostrils flare, his eyes murderous slits on mine. "If you want to take my spot on that pitch, you need to play a lot better than you have been this week." He stands up, drinks his shot, and gestures to Macky and Billy to follow him out. "I tell it like it is, kid, and I don't think you have what it takes to be here. It's only a matter of time before the coaching staff sees it too."

I wince slightly as his words poke the bruise that I've been nursing all week as Finney, Macky, and Billy walk out of the pub. They move with a lot more agility than they should after four hours of drinking. Frowning, I reach over and grab Finney's shot glass off the bar and give it a sniff. With a low growl, I tip back the leftover droplets into my mouth. "It's fucking water."

"What?" Link and Knight slur, barely able to keep their heads up off the bar as they look at me.

"Finney's shots were water." I glower at the bartender, who holds his hands up knowingly.

Link grabs the appletini that's sitting beside his drink. "This smells like booze."

The bartender leans across the bar with a shit-eating smile. "You've had six to his one. And those shots you had earlier…yeah, his were water too."

"He only drank one appletini?" Link exclaims, tucking his dirty blonde hair behind his ears. "I feel so used. How could he have such restraint? These appletinis are delightful."

The bartender laughs, and I shake my head, looking down to see Knight's head propped on his hand, his eyes completely closed with several empty shot glasses scattered out in front of him.

"Definitely going to puke again," he murmurs before lowering his head onto his folded arm.

I exhale heavily and rise, willing myself to be sober. "I live just down the street. You guys can crash at mine."

Link and I manhandle Knight off his barstool. The guy is a giant, and his freshly washed long brown hair is flopping over his eyes. Knight is an entire mood. Luckily, the press doesn't give a shit about us yet, so we don't have to worry about getting photographed as we walk the three blocks to my building and struggle to get Knight up the three flights before he starts dry heaving.

We step back from where he's kneeling on the floor in my bathroom, and I see Link watching him with an odd sort of smile. "He looks kind of peaceful with alcohol poisoning, doesn't he?" A tender look flits over Link's eyes.

"I don't have alcohol poisoning," Knight mumbles into the toilet bowl. "My body is breaking down from the training this week."

I nod knowingly. "I'll get us some waters and order some food to soak up the booze. Fuck the training diet, we need grease to sober up."

Knight lifts his thumb up and I close the door to give him some privacy. I pull up my phone and order three fish and chips from Hubert, the manager at Old George, and then ask if I can pay extra for one of the servers to deliver it across the street. He agrees and I'm relieved because the idea of going in there right now and smelling more alcohol is not an appealing thought.

Link and I sit on the kitchen counter, chugging water as we wait for the food to show up. "Practice tomorrow is going to suck," I offer because it's all I can think about.

"No shit," Link replies knowingly, drinking his own bottle down. "I can't believe those guys were fucking with us tonight. I thought we were finally bonding."

"They don't want us here," I state, my jaw tight with that realization.

Link eyes me seriously. "Did you believe all that shit Finney said about you being a big fish in a small pond back in America?"

"Well yeah. I mean, he's not wrong." I shrug, thinking back to how much tougher this training is than it was back in the States. "I proved that shit this week." I ruffle my shaggy hair and sigh heavily as flashbacks of Finney and Booker doing drills together replay in my mind. They communicate with such ease. It's obvious they've been playing together for a while and Vaughn's words of wanting me to connect with Booker keep repeating over and over in my head. How can I even attempt to connect with Booker if I'm too busy getting my ass kicked all day?

"But that's why we're here, right? To get better, to learn from the best," Link offers hopefully. "It's exhilarating, right?"

"Sure, I guess." A feeling settles in my belly because I feel anything but exhilarated. I feel panicked.

Knight tears our focus off each other when he stomps past us toward my fridge door to grab a water. He has a sheen of sweat across his forehead and my nose wrinkles as the smell of vomit permeates my nose.

"What's with you?" Link asks, staring at me expectantly.

"What?" I turn my attention back to Link.

"You have a weird look on your face."

My jaw clenches. "It just seems like you guys are adjusting to all of this a lot better than I am."

"This is adjusting?" Knight questions, letting out a belch as he holds the cold-water bottle to his forehead.

"In training, at least." I exhale heavily. "I didn't impress anyone this week, that's for damn sure. It's like I shouldn't even be here."

Link nods. "I won't lie to you, bro, I've seen you play way better."

"I know," I grumble, my stomach twisting into knots.

"Is it a mental issue?" Knight asks plainly, and I feel suddenly exposed. "Is there something big going on in your head?"

I hesitate with how to respond because the truth is, I know it's mental. I thought Jude's mantra of football over bullshit would be enough to keep me focused, but it isn't. That Harris family ambush I had in the hallway last Saturday threw me for a loop. Now I can't stop wondering…what if that letter was real? What if I'm related to them? What if Vaughn Harris knows the truth and I'm not good enough to even be here, but he's recruited me as some sort of sympathy ploy for being an absentee dad my entire damn life? What if that's the real reason my mom didn't want me to come here, and I was never actually good enough to be in the Premier League?

I've been obsessing about it so damn much, I even had a nightmare the other night where the press found out Vaughn Harris was my real father and the Harris Brothers had my legs broken so I couldn't play soccer anymore. Now I'm supposed to spend time with Booker and act fucking normal? How the hell am I going to do that?

"Is it your dad?" Link pries further.

I glare at him with a silent warning that he fully grips. "No, it's not about him."

"Then what is it?" Link eyes me seriously like he can see food on my face.

I push myself off the counter. "You know what…maybe you guys should call a cab. You seem like you're sobering up."

"Just spit it out already," Knight barks, pinching the bridge of his nose. "The only way we're going to survive Premier League is if we help each other out. And negative internal or external psychological issues can cause team issues, poor performance, and even lead to injuries."

Link and I both blink at Knight, stunned into a rare silence.

"It's not rocket science," he scoffs, taking a drink of his water bottle before adding, "Read a damn sports psychology book once in a while. Mental health is equally as important as physical health in professional sports. Honestly, it's a subject that's not given enough attention and keeping it bottled up inside is only going to make your performance worse."

My brows lift as Link hops down off the counter and walks over to me, his eyes narrowing. "He's right. And since we're the only ones you can trust on this side of the pond, you might as well just spill your guts." Link pokes me in the stomach and it's that one point of pressure that has my hard-shell cracking.

"Jesus Christ," I groan as the pressure of the past week and a half begins to smother me. It's been hard dealing with this on my own. I've tried to call Jude a couple of times since coming out here but the time difference and our schedules makes that difficult. I can't talk to my mom. I can't talk to my dad. There's no one I can unload this fucking burden on that cares about me here.

Link and Knight seem like good guys, but can I really trust them with this? What if they tell someone and this entire thing blows up in my face?

Then you end up back in America where you belong because your mom was right, and you were never good enough for the Premier League in the first place.

Fuck that voice.

Swallowing a heavy breath, I say quietly, "Okay, what I'm about to tell you guys cannot leave this apartment because it could affect our entire club." I stare seriously at my two teammates whose faces both grow very serious as they nod slowly.

"And I'm only telling you because I don't want my mental block to bring the team down." I slide my hands into my pockets and cringe at the heaviness all around me. "And I'm scared as fuck that if I don't tell someone, I'm going to self-sabotage my ass back to the States."

"You can trust us," Knight says solemnly, his eyes fixed on mine.

Licking my lips, I inhale a cleansing breath and just fucking say it. "I just became aware that there's a chance I might be related to the Harris family by blood."

I clench my teeth as soon as the words are out of my mouth and wonder how long it will take them to start laughing at me.

But they aren't laughing.

They are standing in my kitchen, arms crossed, brows furrowed… not laughing.

Pushing away the knot in my throat, I add, "There's a chance that Vaughn Harris might be my real dad, which would make Booker and Tanner Harris my half brothers."

Link nods rapidly as he processes this information. "I'm going to need more context, dude."

With a low growl, I stomp over to my bedside table where the horrifying letter in my mother's handwriting lives. I've looked at that piece of paper every single night before bed since I arrived in London. I hoped if I stared at it hard enough, it would produce some sort of clue as to its legitimacy or not. It's no wonder I'm having goddamn nightmares.

I hand the letter to Knight and Link because there's no better explanation than that. Turning on my heel, I dig in my fridge for more water, and when I turn around, the two of them are staring at the paper…completely stunned.

"Wait, is your mom British?" Link asks, his face twisted up in confusion.

"That's your first question after reading it?" I walk over and snatch the letter out of Link's hands, annoyed at myself for even opening this can of worms. Jude's reaction was a joke too and I realize that showing this stupid piece of paper to anybody just makes me a joke. "She's not British but she went to college and worked in London for several years before having me."

"Like twenty-five years ago?" Knight asks, his face stony serious. "That's how old you are, right?"

I run a hand through my hair. "Yes. And the letter is dated, so it matches up."

"Fuck," Knight replies with a huff. "What did she say when you asked her about this?"

I exhale heavily. "I never asked her."

"Why?" Link's jaw drops.

"Because my dad's only been dead a year and she's still fucked up over it." I roll my eyes and grip the back of my neck. "She's in therapy and shit. She's…not handling it well."

Link's brow furrows. "So, are you saying you read this letter, got randomly recruited by the club who might be managed by your real birth father, and no one knows that there's a potential genetic connection between you and the Harris family?"

"More or less." I exhale a breath that feels like it weighs a hundred pounds. "I don't even know if my dad knew about this letter before he died, which just makes all of this even more complicated. My mom has been so emotionally unstable since he passed, I can't bring this shit up to her. And we're not exactly speaking at the moment because she didn't want me to take this transfer in the first place but had no real good reason…which basically makes this letter even more potentially real.

"Then again, if this letter is bullshit, me bringing it up to her after my dad died will certainly not help our relationship. And even asking her about this letter feels like I'm shitting on my own father's memory. My dad was a good dad. The fucking best…" My voice trails off as a knot lodges in my throat, but I force it away the same way I have since the day we buried him. "I thought I could come here and play soccer and ignore this letter, but every time I am around Booker, Tanner, or Vaughn, I find myself looking at them and trying to decide if we share any similar features. Or wondering if I'm here because of some sympathy fucking recruit. It's all fucked up, and I'm going to blow my shot at taking Finney's place on the pitch and end up back in the States before the end of the season."

"Jesus, this is like the soap opera my gran used to make me watch," Knight adds, unhelpfully.

I growl a noise of annoyance. "Just forget I said anything. I'm too drunk for this conversation."

The room goes quiet for a moment as I mentally chastise myself for letting these guys in. I just need to burn this fucking letter and maybe then my mind will get the hell out of my way on the field.

"I have an idea," Link says, his finger going up into the air like he's pointing at a light bulb in his head. "What about a genetic test?"

"How the hell do you propose I do that?" I ask like I haven't thought about it a million times already. "Should I just ask Booker Harris if I can get a cheek swab because I think we might be brothers?"

"No, that sounds really awkward." Link winces.

"Exactly!"

"Well, you have to do something," Knight states firmly, his eyes grave. "You have too much at stake right now, and this letter is messing with your mental game. You need to get past this one way or another."

"I know, but how?"

"It doesn't have to be a cheek swab," Links says, his eyes wide and excited. "I listen to tons of true crime podcasts, and there are loads of ways to tie stuff back to the murderers and rapists. I realize we're not trying to catch a criminal here, but if you get a bit of a fingernail or some hair, a used Q-tip. Hell, even some chewing gum could work."

"Are you fucking joking?" I snap, my hands turning to fists at my sides.

"I'm completely serious," Link exclaims. "You said you have to spend some time with Booker Harris for team bonding anyway, right? That's the perfect chance. Maybe even a glass he drinks out of could do the trick. You can buy online kits and mail in anonymous samples, and they'll be able to tell you if there's a genetic connection between your sample and the other subject." Link pulls his phone out and starts searching for God knows what.

"How do you know so much about this shit?" I ask, frowning at the rare intensity on his face.

"I told you, man…true crime. I'm obsessed." He half-smiles, and it makes me kind of want to punch him.

I swallow a knot in my throat as realization settles over me. "What happens if I find out there is a genetic connection?"

"What happens if you find out there isn't?" Knight says, pinning me with a grave look. "What if you're worrying for nothing, and Link's insane idea could actually give you the clarity you need to free yourself of this letter?"

Link nods with a wild look in his eyes. "Exactly. And one way or another, you need answers, right? This is the best way to get those answers and involve the least amount of people. Let me be your Sherlock Holmes and solve this mystery for you. Please."

I watch him closely, waiting for a sign of mischief to cross his face like this is a long-running joke he's trying to play on me, but I don't see it. He's serious. And so is Knight. I've had a lot of teammates in my years of playing soccer, but none have shown up for me quite like this.

"You're seriously willing to help me with this?" I ask because my head needs to hear it spoken out loud.

Link shrugs as he glances back down to his phone. "Yeah, man…I'm your American brother from another mother. And hopefully another father, but without DNA, we won't ever know for sure."

He laughs and even manages to crack a smirk on Knight's face. I can't help but join them because all of this shit has felt so heavy and so serious for over a year. It feels good to bring some lightness to it for once.

A knock on the door thunders in my apartment, causing us all to gasp.

"Who knows we're here?" Link asks, his eyes wide without a shred of humor in his voice.

A husky female voice yells through the thick wooden door, "Come on, Soccer Boy…I have actual tables waiting on me across the street!"

"Oh fuck, it's the food." I jog over to open the door, and the view of Daphney in her shredded jeans and baggy T-shirt is a sight for sore eyes. How is it that just seeing her can lift my spirits? "Boy, am I glad to see you."

"How you got Hubert to agree to delivery is beyond me," Daphney snipes, holding a bag of food with three Styrofoam boxes inside. "I don't think he'd even deliver to me if I asked!"

A grin spreads across my face. "Have you missed me, Ducky?"

Her blue eyes shimmer as she lifts her dark eyebrows. "No, but you've still definitely been missing your alarm."

I grip the doorframe and can't hide my smile. "But I'm getting better. I told you I'm like a retriever and very trainable."

"And I told you I'm a cat person." She hates me.

"I'm trying to forget that depressing fact." I love her.

She thrusts the bag into my chest. "Here's your food. It's thirty quid."

I take the bag and head nod behind me. "Come on in while I find my cash."

I turn to head over to my backpack, and I can see Link and Knight's eyes on Daphney.

"Hiya," she says noncommittally.

"You're the delivery girl?" Link asks, and I bristle as his tongue basically hangs out of his mouth while ogling Daphney.

"Among other things," she replies, crossing her arms. "I live next door too."

"The delivery girl and the neighbor. My God." Link's drooling now, and it's annoying as fuck.

She frowns at him as I rush over to give her forty. "Keep the change."

"Thanks, Soccer Boy." She smiles and winks. "Try to catch that alarm on buzz one tomorrow. Just for something new and different maybe?"

I grin, still feeling the effects of the alcohol in my body. "Maybe you can crawl in bed with me tonight and help rouse me in the morning?"

"Ha!" she barks out a laugh as she turns to leave. "I think I liked your duck sampling pickup line better."

"So you did like it!" I exclaim, hanging out the door and watching her go down the steps. "I'm growing on you, Ducky. Just admit it."

"Like a fungus on your rubbish that still seems to get left in the hallway."

I wince. "I'll take it out tonight."

She waves, and I return to my apartment to find my two teammates staring at me with their jaws dropped. "That's your fucking neighbor?" Link says with his eyes wide.

I nod and sigh. "Tell me about it."

7

No More Treats

Daphney

"**O**F COURSE, YOU'RE HERE," MY FRIEND PHOEBE SAYS AS SHE comes barging into Old George like she owns the place. "I don't know why I bothered buzzing your flat because this is pretty much where you live now."

"Well, some of us have to work for a living," I reply as I pull out a rack of pint glasses and stand back so my face isn't assaulted by the steam billowing out.

"I work," she exclaims defensively, her inky black hair spilling over her right shoulder. "I'm just…waiting for my next spicy project."

I laugh and roll my eyes. Phoebe is a freelance journalist slash influencer slash blogger slash jack-of-all-trades. Recently, she started narrating some romance novels for a studio in London. She's one of those women who has the Midas touch with absolutely everything.

Phoebe and I grew up together in Essex, and her family is beyond loaded so the girl doesn't even need to work. However, that also means she has the luxury of taking a lot of chances and dabbling in a bit of everything.

Honestly, she's everything I wish I could be. She moved to London almost immediately after completing school. She's got a gorgeous little flat in Notting Hill, and she's constantly dating.

Like constantly.

She slaps her hands on the bar. "I might need to borrow your flat Friday night."

"Oh?" I reply knowingly.

"I have a date."

"Of course you do." I roll my eyes.

"And we're meeting at a cute place in Shoreditch, and well…if things go well, yours is a lot closer than mine to…"

"Shag and bag?"

She winks and does finger guns at me.

"You really are such a bloke."

"I know! You should join me in my blokeness. It's fun, and you've clearly earned it." She smiles, her emerald eyes sparkling with mischief. "Any updates on the naughty neighbor?"

"He's still being his normal, irritating self," I snap, my nerves sizzling with annoyance because just this morning I swear he was herding buffalo out of his flat. "I've been practicing in my tiny sound booth out of respect for him…but his alarm issue is still very much alive, and I swear he's doing it on purpose to mess with me. And then his telly is constantly on maximum volume, even when he's not there. I tried to be nice in the beginning, but every day since he's moved in feels like bloody *Groundhog Day*, and I'm going to lose my mind if he costs me this jingle." I finish nearly out of breath as the image of his stupid smile from last night continues to reappear in my mind.

Phoebe smiles at me. "I think you're spoiled."

"Spoiled?" My jaw drops. "How?"

"That flat has sat empty the entire time you've lived there, and you got used to having the floor all to yourself. Welcome to London, love. This is how it goes. I once had a neighbor who walked down to the laundry room in his knickers…and they were supposed to be white…but… they were not white."

"Bollocks," I mumble under my breath, ignoring her fake gagging. "Zander is maddening. One day we passed each other in the hallway, and he started tiptoeing obnoxiously in front of me. He really is a wanker."

"What are the other tenants saying about him?"

I sigh. "He's right above Miss Kitchems, and she says when she takes out her hearing aids at night, it's as if she's sleeping in a grave."

Phoebe's nose wrinkles. "That's morbid."

"I know. Peter below me is never home, and I haven't bothered asking the two tenants below them. It's just me he's making miserable." *And annoyingly aroused but I leave that bit out.* "Last night, he actually got Hubert to have me deliver food to his flat across the street. We don't do delivery here…never have."

"He sounds charming." Phoebe props her chin on her hand and waggles her brows at me.

"He sounds entitled," I retort. "And it's affecting my work. I have to be sure I'm not recording anything when he's around because he's so loud over there that it seeps in through the sound booth."

Phoebe giggles, and then both of our attention is caught by the newcomer entering Old George.

"Speak of the devil," I murmur under my breath as Zander strides toward the bar with his backward baseball cap and crooked smile. God, why does my body instantly warm every time I see him? It's easy to dislike him when he's on the other side of the wall in his flat. But I need to remind myself he's a nuisance every time I come face-to-face with him.

"Daphney Adelle Clarke…what the bloody hell?" Phoebe nearly falls off her barstool as she gapes at him. "How have you not mentioned that he's fucking gorgeous?"

I scoff, and she swivels around to reach across the bar and yank me toward her so we're face-to-face, her breath mingling with mine.

"I'm dead serious, Daph." She eyes me. "You and I are framily, friends who choose each other as family…which means you were keeping this from me for a reason, and I want to know why…right now."

I open my mouth to respond, but nothing comes out.

"Say it," she says, her green eyes turning to slits. "You fancy him."

"I do not!" I jerk out of her grasp, feeling my face redden at her blatant way of calling me out.

We both go quiet as Zander sidles up to the end of the bar. He eyes Phoebe with a look of amusement and then turns to me. "Am I interrupting something?"

"No," I snap like a petulant child refusing to admit anything.

His chest shakes with silent laughter. "I was just going to order some food."

"What'll it be?"

"My usual."

"Zander, you've only ordered in here twice…I have no clue what your usual is."

He licks his lips, and his eyes drift down my body like he wants me to be his usual. When he finally drags his eyes to meet mine, he flashes a devilish grin that makes my stomach tighten. "I'll have the fish and chips and a beer."

Ignoring Phoebe's blatant gawking in my peripheral, I ask, "Don't you have a game tomorrow?" My traitorous eyes drift down his fit body as well.

Zander nods. "We play Manchester City."

"Is a beer really a good idea then?" I grab a pint glass and begin filling his draft. "Also, it's just Man City. You don't have to say Manchester."

He shrugs. "Well, it doesn't matter because I won't be playing against them, so a beer and some bar food aren't going to hurt me. But thanks for worrying about me, Ducky. It means a lot." He shoots me a wink.

"Ducky?" Phoebe sputters, and I cut her a murderous look before redirecting my attention to Zander.

"I'm not worrying about you," I reply through clenched teeth as I hand him his beer. "I'll put your food order in."

"Thanks." He shoots Phoebe a wink before turning to find a table, and I try to ignore the fact that I'm bothered that he winked at both of us.

Phoebe turns to me with grave eyes. "It's a good thing you don't fancy him because I'm going to shag that bloke senseless."

"No, you're not," I stammer, my face heating as I try to come up with a plausible reason my friend can't sleep with a man I don't have a thing for. "I mean…you can't. He's my neighbor. It'd be awkward."

"Not for me." She eyes him like a piece of steak while jealousy surges through me. "I'll just go introduce myself since you so rudely didn't."

"Don't!" I say too quickly and flinch at the volume of my tone, and my cheeks heat with mortification. Phoebe can get any man eating out of her palm within seconds, and the idea of those two together causes a strange pit to form in my stomach.

Phoebe smiles. "I knew you were lying. You fancy the shit out of him."

"He's a footballer." I roll my eyes. "And he's annoying."

"The best ones always are." She tilts her head, and her eyes lock on me like a couple of laser beams. "I can see the hamster wheel spinning in your brain, Daph."

"What are you talking about?"

"You're overthinking like you always do." She shakes her head, a look of judgment marring her striking features. Phoebe leans across the bar and thrusts her finger in my face. "That little dimple on your chin is showing, and that thing only shows up when your brain is moving a mile a minute."

"My brain is focused on these glasses," I lie, holding up one I just finished wiping down.

"Bollocks," she scoffs and turns to stare at Zander. "And I know exactly what you're thinking. But no one said you had to marry the footballer. We decided after Rex the Hex, you need to be on a relationship hiatus."

Just the mention of Rex's name causes a chill to run up my spine. And not the good kind of chill. The kind of chill that makes your nose wrinkle and your body feel like it wants to shit and vomit at the same time. Goodness, why am I having to think about him so much? It's been a year since I've laid eyes on the arsehole, and now, I've had to think about him twice in two weeks.

This is not good.

The last time thoughts of Rex were running nonstop in my head, I couldn't write or record music for weeks. Which meant I had no money coming in, so my big plan to move to London to find myself and be a successful, independent musician living on my own turned into my brother hiring me as his building manager because he felt sorry for me.

Thankfully, working odd jobs for my dad's furniture business all these years made me qualified for the job. But it still wasn't enough. And I refused to let Hayden cover all my rent. That was when I decided to get a job at Old George to have some type of income.

But all this means my plate is full, and I don't need another man-whore turning my life upside down, especially with this big jingle opportunity that's just landed on my lap.

"This is the perfect situation for you, Daphney. A footballer is not boyfriend material in any capacity. Footballers are for fun, not for relationships. And if anyone deserves a little fun, it's you."

"Well, I don't have time for fun right now, so none of this even matters," I retort and attempt to relax my tight grip on the pint glass before it breaks. I take a deep breath and look over at where Zander is sitting playing on his phone. As if he can sense me looking, he glances over, so I quickly avert my eyes.

Phoebe drops her chin. "Everyone should make time for fun."

Phoebe's focus is distracted when her phone trills in her bag. She rushes out of the pub to take the call, so I do my best not to glance over at Zander anymore. I know I'm acting like a child, but he doesn't need to think I'm checking him out. He's like a dog looking for attention, and any slight glance will send him sprinting over and asking for a bloody treat.

I am all out of treats for men like him.

There's a laundry list of reasons I shouldn't hook up with Zander Williams. For starters, I've only ever been a relationship person, and footballers are notorious for not being that. Secondly, we're neighbors, so that's asking for awkwardness if things go wrong. Thirdly, the last relationship I got burned on affected my livelihood, and I refuse to let that happen again. And finally, I don't even know if he genuinely likes me or if he's just flirting with me to be an arse.

I'm inclined to think it's the latter.

When Zander's food is up, I bring it over to him and nearly go arse over tea pot when I see what's in his hands. "What are you doing?" I ask, lowering his food down in front of him.

"Reading," he replies distractedly, not even looking up as he finishes the page he's on.

"Why?" I'm certain my face is contorted with shock.

He grabs a bookmark and slides it into place as he reveals the iconic *Bridget Jones's Diary* cover. Smiling up at me with that stupid crooked smirk, he responds, "I'm trying to get some British terminology down. I really did live under a rock, which is nuts because one of my closest teammates back in the States was British. Hey, you guys don't serve chardonnay here, do you? It's what Bridget Jones likes to drink."

"I'm going to pretend you didn't ask that." I try to school my features so I don't look impressed that he actually took my advice.

Zander nods thoughtfully. "It doesn't sound that good anyway. Hey, there wasn't a package for me in the building that you grabbed by mistake, did you?"

"No, why?"

He sighs. "I thought my mom might be sending a package."

"Did you run out of clean underpants already?" I tease.

"I rarely wear any, so that wouldn't be an issue." He waggles his brows, and I hate the fact that my eyes drop down toward his denim-clad groin area. "Actually, I was hoping she would be sending me some of her oatmeal raisin cookies. I know I won't get any play time this weekend, but not having one in my locker makes me really nervous."

"Can't you just buy some? I could give you the name of a bakery."

He shakes his head. "They have to be homemade. You can taste the love and shit."

"Taste the love and shit," I repeat in his American accent. "Well, I'll let you know if I see a package."

"Cheers."

My brows lift. "You actually *have* been reading."

"Yeah, but I got that one from you, not *Bridget Jones's Diary*." He winks, and I hate how charmed I am by him as I bite my lip and attempt not to smile. Before I turn to leave, he adds, "Daniel Cleaver seems like a douche, but it's hard to tell. Can you just spoil it for me? I've never watched the movies."

"No," I reply, horror encapsulating my entire body at how he's lived his whole life and never even watched the movies.

Zander exhales heavily. "Fine, I'll keep reading."

"You do that, Soccer Boy."

8

Discreet DNA My Ass

Zander

DISCREETDNA.COM. IT'S HARD TO BELIEVE SUCH A WEBSITE EXISTS but, in a world where a Harris Ho and Proud site exists, I don't know why I'm surprised. Discreet DNA gives me all the instructions I need to create my own DNA kit so there's no need to wait to extract my samples. How convenient. The site also says there's a twenty-five percent reduction of accuracy with anything other than a saliva swab, but considering it might be a little difficult to get Booker or Tanner Harris to rub a Q-Tip on their cheek, I decide to take my chances.

I still can't believe I let Link and Knight talk me into this.

And here's a shocker, extracting DNA from someone without them noticing turns out to be wicked hard. I stupidly thought sharing a locker room with Booker would make this plan easy peasy. Grab a hair from his hairbrush, or hell, maybe even a sweaty towel or something, but Booker Harris is a tidy motherfucker. He leaves nothing behind in his cubby after training, not even a tissue. And Tanner Harris's office is communal, so who knows whose DNA I'd get ahold of if I rummaged around in there.

The next day, I decide to watch Tanner a bit more closely. With the beard and the long hair, surely something will fall out. Or maybe I can pluck a hair off his shirt?

After training, I see him toss a sports drink bottle into the trash can and think…here we go. It's on. I walk over to grab it when the voice of Vaughn fucking Harris himself causes me to nearly jump out of my skin.

"Oi, Zander! What the bloody hell are you doing rummaging through the bin?"

Bin means trash, I think to myself before replying. "I, um…dropped something." I fight against a cold sweat, hoping that sounds like a good enough reason for me to be diving in the trash.

"What on earth is so important you'd wade through rubbish?" Vaughn's severe eyes make me feel about two feet tall.

"Um…my retainer?" I blurt out like an idiot because I remember as a kid mucking through a Pizza Hut trash can with my dad looking for my retainer that was, thankfully, never recovered.

Vaughn scowls at me. "Aren't you a little old to have a retainer?"

I clear my throat and force myself to sound professional. "They say the longer you wear them, the better your teeth."

"Well, surely we're paying you enough to buy a replacement. Who wants to put something that's been in the rubbish in their mouths?" (Apparently my dad) Vaughn scoffs. "Ask the gaffer for a dental referral if you need someone local, and for heaven's sake, get away from that bin."

I glance at the trash and resign myself to give up on the search for the bottle as I've already forgotten what it looked like. Sighing, I reply, "Will do, sir."

On day four of Plan DNA Extraction, Link suggests I offer gum to Tanner, and this time, he and Knight will be on the lookout while I fish around in the trash for a chewed-up piece of candy. It's fucking disgusting and horribly desperate, but the sooner I get this over with, the sooner I can get on with my life.

"Gum?" I hold a stick out to Tanner as he tosses a bag of soccer balls over his shoulder before we head out for practice.

He lifts his blue eyes to me and takes the stick. "It's called chuddy in some parts of England."

My brows lift. "That one has not been covered in *Bridget Jones's Diary*."

"What?"

"Nothing." I smile awkwardly and hope I'm coming across as somewhat casual.

"How are you feeling, mate?" Tanner swats me on the shoulder as he chomps on the fresh piece of gum, stepping back to allow the team to file out of the locker room toward the training pitch.

"I'm feeling pretty good, actually." I grip the back of my neck and exhale as I realize the heaviness that I'd been carrying around since I arrived in London is gone. Strangely enough, having an attack plan for my situation has really given me some mental relief. And I hope that the DNA test will reveal no genetic connection so I can get back to focusing on bloody football and nothing else.

Goddamn, I'm British as fuck now…even in my own thoughts.

"You've looked great on the pitch these last few days. You've really turned a corner," Tanner points out. I straighten, standing a little taller at his compliment. "I don't know if you're getting laid on the regular or what, but you're finally starting to adjust, so keep doing whatever it is you're doing."

"I'm definitely not getting laid," I reply with a sad laugh as images of Daphney instantly invade my thoughts.

"Pity," Tanner says, and then I see his throat move.

"Did you just…?"

"Swallow the gum?" he finishes my thought and smiles. "I did. I have a thing for sweets." He pats his slightly protruding belly. "My sister, Vi, is an amazing cook. My wife, not so much. Luckily, we have these big family dinners on Sunday evenings at my dad's. My sister always cooks, so I stock up on leftovers to sustain me throughout the week. Vi's Swedish pancakes with lingonberry jam are to die for."

I nod slowly as I see Link's wide eyes in the doorway looking as disappointed as I feel. So much for gum DNA. For fuck's sake, it's as if the universe doesn't want me to get on with my damn life. This is going to be trickier than I thought.

"Hey, why don't you set up a time with Booker to do that team bonding thing you said Vaughn Harris wanted you to do," Link says as we lay out on the grass and stretch before Coach Z begins to inflict bodily harm.

"I thought about that." I glance over my shoulder at Booker, who's stretching out in the net behind us. "I wondered if it was too soon to do the teammate bonding thing when I'm not even a starter yet? I mean, he hasn't exactly reached out to me."

"I think you'll be starting sooner than you think," Knight says as we glance over to where Vaughn, Coach Z, and Tanner stand with a clipboard, pointing at various players on the field. "I overheard Tanner say they were going to do some shifting around on defense today and look at Finney's face right now." The three of us glance over and Finney's face looks like he's smelling a really rancid fart. "I think he knows something we don't."

"Fuck, that would be awesome." My voice rises with hope as a rush of adrenaline pumps through me. I'm ready to prove myself.

"So, there's no better time to start your bromance with Booker." Link shoves me. "Go invite yourself to his house after practice. You can get all sorts of DNA there."

"Okay, okay. No need to manhandle me." I stand, ignoring the nerves taking flight in my belly as I jog over to where Booker is sliding on his keeper gloves.

As I approach, he offers me a wide smile. "Zander! Well done the past few days. You're looking fast out there."

"Thanks...um...I'm trying." I huff out a laugh, my confidence growing over another teammate recognizing my improvements. "Hey, I was wondering if you wanted to get together sometime and get to know each other or whatever...what your dad said, I mean. Bonding?"

Booker lets out a hearty laugh. "Zander, if this is how you pick up women, I wouldn't be surprised if you're still a virgin."

I grimace as I recall my first meeting with Daphney. "Unfortunately, it's not far off in these parts. London seems to have broken my game in more places than one. But, um...maybe I could come to your place? Whereabouts do you live? I could take a cab there sometime." *And we could share a meal, and I could steal your fork or poke around your bathroom like a stalker.*

Booker's brows furrow. "Mine is no good. I have five-year-old twin boys, and well...let's just say you're not ready for Teddy and Oliver."

"Okay...how about my place?" I offer because going out won't help me get any DNA left behind. "I'm not far from here."

"Your place would be brilliant. How about tonight?" Booker asks, and I'm a bit shocked at the urgency but don't have any reason to say no.

"Tonight sounds wicked."

"Is nine too late?" Booker eyes me thoughtfully. "I have to help Poppy put the boys down, or she'll never forgive me."

"Nine works."

"Great, I'll get your mobile number after training. Looking forward to it, Zander." He reaches out to fist bump me, and I do the same.

"Me, too." *I hope.*

9

Date Night Debacle

Zander

"**O**I! YOU CAN'T PASS WHEN YOU HAVE A CLEAN BREAKAWAY LIKE that!" Booker shouts, his hands gripping the game controller so hard, his knuckles are white. "Is this your first time playing FIFA?"

"No," I snap and shift uncomfortably on my sofa as I fight back the swamp-ass situation happening in my jeans. I've been a nervous wreck since Booker arrived, trying to figure out a way to get his DNA before he leaves. "I've played tons of times, but this new version is throwing me."

"Clearly." Booker laughs, sitting back and wiping the beads of sweat off his forehead. "Christ, it's a workout kicking your arse."

"I'd say." I glance at the water bottle that's been sitting in front of him all night. I made a conscious effort to serve him water in a plastic bottle so I could send it in later. I just hope it's enough for the DNA sample.

"You don't need to get home to your kids or anything, do you?" I ask, glancing at the clock to see it's after midnight.

"Eh, it's alright." Booker sits back on my sofa and looks around my place. "They're in bed, and I'm in heaven. I'd forgotten what it's like to have the telly on as loud as you want after dark. I'm reliving my youth here, so you'll have to kick me out, mate." I catch him wincing out of the corner of my eye before he continues, "My wife, on the other hand, might throttle me when I try to slink into bed later. But I'll gladly take it after a night like this."

I laugh. "You're not even that old to be reliving your youth."

He sighs heavily and runs a hand over his dark brown hair that's the same color as mine. "I'm just over thirty, but the days before I was chasing after five-year-old boys and telling them to stop weeing in Mummy's plants feel like a lifetime ago."

"Parenthood sounds fun," I deadpan.

"Actually, it is," he replies with a fond smile. "And luckily, my boys are carbon copies of their uncles, so I know how to handle them."

"Are you referring to Tanner and Camden? They're twins, right?"

He nods. "Yes. And they were hellers growing up. Always picking on me. Bloody awful. Honestly, once I realized we were having twins, I told Poppy I don't want any more because I know all too well what it's like to be ganged up on by twin brothers who share a bond you can't even begin to comprehend."

"Didn't your parents try to put a stop to them ganging up on you?" I ask, treading into foreign territory because I don't know shit about having siblings.

"Not really." Booker's eyes bend with sympathy. "My mum died when I was one, so I never really knew her. And my dad…well…let's just say it took him years after her death to become even remotely normal. The man he is today out on that pitch managing the club is not the man I grew up with."

"How do you mean?" I question, feeling my body tense as I realize I'm far more interested in this answer than I should be.

A thoughtful expression crosses Booker's face. "The memories I have of my father are mostly of him being very cross and very controlling. Stoic and cold. He really only ever cared about one thing."

"His kids?" I offer as images of my own dad flash across my mind.

"God, no." Booker barks out a dry laugh. "He only cared about football."

I suck in a breath through my teeth. "I probably should have guessed."

"He treated me and my three brothers like his own personal football club. Micromanaged our careers, pushed us to our breaking points a lot. Which was okay, I guess. I'm sure there are worse ways to grow up, and I obviously have a successful career out of it. But that affected us all a bit differently. My eldest brother, Gareth, hated it. He and my dad…oof…loads of blowouts between those two. Especially when Gareth said he was done playing for my dad at Bethnal Green and going to play for Man United, the club my father left when my mum got sick."

"That's intense." I frown as I digest some of this new information. "Your dad's whole life has been football, hasn't it?"

Booker nods. "He keeps threatening to retire, but at this point, it's a family joke. We're going to have to force him out. But he's good at football and has a bit more balance with it all now. Becoming a grandfather softened him tremendously. He missed a lot of our childhood while being so laser-focused on our football careers. With his grandchildren, he's so much better. It's as if he's reliving our youth through his grandchildren's eyes."

My brows furrow when I think about how much time Booker must spend with his dad playing for him his whole life. "Did you ever want to play for another club like Gareth? Get a bit of space from your dad?"

Booker shakes his head. "No, once I became the starting keeper, I knew I'd live and die at Tower Park. Love that bloody pitch. They'll have to kick me out. And you know, my dad and I don't have the issues he does with my older brothers, so I suspect it's easier for me."

I huff out a noise, thinking maybe I dodged a bullet with Vaughn, even if I do discover that I share DNA with him. My parents never pressured me when it came to soccer. In fact, my mom often pushed me to take some time off, which might be a little suspicious after that letter. Maybe she was scared my paths would cross with this family if I kept pursuing this career?

But hearing about how hard Vaughn was on his kids and how Booker was basically targeted by his twin brothers when he's literally the nicest guy on the team doesn't sound like a family I missed out on being a part of.

Booker reaches out and grabs my arm, snapping me out of my thoughts. "Christ, Zander. I was so busy running my mouth, I completely forgot about your father's passing."

"Oh, it's fine." I clear my throat and stand to grab the pizza box and plates off the coffee table. I use my other hand to grab Booker's water bottle, careful not to touch the rim of it as I add, "It's been a year, so I've dealt with it."

Booker follows me into the kitchen as I stand in front of the sink, my eyes glazing over as I think back to the memories of my dad trying and failing to kick a soccer ball around with me. He had zero athletic ability, but it wasn't for lack of trying. I wonder what it would have been like growing up with a dad who was actually good at soccer?

Booker props himself on my kitchen counter and eyes me thoughtfully. "It's been thirty years since my mum passed, and I still don't think I've fully dealt with it. Then again, I'm what my family calls the sensitive one." He laughs and shakes his head. "Gareth is the brooding one. Tanner is the ridiculous one for obvious reasons. Camden is the wild one...and my sister, Vi, is the sensible one. We like labels in our horde."

"I'm not sure what I'd label myself with." I blink over at him in confusion, wondering why the fuck I even want a label. It's not like I'm a member of the Harris family. Nor do I want to be.

Booker tilts his head. "Do you have any siblings?"

"No…only child."

He nods. "We'll call you the surprising one. You surprised me this week on the pitch. And I think you're turning Finney into a new shade of crimson."

We both laugh at that image, but mine is forced. I wonder how surprised the Harris family would be if it turned out we were related. Would they be apt to give me a label then? Or would they shut the door in my face?

Shaking that thought away, I turn the sink on to rinse my plate, and the water begins to sputter out from the faucet in an odd way before making a hissing noise. My head dips low when the hissing sputters, and everything goes very quiet before a clunk thunders under the sink. I squat down to open the cupboard and see what's going on only to be nailed in the face by a huge gust of water shooting out of a pipe.

"Shit," I exclaim and brace myself to stop from falling.

Booker jumps off the counter to help me up and accidentally brings the pizza box, two plates, and his water bottle down with him. The stone plates shatter all around me. "Bloody hell, sorry, mate!" He points at the floor between us. "Watch your hands. There's broken glass everywhere."

"I can see that," I reply through clenched teeth while staring at his water bottle on the ground. I grab it quickly off the floor and set it on the counter away from the mess as I make my way over to a drawer for some towels.

"Here, hand me one," Booker says, and I toss it to him as he squats down to wrap the cloth around the leak. "I am sorry to tell you this, but I know fuck all about plumbing. Do you have twenty-four-hour maintenance here?"

"Oh shit, I think I might. Let me find the number." I carefully walk over the glass and water-covered floor to dig in the drawer for that folder Daphney left me. I fire off a quick SOS text to the handyman number and find a bowl in the cupboard. I squat by Booker and put it under the water running down over his hands.

"This is certainly an interesting way to bond," Booker teases as a burst of water finds its way through his fingers and into our faces.

I bark out a laugh, hoping like hell I can still retrieve some valuable DNA from that water bottle. Goddammit, the universe really seems to be working against this stupid plan of mine.

Moments later, there's a loud knock on the door, and I yell for the knocker to come in. When I turn around, I expect to see a heavy-set white dude with a mile-long ass crack. Instead, I see Daphney. She's wearing those silk pajamas again with her floral robe over the top of it, the belt knotted at her waist. Her hair is in a messy bun, eyes free of any makeup, and she has a red toolbox in her hand. I'm ashamed to admit that my dick twitches at the vision before me.

"I didn't mean to text you," I yell over the water.

"Did you text the handyman number?" she asks, inspecting the mess all over the floor.

"Yeah, I thought so."

"That forwards to my phone. Step aside."

"Careful, there's glass," I shout a bit too forcibly.

She glances down and steps over the big pieces before shooing Booker and me out of the way. We both stand on opposite sides of the sink as we watch her drop her tools on the floor and dip her head under the sink, getting drenched before coming back out to dig in the box. Maybe the universe doesn't hate me after all because I have a very good vantage point of Daphney's face and chest covered in water. Her robe has been forced open to reveal some very delectable cleavage and a quick glance downward shows that the water is very cold indeed. A thrumming begins in my groin, and I force myself to look up at the ceiling as she works so I don't pop a fucking boner in front of my teammate.

Within minutes, the water stops, and the only noise left in the kitchen is the faint trickling of excess water dripping out of the cupboard and onto the floor. Daphney stands and turns her back to the sink as she swipes her hand across her face, pushing back the damp strands as she rewraps her robe over her chest.

She drops a wrench in her toolbox. "Old building means old pipes. I've told my brother that some of the fittings need to be replaced by a proper plumber, but he hasn't got around to it yet."

It feels as though my tongue is hanging out of my mouth because Daphney just came in here and handled that pipe like a boss. I wonder what else she could handle.

"Figures this is Hayden's fault," Booker says knowingly. "But at least I got to see you, Daph." He leans in and presses a swift kiss to her cheek. "How are you?"

"I'm good, Booker. What on earth has you out so late? I thought Teddy and Oliver weren't sleeping through the night yet."

"The little buggers aren't." Booker mock cries. "And Poppy is going to kill me for staying out, but I lost track of time."

My face twists with confusion as I stare openmouthed at the two of them talking like old friends. "How do you two…?" I point between them, unable to finish the sentence because I think I've been stupefied.

"Booker's sister is married to my brother," Daphney answers like it all makes perfect sense.

"My sister Vi, her brother Hayden," Booker offers when I continue to stare at them like I don't speak English.

"Wait, are you telling me the landlord Hayden is married to Vi Harris?" I ask, putting it all together in my own words.

Booker nods. "Vi goes by Clarke now."

My eyes twitch as I scramble to figure out if that means Daphney is related to Booker. Because if I turn out to be related to Booker, that means I'm having sexual thoughts about someone I'm potentially blood related to. *I'm a fucking pervert.*

My mind is messier than the floor we're standing on, so I just flat out ask, "Are you two related?"

"Not by blood," Daphney replies casually and glances at Booker. "I guess you could say we're in-law, in-laws? Is that a thing?"

"It can be if we want it to be." Booker shrugs. "Although it sounds a bit distant. You're pretty much family now."

Daphney reaches out and rubs Booker's arm. "Aw, thanks, Booker. You were always my favorite Harris Brother, so the feeling is mutual. Although, I think you could call me 'framily.' That's what my friend Phoebe calls me. It's basically like friends who are chosen to be family."

"That's perfect, actually." Booker smiles. "I have loads of framily now that I think—"

"I just…I didn't…I had no…" My mouth can't find words.

Booker and Daphney eye me warily before Booker says, "Well, while Zander digests this apparently shocking bit of info, I'm going to duck out to get home before the boys wake up for the first time tonight. Sorry to leave you with a mess, mate." Booker pats me on my frozen shoulder. "But thanks for the fun night. It was exactly what I needed." He turns his focus to Daphney. "See you Sunday?"

"I can't turn down Vi's cooking even if I tried. She'd literally drag me out of here if I didn't show up."

"That she would." Booker laughs and makes a hasty departure.

As he leaves, Daphney turns to double-check the pipe one more time, so I grab a broom and start cleaning up the mess. This new information has me reeling more than it should. I'm not sure why I'm so affected by it. I guess the crossing of two worlds, maybe?

Daphney holds the trash can for me as I dump the glass into it. "I'll get a plumber in here tomorrow so this doesn't happen again."

"Sounds good." I grip the broom and pull awkwardly on my wet shirt, feeling a chill run down my body. "So, you're like…close with the Harris family?"

Daphney shrugs. "A bit, I suppose. When I moved to London last year, they all but demanded I come to their Sunday dinners at Vaughn's house. And the Harrises aren't exactly a family you can say no to. They've really mastered that whole Harris Shakedown thing they're famous for."

I blink back at her, my eyes widening. "You go hang out with all of them every Sunday? At Vaughn Harris's house?"

"Not every Sunday. Just when I can." She laughs and shakes her head. "I can't believe you're still fangirling over the Harrises. You've been training with the team for a couple of weeks now, right? Don't you see Booker, Tanner, and Vaughn every day?"

I roll my jaw from side to side. "Yeah, it's not that…I just…I didn't realize your brother was married to a Harris. It just threw me, I guess."

Daphney sets her toolbox on the counter. "Well, the Harris clan all sort of perpetuate each other's business endeavors in many ways…fashion, housing, philanthropy. Whatever any of them have a hand in, they all find a way to support each other. Hayden owns a few properties, so I'm sure when Vaughn needed a place for you, he thought he'd see what Hayden had vacant first."

"I see." My brow line feels permanently crinkled so I roll my shoulders to try to relax. "Sorry for calling so late."

"Are you?" she asks before grabbing her toolbox. "Because if you were sorry for calling so late, maybe you could have been sorry for your loud telly that's been blaring straight into my flat all night long, making it impossible for me to hear anything else."

"Fuck," I reply, scrubbing a hand over my face. "I'm sorry about that."

"I know you are." A rueful smile spreads across her face. "Although I wouldn't have been so cross had I known there was a Harris in here."

"So, a Harris can be noisy, but I can't?" I place a hand over my chest, feeling a dagger pierce right through it, but she shoots me a wink that's so adorable I'm not even annoyed by the double standard. "What do I have to do to get into your good graces like Booker has? I'm a desperate man."

"You're anything but desperate." Her cheeks flush a rosy hue as she glances down at my chest. "But your wet T-shirt isn't the worst wake-up call I've ever had."

My jaw drops. If I was a keeper and Daphney a striker, she would have caught me totally flat-footed with that kick. "Come again?"

She laughs nervously and makes a move to leave. "Only joking."

"No, no," I respond with a genuine smile and move into her path. "Were you…?" My voice gets caught in my throat as excitement courses through my body like a damn teenage boy. "Were you just flirting with me, Ducky?"

"No," she snaps and rolls her eyes. "You drive me mental too much to flirt with you."

My brows lift, and I point at her face. "But you're kind of smiling when you say that, so surely you can understand my confusion."

"I'm not smiling," she says around a smile. "Would you get out of my way? I need to go to bed. I have a tire shop jingle I'm desperate to finish."

"Seems like we're both a bit desperate these days." I bite my lip and can't help but notice how intently she watches my mouth. My eyes dip to her lips that are the perfect shade of pink that I really would like to taste right about now.

A small dimple appears in her chin as she jerkily shakes her head. "I really do need to get on."

I nod and step back, flexing my chest and not even trying to hide my pleased smirk when I catch her checking me out…again. She's like a dude, and I fucking love it.

I lean out my doorway as she makes her way back to her place. "I think I'm wearing you down a bit, Ducky."

"In your dreams, Soccer Boy."

I close my door with a really cocky smile on my face because I think the score just changed to Daphney: one, Zander: one. I can have all sorts of good dreams about that new development.

10

No Knickers

Zander

TOMORROW, WE PLAY EVERTON, SO IT'S ANOTHER LONG-ASS BUS RIDE where Link won't shut the fuck up and Knight will sleep the entire trip. Hopefully, I can sleep on the bus too because I should have been out hours ago. My mind is fucking racing, though, and for a good reason.

Earlier today, I mailed off a large envelope that contained the water bottle Booker drank out of last night plus a cheek swab from me. There were also several forms I had to fill out for the sibling-to-sibling DNA test at discreetdna.com, and the fact that I actually pulled the trigger and sent this shit has my stomach in knots.

In a week or so, I'll find out if I've been lied to my whole life. No pressure.

On top of that shit show, I don't know if I'm starting tomorrow. Coach Z had me training with team A earlier today, but he said it was just training, so I shouldn't get my hopes up.

He's real inspiring.

I grab my phone off the end table and pull up my mom's number. It's eleven here, which makes it like six in Boston. She's probably just getting back from work, having a glass of wine, and sitting all by herself. That entire vision causes a pit to form in my gut.

Being so far away from her was never a big deal when my dad was around. Those two were best friends. They watched all their TV shows together and had happy hours in the sunroom every day. They even did their grocery shopping together. And they weren't the type of couple who scrolled on their phones at dinner. They always had something to talk about. Gossip around town, work drama, me. They talked a lot about me. My mom would cry at every game she came to of mine. The moment I stepped onto the field and looked up in the stands, it was a guarantee she'd have tears in her eyes, and my dad would be patting her back while holding whatever video camera he happened to own at the time.

Which is why I feel like a fucking asshole for not speaking to her since I arrived in London. She's called me a few times, but I usually text her back and tell her I'm swamped with training. It's technically true, but the truth is, I'm just not ready to talk to her.

No matter how hard I try, I can't forget about her telling me that I wasn't good enough to be here. And with how much my game struggled from week one, I didn't need someone putting more doubt in my mind. After week two, I've finally found my stride, and calling her to tell her my good news could mess all that up.

Plus, we rarely talk soccer anyway. That was always my dad's thing. He'd ask me about my training, stats, games, all of it. He even had a spreadsheet of every one of my seasons, and he'd graph shit out and show me where I improved or where I needed to work harder. The man couldn't kick a ball for shit, but he was a numbers guy and my number one fan.

I rub my thumb along the tattoo inside my bicep and close my eyes, just barely able to hear his voice calling out, "Hey there, buddy boy!" Fuck, I miss him.

And I miss my mom. She's not the same person she was when he was alive, and while I know she's doing the best she can, I still can't help but think that if things were normal between us, I would have given her a video tour of my apartment by now and she would have ordered me all sorts of random shit I would never have known I'd needed. And I would have had a damn freezer full of oatmeal raisin cookies. My apartment is currently sans cookies, so I know things between us aren't right. And I'm not sure when that will change.

I close my phone and roll to my side to quiet my mind for some much-needed sleep. Hopefully, once I get these DNA tests back, I can get my life back on track, no matter what the results are.

Just as I begin drifting off, I hear a door slam loudly down the hall followed by some commotion. I sit up, my body on red alert because it's rare I hear anything but music come from Daphney's apartment. I wonder if maybe she needs help carrying something when I'm silenced by the sound of feminine giggles. The giggles are shushed by a male companion and then…silence.

I swallow the knot in my throat. Does Daphney have a guy over there? My hands fist around my duvet at that strange thought because I haven't seen any signs of a social life from Daphney since I arrived two weeks ago. Then again, I'm gone on the weekends, so who knows what she gets up to then.

A long female moan fills my apartment, causing my stomach to lurch. Jesus Christ, no wonder Daphney hates my alarm clock and television so much. It's like I'm in the room with them. The dude makes a grunting sound, and I cringe when I hear him say, "No fucking knickers, you naughty girl."

Then there's some gasping and more giggling that I don't fucking like. Not one bit. Daphney doesn't giggle like that. I should know, I've made her giggle. Whatever laughing she's doing with him is clearly fake and forced. It doesn't even sound like her, honestly. Then again, I probably don't sound like me when I'm having sex either. Sex voices just hit different.

Seconds later, I hear the creak of a bed and then a rhythmic rocking sound. Oh, fucking hell, are you kidding me?

"Oh God," Daphney utters, and I hate that my dick twitches in my sweats. Another guy is railing her over there, and I'm sitting here getting turned on? Jesus fuck, I need to get laid.

"Deeper," she cries loudly.

Deeper? If a girl has to tell you to go deeper, then this guy is clearly not equipped. I can tell you with absolute certainty no girl has ever told me to go deeper.

"Yes!" she cheers, and I cringe because I'm annoyed whatever he did worked, and he's getting praised for it.

Jealousy niggles in my belly, so I hop out of my bed and stomp into my bathroom to try to get away from the noises. Now the dude is moaning and groaning, and it's not as enjoyable to hear as Daphney.

Who is this fucking guy anyway? As much as I've flirted with Daphney, she would have mentioned having a boyfriend, right? Especially after last night. I'm not crazy. She was checking me out. Surely, she wouldn't be checking me out and flirting with me if she had a boyfriend.

Maybe it's just a random dude she brought home from the pub? Maybe she does that a lot, and I'm going to have to get used to the idea of listening to her banging dudes next door.

Fucking hell, this is messed up. I'm the professional athlete here. Aren't I supposed to be the one getting laid on the regular? This is some bullshit.

To be fair, I haven't exactly gone out looking for girls. Link and Knight have hit the clubs in West London a couple of times, but I always pass. I was playing too shitty to push myself like that. Plus, I wasn't in the mood for random hookups. I just wanted to get my shit together and not get kicked off this fucking team.

Daphney and this guy don't seem to be slowing down any, and the more I stand in front of my bathroom sink and listen to them, the more on edge I feel. My palms are sweaty as I grip the porcelain sink. Sex used to help my soccer game. I sought it out after every match like a fucking oatmeal raisin cookie. My little treat for a big victory. Maybe not going out with Knight and Link was a bad idea.

"Fuck it," I growl. Slipping my hand into my lounge pants, I fist my rock-hard dick. "Jesus," I utter because I haven't been this hard in months. It's nearly painful to stroke it's so goddamn hard. But the pain of it feels good, too. Rewarding in some sick way.

I pump my cock and picture myself in there with Daphney, bending her over that tiny sofa, pressing her up against that sound booth of hers, clanking notes on her keyboard as I fuck her brains out and hear her call out my name…not whoever that asshole is in there with her.

Daphney barely tolerates me, so jerking off to her fucking some guy next door makes me a low-key perv, but I deserve this for all the nasty looks she cuts me every time she sees me. For all the times she yells at me about my alarm or has texted me a reminder to take my trash to the dumpster and not leave it in the hallway to rot. She's been nothing but a nag since the moment I stepped foot in Old George while I've been nothing but friendly.

"Fuck!" I exclaim as my climax catches me off guard, and I splatter my release all over my bathroom sink. I exhale heavily, my stomach tensing with each frenzied breath.

I pause to listen and realize there's no more noise coming from next door. They must have finished before me. Fucking amateur.

I clean up and slip back into bed, and it's the thought that I could please Daphney ten times better than that cum stain next door that sends me into a deep, restful slumber.

11

Cat's Away, Mice Will Play

Daphney

Phoebe: So, did the music flow like the beautiful country hills of Essex?

Me: Not the way I'd hoped. I wrote lyrics for an entirely different song, not the jingle that I stand to make some decent money on.

Phoebe: Well, you're writing again! That's something to celebrate.

Me: I suppose. I'm just frustrated. This isn't rocket science. It's Tire Depot. I need to turn in the lyrics in three days, or I'm going to miss out.

Phoebe: Just relax. You'll figure it out. You always do.

Me: Not always.

Phoebe: You know what they say helps with creativity?

Me: Hard drugs?

Phoebe: Sex, Daph…which might be a bit easier to locate than hard drugs. I know a naughty neighbor who would probably be all too willing to provide you such a service at a much cheaper rate than a drug dealer.

Just the mention of Zander causes my entire body to heat. Ever since I saw him reading *Bridget Jones's Diary*, my disposition to him has shifted. It humanized him or something. Made him a lot less wanker and a lot more adorable boy next door. And while I know there's a mile-long list of reasons I should stay far, far away, I can't help but admit that I was excited when I saw he was the one with the plumbing issue the other night.

I mean, he's a sexy footballer who's my neighbor. A girl can only deny an attraction for so long.

> **Me: Do you really think I can pull off a one-night stand with him, Phoebe? He's my neighbor, so it could be awkward. Plus, I'm a relationship girl. Always have been.**
>
> **Phoebe: People change, Daph. I'm a romance narrator now! No one saw that coming.**
>
> **Me: Fair point.**
>
> **Phoebe: Plus, it's only awkward if you let it be. And you won't know if you don't try. You need a rebound to get back to your old self. Just see what happens when you let yourself have a little fun.**
>
> **Me: Easier said than done.**
>
> **Phoebe: I have the utmost faith in you, Daph. XX**

I laugh and slip my mobile into my pocket as I climb the three levels to my floor. It's late Sunday evening, and I feel a bit defeated after a wasted weekend at my parents' home. I thought going back to Essex where I wrote tons of songs in my youth would remind me that I'm capable of this.

Unfortunately, the trip inspired too much of my youth because I ended up writing lyrics to something that had nothing to do with Tire Depot. Creativity is a fickle bitch. Maybe Phoebe's right, and having a bit of fun would help?

When I hit the third floor, and my eyes catch sight of a mouse darting away from a rubbish bag sitting in front of Zander's door, my hopeful outlook toward Soccer Boy plummets to the filthy ground below my feet.

Abandoning my suitcase in the hallway, I march over to Zander's door and loudly pound on it. I don't give a toss if he looked cute reading *Bridget Jones's Diary* at Old George or if his pecs looked ridiculously fit in that wet white T-shirt the other night. He's just completely screwed up my week by bringing vermin into our building. God, I should have never let my guard down with him! You give dogs an inch, and they take a mile.

It takes ages for a sleepy-looking Zander to open his door. He's dressed in a pair of low-slung gray loungers, and the angles of his hip bones jut out inhumanely, but I bury that ungodly image to a deep vortex in my body as I poke him hard in the chest, ignoring how firm he is.

"How many times have I told you that you can't leave your rubbish in the hallway?" I seethe, my fists clenched tightly beside me.

"I was sleeping," he mumbles, rubbing his fists over his dark-rimmed hazel eyes.

"I don't care!" I exclaim, hating how cute he looks while I'm cross at him. I stamp my foot in frustration. "I saw a mouse in our hallway just now!"

"Set some traps. It'll be fine. I'll take it out in the morning." He turns to close the door in my face, and I move my foot in its tracks.

How rude is he? "You'll take it out now."

Zander narrows his eyes on me. "Look, I know you take this building manager job very seriously, but unless there's a damn zombie apocalypse out here, I can deal with this in the morning. I had a really rough week-end, and I need to crash."

"Fine, I'll do it myself!" I let out a harsh growl as I bend over and pick up his bag. I turn to walk down the steps and feel a warm hand wrap tightly around my elbow and jerk me backward.

"You're not taking out my trash." Zander releases his hold on me, then reaches down to yank the rubbish out of my hand. His crinkled eyes look severe in the harsh hallway lighting as he bows over me with agita-tion billowing off his fit body.

"Try to stop me," I snap, refusing to let go of the bag. "You clearly think you're too good to take your own rubbish to the bin. And since I don't fancy a mouse in my flat, I'll have to bloody well do it myself!"

"Why can't it wait until morning?" He yanks the bag out of my hand and grips the back of his neck as he takes a step back. My eyes are drawn to his bulging bicep and a small tattoo I never noticed before. His voice is flat when he adds, "I see other people leaving their trash bags in the hall overnight. Are you up their butts too?"

"I am hardly up your butt. And what a ridiculous phrase," I scoff, annoyed at how gruff his tone is with me right now. This isn't the type of Zander I'm used to. But that muscle in his jaw that's moving angrily is re-ally attractive.

"Oh please, Daphney. You've been so far up my ass since I arrived that you can probably talk for me by now. I can't get away with anything over here. Meanwhile, you get to fuck random dudes as loud as you want all night long without a care in the world."

"Fuck random dudes? What on earth are you talking about?"

"Friday night, the night before my first match that I got to start in, by the way, I heard you railing a guy next door. Woke me up four fucking times throughout the night. I didn't think the guy had the stamina, but he proved me wrong. Please be sure to pass along my props to him. You sure know how to pick 'em."

Flustered, I stare at him, trying to comprehend what he just rambled on about. "Wait…you started in the football match?" My chest tightens as I search his face for confirmation. I didn't let myself watch because I needed to work, and I didn't think there was a chance Zander would play after our conversation in the supermarket. If I'd known he was on the pitch, I would have flicked on the telly. "You actually started the football game? Zander, that's brilliant!"

"I know! And I fucked it up, thanks to you," he snaps, his jaw tight as disappointment streaks across his face. "I was playing a second center-back alongside Finney, and I challenged a striker to prove myself, and I got beat like a bitch. They scored on me and won the fucking game right at the end."

I blink away my confusion. "And that's somehow my fault?"

"Yes! I got shit for sleep Friday night because it sounded like a kinky horror movie over there. I didn't realize you were such a screamer, Duckmeister."

"That wasn't me!" I exclaim defensively, finally figuring out what he's been going on about.

"Okay, sure." He rolls his eyes.

"It wasn't!"

"Then who was it?" A jealous look flits across his eyes, and my chest lurches with excitement over that realization.

"That's none of your business, but I assure you it wasn't me." Swallowing the knot in my throat, I cross my arms over my chest and ignore the warmth spreading through my body. Even if it was me, it doesn't give Zander permission to ignore the very simple rules of the building. "I was back home in Essex visiting my parents and working because you are literally the loudest neighbor in the universe."

"So you rent your room by the hour while you're away?" He barks out a dry laugh. "I'm sure your brother would be glad to hear you're turning his building into a brothel. Maybe I'll just text him."

"You have some bloody nerve!" I seethe as he turns to walk back into his flat. I grab his arm, whirling him back around to face me. My hand instinctively squeezes the muscly flesh, and I feel a flame lick up my entire arm from the direct contact. "Not that you have any right to know, but it wasn't just some random person. It was a friend," I grind out, feeling irritated at myself for wanting to clear this up because I care about his opinion of me. "I'm not going to tell you who because that's an invasion of her privacy and none of your bloody concern, but she asked for permission to use my flat, and I said yes."

"She asked you for permission to fuck someone in your flat?" Zander glares at me in disbelief. "Classy friend."

"Guys would do the same thing without even asking," I snap back as I'm painfully reminded of the Zander I met at the pub who was a complete pig. Forget the guy who looks nervous when he talked about football or the one who bought a *Bridget Jones's Diary* bookmark to go inside his book. He's long gone now. The man in front of me looks dangerously like the arsehole who screwed me over not long ago. "That is such a misogynistic double standard."

"Look, I don't care who or where your friends get nutted. In fact, I sort of wish it was you because then maybe it'd help get that stick out of your ass."

"I do not have a stick up my arse!" I practically squeal as I take a step toward him.

"You sure as fuck do because you fucking like me, Ducky! And you're telling yourself you don't, for God knows why. A good-girl complex? Think fucking the footballer will make you bad? Well, it won't. The only thing that makes you bad is lying to yourself about what you want."

How does he know what I want? He can't possibly know the way his stupid backward hat makes me feel.

"That's not…I don't…this isn't…" For the love of God, he could stop smiling at me with that stupid crooked smirk just long enough for me to get my thoughts straight.

My fingers tremble as Zander looms over me all big and cocky and pushy like he knows exactly what he does to me. I don't think having sex with Zander Williams will make me bad. That's ridiculous. I'm a grown woman, and if I want to sleep with a footballer, I can.

He scoffs and hits me with a demeaning smirk. "That's what I thought. Little Miss Perfect."

Little Miss Perfect, my arse.

He bends over to pick up the rubbish, and the proximity coupled with the rage coursing through my veins causes something shocking to happen to my body. A demon possession, a judgment lapse, temporary insanity? I'm not sure…but the next thing I know, my hands wrap around his neck, and I yank him down to me for a very surprising, very unexpected, very off-brand for Daphney Clarke…kiss.

Zander's lips are hard on mine as I snake my hands up around him and fuse our mouths together. He smells like a mixture of citrus and toothpaste. In a flash, I realize I haven't kissed a bloke since Rex, and I hate that he's even entered my mind *again*. I want Rex the Hex erased from my memory forever. And well, Phoebe does always say the best way to get over someone is to get under someone else.

And thankfully, Zander does not kiss like Rex at all. Zander feels foreign and new and a bit hard now that I think of it. On second thought, the kiss is rather odd because I'm only now just realizing *he's not kissing me back.*

Oh fuck…is this consensual? Should I have asked first? If he doesn't want this and I'm kissing him against his will as the building manager, this could be very, very bad.

I yank my lips off his, sucking in a ragged breath as I stare at him with horrified eyes. "My God…I can't believe I just did that. That was so inappropriate. We should—"

My voice is cut off when he presses his warm palms against my cheeks and lowers his lips back over mine, swallowing my words up into his beautiful, soulful mouth that's definitely kissing back this time. He plunges his tongue inside, and a deep growl vibrates his chest as his hands slide down my arms to wrap firmly around my waist, pulling me against his broad frame.

Okay, what we were doing seconds ago wasn't kissing. This is kissing. My fucking God, this is kissing. This is a proper snog like I've never had before.

Which likely means my kiss before was consensual but just stunned him a bit? Or if it wasn't consensual, it is now…so…all good, I think? God, brain…shut the hell up and kiss him back. You deserve this!

My hands splay out on his bare chest as he walks us backward and bumps me up against the nearest wall. When his body is flush against mine, there's an instant zinging that happens between my legs that causes a moan to escape my lips. Rex and I never had this level of passion. Not even close. In fact, none of the men I've dated had this. Maybe because we dated so long before we ever really got intimate? Hell, maybe Phoebe's right, and shagging and bagging can be fun.

Zander's hands slide around my back and move downward to my bottom. He pulls me into his groin greedily, forcefully. Like any millimeter of space between us makes him angry. Our lips never stop moving, and my thighs clench with desire when I feel the excitement happening below his waist as well. My skin is on fire, and Zander's lips are the petrol fueling the flame.

Zander breaks this kiss, his voice ragged and rough as he murmurs against my ear, "Tell me that you haven't been sitting in your apartment and looking at that thin wall that separates us and wanting to break through it to fuck me."

A nervous noise squeaks out of my throat. "Erm…"

"Because I have." He runs his whiskered chin across my neck to whisper into my other ear, his hot tongue teasing me. "Nearly every fucking night since I got here, I've wanted you…thought about you."

"Oh my God," I groan at the overly sexual tone of his voice, my body positively melting in his arms as my nipples pebble beneath my shirt. Honestly, if he wasn't holding me up against this wall, I'd be pudding on the floor.

"Tell me you want me, Daphney." Zander's voice is so confident, so certain. Like he's done this before. Multiple times with multiple women.

The entire image of that assaults all my senses. If I were Phoebe, this would be an easy answer. Just say yes and let him shag the shit out of you, Daphney! You deserve this! You need a rebound.

Unfortunately, I'm not Miss Casual. I'm Miss Monogamous. Getting naked and sleeping with a bloke I'm not in a relationship with is sure to mean awkward and clumsy sex. I'll be embarrassed about my body, and he'll look like the fit footballer he is. Then we'll have a strange goodbye and the whole *will he call or won't he call* moment will make me want to die.

When you really think about it, casual sex is anything but casual. Sex with a boyfriend is truly casual. He knows what you like and don't like, so you can just relax and enjoy yourself…worry-free. You don't even have to worry about having an orgasm because you're not trying to impress each other if you're in a committed relationship.

What if I'm shit at casual sex? What if I freak out and can't climax and have to fake it? I'm a crap actor…always have been. I can't even lie properly! Phoebe could tell within seconds that I was fancying Zander, and I don't think I even knew that myself yet!

Oh God, this is a terrible, terrible idea. I can't do this.

"I want…" I rip my lips from Zander's and press against his chest as I mutter, "You to take out your bloody rubbish. It's called trash in America."

Zander's face falls, and I use his shocked reaction as an opportunity to detach myself from his grasp. I stumble over to my suitcase by the opposite wall and wheel it behind me as I scamper to my door. Once inside my flat, I collapse on the floor and consider hitting my head to try to give myself a strong dose of amnesia, so I never have to remember that embarrassing moment again.

I guess I know what happens when I stop thinking.

12

Cat and Mouse

Zander

"**A**RE YOU OBSESSING ABOUT THE DNA TEST?" LINK MUMBLES OVER a mouthful of protein pancakes.

"What?" I ask, my thoughts completely distracted as I sip my protein shake. It's early Monday morning, and the three of us met up for breakfast at a café located directly across from Tower Park called The Full Monty. We have training in an hour, and I have to admit, I have no idea what they've been talking about because I've been seriously distracted.

"You haven't got the results yet, right?" Knight inquires, cupping his mug of coffee.

"God, no. It's only been a couple of days." I shake my head to clear my thoughts as Link and Knight train their eyes seriously on me.

"Are you thinking about Saturday's match?" Knight asks, a knowing look spreading over his face.

I wince and debate if I should lie and pretend that is what I've been distracted with, but then I say fuck it and go for full transparency. "I'm in the middle of a bizarre, sexual cat and mouse chase with my hot, handy neighbor who I'm pretty sure hates my guts but also wants to fuck me."

"Come again?" Knight replies flatly.

Link's brows furrow. "Is this the girl who delivered the food that night we were drunk at your apartment?"

I nod and prop my chin in my hands, gazing out at the traffic on the busy Bethnal Green road. "She's been riding my ass super hard about being noisy and not following the building's rules. There's been some yelling, and I think I might be in love." Not love love…but fuck, if I can't stop thinking about that kiss, I have it bad.

"You sound like a creep, man." Knight shakes his head.

"I know." I stare up into the sky. "She inspires me."

"Does she even like you?" Link cuts into my daydreaming with an annoyingly obvious question. "I didn't pick up great vibes between you two at your apartment that night."

"That was before." I lean forward with a sneaky smile.

Link mimics my posture, his eyes blazing with curiosity. "Before what?"

"Before she pounded on my door last night and woke me up out of a dead sleep to yell at me about my trash in the hallway. Then out of nowhere, she shock tongues me."

"What's shock tongue?" Link asks, staring at me with wide, enraptured eyes. "Sounds aggressive."

The corner of my mouth curls up on one side. "A shock tongue is the kind of kiss you don't see coming, but once the shock wears off, you're glad it's happening."

"Sounds lovely," he croaks and then clears his throat awkwardly and pitches his voice low. "I mean…sounds fucking hot."

"Oh, it was." I can't wipe the smile off my face if I tried. Pretty sure I woke up smiling today.

"What happened after?" Knight grunts, showing more interest than I expected of him this early in the morning.

"She stopped the kiss, yelled at me to take my trash out, and disappeared into her apartment. Fucking hot."

"She sounds nuts," Knight huffs.

"She sounds perfect," Link corrects.

"She sounds like she wants me but doesn't want to admit she wants me." I drop my fork and push away my food, sitting back in my chair to think. "What can I do to get this shock tonguing to happen on a regular basis?"

"Can we stop saying shock tongue?" Knight grumbles, staring into his coffee mug. "It sounds rapey."

"I have an idea," Link says, and I can't help but wince because it reminds me that it was Link's idea for me to send in the DNA, and every time I think about what those results might be, my anxiety spikes. "What if tonight, we come over and break something in your place, so she has to come fix it like she did when you had Booker over? We're basically setting up the perfect porno film."

"Right," I reply slowly. "Except we're not doing an orgy scene so why would I need you guys there?"

Link deflates. "Really?"

I blink back at him. "You'd want to three-way one girl with me and Knight?"

"I'm open-minded." Link shrugs.

"I'm closed-minded," Knight barks. "To you. And other dicks in general. I'm not closed-minded to men who like dick. Play with whatever balls you like. But don't feel the need to pass them over to me, you know?"

"Well, I don't need them passed to me either," Link defends, looking hilariously rejected. "I'm just saying if I was tossed into the middle of a porno, I wouldn't be that disgusted at the idea of being with a couple of shredded pro soccer players. I think I'd be gay for you! Are you telling me you wouldn't be gay for me? Have you seen my abs?"

He lifts his shirt up, and while the man is rocking a solid six-pack, I fear this conversation is getting away from us. "How about I just stop by Old George after training today and see if she's working?"

Link sighs defeatedly. "Always the bridesmaid, never the bride."

"Or..." Knight leans across the table to point his fork at me. "You focus on the match we have at Tower Park Wednesday night. You have a chance to start at a home game, and that's one hundred percent where all your focus should be directed. Not some girl."

I sigh heavily and rake my hand through my hair. "Fuck, you're right. But after what happened Saturday, I'll probably be back on the bench." My jaw tightens as I replay the moment in my head. "God, I know I shouldn't have pushed forward. They put me in as a center-back, but I was so fucking close to stealing, I couldn't help myself. I left Booker hanging with his nuts out. Rookie move, for sure. Coach Z is going to have my ass for breakfast today."

"I wouldn't be so sure about that," Knight replies with a knowing look. "You may have been overzealous at one point, but up until then, you played more like a sweeper than a center-back, and that's what Vaughn recruited you for."

"You think?" I ask, still kicking myself. "I lost us the fucking game, Knight."

"I know, but you and Booker were totally in sync. That's what Vaughn Harris wants from you. A sweeper who sits back and protects the penalty box when necessary and has his keeper's back...or front. I think your instincts for most of the match were spot-on. You just got burned because Finney didn't have your back. Didn't you notice how Vaughn pulled Finney aside after the game instead of you?"

"Yes," I respond, feeling a nervous tingle start in my fingers. "I figured that was because he was too disgusted by me to talk."

Knight shrugs. "Or you're doing exactly what he wants, and now he just needs to shift things around to speed up the new game plan."

"Well, fuck me." I huff out a laugh, feeling ten times lighter than I did when we sat down earlier. "Knight, if you're right, I might just have to shock tongue you."

"I'll watch!" Link exclaims, and the eerie twinkle in his eye makes both Knight and I burst out laughing.

13

Mousetrap

Daphney

I'T'S TUESDAY EVENING, AND I'M SEATED INSIDE MY TINY, CLAWFOOT bathtub with my guitar clutched tightly to my chest while the acoustical chords reverberate loudly off the tiled walls. I sing out the last bar of the Tire Depot jingle that I finally completed and feel a euphoric rush hit me.

"Oh, my God," I exclaim, and my guitar makes an angry noise of protest as I grab it by its neck and hurl myself out of the empty tub. "That's it!"

I grab my notebook with the lyrics I've just come up with and glance around for my pen, only to remember it's stabbed into my messy bun. I pull it out and make the final note that just came to me as I shuffle out of my loo to put my guitar back on its stand.

It's been two days since I snogged Zander in the hallway, and I haven't had a moment to even think about it. Apparently, it doesn't take sex to unlock my creativity—a steamy hallway kiss will also do nicely.

At first, I was messing with some lyrics that had nothing to do with work. Then out of nowhere, the melody for Tire Depot just popped right into my head, and I didn't leave my loo until I had it perfect.

I've always practiced my music in the loo, and it drove my siblings absolutely mental when we were growing up. The four of us shared one bathroom on the second floor of my parents' country home, and after school, I would take my collapsible music stand into the loo along with my French horn and practice my sheet music until teatime. I really was the most annoying youngest sister.

It got a bit more tolerable for everyone when I switched my focus to the guitar, but they still moaned to my parents every night about me occupying the loo for hours. My parents never told me to stop, though, so the habit has stuck with me.

Vocals were never my focus, but if I must do something vocal, like a jingle for a tire shop, I feel like the loo makes me sound better than I am. Phoebe says my husky tone is like a mix between Adele and Janis Joplin, which she obviously only says because she's my best mate, and that's what best mates do. They lie through their teeth to make you feel better about yourself. But I know I'm not an awful singer. I'm at least on pitch, and that's half the battle. It's just not something I like to do for attention if I can help it.

I sang at Hayden and Vi's wedding and I didn't mind that because the focus was entirely on the bride and groom. No one was looking at me for a performance. The music just provided an emotional backdrop. That's the kind of singing I enjoy. Or this kind where I record it in the privacy of my flat where no one else can hear me.

Once I've got my lyrics perfect, I step into my small recording booth and fire up my equipment while slipping on my headphones. I pull up the original track of the instrumental version that I submitted to Commercial Notes ages ago and tap it into my ears, so I have accompaniment to sing along to.

Recording the sixty-second vocal bed only takes me twenty minutes because it's all so fresh in my mind. Honestly, this is what I love about promotional tracks. They're short, sweet, and to the point. We're not looking to impress some big record label or get a room full of opinions. I've whipped up my Big Mac and fries of the music industry, and after a few minor edits, I've zipped this track off to Drake and will sit here with bated breath, just waiting to hear what they think.

I'm trying not to get my hopes up. Ten thousand pounds would be incredible money, but with my voice on the track, it might not be the feel they're looking for. Hopefully, they'll at least buy the instrumental version for a nominal fee so it's not a total loss.

As I step out of my booth, I hear a loud snap from out in the hallway, and my eyes go wide as realization hits. Steeling myself, I tiptoe over to my flat door and peer out to confirm my suspicions.

A tiny, brown, beady-eyed creature has been trapped inside the neon pink humane mousetrap that I picked up at a pet store yesterday morning. I bought a no-kill trap because I couldn't stomach the idea of handling the remains of a dead mouse, but now that I'm looking at this thing alive and very much irritated for being stuck inside a teeny tiny mouse hotel, I think this might be far worse than I anticipated.

With a light squeal, I duck back into my flat and pace the small space, trying to muster up enough courage to go out there and get rid of the thing. If certain people would be courteous enough to take out their rubbish, I wouldn't even have to be dealing with this mess in the first place.

Narrowing my eyes, I walk over to the wall that separates mine and Zander's flat. I press my ear up against it to see if my naughty neighbor might be home because this should be his problem.

Naturally, for the first time in the three weeks since he's arrived, it's dead silent over there, so he must not be home.

"Figures," I huff to myself.

My stomach churns at the idea of that thing out there…getting angrier and angrier by the second. My guess is that neon pink isn't exactly a soothing color.

I shake out my arms and jump up and down to pump myself up. "You're the building manager, Daphney. You're independent. You're strong! You can handle this. Not to mention, this is part of your job and why your brother gives you a discount on rent. So, just go out there and take care of business!"

With a growl of determination, I march into my kitchen and grab a pair of yellow rubber dishwashing gloves from under my sink. Still feeling a bit exposed in my leggings and T-shirt, I decide that the red poncho I had to buy from a street vendor one night when I got caught in the rain at the Columbia flower market might offer some decent protection from the vermin. Oh, and my wellies. Knee-high rubber boots and elbow-deep gloves will keep all my wobbly bits safe from any diseases that awful creature might be carrying. For good measure, I also add my giant sunglasses—you never know what those creatures might expel from their body.

I grab an empty Amazon box and tiptoe out of my flat, hoping the tiny thing is sleeping and I might be able to gently place it in the box, move it outside, and open the trapdoor all without waking it.

Good God, could I be any more of a girl?

I realize I grew up in the country, but we weren't the farm animal types. We were the dirt bike and quad types. We were the types who went for long walks outside, not horseback riding and tending to livestock.

Plus, I had a father and two strapping brothers who dealt with the unsightly horrors one might expect to find in nature. And sure, I might be handy with a plumbing wrench, and I fixed Miss Kitchems's water heater with a healthy number of YouTube videos to assist me, but none of those skills qualify me to handle this mouse in a mature fashion.

So...girlie girl or not, I will get rid of this mouse.

I hold my breath and move slowly over to the trap, careful not to make eye contact because I'm quite sure I read that wild animals feel threatened by direct eye contact. When the little guy doesn't move a muscle, I gently bend over to pick it up, and the tiny bugger goes demonic as it bounces off the plastic walls and flips the mouse hotel upside down. I screech like I've been shot in the arse and turn to flee out the building, and maybe even the bloody country, when I smack right into a large, firm body that was not standing there a second ago.

"Oof," a male voice utters as my elbows slam into an abdomen.

I scream because well, I'm basically a live wire of nerves at this point, and I wasn't expecting another human in my vicinity so the image of a giant, man-sized rat enters my brain for a fleeting, neurotic second.

"Calm down, Ducky. It's just me!" Zander grabs my arms as his voice breaks into my internal freak-out, somehow calming me as I exhale a huge breath.

"Where did you come from?" I ask, looking up at him with wide eyes that he probably can't see behind my glasses.

"My apartment," he says with a laugh. "Where did you come from? Mars?" His eyes travel down my entire body, and his look of complete and total amusement isn't even mildly concealed.

"Something funny?" I tut, stepping out of his embrace to prop my rubber-gloved hands on my poncho-covered hips.

"I didn't take you for a cosplay girl, but this image right here has unlocked a whole new catalog of you in my mind."

A dirty look flits across his face, and I reach out and smack him on the chest, not at all noticing how firm it is. "Stop it. Stop whatever is going on in that thick head of yours. I'm just...protecting myself."

"From an epic paintball battle?"

"From that bloody mouse you brought into our building. I've actually caught the little bugger, and now I'm trying to get rid of it."

"What mouse?" Zander asks with a look of confusion.

I turn around to check the trap, and my stomach sinks with despair when I see the mouse hotel door somehow opened in the scuffle, and the little beast is gone forever now. "Oh Zander, this is all your fault again!"

"My fault? I was just standing here! You were the one who flipped out."

"I didn't flip out. The mouse flipped out. Scared the bloody life out of me." I place a gloved hand on my chest and feel my heartbeat thundering beneath my palm. "What are you doing sneaking around behind people when they're working?"

"I didn't know you worked in pest control," he replies with a laugh, and an affectionate look casts over his face as he stares back at me. "I thought maybe that zombie apocalypse was happening out here after all, so I came out to investigate."

I shove my sunglasses on top of my head and hate the fact that he's seeing me in this state while he's standing over there in sexy jeans and a fitted green T-shirt that really brings out the mossy color in his eyes.

I swallow the knot in my throat as I look away and yank my yellow gloves off. My palms are sweaty, and this poncho is causing my body to break out in a nervous sweat. Or maybe that's Zander.

"You sounded good in there earlier, by the way," Zander says, his voice soft and soothing like melted chocolate as he points at my flat door.

My face falls. "You could hear me?"

He nods and smiles. "Yeah, thought it was a radio at first until I heard you muttering and cursing."

I cover my eyes with my hand. "I didn't think you were home, or I wouldn't have rehearsed in the loo."

"Pretty sure my alarm issue earns you unlimited bathroom rehearsals…if that's your thing." He shrugs and shoots me a rueful smile.

Rubbing my lips together, I reply, "It's where I like to rehearse."

"Because the acoustics are wicked," he confirms.

I roll my eyes. "This is embarrassing."

"What?"

"This." I gesture to my outfit. "You seeing me like this, hearing me sing…Sunday night."

"Sunday night was embarrassing?" His face goes serious as he steps closer to me, and I get a whiff of his body soap that I desperately want to rub my face into.

"Sunday night was mortifying!" I shove my hand into my hair and realize I stuck my pen back in there before. My God, I'm giving him a lush view to feast on. "I don't know what came over me. One minute, I was mad at you, and the next minute, I was—"

"Shock tonguing me?" he finishes with a laugh and then reaches out to touch my arm. "I wasn't mad about it."

"I was." I jerk back, needing space between us because clearly, I'm not someone who can be trusted around the likes of Zander Williams. I cringe as I recall the stunned look in his eye when we broke apart for the first time, and I thought the kiss wasn't consensual. What a horrible, horrible fear to even consider. "That wasn't the way I wanted to start this."

His brows shoot into his hairline. "There's a this?"

"No," I bark and expel a nervous seal-like laugh, moving even farther away. "Clearly not."

He moves with me, his hands reaching toward me again. "There could be a this."

"But I don't want a this." I do a small circle with my hand between us. "I want a that," I say, pointing at my flat. "And a that," I state, pointing toward Old George out the side window. "And I want to take care of this." I point at the mouse trap and sigh heavily. "My plate is full, so *this* should not happen."

"What is *this* that you're even referring to, Ducky? This doesn't have to be something to add to your list of things that stress you out. This can be easy. This can be casual. In fact, casual is kind of my specialty." He grips the back of his neck, and a look of nervous hope flits across his face. "Plus, we're neighbors, so the convenience factor should not be ignored."

I laugh nervously and shake my head at the idea that sex can be called a casual convenience. It's so different from everything I've done in the past. In the past, I'd have to date someone for at least a month before I'd sleep with them. I needed time to build trust and comfort. To make sure I knew who they were before we could be intimate together.

Then again, I waited an entire month to sleep with Rex, and look how brilliantly that turned out. I was in love with him, and I didn't even know him. Maybe knowing a bloke before you get naked together is overrated.

I mean, look at Phoebe. She makes casual hookups look easy and carefree. She never moans about guy problems. She is fulfilled by not knowing the men she sleeps with.

Zander Williams is likely the male version of Phoebe, and he clearly doesn't get troubled by anything or anyone. Maybe I'm doing this adulting thing all wrong.

Zander steps closer to me and reaches out to tuck a stray hair behind my ear. The sensation sends shivers beneath my poncho, and I turn into his warm touch. It's a heady sensation having him this close again. I don't want it to stop.

"This can be fun, Ducky," he says, his voice low and sultry. "We are consenting adults, and we can make our own rules. So just think about what you want and let me know." He hits me with a soft, crooked smile that I really would love to kiss right now. Then he leans in, and I hold my breath as he tenderly brushes his lips over my cheek. "I'm only a wall away."

14

Double W's

Zander

"**T**HAT'S HOW YOU FUCKING DO IT, BOYS!" COACH Z YELLS AS THE entire team files into the locker room, sweaty, screaming, and flying high from a home game win at Tower Park.

After training the entire week in the official sweeper position and doing drills with Booker over and fucking over, I still couldn't believe it when Vaughn told me I was starting. The guy actually pulled me aside before the game, looked me in the eyes, and said, "The improvement I've seen in you the past week and a half has been so incredible, I'd be a fool to clip your wings tonight. So go out there and fly, son."

Hearing him call me son at that moment hit me in a way I didn't expect. I've been doing such a good job with focusing on soccer and not giving any real estate in my mind to the DNA results I'm still waiting on. But at that moment, when my manager and possible birth father told me in so many words that he was proud of me, a fantasy took flight in my mind. I allowed myself, just briefly, to imagine what it would be like to play for Vaughn as his actual son.

The scariest part of that image? I actually liked it.

The guilt over that realization was nearly crippling. I felt it hovering over me as I marched out of the tunnel and onto the pitch to warm up. I had a dad. He is who I should play for today and no one else.

Before the game started, I pointed up to the sky and repeated my mantra, football over bullshit. My first starting game isn't the time to play make-believe. It's the time for focus.

And that's what I did until the referee blew the final whistle.

When Knight and Link both tackled me onto the field with celebratory hugs, I realized that somehow, someway, I just finished the best game of my career. Suddenly, Link and Knight are shoved away from me by Booker Harris. He holds his gloved hand out and helps me up before pulling me into a long hug.

"Let's do this all season, Williams." He pulls back and shakes my shoulders before stabbing me in the chest with his fingers. "We're celebrating tonight."

"Fuck yeah!" Link bellows and wraps an arm around Booker, who doesn't look like he was planning to celebrate with Link. He laughs and shoves him off, then points at me one more time before jogging over to the sidelines to embrace Vaughn and Tanner.

I stand frozen on the grass, watching the three of them embrace and talk animatedly, their hands gesticulating plays that had happened throughout the match. At one point, all three of them look over at me, and Tanner offers two big thumbs-up while Vaughn directs a round of applause my way.

A knot forms in my throat as I wonder once again if my connection to these men is only soccer related? Or blood related? I'd all but forgotten about the DNA results I'm still waiting on the past few days, but experiencing a win like this has shifted something inside me. I feel a bond to them I hadn't felt before. Maybe I actually want to be related to them?

After we've showered, changed, and completed a few media interviews, we make our way into the player parking lot. Bethnal Green fans crowd the sidewalk, cheering through the gate, and several of the players stop to sign autographs and take selfies.

Once we're done, we begin loading up into various cars. "Where are we going?" Link asks Booker as we slide into his large SUV.

"We're going to Old George by your flat, Williams," Booker replies, glancing at me in the passenger seat. "That's a family favorite. And if we end up back at your place to play a little FIFA afterward, that wouldn't be the worst thing in the world."

I laugh and pull the bill of my cap down low, amazed that this pro soccer player would even consider sitting on a rookie's couch playing video games over hitting up a posh nightclub with a million fans to soak up all his glory. Booker Harris is kind of the shit.

Minutes later, we stroll into the Old George, and the patrons instantly start chanting the Tower Park pride song, forming a semi-circle around us. Loads of patrons are decked out in green and white Bethnal Green jerseys and T-shirts as they give all of us a round of applause for the big win tonight. Several fans come over and take selfies with the team, and when one asks me to jump in the shot with him and Booker, I can't help but smile. To be on top again feels wicked, and the atmosphere of the community all rallying around the team is amazing. We really are the people's team, just like Daphney said.

Once the crowd clears out and gives everyone some space, my eyes go to the bar in search of good ole Duckmeister to see if she's working. I couldn't stop thinking about her last night after our second little hallway tryst. She looked so fucking ridiculous in that mouse-catching getup yet still just as adorable as always. It's been a while since I've had to chase a girl, but I have to admit, I like that she's not making this easy.

However, I'm not sure what will come of us. I can tell she's a relationship girl, and I honestly haven't ever been in much of a relationship. One girlfriend in high school that I dumped to focus on my soccer doesn't really count, does it? And with all I have going on at Bethnal Green, getting involved in something serious isn't what I want, either. But just the thought of a missed opportunity with Daphney makes my balls fucking ache.

When Hubert appears behind the bar, I, along with Link, Knight, Booker, Roan, and a few other teammates, sidle up to order some drinks. My head jerks when my phone buzzes against my thigh. I pull it out to see a missed call from my mom. She left a voicemail that I wonder if I should even listen to. It might bring down my good mood.

Unable to stop myself, I press play and move down to the end of the bar to listen. "Hey Zander, it's Mom. Saw the game online…I was able to buy this package that lets me see the matches, but since I'm not in the right region, my neighbor had to do some sort of hacker thing to hide the location of my computer. I was slightly worried that he used my computer to get on the dark web, but in the end, I was able to watch and… wow…what a game, buddy." Her voice pauses for a moment, and I hear a soft gasp of breath as she adds, "Dad would have been so proud." My eyes tear up instantly as my grip tightens around my phone. "Anyway, I took a long lunch to watch, so I've got to get back to work before they realize just how long a soccer game actually is." She laughs and adds, "I love you," before hanging up.

My heart thunders inside my chest. She watched. She got over herself and she fucking watched me play. There was no apology in there for words said in the past, but it's a step in the right direction at least. I'd better give her a call tomorrow.

"Zander, we're going out to the beer garden!" Booker says, handing me a drink and gesturing for me to follow.

I take the beer and swipe at the stinging in my eyes, hoping he doesn't notice anything is off. It might not be tears, but it's the closest thing I've felt to them in a long time. I nod toward the bathroom first. I just need a minute. One minute and then I'll be ready to celebrate with my new team.

When I finally get my shit together, I walk through the small hallway that leads back into the beer garden to look around for my teammates. My eyes take in the space with appreciation. The beer garden looks a lot nicer from this vantage point than from my apartment window, that's for damn sure.

It's scattered with an array of picnic tables illuminated by Edison bulbs strung up overhead. People are huddled around a large fire pit in the center and some propane heaters along the ivy-covered walls to keep warm. I zip my coat up to my chin and glance over at the outdoor bar off to the right in search of the guys.

"Z, over here!" Link calls out from the far corner.

I begin to head over but my boots falter on the cobblestone when a familiar voice breaks through on a microphone. "This is so not my thing."

With a frown, I turn to the right to find the source of the voice and spot a small, empty stage. It's got a few lights strung over it, some large speakers, and an empty microphone stand in front of a wooden stool. There's no sign of life up there, so I look down at the crowd to see where the voice may be coming from.

"I hate singing in public almost as much as I hate my best friend, Phoebe," Daphney's voice utters from the speakers, and chills rush over my body because it must be her. No one has a voice like Daphney.

Daphney emerges from the crowd as she steps up onto the dimly lit stage with the microphone in hand. "This is what happens when you lose a bet."

The crowd replies with sympathetic murmurings as she thumps the mic into its holder and grabs an acoustic guitar off the nearby stand. She thrums a quick chord on the guitar as she adjusts the tuners at the top.

With a rueful smile on her face, she steps back up to the mic and says, "This one's for Phoebe. You bitch."

A loud cheer echoes from the crowd, and I catch sight of what looks like her friend's dark black hair that I saw at Old George the other day. The crowd pushes in closer as Daphney situates herself on the wooden stool and adjusts the mic to her level.

I freeze as I take a moment to check her out because she hasn't seen me yet. It's dark where I'm standing, so I feel a bit like a voyeur as my eyes travel over her oversized coat. Her blonde hair is loose and curly around her shoulders, blending in with the tan faux fur jacket. Her lips are a dark red, and her eyes have more makeup on them than I've ever seen before. She looks stunning.

She crosses her legs on the stool and positions the guitar on her thigh, revealing a short black skirt, and patterned tights with black ankle boots. She looks edgy with a touch of glam, and I'm not ashamed to admit that my cock thumps with attention. And the fact that she's about to sing makes me wonder if I am dreaming right now.

She begins strumming the guitar, and the beginning of John Legend's "All of Me" projects loudly through the speakers. When she leans into the mic and her husky voice echoes through the beer garden, the patrons all grow quiet, clearly caught off guard by her ability.

I was already aware Daphney could sing. Even hearing her through the wall of my apartment, I got chills, and I'm pretty sure she was singing about tires. Not that it matters. The girl could sing the alphabet, and her unique tone would enrapture me.

But tonight, what she's doing now…this is bone-chilling. Her raspy tone is like a cry as she sings the soft melody, yet her face is cool as a cucumber, despite her mentioning she hates singing in public.

The performance is intense. And the fact that I'm able to sit here and take it in is a gift I did not expect tonight.

As she finishes the song, I have to physically shake off my stunned reaction when the crowd goes wild. Her friend joins her up on stage, and the two hug and laugh while Daphney rolls her eyes.

They move off the stage, and I attempt to make a beeline to them when an arm wraps around me. "Is that your neighbor?" Link's voice booms in my ear as he takes a drink of his beer.

"Yes," I reply through clenched teeth, wishing I didn't have to go join my teammates right now.

"Fucking shit, she was hot before, but she's off the charts now," Link states, and I grind my teeth at the realization that every guy in this pub is probably thinking the same thing. "You going to do something about it?"

"I'm not sure yet." I turn my hat backward as strange nerves take flight in my belly. "Hey, let's go get another beer."

I've never needed liquid courage with a girl before, but after listening to Daphney sing, I fear she might be painfully out of my league. When we make our way over to the team, my heart leaps up into my throat when I see that Daphney is seated on top of the picnic table next to Booker, looking perfectly at ease as she visits with everyone.

When her eyes find mine, I give her a slight head nod, and she shoots me a secret smile that I think might be saying something, but I don't know what exactly.

My head jerks back when her friend steps in front of me. "Hiya there, naughty neighbor. I'm Daphney's best friend, Phoebe."

My focus shifts from Daphney to her raven-haired friend. I offer her an easy smile. "Hi, Phoebe, I'm Zander."

"Oh, I know all about you," she says with a wicked glint to her eye. "And who might this bloke be?"

"I'm Link Conlin. Striker from Arizona." Link reaches his hand out, and she takes it with a laugh.

"Is that how you always introduce yourself? Well then, I'm Phoebe Oxley of Essex, romance narrator to the stars."

"Come again?" Link asks, his brows furrowing curiously.

"I narrate romance novels." She winks up at him. "Do you want to hear an excerpt?"

"Abso-fuckin-lutely," Link answers and shoulder-bumps me out of the way.

I gladly give them some space as I walk over to the table and try not to stare at Daphney like I haven't pictured her naked four hundred and twenty-two times.

"Congratulations on the win, Soccer Boy," Daphney says with a bright smile, holding her glass of beer out to me. "You played the whole match."

"Bloody hell right, he did!" Booker bellows, holding his beer up. "Welcome to Bethnal Green, Williams!"

The guys all cheer and clink glasses with me before taking a sip. I swallow the knot in my throat and move closer to Daphney. "So, you watched?"

Her cheeks turn a rosy hue in front of me, and I swear I have tunnel vision right now because all I can see is Daphney. She wrinkles her nose and shrugs. "Nothing else good on the telly."

I laugh and nod. "Oh, I see how it is." She giggles, and it's too fucking sexy for her own good. I turn to sit beside her on the table and nudge her with my leg. "I wouldn't have pegged you as a beer drinker."

"Why not?" she asks, and I have to force myself not to stare at her dark lips.

I shrug. "I don't know. Most chicks I know drink wine or liquor, I guess."

"Well, I'm not like most chicks."

"I couldn't agree more," I reply quietly as I watch her take a drink, her eyes slightly hooded in a way that makes me think about her in my bed. Pushing back my dirty thoughts, I ask, "So what was the bet you lost?"

She loses all good humor on her face. "You were here for that?"

"Oh yeah," I confirm, and my cock presses against the seam of my jeans as an image of her singing flashes in my mind.

She covers her eyes with her hands. "That was embarrassing."

"Nothing to be embarrassed about. You sounded…" I exhale a heavy breath and shake my head, my entire body vibrating with awareness. "Amazing."

She shrugs. "It's an easy song."

I roll my eyes. "Just take a compliment, Ducky."

"Sorry," she exclaims and holds the beer in her two hands, unable to wipe the smile off her face. "Thank you."

I watch her curiously for a moment. "Why are you so smiley tonight?"

"I'm not smiley," she replies with a smile.

"Yes, she is," Phoebe bellows across from us. "And she's smiling because she sold her first jingle today and made a boatload of money! You are now looking at the voice of Tire Depot!"

Everyone's eyes turn to Daphney with a mixture of amusement and genuine appreciation. Booker holds his beer out. "Congratulations, Daph! That's brilliant."

"Thanks, Booker." She tucks her hair behind her ears, clearly not liking all the attention. "Phoebe demanded we celebrate tonight, but it was only then that I realized it was so she could make me pay up on our bet."

"What was the bet exactly?" I ask again, watching her with rapt fascination because she seems lighter than I've ever seen her before, and hell if I can't tear my eyes away. I'm not even trying anymore at this point.

"She didn't think she'd sell the bloody song, and she did because she's brilliant," Phoebe answers with a knowing glint to her eye. "Now she's rich and buying all of our drinks tonight!"

Phoebe cheers along with the rest of the guys, and Daphney's face falls. "I am not paying for drinks," she exclaims, losing all good humor on her face. "I wrote a song about tires, not jewelry!"

Phoebe laughs good-naturedly and shoots her friend a wink.

I nudge Daphney with my shoulder. "Relax, these guys can definitely afford their own drinks."

She huffs and takes another drink, her smile from earlier returning.

"Congratulations on the jingle," I say quietly.

"Thank you. It's silly but also kind of exciting to actually make decent money at it." She turns her stunning blue eyes to me. "And I'm desperately trying to forget the fact that I might be hearing my voice on the telly sometime. Maybe even after one of your football matches."

"That's wicked." I lift my brows with interest. "With a voice like yours, you should be singing on stages."

"Pass." She cringes. "Not all of us are meant for the spotlight." She hits me with a dazzling smile and adds, "Hot new American footballer takes Premier League by storm. Now that's a headline."

I bark out a laugh. "Did you just call me hot?"

She rolls her eyes. "It's an expression."

"It's a compliment." I waggle my brows. "And I could give the very same one to you. You look stunning tonight."

Our eyes lock, and the smile on her face falls as her gaze dips to my lips. The look in her eye is unmistakable, and I have cause to hope that I might pull home two W's tonight.

15

Taste the Love and Shit

Daphney

OPERATION: SHAG THE SLUTTY FOOTBALLER IS IN FULL EFFECT.

This is a ridiculous plan, which obviously means it came from Phoebe. After telling her all about my kiss with Zander and his blatant proposition, she was certain that an affair with a slutty footballer was exactly what I needed to forget about Rex for good. Which means my quiet evening of sitting at home in my pajamas to watch the Bethnal Green match on my telly was thwarted when she burst into my flat and yelled, "Tart up, we're going out!"

I actually was a bit relieved for the assistance because I wasn't sure what my next move with Zander would be. I just knew that ever since that kiss, well, honestly, ever since he arrived in London, I have not stopped thinking about him. Zander Williams gets under my skin like no other bloke. I'm quite certain he's ninety percent spoiled man-child and ten percent manwhore.

However, I'm twenty-six, single, and living next door to a man who may very well be my muse—not that I would *ever* tell him that. His bloody ego wouldn't fit under that stupid backward cap he always wears. But it's undeniable that the kiss I shared with Zander, dysfunctional as it might be, ignited something inside me. It's as if it awakened a part of me that had been sleeping ever since Rex. Maybe even before Rex. I'm keen to explore that part of me, even if it is a bit outside of my comfort zone.

Plus, look what happened after I stepped out of my box and snogged him in the hallway. I finished my jingle, submitted it to Drake, got a rave review, and made ten thousand pounds.

All signs are pointing to…live a little, Daphney Clarke!

Phoebe's plan for tonight was to hunker down with drinks at Old George and hope for a Zander sighting. The Harris family often frequents the pub after a home match. It was the twin's wives', Indie's and Belle's, favorite hangout when they worked at the same hospital together, and I guess it was sort of claimed as a Harris hangout after that. Hubert reminds the patrons to give the footballers space or they will be asked to leave, so everyone plays it pretty cool. And after how well Zander and Booker played on the pitch, I had a feeling Booker might drag him here.

I knew they'd show up, yet still, my heart leaped up into my throat when I spotted him walking over to our place on the corner picnic table. He looked so fit in his tight jeans and gray long-sleeved top peeked out from his puffy black coat. His shaggy brown hair was tucked under that American baseball cap he's always wearing, but thankfully, it was turned backward to reveal his bright and alive eyes. He is most likely still riding a high from their big win. He played a perfect game, and while I greatly admired how he looked on the telly in his football kit, the lace-up tobacco leather boots he's wearing tonight are giving me lumberjack fantasies that have me squirming in my seat.

So, the plan was first to run into Zander. *Check.*

Next, I was to flirt with him and not yell at him for something annoying he may have done in the past twenty-four hours. That was tricky because his alarm went off four times this morning, but I do have some flirting capabilities left inside me. Therefore, flirting mission accomplished. *Check, check.*

The rest of the night, I was to play it cool as we all ate and drank and enjoyed the band that returned to the stage after my solo performance. They sound incredible, and between the moonlight, the firelight, and the air of possibility, my body feels more alive than it has in ages.

Booker's wife, Poppy; Tanner's wife, Belle; and Roan DeWalt's wife, Allie, the Harris Brother's cousin who moved here from America a few years ago, all joined us at the pub to celebrate the win tonight as well, so it's a proper party at Old George. I see most of this lot at the weekly Sunday dinners at Vaughn's house, but watching them interact without their children and letting off some steam is another story altogether.

All the couples are out on the dance floor, completely enamored with each other, dancing in their own unique ways. Tanner, like a child while Belle is his scolding mother. Booker and Poppy are slow dancing to a fast song. And Roan is spinning Allie around like a pro. It's adorable.

Phoebe dances beside me and nudges me in the ribs. "Don't get any bright ideas."

"With regard to?" I ask, rubbing the tender spot she hit.

"The Harris Brothers are the exception, not the rule." Her green eyes sparkle from the nearby firelight as she wiggles her hips to the music.

"I don't know what you're going on about." I grab Phoebe and force her to look at me.

She pins me with a serious look that's a rare sighting on her. "Footballers are slags. All of them. Even the Harris men were slags in their time."

"Okay…" My face has to be the picture of confusion because I'm not following what she's going on about.

"Zander Williams is no Harris Brother," she states through clenched teeth. "He's Rex 2.0. So don't think you can turn him into a boyfriend, okay? Zander is for fun, not for the future."

"I know that." I step back, my body tense with annoyance at the mention of Rex. "Can we get to a point in my life when all signs don't lead back to Rex Carmichael please?"

Phoebe holds her hands up in surrender. "Sorry!"

"I'm here tonight following all your silly rules, so give me a little credit."

"Fair enough." She moves closer and wraps an arm around my shoulders. "I'm just looking out for you. You have a tender heart, Daph, and I want you to protect it as you attempt your first casual fling."

"You make me sound pathetic," I sulk, crossing my arms over my chest. "I'm not looking for a boyfriend any more than you are."

"Okay." She gives me a wry grin. "And we still have our rule that if we're still single by the age of thirty-eight, we're marrying each other and using a sperm donor, right?"

"Right, but I still don't want to be pregnant."

"Neither do I," she exclaims defensively.

"Which is why we're both getting turkey-basted at the same time." I waggle my brows excitedly.

"And may the odds be ever in our favor."

She clinks her glass with mine and reminds me to keep making occasional eye contact with Zander from my position. That task is not difficult because Zander feels like a piece of metal, and my eyes are two giant magnets. Every time our gazes connect, the swirling in my belly is so intense, I'm forced to look away, or I might faint.

The last little technique Phoebe told me to accomplish was to try to give attention to another bloke. Booker Harris would be the easiest choice since I know him, but he's too enraptured with Poppy to even play that game with me.

So, when I end up cornered by the Scottish midfielder named Banner, I figure he'll get the job done.

"I'm from Edinburgh," Banner says, his eyes staring blatantly at my chest.

"That's nice. I've been there a few times," I respond, doing my best to look into his steel-blue eyes, but it's hard when his gaze isn't on my face.

"You haven't been to Edinburgh with me, though," his growly voice replies creepily.

I frown at that strange remark. "Well, no, because we've just met."

"Aye, if you come to Edinburgh with me, I'll show you a part of the city you never even knew existed." Banner nods proudly, his chest puffing out like he's striking a pose. "Things your mind can't even imagine. The seedy underbelly."

"Sounds scary." I laugh nervously and glance over Banner's shoulder to see Zander standing at the bar and watching me with rapt fascination. I can't help but smile victoriously. Bloody hell, maybe Phoebe's crazy ideas actually work.

I redirect my attention back to Banner. "I'm from Essex. What you see is what you get there, I'm afraid."

"I don't know about that," Banner says with a laugh. "I'm quite certain you have some surprises hiding under that fur coat of yours."

My brows furrow at his bizarre reply. What is it with footballers and horrible pickup lines? I mean, I know the fact that they're footballers pretty much makes them hot by default, but they surely can do better.

When I look past Banner again, a group of girls has joined Zander. A tall blonde leans up and whispers something into Zander's ear, and my spark of jealousy is instant. When her hand slides up his arm and wraps around his bicep, my mind implodes.

This is stupid.

Playing games with men is stupid. Why did I let Phoebe talk me into this? I already knew Zander wanted to sleep with me. He all but said so in the hallway. And my original idea was much, much easier. I was going to hang out in my flat until I heard him come home and then invite him over for the little surprise I made him. Now there's a girl who looks like she's about to win Operation: Shag the Slutty Footballer, and I don't fancy the idea of losing.

"Will you please excuse me," I bite out to Banner, and without waiting for him to respond, I march straight over to where Zander stands at the bar with three girls pressing in on him.

His eyes widen as I approach. "Can I see you for a sec?" My voice is clipped as I tap my boot impatiently on the cobblestone.

"He's busy," some girl slurs, but I ignore her because Zander's eyes don't leave mine.

His brows flicker with concern as he detaches the woman's claws from his arm and is nearly forced to shove his way out of the gaggle of women. "What do you need?"

I grab his hand and drag him toward the pub and hang a right into the narrow hallway by the toilets. I swerve around on my heel and inhale a sharp breath at our proximity. He's all tall and smoldering, a curious glint in those hazel eyes. I shake off my traitorous thoughts and ask firmly, "Are you having a nice time tonight?"

His eyes dance over my face, and I swear he's fighting back a smile. "Yeah, sure. How about you?"

"I was until a couple of minutes ago." I chew my lip, tasting the chalkiness of my lipstick.

"Anything I can help you with?" Zander asks, hitting me with that annoying crooked smirk.

"Are you planning to shag one of those girls tonight?" I bite, shocked at how angry I sound. I swear this man gives me a personality transplant. I'm not normally this confrontational.

"Come again?" Zander's face is a mixture of humor, confusion, and shock.

"What is your plan?" I snap through clenched teeth. "Because it would be nice to know so I can stop doing the stupid things Phoebe told me to do and just go home."

Zander steps back and removes his backward hat to fork a hand through his hair that's curling at the ends. I get a fleeting urge to run my fingers through it, but stuff that thought into the dark vortex that houses my temper.

"I don't even know what you're talking about, Ducky," Zander's tone is casual as he stares down at me in that big, overbearing way of his that makes me feel petite and feminine.

My face heats as I force myself to break eye contact so I can focus on what I'm about to say. Taking a deep breath, I make the rash decision to throw all of Phoebe's advice out the window and go for brutal honesty instead. "I'm doing these stupid things to seduce you because I want to try some casual sex with you." I cringe and cover my face, feeling his hazel eyes boring into me like I'm a circus freak. "But if what you said in the hallway yesterday was utter bollocks, then tell me now so I can go home and resume hating you for all of space and time. I think I was quite exceptional at that, as it turns out."

I finally lower my hand and glance up to see delighted amusement on Zander's face. His full lips purse together as he fights back a smile. "You want to try some casual sex with me?"

My fists clench with the urge to punch him square in the nose. It'd be nice to give him a crooked nose to match that crooked smile. Unfortunately, images of him naked in that stupid pink tea towel live rent-free in my mind, so I'd much rather he thump me…in the casual sex sort of way.

"I thought casual sex was the original idea," I croak, my breathing growing shaky as flashes of his abs alight in my mind. "No strings and all that." Christ, I sound like I'm ordering a Big Mac. Better go ahead and add a side of fries while I'm at it, so I'm sure to be full by the end of the night.

Zander cocks his head, his eyes darkening as he glances down at my body, causing my nipples to pebble beneath my coat. "I already told you that was my specialty."

"Then what were you doing out there?" I thrust my finger back toward the beer garden where he was just surrounded by Harris Ho wannabes.

"What were you doing out there?" he volleys back, and the vein in his neck looks ridiculously sexy. "I was only talking to those girls because you were talking to Banner."

"Well, fine," I retort, my chest heaving as he moves closer to me.

"Fine," he repeats, forcing me to look up as he bows over me. His delicious scent assaults my senses, and I lick my lips, desperate to feel his on mine again. His voice is deep and controlled when he adds, "Does this mean you're ready to admit that you want to fuck me as bad as I want to fuck you?"

My balance wavers as all the blood in my body rushes to my nether regions. I force myself to maintain eye contact with him when I reply shakily, "Unfortunately, yes."

Zander tilts his head and allows his eyes to do a long, languishing inspection of my face. "Nothing unfortunate about that."

A moment of tense silence casts over us, and I briefly wonder if I should just drag him into the loo and let him take me up against the wall. This ache inside me is so intense, I'm not sure I'll be able to walk out of here without my knees buckling. But I need to play it cool with Zander. I'm sure he does this with women all the time, so there's no need to inform him how desperate and starved for sex I actually am.

I chew my lip and pull my mobile out of my bag to shoot off a quick text to Phoebe.

"What are you doing?" Zander asks, his breath warm on my neck as he glances down at my phone.

"I'm telling Phoebe that we're leaving." I press send and look up to see an impressed smirk on Zander's face. "That okay with you?"

"You're the boss." He waggles his eyebrows playfully as I grab Zander's hand and pull him toward the side exit of Old George.

My mind is whirring with annoyance and irritation for how horribly I played that game tonight. Honesty is always the best policy. I should have never let Phoebe get in my head. And besides, if Zander and I are truly just going to have casual sex, there's no need to play these stupid games.

As we make our way up the three flights of stairs, my crossness shifts into arousal with every step I take. I can feel his heat and presence looming behind me. I don't have to glance back to know that his eyes are on me. And it's a heady sensation to realize that I want them to be. I want his eyes on every part of my body.

This is really happening. I'm really going to have sex with my footballer neighbor. The last boy who made my vagina dance like this was Sam Thompson in year nine. I was too young and stupid to do anything about that. Now I'm older. I'm mature and independent. I've earned this experience, and I'm going to stuff away all our past drama to enjoy this.

When we reach our hallway, I head toward my door and call over my shoulder, "I have something for you, but you can't come inside."

"Seriously?" Zander hesitates in front of my door with a confused look on his face. "What is it with you and this hallway?"

I roll my eyes at his little joke. "My nieces were over today and left it a total pigsty. I'll just pop in and grab it, and we can go over to your place."

Zander smiles and takes a step toward me, his hand propping on my door as he leans in with a sultry look on his face. "I like a pigsty."

"No one likes a pigsty," I deadpan, totally immune to his charms for once and annoyed that Phoebe didn't give me any time tonight to clean up before she dragged me over to the pub. My saving grace was that we would hook up in Zander's far superior flat, but of course, his pushy-arse isn't easily persuaded.

Zander pulls back and crosses his arms over his chest. "Just let me come inside."

My brows lift at that double entendre, and I cringe when I'm pretty sure he just read my dirty mind. With a growl of acceptance, I unlock my door and let him into the chaos. What do I have to impress him for? It's not like this is a relationship.

"Just don't look too closely," I call over my shoulder as I flick on my twinkle lights that wrap around my living area and cast the flat in dim lighting. I shuffle into my dark kitchen to quickly toss all the baking dishes into my sink and corral all the items I left out earlier. Housekeeping has never been my forte. And my nieces are wild little beasts when they come over. I don't even think they like baking all that much, but I do it with them so they stay out of my living room and away from my music equipment.

I find the small dish with the item I have for Zander and turn to see he's watching me from the entry of my kitchen with an amused look on his face. "Don't make fun of me, or you won't get this present."

His face goes serious. "It's a present?"

I grip the plastic dish nervously in my hands. "I can't promise it's as good as your mum's because I've never made oatmeal raisin in my life, and the girls said the raisins look like sheep poo, but I assure you, they're not."

I thrust the container that houses one oatmeal raisin cookie toward him. The cookie is resting on top of a neon green piece of tissue paper and the girls decorated a small card that says, "Great Game, Soccer Boy" but they ended up scribbling over the top of my text, so I'm not sure he can even read it anymore.

Zander holds the container up to his eye level as he stares at the cookie with an unreadable expression on his face.

"The mess should tell you it's homemade, so hopefully, you can 'taste the love and shit." I laugh nervously because I don't know what he's thinking. Surely, he understands the love and shit comment was a joke. I was just repeating what he'd said earlier about his mum's cookies. I don't even talk like that. It's a very American-sounding phrase, but the longer he goes without talking, the more I fear he thinks I'm a level-ten stalker and trying to make him my boyfriend!

Finally, his eyes flicker from the cookie. "You made me a cookie?"

"Yes, but the *love and shit* thing was a joke," I stammer nervously. "In fact, that cookie was made with a fair amount of frustration and probably plenty of germs. I made Marisa and Rocky wash their hands, but you know little kids. They're really disgusting, and their hands always seem permanently covered in jam. You know what…on second thought…maybe take a pass on the cookie. We don't need Bethnal Green's new star defender feeling poorly from a dodgy cookie."

I reach for the container, but Zander pulls it out of my reach, causing me to stumble into him. He wraps his free arm around me as a giant smile spreads across his face. "You made me a cookie."

His awestruck expression causes butterflies to erupt in my belly. I bite my lip, feeling strangely giddy at how pleased I've made him. Inhaling a cleansing breath, I narrow my eyes. "I also asked to have casual sex with you, and it doesn't seem like that was a good idea either."

His shoulders shake with silent laughter as he releases me to pull the cookie out of the container. He takes a massive bite, making a big show of moaning around every single morsel. I hate that I love watching this.

He mumbles around a mouthful, "A true triumph."

"Don't be an arse." I roll my eyes and swat at him.

He licks his lips and swallows, his face growing thoughtful for a moment. "No girl has ever made me cookies before."

I quirk a brow. "Your mother is most likely a girl."

"You know what I mean." His eyes sweep over my face, and a warmness creeps up inside me at the look in his eye.

"You're welcome." A sheepish smile spreads across my face. "Don't let it go to your head."

He shoots me a cocky smirk. "Too late."

16

Cookie for the Road

Zander

DAPHNEY POURS ME A GLASS OF WATER, AND THE ENTIRE TIME I watch her moving around her messy kitchen, making excuses for the clutter, I can't help but think this situation is fucking perfect. We're neighbors, she doesn't like me, and she still wants to have sex with me.

I just scored the best goal of my life. That brings our score up to Zander: two, Daphney: one.

Knowing I need to make a move before she comes up with some ridiculous reason to call this whole thing off, I toss my hat on the counter along with the cookie container. I position myself behind Daphney at the sink and snake my hands around her hips. She inhales a sharp breath as I turn her around, so her ass is pressed up against the counter and our bodies are flush.

"Do I get my second present now?" My gaze dances from her full lips to her sparkling eyes, unsure which I want to stare at more.

Her voice is raspy when she replies, "What present are you referring to exactly?"

I fight back a smile as I circle my thumbs over her hip bones and watch a flush crawl across her cheeks. "Oh, what did you call it again? Casual relations?"

She covers her face with her hands. "That sounds just as bad as the first time I said it."

My body shakes with amusement. God, she's cute. And sexy. And when she was all flustered and jealous, asking me if I was going to sleep with those girls at the bar, I about pushed her into the bathroom and took her right then and there. And the fact that she admitted she was only talking to Banner to get my attention is even cuter. She really is a good girl.

"Maybe we should have some rules?" she croaks as I move my hands up to her shoulders and pull her faux fur coat off.

I toss it to the side and my eyes drift down to see that she's wearing a long-sleeve sheer black top that shows a black bra underneath. That with the skirt and tights has my cock already thickening in my jeans.

"I get enough rules on the pitch, Ducky," I reply, removing my own coat and discarding it on the floor with hers. "Let's fuck the rules."

Her eyes flare with excitement, so I reach back and pull my shirt off over my head. The little noise she makes in her throat makes for an uncomfortable situation in my jeans.

"My God." She sighs, her eyes roving over my chest and abdomen. "You really are quite confident, aren't you?"

When it comes to Daphney, I don't know what I am, but right now… this second…I want her, and by the look in her eyes, she wants me too. That's all that matters.

"Your turn." I glance down at her body and step back to give her space.

She smiles shyly, and with a slight eye roll, she peels the thin fabric off her body as she stands before me in a black bra. Her skin is pale against the fabric, and I can see the outline of her nipples through the lace.

My heart speeds up as I hold myself back. "Need help with that last bit?" I ask, pointing at her chest and dying to touch her. "I'm kind of an expert."

"An expert at being a cheeky arse." Reaching behind her, she unclasps her bra in Mach speed and flings it off to the side. She props her hands on her narrow hips. "Happy?"

My smile falls as I stare down at her breasts. They are fucking perfect. Even better than my dreams. Petite, teardrop shapes with tiny, pale pink nipples that I…*oh fuck it, what am I waiting for?*

I reach out and gently stroke her breasts, my hands testing the weight of them in my grip as my thumb glides over the hardened buds. She's a petite girl, but these breasts are still an admirable handful. And I have big hands.

My mouth practically waters as I dip my head and wrap my lips around her right nipple, sucking the hard flesh deep into my mouth. Her perfume invades my senses as I flick my tongue over her, and she cries out as she forks her fingers into my hair, scoring her nails over my scalp. The sensation causes my entire body to tremble.

Annoyed at the uncomfortable angle, I grab Daphney around the waist and hoist her up to the counter. A cloud of flour puffs out around us as I move my lips to her other breast. How is it possible that this one tastes even better than the other? *Fuck, I'm not going to last long.*

"Zander." Daphney sighs, and her legs circle around my hips as she pulls me closer.

She grabs my jaw and pulls my mouth to hers. Our lips connect, and she swirls her tongue deep into my mouth, taking me the way she did in the hallway. I can taste the desire on her lips, and it makes me desperate to taste more of her.

"I want to touch you," I murmur against her lips as I slide my hands up her legs, frustrated by her tights. "We need to get these off."

Nodding, she braces herself on my shoulders as she slips off the counter and kicks out of her boots. I do the same and then laugh when she turns her back to me because her ass is covered in flour.

"What are you laughing at?" she hisses, turning around with a frown.

My abs contract with poorly concealed amusement as I walk over and swat at her bottom. She looks confused at first but then the cloud of flour wafts all around us.

"You said you liked a pigsty, Soccer Boy," she giggles as she unzips her skirt that now has my handprint outline on it. She shimmies it down her hips and says, "Let me grab my robe, and we can sneak over to your place."

"No way." I shake my head adamantly and step back, taking in her half-naked body donning nothing but black tights as she stands in her kitchen. "This is how I want to picture you in all of my fantasies from now on."

She levels me with a lethal glare. "I've had about enough of your cocky mouth."

I close the distance between us and tilt her chin up to mine. "I'm only getting started with yours."

I crush my lips to hers and take a moment to explore her mouth, neck, and shoulders as we stumble toward her unmade bed, kicking out of my jeans on the way there. We pause at the sofa on the foot of her bed as I slip my hands down the back of her tights, palming her fleshy bare ass. It's soft and supple. And I realize that no panties under tights may just be my new favorite thing.

Daphney gasps when my erection grazes her center. My black boxer briefs are the only barrier as she reaches between us and slides her delicate fingers over my shaft. The gentle stroking overwhelms me, and I stop kissing her to rest my forehead on her shoulder for support. I can feel the precum seeping out of me already. Fucking hell, this woman is going to kill me.

"Do you have a condom?" Daphney asks, her voice deep and husky and causing all the blood in my body to drain to my cock.

Painstakingly, I turn around and grab a condom out of the pocket of my jeans. I had high hopes for tonight, and the fact that Daphney has already exceeded all of them before I've even entered her is a pretty alarming thought.

Daphney's eyes are trained on me as I slide my boxers off and roll the condom over my bulging erection. It's been a while since I've been laid, and I'm painfully aware of the fact. Therefore, I know I will need to distract myself if I want any chance of this lasting.

Daphney doesn't make it fucking easy.

She bites her lip and ditches her tights before positioning herself on the bed. Her blonde hair cascades over her white pillow as she spreads herself open to me. Her smooth mound glistens in the dim overhead lighting. She looks like a goddamn angel, and I'm the devil dragging her over to the dark side.

The bed dips as I move toward her, and a fleeting look of anxiety crosses her features. "Do you want me to stop?" I ask, my cock weeping inside the rubber.

She shakes her head as her cool, soft hands reach out to pull me closer causing her breasts to brush across my chest. "Don't stop."

Swallowing the lump in my throat, I reach down and drag my fingers along her hot center. "Daphney, you're fucking soaked," I croak, my voice sounding like a completely different person.

She squirms against my gentle caress, and with her eyes closed, she reaches down and grabs my hand, thrusting my fingers inside her.

"Holy fuck," I groan as she rides my hand for a moment, her lips parted, her noises unbearably sexy.

She's more than a fucking fantasy. She's a goddamn wet dream come true. She's immortal. She's legendary. She's all the things. Soft and supple. Sweet and innocent. Brave and spicy. And best of all, needy, wanting, and not afraid to show it.

The best fucking combination.

I thrust my fingers into her slowly, enraptured by the way she moves. I want to take this slow so I can savor it. I also want to race to the finish line because I'm so fucking turned on.

My dick hardens painfully as she arches her chest toward me, begging my lips to give her breasts more attention. Leaning down, I lick my way around her nipple, enjoying the surprise in her moan as I latch on and suck hard while my fingers speed up. Her slick heat drenches my digits as my cock strains between us.

I focus on my breathing, determined to make her come when she pushes my head away from her breast with a wild look in her eyes. "Now," she says, her head nodding as she hooks her heels around my ass and pulls me close. "I need you now, Zander."

I'm at a rare loss for words as she moves my fingers out of her center and positions my cock at her apex. When I begin to push inside her, her head flattens against the pillow, and she bites down hard on her lip. I push in to the hilt and freeze. Fuck, she feels amazing. Tight and warm, like the perfect hug for my cock. I pull back and thrust again, this time going even deeper as her wetness coats me. Her back arches off the bed, and her tits thrust up toward my face. My control snaps as I devour her nipples and neck and begin pumping wildly inside her as I do it. I want to taste every inch of Daphney's body.

She cries out, but I do my best to block out her noises so I don't come too soon. Can't come too soon. Need her to come first or I'll never fucking forgive myself.

I begin outlining the Bethnal Green playbook in my head to tear my focus away from her. I've been studying them every night since I arrived, but a refresher never hurts.

Goddamn, tonight's game was epic. My connection on the field with Booker—and Finney's eyes when he realized I was here to stay—was everything I wanted my first week I arrived. Now I get to top all of that off with a great lay from my neighbor who made me a fucking cookie.

Which was awful, by the way.

Tasted like playdough.

But it was oatmeal raisin, and I gutted it down like a champ because the fact that I didn't have to break my ritual of a cookie reward after every win means more to me than I'll ever tell her.

I'm jolted back into the moment when Daphney's nails stab into my back, and the sensation of her sex clamping down around me is the most intense female orgasm my cock has ever felt. She groans my name, and the hoarse tone of it sounds way too fucking good for me to last a second longer.

With a guttural moan, I press my face into her neck as I empty myself inside her with shocking savagery, my cock pulsing inside the tight condom as every nerve in my body gyrates over top of her.

Once my brain revives itself, I roll off Daphney, sweaty, out of breath, and in desperate need of some sleep. I sit up and make my way into her bathroom to dispose of the condom and clean myself up. That was fucking intense. More than I expected of my cute, nagging neighbor, who I'm pretty sure still hates my guts even after sex.

When I return a few moments later, Daphney's sitting up in bed, fully dressed in her silk pajamas that she wasn't wearing a second ago. She has a notebook and pen clutched tightly in her hands, and she looks like she's making a damn grocery list.

My brows furrow as I stand naked in her apartment. "You good?"

She hits me with a bright, toothy smile. "I'm excellent. You?"

"Um…I'm good," I reply, feeling a bit bewildered. "Should I…?"

"Go back to yours? Yes, that would be perfect," Daphney says brightly, her eyes not even glancing at my cock that's still semi-hard and not totally ready for bed. "Do you want another cookie for the road?"

My head snaps back. "Um…no. Just one is good."

"Cool. I'll see you later then, yeah?" She brings the pen to her mouth and stares intently at her notebook like she's trying to solve some sort of puzzle.

"Um, okay." I run a hand through my hair that feels like it's grown two feet from her fingers running through it all night. As I stumble around and get dressed, I wonder if I'm getting blown off? Was it not good for her? It was good for me. Mind-blowingly good for me, even if I did have to think about corner kick formations that have zero fucking sex appeal. But I did that for her benefit. So I could make sure she got off. And she one hundred percent got off. Her pussy was like a vise-grip on my cock. It was so tight, I wondered if I might have been trapped there forever.

I could think of worse places for my cock to be stuck in.

But seriously…the parts I was fully present for were wicked hot. I should at the very least get a good game pat on the butt or something, right? I'm her Soccer Boy, for fuck's sake.

When I retrieve my coat from the kitchen floor, I glance over, considering a quick kiss goodbye, but her body language indicates she just wants me out of her space.

Trying to sound casual as the sex we just had, I offer, "Good night?"

"Night!" She waves at me like she waves at the deliveryman.

I walk out into the hallway and slump against her door when a horrifying thought crosses my mind: *Am I bad at sex?*

17

Bye Bye Snoregasm

Daphney

"PHOEBE, I COULD STRANGLE YOU!" I EXCLAIM, MARCHING INTO Phoebe's bedroom at eight o'clock the next morning.

She shoots up out of bed, her teal silk eye mask still fully in place as she flings her hands out wide. "I only consented to choking that one time!"

I blink at that odd response but figure we can unpack that conversation at another time. We have bigger fish to fry this morning. "Well, prepare for my wrath regardless because I am coming in piping hot," I growl and drop my key for her flat back in my purse.

Phoebe pushes her mask up into her hair, revealing green eyes that are still just as vibrant in the morning as they were last night. How does she wake up like that?

"What did I do?" she asks, shoving her stray black strands of hair out of her eyes.

"Oh, where do I begin?" I start pacing the floor of her very girlie bedroom. It's decorated in all white and pale pinks, just like it was when we were children. It's like an adult baby room. Flowery, fluffy, girlie, the very opposite of the rage boiling inside me right now. "First, you made me do all those stupid games with Zander at the pub last night."

"Which clearly worked because you slagged off without me last night." Phoebe waggles her eyebrows.

"I bailed on your plan and told him I wanted to sleep with him," I state, propping my hands on my hips.

Phoebe shrugs. "So, you were inspired to go rogue. What's wrong with that? Did you guys not have sex?"

"Oh, we had sex." I laugh, and my cheeks flame at the flash of memory that assaults me.

"Good!" Phoebe nods excitedly.

"Not good!"

Phoebe's face falls as she grabs a pink pillow and clutches it to her chest like a coat of armor. "Was it that bad? Soccer Boy has tons of big dick energy. I thought for sure he'd come packing."

"Oh, he has a big dick. A very nice dick. In fact, probably the nicest I've ever had." The image of him rolling that condom on with deft ease is burned into my brain for all of space and time.

"That's brilliant. A good cock is half the battle," Phoebe offers.

"But you never told me." I run my hands through my tangled hair that I didn't even brush before rushing over this morning. I tossed and turned all night so I'm sure I look a fright.

"Never told you what?"

"What it actually feels like!" I exclaim back at her, my entire body heating at the memory. "You and I have talked about sex ad nauseam. And I've described my past experiences to you in intricate detail. And you never ever told me."

"Told you what? I am so confused." She tosses her pillow at me. "You're not some closet virgin, are you?"

I catch it and bite my lip. "I might as well be."

"What the bloody hell are you talking about, Daph?"

I inhale a cleansing breath and hit Phoebe with the harsh reality I only learned mere hours ago. "Until last night, I had no idea that I'd never had a proper orgasm before." I gesture toward my vagina like it's going to nod its solemn approval with me.

Phoebe rises to her knees to grab my wrist and yank me down onto her bed. She touches her temples. "Wait, clarify for me because I have a crippling hangover, and I'm not sure I'm following. Did you have an orgasm with Zander Williams last night?"

"Yes." I drop my chin and eye her sternly.

"Then what is the problem?"

"My problem is, I thought I've been having orgasms my whole life. I've had five semi-serious boyfriends and had multiple sexual relations with all those blokes. I thought I'd been climaxing every time we shagged! However, I did always think it strange that I never moaned and groaned like people on the telly did. Nevertheless, I thought I was coming right along with my partners! I had no idea until last night that I never moaned before because I wasn't even orgasming!"

Phoebe's eyes turn to saucers. "Daphney Clarke, are you telling me that Zander Williams is the first bloke you've ever reached climax with?"

"Yes!"

"Oh, my God!"

"I know! That's why I want to strangle you!"

"What did I do? I wasn't even there!"

"You just…you never described it to me. You described everything else! I think I know every freckle on your nipple after last year."

"Well, I thought I felt a lump. I needed a mate to have a proper look." She crosses her arms over her chest protectively.

I sigh and rub her shoulder affectionately. "I understand, but Phoebe, somehow, in all the years of our friendship, you and I never descriptively discussed what an orgasm felt like. Which means I've spent the majority of my adult life thinking I knew…but after what happened to me last night, I now realize that everything in my past sexual experiences was a complete and utter lie. I mean…did I even have sex? Is it sex if you don't climax?"

"Of course it's sex. Don't be daft."

I exhale heavily. "I know, but Phoebe, what happened to my body last night was…mind-altering."

Phoebe's eyes alight with interest. "What did he do?"

I bite my lip and shake my head from side to side, still feeling stupefied by the whole ordeal. "I don't think he did anything all that special. It just bloody worked. I felt like I'd been electrified. It was like this powerful current swept through me, and it was such a huge gush of release that I thought I wee'd."

"Fucking brilliant."

"I know!" I huff out an awkward laugh. "I couldn't sleep last night thinking about how brilliant it was. And you're a twat because we're framily, and you should have set me straight years ago. What have I been missing all my life?"

"Well, you're only twenty-six, so it's safe to say you're being a tad dramatic."

I frown at her. "I feel like a new woman."

"This conversation needs champagne." Phoebe rises from her bed and walks out of the bedroom, her long satin nightie flowing dramatically behind her. I follow her into her whitewashed kitchen, where she grabs a bottle of champagne from her wine chiller and two flutes from her cupboard.

She tops the bubbles off with a dash of cranberry juice and hands me one. "To your first sexual climax."

Our glasses clink, and we both take a longer than appropriate drink for eight in the morning. Phoebe lowers her glass and hits me with a severe look. "Have you never masturbated before?"

"No," I reply and take another swig. "I tried when I was younger, but it felt weird."

"What did you try with?"

I wiggle my fingers at her.

"That's your first mistake," she scoffs and takes another sip. "You need a toy. It's much less cardio. I'll send you a link for a good vibrator. I have a voucher code for one and everything because I'm one of their influencers."

"I don't need a vibrator, Phoebe," I snap, feeling frustrated at how I feel like a virgin all over again. "I don't know what I need."

"Well, you obviously need to thank me for encouraging you to have casual sex with the slutty footballer." She crosses her arms as she holds her glass in front of her. "I mean, if it wasn't for me, you'd still be having snoregasms."

"God, you're right." I slump down onto one of her plush white barstools. "It's just so weird because I thought all this time I was climaxing. I guess it just…felt good? And the fact that my first orgasm was with someone who pretty much drives me mental every day is messing with my mind. Do you think that makes me crazy? Like is this some weird kink I have?"

Phoebe props her chin in her hand. "No, I think it means you're letting loose and having a bit of fun for once, Daph. I've been having fun for years, and my skin has never looked better."

She gestures to her beautiful, flawless skin, and my brows lift.

"So how many times did you do it?" She waggles her brows.

I pull my lips into my mouth and wince. "Just once. And then I sort of flipped out and told him to go home. I can't imagine experiencing that sensation multiple times! I'd explode into a million pieces."

"That's kind of the idea! You climax so many times that your body turns into jelly, and you can't move a muscle for hours. It's fantastic." Phoebe shivers as an apparent memory assaults her. "Did he want to go again, you think?"

"Maybe? I'm not sure. He looked kind of sad when he left. I feel bad if he was expecting a round two. I just sort of shagged and bagged, I guess."

A shocked look casts over Phoebe's face. "My God, I couldn't be prouder right now than if you offered to carry our future sperm donor children."

18

Nervous in the Service

Zander

"I THINK I MIGHT BE BAD AT SEX," I STATE OVER BREAKFAST THE next day at The Full Monty with Knight and Link.

Link leans in, his eyes rapt with interest as he replies, "Gonna need a bit more context again, my dude."

I swallow the knot in my throat and wonder when the fuck I became such a sharer. I'm an only child. I don't need someone to help me make life decisions. But ever since my dad died, I can't seem to figure anything out on my own...so here I sit, having breakfast with Knight and Link and sharing my innermost thoughts with them before we head over to Tower Park to watch game footage of last night's match with the team. I'm such a weakling.

I level them both with a serious glower that says I'm being dead serious. "Last night, I hooked up with Daphney, and after we finished, she sort of...kicked me out."

Link's head snaps back. "Did you want to stick around and spoon or something?"

"Fuck no," I bark. "But I probably could have gone for a round two. I mean, it's been a while since I've been laid, so I was up for it. In fact, I don't think I put my best foot forward because I was too busy trying to distract myself from what we were doing so I wouldn't..."

"Be done in sixty seconds?" Link finishes with a laugh, holding his coffee mug out to me. "Been there."

I roll my eyes and shake my head. "Yeah, I mean, I wasn't totally focused on her while we were doing it because I was trying to make it last, but I know she fucking came. What more did she want?"

Knight props his elbows on the table. "Maybe she faked it."

"She didn't fake it," I nearly growl.

Knight shrugs. "Maybe she thought fucking a pro athlete would be more exciting?"

The response feels like a sharp knife in the gut. "I'm exciting."

"Are you?" Knight volleys back.

My brows furrow. "I'm Zander fucking Williams. I'm as exciting as it gets."

Link huffs out a laugh. "You're trying to convince the wrong people, dude."

Knight nods in agreement, and my body recoils at the idea that it just wasn't good enough for her to want me to stick around. Jesus Christ, this is humiliating. How am I going to show my face in front of her again?

Link snaps his finger at me. "My sister reads a lot of romance novels, and she's always saying what's sexy about them is when the hero goes all alpha and just takes the woman without asking."

"That's called rape," Knight deadpans over his mug of coffee.

"Not if it's with a consenting party," Link insists.

Knight shakes his head, clearly not convinced.

"They just like you to be a man," Link explains. "With their permission obviously."

"Did your sister tell you all this?" I ask, my head tilted curiously at my brother from another mother. "'Cause that's a really weird convo to have with a sister."

Link smiles smugly. "I eavesdropped on her book club one time. You can learn a lot of shit about what a woman likes at a romance book club."

Knight takes a sip of his coffee. "That's really weird, man." The two of them begin arguing about romance novels causing unrealistic expectations on men while I brood over my coffee.

I mean, Link's not wrong. I do need to show Daphney that I'm a lot more than what we did last night, which I didn't think was bad. It felt wicked good actually. But maybe my head not being fully focused on her was too obvious. I can't remember the last time I went a year without sex. I'm sure I was just a little rusty. Now that I've jumped back on the saddle, I'll be much better the next time.

However, I'm not even sure Daphney wants a next time. We didn't exactly discuss our situation. Was it a one-time thing? Or could we be regular starters in each other's lives?

Either way, I need a redo. I can't face her in the hallway every day and have her thinking I'm bad at sex. No goddamn way. I have a reputation to uphold. Maybe Link's idea of *taking her* isn't as crazy as it sounds. I just need one chance to show her that I can jerk one out of the park and have her begging for more.

19

Premier League Sexpert

Daphney

M Y FINGERS FREEZE ON MY KEYBOARD WHEN I HEAR A KNOCK ON MY door. It's two o'clock on Friday, and I've been hiding out in my flat for the past two days, trying my best not to run into Zander. After how mental I behaved a couple of nights ago, I'm sure the last thing he wants to do is see his one-night stand again.

Of course it's just my luck that Bethnal Green has no matches this weekend, so the odds of avoiding him are not in my favor. I'd go back home for the weekend if I didn't have a shift at Old George tonight and tomorrow night.

I begrudgingly rise from my piano bench and make my way over to the door, hoping it's just my brother or Phoebe stopping by. When I peer through the peephole and spot Zander on the other side, my heart leaps into my throat.

"I heard you playing your piano, Ducky. Just open up and stop avoiding me." His voice is gruff and sexy, causing my vagina to dance again. Damn him.

I exhale heavily and open my door to see Zander standing there in workout gear consisting of Adidas training trousers and a zip-up hoodie. His hat is facing forward, and the moody look in his eyes has my body clenching with desire.

"Hiya." I cringe at the weird tone in my voice. This moment right here is why casual sex is an awful idea. It's never awkward to see your boyfriend after shagging him. But a one-night stand? Awkward city!

Zander steps toward me, a glacial look in his eye as he says flatly, "I'm going to kiss you, okay?"

"Sorry?" I croak, and the next thing I know, his lips press on mine as he holds my face in his large, calloused hands and thrusts his tongue greedily into my mouth.

In most circumstances and with any other man, I would be offended. I'd shove him away and tell him that he has no right to just kiss me like that. But this isn't most circumstances, and Zander isn't just any other man. He's…Soccer Boy. And the trembling of my limbs right now is a clear indication that he can do pretty much whatever he wants with me.

My puckered lips whoosh forward when Zander yanks back, his eyes frantic with worry. "Shit, you didn't say yes."

"What?" I rasp, my mouth feeling like it's been teased in the cruelest way possible.

"I-I just thought you'd say yes," he stammers, his words ragged as he stares hungrily at my lips. "Is this consent?"

"What on earth are you talking about?" I grip the sides of his jacket and feel annoyed that we're not still kissing.

He releases my face and steps back, and my body nearly falls forward at the loss of him. His chest rises and falls with rapid breaths. "I want to take you."

"Take me where?" I ask, staring up at him like he's a bloody alien speaking another language.

"Here…sexually," he barks, his voice laced with frustration.

My eyes nearly pop out of their sockets. "Zander, I can barely understand you. What is going on?"

"Yes or no, Ducky?" He pulls his hat off his head to run an agitated hand through his hair.

"Yes," I croak because my body has been practically screaming to be touched ever since I experienced my first orgasm less than forty-eight hours ago.

In a breath, Zander rushes me, grabbing my bottom and hoisting me up so I have to wrap my legs around him. He kisses me wildly, banging me into the door as he closes it behind us. His tongue moves down my neck as he nips at my skin. The sensation causes every muscle in my body to tense, and I feel my hips rolling into his.

He pushes us off the wall and stomps over to my bed. "Take your clothes off," he growls as he drops me on the mattress like a sack of potatoes.

Confused but also insanely aroused, I do as he says and watch him as he also ditches his own clothing. My eyes are saucers when I see he's rock hard already. His bare cock is pointing right at me, and in the broad daylight, I dare say it's the most beautiful cock I've ever seen.

I perch on the edge of my bed, naked and slightly confused as he rolls on a condom. My body shivers as his hands grip my ankles to yank me to the edge of the bed. I let out a little yip that sounded embarrassingly like a frightened Yorkie, but Zander doesn't notice as he places my legs on top of his shoulders and centers himself at my entrance.

"Fucking wet again," he groans as he pushes his long finger deep inside me. He bites his lip as he pumps slowly and steadily into my channel. He looks like he's in pain, and it might be the sexiest thing I've ever seen.

Without warning, he pulls his finger out and replaces it with his cock. The abrupt invasion has my entire body tensing. "Oh, my God," I cry out because the pressure is overwhelming.

Zander jostles me as he throws one of my legs over his head and pivots me onto my side. He's now gripping both my calves on his left shoulder as he hunches down and pulls out before driving back inside me. The new angle pushes him even deeper, and with my legs closed, I can feel every ridge of him as he hits a new spot that's never been stroked before.

"Holy shit," I bark out unattractively as I grip the footboard for support. Zander is moving so fast, so recklessly, and without abandon, it's sending my body into overdrive. The pressure building in my core is so intense, my legs tremble uncontrollably as my senses take over.

Without warning, I start to spasm under his firm grip, and the concentrated look in his eyes as he watches himself pound into me is so erotic, I begin to lose myself.

"Zander, I'm going to…"

My voice is cut off because he moves his hand between my legs and presses his thumb to the hood of my clit. He slides it back and forth rapidly, and an orgasm hits me with such unbridled violence, I nearly buck him away.

But his hold is strong, and he's not done. He's still pounding relentlessly into me, and when he brings his thumb that was just touching me to his lips and sucks on it, I think that I must be in the middle of the dirtiest sex dream of my life because this cannot be real.

I'm jostled when he pulls out of me and flips me onto my back. I hold my breath high in my lungs as he spreads my legs and drops to his knees. His lips and tongue are now assaulting my sex, and my body feels like it could crawl out of its skin. It's all coming so fast, so hard, so frantic. He shakes his head from side to side, savagely feasting on me as his fingers dig into the meat of my thighs. The noises he makes vibrate through my core, and I feel as if I've been launched into another dimension. I don't even have a chance to catch my breath, to catch my mind, my heart…all of it is gone, emptied to the depths of my dancing vagina that's gearing up for another…

"Not again…" I croak as the release hits me like a sharp branding iron, and I scream out, "Zander!"

He moans his approval into my sex, lapping at my sensitive nub as I shudder and go limp beneath him. He stands to push back inside me. His cock is still gloriously hard as he holds himself up over top of me and pumps with a smooth, sultry rhythm. I try to lift my head off the bed to kiss him, but every ounce of muscle is drained from my body, and my sex seems to be the only thing left as it pulses between my legs with its own bloody heartbeat.

Zander's eyes are trained on me, but I can barely see past the stars dancing in my vision. "Do you want to taste yourself, Daphney?" he asks, his voice husky as he licks his moist lips.

I nod and find the strength to reach up and grab his neck. I pull him down to my lips, and he swirls his tongue deep into my mouth. He tastes naughty and sensual, and the entire act has my pelvis greedily grinding up to meet his thrusts. A third orgasm approaches, and I can't even believe it's possible.

How did I live my entire life, never realizing this was what I was missing? How will I live my entire life, potentially never having this again? That thought causes a pang fear to surge through me, and it's apparently triggered a domino effect because the next thing I know, I'm toppling over the cliff for the third time.

I cry out as Zander pushes through my trembling aftershocks. It feels like I'm practically milking him, and I fear he's going to try to make me come again, and I'm not sure my body will survive another.

Finally, he lets out a frustrated growl, and when I see his jaw go taut and his arms turn to rock-hard boulders around me, I exhale with relief. Seconds later, he expels a savage groan and freezes as he releases inside me.

With a huff, he drops onto my body, and the dead weight of him is like a delicious, weighted blanket I'd love to own.

Finally, he comes to and glances down at me with a smug look I'm surprised he has the energy to express. "See? I'm not bad at sex."

His comment causes a confused jolt to shoot through me as he rolls off and stands, giving me a perfect view of his sculpted arse as he walks toward my loo.

"What did you just say?" I prop myself up on my elbows and watch his profile through the open bathroom door as he discards the condom and washes his face and hands in my sink.

He wipes his hands with a towel and turns to prop himself in my doorway. He quirks a pleased brow. "I showed you, didn't I?"

"Showed me what?" I sit up and push my tousled hair out of my face.

"That I'm a good lay."

My body tightens. "Who said you were a bad one?"

He laughs and shakes his head as he returns to stand in front of me. He grabs his boxers off the floor and pulls them on. "No one. Ever. That's why I had to prove it to you."

Frowning, I grab my robe off my bedpost and slip it on, cinching it tight around my waist as I stare back at him. "Zander, what are you going on about?"

He hits me with a flat look. "I could tell the other night you weren't impressed. Which is really unfair because I'd just finished playing ninety minutes of soccer. What did you expect of me? It's fucked up, ye know. Women get mad at men for being misogynists, but one mediocre performance, and you're ready to write a dude off. It's a double standard, Ducky. I expected better of you."

"Zander, I swear on my life I have no clue what you're going on about." I stand and stop him from putting on his shirt because I need to understand what he's saying.

He narrows his eyes on me. "Just admit that you sent me packing the other night because you thought I was a bad lay."

"I never said that!"

"I can read between the lines," he volleys back at me. "Although I'm surprised I had to. You don't strike me as a girl who can't be honest with a dude."

I cross my arms over my chest, feeling properly annoyed now because he's assassinating my character for all the wrong reasons. "You think I wanted you to leave the other night because you were bad at sex?"

"Yup, which is why I had to prove you wrong." He mirrors my stance and cocks his chin. "I can't have my street cred tainted because of one lackluster performance."

A hyenic laugh bursts out of my throat as I cover my mouth. "I can't believe you're serious right now!" I shake my head and push my hair out of my face. "Most days, your ego is so big, I fear you won't fit in this building. But other times, you're just so utterly human it's…almost endearing." I press my hand to my chest, staring at the half-naked footballer in front of me, who looks as if I've just kicked his puppy.

"Then what was the issue?" he growls, his expression turning from cocky arsehole to boyishly confused in the blink of an eye.

"Not that," I reply honestly, fiddling with the belt of my robe to avoid eye contact.

"Then tell me what it was," he insists.

"It's not something you need to worry about." I sit down on my bed and cross my legs to feign casual, feeling anything but after those three orgasms he just gave me.

"So, there is something?" Zander's tone is challenging as he steps in front of me to use his massive frame to intimidate me.

"Leave it be," I state firmly.

"No."

"Yes."

I glower up at him, daring him to argue with me again, and before I know what's happening, Zander pushes me backward and flattens his body over mine. He clutches my wrists in one hand above my head, rendering me incapacitated.

"What are you doing?" I gasp, squirming against his body, my chest heaving beneath his crushing weight. He situates himself between my legs, causing my robe to fall open.

He eyes my exposed breasts hungrily. "I'm going to get my answer out of you." He blows cool air over both of my nipples, causing them to pucker beneath his greedy gaze.

My pelvis writhes beneath him, and I'm aching for his breath to be in another area altogether. But of course, I can't tell him that. I roll my eyes and sigh dramatically. "Just because you gave me some orgasms doesn't make you some sex god, you know."

His body shakes with laughter, and I see a wicked glint in his eye just before he releases my wrists to assault my sides with his fingers. I squeal in protest and do my best to fight him off as his hands move over my ribs and stomach, relentlessly tickling me until I can hardly catch my breath.

"Fine, I'll tell you!" I scream out, my body wilting under his assault as tears from laughing fall out of my eyes. "Just stop tickling me."

He's like a proud dog with a bone as he hovers over top of me, smiling like a loon.

I sigh and turn away because I can't make eye contact when I say this, or I'll die of embarrassment. "I sent you packing the other night because I had just experienced my first orgasm and was having a bit of a mental freak-out."

I chance a glance at him, and he blinks back at me in shock. "You're lying."

"Why would I lie about something like that? It's not exactly something to brag about."

He shakes his head as he climbs off me to sit on the edge of the bed. I pull my robe closed around me again and sit up to watch him process this apparently very shocking information.

"But you're not a virgin, right?" he asks, looking at me with a puzzled brow.

"No." I laugh.

"But you're saying I gave you your first big O?"

A dejected sigh escapes my lips. "It would appear so."

"So, I'm not bad at sex." A smug grin lifts all the features on his face.

I want to insult him to knock him down a few pegs, but I'm nothing if not honest. "You're not bad at sex."

He bites his lip with a victorious smile. "And just now…" he points at the bed, like a dog begging for a treat.

"You gave me three more orgasms," I state flatly.

"Fuck yeah, I did." He makes a fist and pumps it a couple of times in front of him as his eyes dance with victory.

I comb my fingers through my tousled hair. "I'm glad you're pleased because sex is probably ruined for me forever now."

He stops his mental dance and eyes me curiously. "What is that supposed to mean?"

"Well, I've had five sexual partners in my life that never got it done. So, the odds of finding someone who can do it in my next relationship are probably not good. I'm currently one for six."

Zander frowns as he stares back at me, his voice taking on a surprisingly honest tone when he says, "Well, it's not much different than soccer. You probably just need practice."

"What am I to practice exactly?" I ask, turning to him with confused eyes.

"Practice figuring out what you like. I mean…sex is a team effort, so communication is the first step."

I frown at that thought. "You mean I should just tell the bloke what to do?"

Zander nods. "Basically."

"But I don't even know what to tell them. I didn't tell you anything. You just figured it out."

"That's because I'm a Premier League sexpert." He chuckles like a moron.

"Don't be daft."

"Okay, okay." He wraps one of his muscly-soft arms around me, and my body instinctively tucks into him, inhaling his manly scent for comfort. "What if we keep this going between us?"

"What?" I peer at him out of the corner of my eye, hoping he's not winding me up. "Keep having sex?"

"Yeah…I mean, we can keep it casual. But like, regular. That way, you can figure out what you like. Then someday, when I've provided you with enough sexual healing, you can direct a mere mortal's cock to perform better for your pleasure."

"I really hate that I told you all of this." I groan and drop my face into my hands. "Your ego does not need it."

"I love that you shared this with me." He chuckles sweetly. "I've been a fumbling moron around you since the moment I arrived in London. It's about damn time I got a leg-up for once."

I roll my eyes and glance over at his stupidly cute face. He's like the perfect combination of sexy and adorable. It's really inconvenient.

"Just admit you like my cock, Ducky." He leans in and waggles his dark eyebrows at me.

"Shut up."

"And you like my mouth too." He bites his lip again, and my center clenches with desire. Bloody hell, I do like his mouth.

Honestly, how am I not exhausted from those three orgasms already? It makes no sense.

"Basically, you like everything but the words that come out of my mouth."

"That, I will agree to." I give him a playful shrug.

"So, let's keep this going. Let's have some fun and get to know each other…biblically."

"So would you call this friends with benefits?"

"Friends is a stretch when you just openly admitted you hate everything that comes out of my mouth." He laughs good-naturedly. "But I know you like labels and rules, so let's call us…neighbors with benefits."

"Neighbors with benefits," I repeat the silly label and feel myself nodding slowly. "What's the worst that could happen?"

20

Former Wild Child

Zander

MARVIN GAYE'S LYRICS FOR "LET'S GET IT ON" BOOM THROUGH MY portable speaker as I sit in my living room at eleven o'clock the next day. I've been up since eight and have already worked out and picked up my apartment. I even went to the post office and sent a Bethnal Green jersey to my mom.

And the best part is, I've done it all *quietly*.

Which makes me hope that when Daphney hears my not-so-subtle music through these paper-thin walls, she doesn't stomp over here and rip my head off. I'm genuinely not trying to piss her off. Then again, she's cute when she's mad, so even if it does get her riled up, I'm still pulling in a W. No one ever said I was mature.

I wince to myself as the song continues. This is for sure one of the most desperate moves I've ever made with a girl. But I have a rare weekend off from soccer because it's an international break, and I wasn't called to play for Team USA this time around. It was a damn miracle that the sadist, Coach Z, let us all have the weekend off too. Which means I need to make the most of this. And I can think of no other person I'd rather spend it with.

Yesterday, after I gave Daphney three orgasms, she had to shower and leave for work. I offered to wash her back, but she said we hadn't reached that comfort level yet. That was a hilarious response because she looked pretty damn comfy when I was eating her out and she told me she wanted to taste herself on my lips.

Fuuuck, that was hot.

In fact, it was dirty hot, which is a nice contrast to the good girl persona Daphney projects most of the time. I intend to make many more dirty memories with her. Starting today.

A knock on my door causes a giant smile to spread across my face. When I jump off my sofa and run to see who it is, I'm pleased with the sight before me. Daphney wears a big, girlie, shy smile that I really want to kiss off her face.

I school my features to look aloof as I grab my phone and press pause on the music. "Oh sorry, is my music too loud for you, neighbor?"

She crosses her arms over her chest and hits me with a devilish smirk. "Why on earth would you think that?"

I lean on the doorframe and can't mistake the flare of heat in her eyes as her gaze moves down my body. "Oh, maybe because I was playing it at max volume to get your attention." I waggle my brows at her, making no mistake the dirty thoughts crossing my mind as well.

She bites her lush lower lip. "You are such a cheeky arsehole. You could have just knocked on my door."

"I was trying to be charming," I state plainly and glance down at her appearance. She's wearing a slouchy green sweater and tight jeans with high-heeled boots. Her makeup and hair look freshly done, too. She didn't just wake up. She's been up for a while. What the hell? "How long have you been up? I thought you'd still be sleeping since you worked late last night. I've literally been sitting here quiet all morning waiting for you to wake up."

"I woke up an hour ago." She slides her hand through her loose blonde curls. "I'm meeting Phoebe for brunch."

I eye her seriously. The fact that I wasn't her first priority upon waking is an offense I will not take lying down. "Well, what a coincidence. I love brunch."

She barks out a laugh. "You want to go to brunch with us?"

"I'm ravenous." I narrow my eyes wickedly at her.

"You have met my friend Phoebe, right?" She hooks her thumb over her shoulder.

"Yeah, she seemed cool."

She purses her lips together, and that little dimple appears on her chin. "Very well then, come to brunch with us, Soccer Boy. This should be entertaining."

She turns to retreat, but I reach out to grab her by the sweater and yank her toward me. "Do we have time for an appetizer?"

She stares hungrily at my lips. "They're called starters in England."

I laugh and don't even try to hide the smile on my face as I kiss her smart mouth.

The car ride with Daphney is surprisingly comfortable. Not that I thought it'd be awkward. But I can't say that I've had many experiences hanging out with girls I've had sex with outside of the bedroom. Maybe a night-club, or a bar. But in broad daylight with nary a beer in sight? Not typical.

Then again, nothing about Daphney is typical. Most girls who found out they lived next door to a professional soccer player would have been tripping over themselves to flirt with or impress me. Daphney tripped over herself to yell at me. Until she kissed me, obviously.

And what a kiss that was. I guess what they say is true, the chase re-ally does make things taste so much sweeter. And look, I'm not trying to toot my own horn or anything, but I swear Daphney seems cheerier since we've hooked up. Maybe we're actually alike in one way. Good sex equals a good mood.

Daphney chatters as she drives us to brunch, telling me about the different areas of London and the types of people who inhabit each part. I've gathered she has two brothers who live near our apartments, and it was a big deal for her to move out of her parents' home in Essex last year. It's a bit of a foreign concept to me because as soon as I started college, I basically never went back home. I considered myself close with my par-ents but not in the way that Daphney appeared to be.

We arrive at some fancy-looking brunch place in Soho. The restaurant is covered in white tablecloths with servers bustling around in black and white uniforms. It feels like I'm watching an episode of *Downton Abbey* that my mother made me watch with her for an entire season.

"No fucking way," a voice yells, and I turn my attention to see that it's Daphney's friend Phoebe sitting at a small square table with her eyes fixed on us.

Daphney's eyes go wide as she clocks a woman with two small chil-dren at a table right beside Phoebe. She shoots a furious look at her friend as she grabs my hand and hurries us over to the table. "Watch your lan-guage, Phoebe," Daphney hisses as she all but shoves me down in a seat beside her.

Phoebe gapes at us like we're covered in blood. "I'm sorry, but I didn't expect you to bring the slutty footballer."

"Phoebe," Daphney nearly growls and mouths an apology to the woman who is now openly glaring at us.

"Also known as Zander Williams," I reply with a mock hurt tone. "It's nice to see you again, Phoebe."

She barks out an unamused laugh and sits back, arms crossed over her chest. "What does this mean?" She points between Daphney and me with an angry look on her face, then leans forward and lowers her voice. "It obviously means you shagged him again, but what else does it mean? I mean, shagging is one thing. Shagging and brunch is an entirely different matter."

I can't help but laugh because she's talking like I'm not even here.

Daphney lifts her menu to her face, ignoring her friend. "Do they do a nice eggs Benedict here?"

Phoebe slides her eyes over to me. "Are you going to tell me what's going on?"

My brows lift. "I'm just here for the food and fellowship."

"Mm-hmm." Phoebe reaches out and grabs her champagne flute, sipping her mimosa with a skeptical brow.

Following Daphney's lead, I look over my own menu and decide to order two entrees instead of one. This hot seat has really worked up my appetite.

The server arrives and takes our orders, and as soon as he's gone, Phoebe scoffs. "I knew you could never pull off a one-night stand."

Daphney's face flames red as she shoots daggers at her friend. "Phoebe!"

"Was that the original plan?" I huff out a laugh and glance over at Daphney to find her fidgeting with her cloth napkin.

"I don't know," Daphney snaps. Her nostrils flare as she sputters, "I tried to set some rules, but you wouldn't let me, if you recall."

Phoebe shakes her head. "So, what now? Are you two dating?"

Daphney chokes on her water, and I reach over to pat her on the back, letting my fingers linger on her bare shoulder that's peeking out from her sweater. She shivers beneath my touch, and I can't help but smile at her. She's cute when she's flustered.

When she catches her breath again, she pins her friend with a harsh look. "We're just having fun."

"I'll believe that when I see it," Phoebe says flatly, not breaking eye contact with me as the server sets a coffee in front of me and an orange juice in front of Daphney.

We all take fortifying sips, and Phoebe launches right back into me. "What's your deal, Zander Williams? What's your damage?"

"Damage?" I ask, shaking some Splenda into my mug.

"Background, baggage…let's air out your dirty laundry so I can make sure that my mate is safe in your apparently very 'fun' hands."

I can't help but laugh as I sit back and drape my arm over the back of Daphney's chair. "No dirty laundry here. I'm just a soccer player."

She scoffs. "No illegitimate children back in America? Some baby mamas you're paying child support to?"

"No," I nearly choke on my coffee. We really are on an episode of *Downton Abbey*. "Illegitimate children? Is that really what you call them?"

"Ex-wives then?" Phoebe asks, and I can feel Daphney's eyes burning on me.

I roll my eyes and shrug. "I'm twenty-five, so that's a hard no as well."

"Mummy issues? Daddy issues?"

All humor drains from my body as I shift in my chair and feel painfully reminded of the stupid situation I'm in right now—waiting on a freaking DNA test result. I school my features to look casual. "Like I said, I'm just a soccer player. What you see is what you get."

Phoebe doesn't seem convinced as she glances over at Daphney who looks exhausted after being completely steamrolled by her best friend.

Oddly, I feel protective of her. I jerk my chin up at Phoebe. "What's your deal?"

"Moi?" Phoebe replies, feigning innocence.

"Yeah." I lean across the table and pin her with a serious look. "How long have you and Daphney been friends?"

"Oh, darling." Phoebe sighs dramatically. "We aren't friends. We're framily. And we've been so since nappies."

"That means diapers," Daphney whispers under her breath.

"I know what that means," I hiss back at Daphney, not wanting to look weak in front of her friend here since we're clearly on trial. I pin her with a skeptical look. "If you're so close, what's one of your favorite childhood stories involving Daphney?"

Phoebe's eyes alight with this change in course. "My God, which one should I pick?"

"Don't embarrass me," Daphney whines, and I slightly regret my question.

"Why would you think I'd embarrass you?" Phoebe laughs and turns devilish eyes to me. "Okay…there's the time that Daphney forced me to ditch school."

"It was your idea!" Daphney interjects.

Phoebe waves her off. "We snuck into my neighbor's house and stole a packet of his cigarettes and tried to smoke them in the woods behind his house. We both ended up vomiting and nearly starting a fire. It was completely mental. We went back to school for the last lesson smelling like smoke and sick."

I turn amused eyes to Daphney. "You have a thing for neighbors, don't you?"

Her pink lips part in shock. "I do not!"

"Oh, and then." Phoebe reaches over and grabs my arm to redirect my attention. "She tried to give me a haircut when we were, oh, I don't know…eleven? She swore she could make me look like Reese Witherspoon in *Sweet Home Alabama*. It looked so terrible that my mum had to take me to London to get it fixed."

"It didn't look that bad," Daphney argues, her eyes lighting up with amusement. "I just needed a bit more time."

"Time for it to grow out, you mean?"

"No!" She erupts in a fit of giggles. "Time for you to get some taste."

"Oh, so it's my taste that was the problem?"

"Or your mother's. She never did like me." Daphney harrumphs, crossing her arms over her chest to pout.

Phoebe rolls her eyes. "My mother doesn't like anybody."

"Wait a minute," I interrupt the walk down memory lane, trying to make sense of everything I'm hearing. "Phoebe, are you telling me that Ducky here was a bad girl?"

"Entirely. She was a horrible influence on me."

"Not true!" Daphney interjects.

"This does not compute," I reply, moving my chair so I can turn all my focus to Daphney. "You seem like such a Goody Two-shoes now."

She glares at me. "I'm not a Goody Two-shoes."

I look pointedly at her friend. "Is this the same girl you grew up with?"

Phoebe narrows her eyes at Daphney. "I believe the former dark passenger still lives inside her. It's just quieter now."

"Or maybe I've just grown up," Daphney snaps as the server sets the food down in front of us. "That's kind of what people do, right? We're not children anymore. Nothing is wrong with being responsible."

"Nothing wrong with that at all," I respond knowingly, ignoring my food for a moment. "But it's usually not very fun."

"That's what I've been trying to tell her!" Phoebe exclaims, pointing her fork at me in a moment of silent comradery.

"I have plenty of fun," Daphney says, tucking into her food.

"When you're not working seventy hours a week." Phoebe rolls her eyes and begins cutting up her pancakes.

A sullen look begins to mar Daphney's striking features, so I offer, "You were loads of fun yesterday." A knowing smirk lifts the corners of her mouth, so I lean over and whisper, "Three times, if you recall."

"Three times?" Phoebe squeals around a fork full of food. "Well done, Soccer Boy!"

"Did you really have to share that?" Daphney glares at me but the smile on her lips is unmistakable. "You're skating on very thin ice."

"Speaking of thin ice," Phoebe interjects. "Remember that time Marisa had to pull you out of your father's pond? She told us it wasn't cold enough to go ice skating, and we ignored her. My God, I thought she was going to murder us. Luckily, the pond isn't very deep, so we weren't in any real danger but still, the image of you frozen and shaking while Marisa screamed at you lives rent-free in my mind."

I laugh at the visual. "Who's Marisa?"

An awkward silence descends as I glance back and forth between Daphney and Phoebe and notice all humor draining from Daphney's face.

"Just someone we knew," Daphney replies quickly. She clears her throat and smiles as she redirects her focus to her food. "These eggs are really nice."

Phoebe smiles softly, and there's a marked change in her demeanor. I consider asking more questions, but I get the impression we've ventured into a subject Daphney would rather not discuss.

My hand moves to my leg when I hear my phone ringing in my pocket. I pull it out to see it's a foreign number. Smiling apologetically, I excuse myself from the table to step outside for the call.

"Hello, this is Zander Williams," I state, inhaling the cool air as I stuff my other hand into my pocket.

"Hi, Zander Williams, this is Bernard from Discreet DNA, do you have a moment to talk?"

Chills erupt over my entire body as I freeze in the middle of the sidewalk, not even noticing the people trying to get around me. "Okay,"

I answer woodenly, cringing that I said okay instead of telling him now is a bad time.

"I'm afraid that the sample you sent in on the water bottle has come up as inconclusive. This happens sometimes when the sample is tampered with or contaminated in some way. Do you know if it was exposed to any outside elements before you sent it in?"

I wince as I think about how it fell to the floor when the sink decided to explode, and Booker knocked everything off the counter. The lid was still on it, so I thought it would be fine.

"It might have gotten a little wet," I reply, turning to glance through the window at Daphney and Phoebe. They look so at ease in there, enjoying their breakfast. I'd do anything to trade places with them right now.

"That's probably the issue then," Bernard says jovially. "If you could send in a new sample, we can run it again. But I'm afraid there will be another sixty-pound fee."

I shake my head and snap, "It was hard enough getting the first sample."

Silence descends for a moment before the man responds, "Well, if that's the case, you may want to consider getting a paternal sample. Half sibling tests don't have the same level of accuracy without samples from the shared parent. So, while we could get you results on a new sample of your potential half sibling, the success rate is quite diminished."

"Jesus Christ," I reply and run a hand through my hair. "This was a mistake."

"I apologize for the inconvenience, sir." He pauses for a moment and then adds, "If you do decide to try again, please note that a hair follicle from your alleged father is your best sample option aside from blood or saliva for conclusive results. Much higher success rate than a water bottle. So, if you can ever get hold of a hair follicle, then we'd be happy to rerun the test for you."

I roll my eyes and stare up at the sky. "Oh sure, that sounds easy."

"I'm sorry we couldn't be of service, sir."

I hang up and clench my teeth, annoyed as fuck that all those hoops I jumped through were for nothing. How the fuck am I going to get a hair sample from Vaughn Harris? I'd sooner get Daphney Clarke to fall in love with me.

I exhale heavily and crack my neck. This setback better not fuck up my game. I can't afford to go backward. Not now that I've come this far.

21

Plan B

Zander

"OH, BALLS," LINK YELPS AS HE DROPS DOWN INTO THE METAL BASIN filled with ice water in the physical therapy room at Tower Park. "Why does Coach Z hate me so much?"

"Because you always look so damn happy during training." I turn down the speed on my treadmill and take a quick drink out of my water bottle. "He thinks he's not pushing you hard enough. Try looking miserable like the rest of us."

Link rests his head on the edge of the tub and contorts his facial features into a moronic expression. "How's this look?"

I laugh, and at the same moment, Knight walks in, scowls at Link's face, and walks over to the medicine balls. He lowers himself on top of the biggest one and nods his head toward me. "Where were you all weekend? Feeling sorry for yourself because of the DNA mix-up?"

"No," I scoff and can't hide the smile that spreads across my face. "There was no moping."

Ice clinks against the metal basin as Link turns toward me. "I thought I saw an extra pep in your step at practice today. Did you make good use of my romantic wisdom with Daphney then?"

"Shut up," I laugh, and an image of Daphney in my bed after brunch on Saturday hits me full force. It was one of those epic sex marathons that leave you feeling hollowed out by the end. Fucking mind boggling. "I had a good weekend, and that's all you're getting from me." I glance toward the door and hold my finger to my lips. "And don't mention her name. She's close with the Harris family, and it's just a casual thing, so I don't need that fucking things up here."

"How close?" Knight asks, his brows furrowed curiously.

"Like she went to Vaughn Harris's house yesterday for Sunday dinner with the whole family."

"Holy shit," Link replies with wide eyes. "That's definitely close."

I nod and wipe the sweat dripping down my forehead. "Which gave me an idea."

"Oh?" Link and Knight both look at me with renewed interest.

"Well, that DNA guy who called me Saturday said that paternal hair follicles have the highest chance of accuracy on their tests. And I was thinking maybe if I could get Daphney to bring me along to one of those Sunday dinners, I could stumble into the wrong bathroom and get what I need."

"You want to go to Vaughn—" Link winces when I shush him loudly. He lowers his voice. "You want to go to the home of 'he who shall not be named,' slip into his bathroom, and take a lock of his hair?"

I shrug. "Seems like I'd have a better chance of scoring hair there than trying to sneak something out of his office."

"What if you get caught?" Knight asks, his eyes grave. "This is the manager of our club."

"You guys weren't worried about me getting caught when I was running around the locker room trying to get Tanner's gum out of the garbage. This idea seems way more sane than that. I'll be alone in a bathroom. There's no way I'll get busted."

Link interjects next, "Does fishing for an invite from Daphney indicate casual? What if you send her mixed signals?"

"We're friends-ish." I shrug again.

Link hits me with a dubious look. "Does she think that?"

I roll my eyes. "I'll take her out sometime this week. To dinner or something that doesn't involve sex. Lay down a foundation that exists beyond my bedroom. Maybe one of those double-decker bus tours would be a nice gesture."

"That doesn't sound casual. That sounds like a relationship," Link coos.

"Whose fucking side are you on?" I snap, surprised at my temper but also really annoyed these guys aren't supporting me on this. It was their stupid idea for me to get DNA in the first place. Now they have cold feet? Fuck that.

Link holds his pruney hands up out of the water. "Yours, my dude. Chill out."

I scrub a hand through my hair, annoyance prickling my veins. "I just want to get this fucking thing done. I don't like leaving things open like this. I trained good today, and I want to keep it that way, which means I need to focus on this plan and finish what I've started."

"Alright then." Link nods in solidarity. "I'm here for you, man."

I look over at Knight, who is definitely not the picture of support. "Just be careful," he says, hitting me with a weighty look. "It's one thing to play soccer with a few members of the Harris family. It might be another to share an entire meal with their wives and kids."

I shake my head and turn my treadmill speed back up, effectively ending this discussion. This isn't a bad idea. This is a good idea. And the more I think about it all, the more I expect I'm going to discover that Vaughn Harris isn't my father. It's probably why my mom never sent that letter in the first place. I know who my dad is. I just need to finish this stupid plan to confirm that fact so I can move on with my life.

I lower the speed on my treadmill again and pull out my phone to shoot Daphney a text.

Me: What's your schedule like this week?

Daphney: Madness, yours?

Me: I want to do one of those double-decker bus tours.

Daphney: Are you taking the piss?

Me: I am a man of many talents, but pissing and texting isn't one of them.

Daphney: Siiigh. Taking the piss means having me on. Messing or joking with me.

Me: They didn't cover that in in Bridget Jones's Diary. I'm on the second book, though, so maybe it's coming still.

Daphney: You're reading those fast!

Me: This hot girl I met recommended them to me. I'm trying to impress her.

Daphney: Why are you buttering me up? I already agreed to be your neighbor with benefits.

Me: Can I reap some of those benefits tonight?

Daphney: I'm afraid not. I'm working at Old George.

Me: Well, if you have some free time this week, let me know. I want to do this bus tour thing, and I need you to be my tour guide.

Daphney: Those buses come with a tour guide.

Me: Yeah, but you can give me the stuff they don't cover in Bridget Jones's Diary. ;) Whatcha say, Ducky?

Daphney: Very well, Soccer Boy. I'm free Tuesday after 4.

Me: Perfect. I'll pick you up.

22

Double-decker Confessions

Daphney

I T'S TUESDAY AT 3:50 WHEN I HEAR A LIGHT KNOCK ON MY DOOR. "KEEP going," I tell my niece Marisa as she sits at my keyboard, playing through the lesson I assigned her last week.

I tiptoe behind her and hurry to the door. "You're early," I say to Zander as I peer through my cracked door.

He frowns. "Who's playing your piano?"

"My niece. She has ten minutes left for her lesson. Just go back to yours, and I'll come get you when we're done."

I move to close the door, and he holds his hand out to stop me. "Can I watch?"

"Watch me give my seven-year-old niece a piano lesson? No!" I hiss.

"Come on," he whispers as his eyes dance with interest. "I can already hear her through the wall. I'll be as quiet as a mouse."

"Too soon for mouse references," I grumble under my breath because I still haven't caught that vile creature. He's leaving signs of his existence in the building, too. I roll my eyes and open the door. "You can come in but don't say a word. I don't want her distracted."

He smiles victoriously and walks quietly behind me. I point at the sofa for him to sit, grateful that Marisa is still focusing on her music. We don't need to waste time with introductions. She already talked to me for the first ten minutes of her lesson about her difficulty with pooing at school. I honestly sympathized with the poor girl.

I sit back down on the chair next to the piano bench and cringe when Marisa accidentally hits two notes beside each other. "Okay, Marisa, look at your hands. What's wrong with them?"

She exhales heavily and blows a strand of her auburn hair off her face. "I don't know, Auntie D."

"Yes, you do. Remember you should curve your hands like a little old lady, right?" I crook my voice up into the best impression I can muster of my grandmother. "Show me your granny hands, and be sure to add in a proper granny voice, too."

Marisa giggles and holds her hands up to me. "How's this, my pretty?"

"That's a little Wicked Witch of the West, but it's close enough! Let's try again."

Marisa smiles as she resumes the sheet music in front of her, and I can't help but glance over my shoulder at Zander. The expression on his face isn't exactly what I'd call amusement. I'm not sure what I'd call it, but it's making the hairs on the back of my neck stand.

When Marisa finishes, I tap her on the shoulder and point my thumb behind me. "Did you know you had a professional footballer watching you play just now?"

Marisa's green eyes go wide as she turns around on the piano bench to see Zander. She blinks curiously at him. "He doesn't look like a footballer."

I laugh at that very candid response. "What does he look like?"

Her nose wrinkles. "He looks like he could be a house cleaner? It is quite messy in here, so if he is your cleaner, I don't think he's doing a very good job."

"Oh, you cheeky rascal!" I reach out to tickle her sides, and her giggles are music to my ears. "My flat is clean enough."

When I've finally finished attacking her, she walks over to Zander and holds her hand out.

"Nice playing." He slaps it in a high five.

"Don't you owe me money?" She tilts her head with an adorable furrow to her brow.

"Do I?" Zander asks, glancing at me. "What for exactly?"

"For listening to my performance, of course. Paper only, please. No coins." Marisa holds her chubby hand out to Zander again, and he looks so shook, I bark out an incredulous laugh.

"Okay then." Zander digs into his pocket and pulls out a twenty-pound note. "I don't suppose you have change?"

Marisa sighs heavily. "If you're really a footballer, you can afford it."

A voice clears in the doorway, and I glance over to see my brother Theo. "Oi, where did you get that?" He points at the note in his daughter's hand.

"From this man who claims he's a footballer." Marisa points a finger at Zander. "Daddy, isn't he a bit small to be a footballer?"

"I'm not small!" Zander whines and stands up to prove it. Marisa looks unimpressed at Zander's six-foot-plus stature, and I have to clap my hand over my mouth to conceal my laughter.

Finally, I pull myself together and walk over to my brother. "Theo, this is my neighbor, Zander."

"Ah yes, the new defender from America." Theo adjusts his glasses and walks over to shake Zander's hand. "Sorry about my daughter. She has no filter just like her mother."

"And possibly her aunt," Zander adds with a wink to me.

"Marisa is lucky to have Leslie and me as star influencers in her life. It means she knows her own mind, doesn't it, Mar?"

"Yes, it does," Marisa insists, crossing her arms and giving Zander a punishing glower that positively tickles me.

My eyes connect with Zander's, and there's a certain twinkle in his gaze that wasn't there earlier. It's causing a bit of a carnal reaction in me, which is a bit awkward to be happening in front of my niece and my brother.

I look up and notice that Theo's brows are furrowed as he registers the flirtatious exchange. He clears his throat. "Right, well, we've got to run. Footy practice starts in thirty. I'll Venmo you, Daphney."

"No rush," I reply and reach down to hug Marisa. "I'll see you later, okay? Don't forget to practice this week."

"With my granny hands," Marisa says as she runs over to grab her lesson book off the keyboard.

I smile fondly as I watch Theo take Marisa's hand and hurry out. Once they're gone, I turn to Zander and rub his arm. "Are you okay? Do you need a bit of a cuddle after getting so properly schooled by a seven-year-old?"

"I might," Zander responds, his face crestfallen. "She's a savage little thing."

"She really does take after me." I stick my tongue out and walk over to my wardrobe to grab my coat. "And you deserved it for showing up early. I told you 4:05 and not a minute sooner."

"Who chooses time increments of five minutes?" Zander scoffs.

I prop my hands on my hips. "Your alarm clock, apparently."

Zander shoots me a sheepish smile. "Well, you didn't mention you taught piano to your niece."

"Why would I?" I volley back. He shrugs and hits me with a curious expression I still can't quite read.

He clears his throat. "So, are you still game for the bus tour? If you're tired from working, I understand."

"I'm actually looking forward to this. I've never done a proper bus tour. Well, not as an adult at least."

"Then how are you such a British expert?" he mocks.

I level him with a glare. "Don't be cheeky."

The bus is touristy and corny and all the things I thought it would be, but it was also loads of fun. Honestly, I don't think I've laughed this much in ages. Zander's silly Americanisms always catch me off guard. And the way he asks questions to the tour guide like the man is here solely for us really amuses me. But I am, in fact, learning some things I never knew before. When we were kids, we often did field trips into London, but I guess I was too young to really absorb anything useful back then. This has been a nice refresher, and the fact that I'm sitting next to a professional footballer for the entire thing is a memory I never thought I'd have in my life.

"Do you think at some point you'll start getting recognized by people on the street?" I ask as I zip my coat up to my chin to try to stay warm. It's February in London, so of course it's brass monkeys out, but Zander begged me to sit on the top deck of the bus so he could have the proper tourist experience. And honestly, with those puppy dog eyes of his, it's nearly impossible to say no. "You are Premier League now."

Zander notices my shivering and wraps his arm around me like he's done it a hundred times before. "Doubt it. I'm defense, and fans usually fawn over the strikers. Plus, I'm still way too new for anyone to care about. It's the legacy players who get stopped on the streets. Ones with lots of sponsor deals and TV ads. I have none of that happening."

"Did you have any sponsor deals in the States?" I inquire, tucking my hands into my pockets.

"A couple back in Boston that my dad set up." Zander flinches like he said something he didn't mean to say.

"Do you need to find an agent over here? Or is your dad still able to manage you from the States?"

The muscle in Zander's jaw tics nervously as he removes his arm from around me and glances down from the top level of the bus to the street below. His voice is clipped when he replies, "He passed away last year."

My lips part as I register what he just said. "Oh my God, I had no idea."

"How would you?" He huffs out a dry laugh and tries to offer me a smile, but it's strained.

I remain silent, feeling the full effects of what he's just revealed. I purposely never googled Zander because I didn't want any preconceived notions about him before he moved in next door to me. Though, in all honesty, I was already stereotyping him before we met. And then when he made a pass at me in the pub, he seemingly confirmed those thoughts I already had.

Now I'm seriously regretting not looking into him because I would have treated him differently had I known he's just lost his dad. Been less harsh, less demanding. I certainly would have been more forgiving of his struggle to transition to a new city. My stomach swirls with regret.

I swallow the painful knot in my throat. "Can I ask how he died?"

Zander scratches his jaw and sits back in his bus seat. "Car accident. He lost control on an icy freeway and flipped his vehicle. Died instantly, or so they said."

"That's awful." I blink away the burning sensation in my eyes. "Were you two quite close?"

"Yeah, you could say that." A half-smile lifts the corner of Zander's mouth. "I was an only child, so I was kind of my parents' whole world. With that said, I was always a little too much of my mom's whole world. We butted heads a lot. Dad was always the one to come in and calm the storm. He was a total peacemaker."

That comment brings a smile to my face. "He sounds lovely."

"He was." Zander nods, licking his lips thoughtfully. "We talked a lot. Never about anything deep or profound…just…stuff. I miss that."

His eyes fix off into the distance, and I wonder if I'm interrupting a memory when I ask, "Are you close with your mum?"

Zander's demeanor shifts instantly at that question, and I see the muscle in his jaw tic before he answers, "Not as much, no."

My lips thin at that answer because I know how important being close to family is after a loss. "She must feel very lonely now that you've moved so far away."

Zander huffs out a dry laugh. "She didn't want me to come."

"Really?" I say, feeling both shocked and empathetic over that admission. I'm sure she didn't want Zander so far away, but she must know that an American getting recruited to a Premier League team is a tremendous opportunity.

Zander gets a pensive look in his eyes. "She's the reason I delayed my transfer six months ago. She was in pretty tough shape after my dad died. Still is, honestly. Not many people know this, but she came upon the accident shortly after it happened. The traffic was at a standstill on the freeway, and she had a strange feeling, so she got out of her car and approached the ambulance. They had just put him on a stretcher, and… well…it was bad, I guess."

My body shivers with that image. "I can't even imagine."

"I wish I couldn't." Zander's nose wrinkles. "My mom was pretty descriptive after I flew home to be with her."

"I'm so sorry."

He shrugs. "She's doing the best she can."

"Will she come out for a visit?" I ask. "I bet she'd love a bus tour like this."

He shakes his head, a sad look fleeting across his face. "Nah…it's not likely. My dad always kind of had to drag my mom to my soccer matches. With him gone, I just don't see her being brave enough to do it alone. Especially in a foreign country."

A moment of silence grows between us, and I feel at a loss for words. I learned long ago that when it comes to loss, sometimes the less you say, the better.

Finally, I say, "My niece is named after my sister, Marisa, who passed away about ten years ago now."

Zander's eyes snap up to meet mine. "Jesus, really?"

I purse my lips and shrug. "I was sixteen at the time. She was twenty-six. It was a freak accident at my parents' home. My two brothers and my sister and I were all riding quads on my parents' property, and Marisa was tossed and died instantly." I cringe because I'm certain I'm oversharing right now. Then again, he started it.

Zander blinks slowly back at me. "Did you see it happen?"

I shake my head. "No, my brother Theo shielded me from everything. Hayden was right there, though. And while I couldn't see much, my mother's screams told me it was really bad."

"Fuck." Zander huffs, leaning forward and shaking his head as he processes what I've just unloaded on him.

"She was the same age I am now." I rub my lips together. "It's kind of sad to think about that. Our family was messed up for years."

"I can imagine." Zander looks back at me over his shoulder. "I hope it doesn't take my mom years to come around. I feel like I've dealt with it. Now I want that for her."

My lips purse together in curiosity. "I'm still not sure I've dealt with the loss of Marisa. Grief feels like a forever kind of thing to me. It's just varying degrees at different stages in your life. I think it's even harder to cope with when it's an accident with no sign of it coming."

Zander nods slowly as he sits up and turns to look out the top of the double-decker bus again. His brow is furrowed, his mind clearly deep in thought. It's interesting how you can look at someone and have no idea what's going on in their mind. I had no idea how much my brother Hayden struggled with Marisa's loss back when I was a teenager. He hid his pain from me, and my parents and Theo never let on how much they were dealing with him and the blame he put on himself.

They were all struggling but felt I was too young to burden with their pain. In many ways, I felt like a voyeur, watching from the outside as everyone grieved the loss of Marisa. It wasn't until I was older that I truly felt the loss of her. My only sister. It's been ten years, and I still find myself wishing I could talk to her about boys or my music or my work. Grief isn't something you "deal with." It's something you live with. The fact that it's only been a year since Zander lost his father makes me doubt that he's realized that fact. Perhaps Zander needs more than just a neighbor with benefits. Perhaps he needs a proper friend who understands.

I wince when the tour guide blares through the speaker, and we both shift our attention back to the announcer, grateful for the reprieve from a surprisingly serious conversation.

We listen to the guide's description of the next stop, but my eyes are drawn to Zander. I feel almost kindred to him now, which is never something I expected to feel with Zander Williams.

23

The More Things Change,
The More Things Stay the Same

Zander

"Hey, Mom." My voice is tense when I find myself calling her out of the blue after training the next day. After talking through the loss of my dad with Daphney yesterday, I knew I needed to put my ego aside and reconnect with her. It was time.

"Zander?" My mom's voice is hoarse, and I flinch when I realize it's only six o'clock over there, and I probably woke her up.

"Shit, sorry. I didn't think about the time difference."

"No, it's okay," she murmurs, and I hear the rustling of her bed and the clicking of her bedside lamp. "I'm so glad you called."

"Just got done with training," I offer because I'm not sure what else to say.

"Oh?"

"Yeah, we go to Leicester on Saturday. Coach is going to start me as a sweeper, officially."

"Oh buddy, that's so amazing," my mom coos, and I'm surprised to hear she actually sounds happy for me.

I struggle with what to say next. "One of my teammates told me that Leicester is where Walker's crisps originated from."

"What?"

"Crisps means chips here. They call fries chips. It's hard to get the hang of. The Walker's brand is like our Lay's potato chips."

"Yes, I'm aware. I lived there, remember?" She laughs, but it's strained.

I bite my lip nervously. "You good?"

"Oh, you know me." She huffs into the line, but her voice sounds weak.

I rub my lips together, waiting for her to ask me how I am, but she doesn't.

"Are you still seeing that doctor?"

"Yes," she replies but doesn't sound happy. "I'm starting a new medication again."

I flinch at that response. It seems like she's always starting a new med, which basically feels like she's always starting over. "I hope it helps."

"Me too," she says quietly. "Oh, I wanted to ask you something."

"Yeah?"

"Do you want these old baseball cards of your father's?"

"What?" I ask, my brows furrowing in confusion.

She inhales sharply, and her voice is garbled when she responds, "Your father's baseball cards are still sitting in his office, and I can't stand to look at them every day, so I need to get rid of them."

"Seriously?"

"Yes, seriously," she blubbers into the phone line. "I know I should be stronger by now, and I am trying, Zander. I just can't keep looking at these things because I picture him looking at them with that stupid magnifying light mounted to the wall. My therapist said I should remove items that trigger me. If you don't want them, I'm going to sell them."

"Mom, of course I want them," I cry, my hand gripping the phone tightly. A knot forms in my throat because I have countless memories of my dad making me wear white gloves before he'd let me even touch one. He was nutty for those things.

"Great, I'll get them packaged up to ship to you," she tuts, her voice distracted.

"They can't just sit in a closet or something? They're pretty valuable. Shipping them is risky."

"No, Zander, that's not what my therapist told me to do."

My jaw clenches as I silently scream to myself before replying stiffly, "Fine, Mom. Mail them over the ocean."

"Okay. Thank you, buddy."

"No problem."

"And hey, I'm proud of how well you're doing out there. Keep it up, okay?"

"Yep, sure."

We hang up, and it takes everything in me not to throw my phone into the damn street. I'd hoped the fact that she was watching my games meant that she was doing better, but she's clearly not. She's no better than when I left.

It's no wonder I haven't cried over the death of my dad. There's no damn time to. I had to plan the funeral, pick out her funeral dress, pick out the urn. Buy burial plots. Did you know a family plot is a wise investment because they appreciate in value over time? I sure as fuck didn't. So, I bought three plots next to my grandparents. One for my dad, my mom, and me whenever I kick the fucking bucket. Which better not be before my mom because she's clearly incapable of burying me, and I'd rather not rot in some morgue somewhere.

And why wouldn't I want to store valuable memorabilia in my tiny apartment in London? I'm only a professional soccer player with a brand-new team who has no idea if I'll still be with this club next year. But sure, Mom, send me all the things from my dead dad, who, oh by the way, might not even be my dad. He might just be a fucking liar, like you.

I glance down at my feet and wonder when I started running? I have no memory of deciding to run. But the burning in my lungs indicates I've been running for a while.

There's only one thing I can think of to make this ache inside me go away. At least for a little while.

24

Rules of Seduction

Daphney

"ALRIGHT, LET'S LAY OUT SOME RULES," ZANDER STATES AS HE WALKS into my flat without knocking. He drops his backpack on the floor and hunches over with his hands on his knees, clearly out of breath.

"Did you run here?" I ask, removing my guitar from around my neck and setting it in its stand.

"Yes."

I stand and walk over to him with a frown. "Well, rule number one. Knock."

He huffs out a laugh and stands to his full height, hitting me with those eyes of his that smolder, especially right now. He cocks his head to the side, a clear look of annoyance marring his boyish features. "Really? I can eat your pussy, but I can't enter without knocking?"

"Zander!" I snap and cross my arms over my chest. "Why are you being vile?"

He exhales heavily and turns his baseball cap backward. "Fuck, I'm sorry. That wasn't directed at you."

"Pretty sure I'm the only other one standing in the room." I take three steps backward to give him and his mood some much-needed space.

His face bends with sympathy. "I'm sorry. I've just had a bad phone call with my mom, and I'm...on edge." He walks over to me and grabs my hand in his. "I'll knock from now on, I promise. We can even come up with a secret code if you want. Knock once for oral. Twice for sex. Three times for..."

I press my hand over his mouth. "Don't finish that thought if you ever want me to open the door."

His breath is hot on my palm as he laughs and pulls my hand off his face. He kisses the top of it sweetly. "Okay, knocking is rule number one. What's rule number two?"

I pull out of his embrace and walk toward my kitchen, surprised at his sudden urgency for rules. But honestly, I'm a bit grateful for it. Since this is my first casual relationship, I think I'm better with boundaries, especially after our deep feelings talk on the bus yesterday.

Reaching into my refrigerator, I grab two bottles of water and offer one to Zander. We both need to stay cool as we figure this out. "I don't think we should spend the night with each other," I state, flinching as I await his reaction.

"Okay." His eyes flare in surprise as he untwists his cap. "That's probably a smart rule. Plus, you picked out a really nice bed in my flat, so I'm good with that."

I can't help but smile. "You said flat, not apartment. Well done you."

"I'm British as fuck now." He waggles his eyebrows.

I cringe and shake my head. "A lot less British after that last remark."

He laughs and takes a large swig of water, his Adam's apple sliding down his thick neck in a way that makes me really…aware of his body. He wipes the liquid that dribbled down his chin. "Rule number three…no getting offended for late-night booty calls. We both know what this is, so why bother letting our pride feel smited over a last-minute decision to bone."

"How you managed to use the word smited and bone in the same sentence is either a true mark of genius or an offense on all mankind."

"I'm gonna go with the former." He winks at me. "Your rule next."

I lick my lips and nod as I lean against my kitchen counter. "I'd like to keep this a secret. I know Phoebe already knows, but I don't want anyone else to know. My brother would not like me sleeping with a tenant, and I'm pretty sure the Harris Brothers would not like me sleeping with one of their teammates. Especially casually."

Zander cracks his neck, a look of annoyance marring his features. "Fine." The muscle in his jaw tics.

"We can still go out together if we want. Just maybe avoid the usual hangouts," I offer because he seems agitated.

"Got it," he replies, his nostrils flaring. "And I think this should be exclusive."

"Really?"

Zander avoids eye contact with me as he adds, "I don't really like the idea of sharing."

"Are you talking about me?" I can't help but laugh. It's a rather possessive statement from someone who seems to be well acquainted with the idea of random hookups.

"Yes, I'm talking about you," he responds firmly, and our eyes lock for a tense moment of silence. It's the kind of silence that feels like the calm before the storm. It's...really hot.

"Very well then," I reply because if I'm being honest, I don't like the idea of him with other women either. Not that his ego needs to hear me say that out loud.

"Good." He nods briskly.

"Good," I repeat, crossing my arms over my chest and feeling strangely naked right now.

"We're settled then."

"It appears we are."

"We have work to do anyway," Zander says and begins stalking toward me.

"What do you mean?" I ask like a moron because I have no idea where he's going with this.

Zander stops in front of me and brings his fingers up to tuck a strand of hair behind my ear. "We have to figure out what revs Daphney Clarke's engine." I roll my eyes and move to push him away, but he uses my momentum to pull me in close to his chest. "The last couple of times we've slept together, you've been very quiet."

"I have?" I balk because I'm pretty sure I've never been more vocal with any man in my life.

"Not in all ways." He tilts his head, and his eyes lower to my lips. "But you haven't been telling me what you like. And that was sort of the whole point of this neighbors-with-benefits arrangement, wasn't it?"

I bite my lip, and my voice is quiet when I reply, "Well, you haven't needed much direction."

"That's because I'm a professional." His chest vibrates with laughter, and as much as I'd love to wipe that smug look off his face, he's not wrong.

"Your ego isn't going to fit in my flat if you keep that up."

He smirks down at me, his eyes hooded with arousal. "What do you say we go take a shower and get to know your body?"

His proposal has my heart lurching into my throat. A shower is so intimate, so exposed. I wouldn't say I'm self-conscious about my body, but I've never showered with a professional footballer before either. Then again, Zander has seen pretty much every part of me, so what difference does it make if we're standing in a brightly lit shower?

Zander's lips descend onto mine, and my mind is a flutter of arousal as he walks me backward toward my tiny loo. I just have a small glass-walled shower, nothing like his. But swapping flats might ruin the moment, and I'm quite enjoying what's happening right now.

When we step onto the cool tile, Zander pulls back and begins removing my shirt when his puzzled eyes look past me to the countertop. "What is that?"

My eyes practically bulge out of my head as I turn around and yank my shirt off my arms and use it to conceal the gift Phoebe left on my doorstep this morning. I was looking it over earlier, and I completely forgot that I didn't put it away.

"It's nothing," I exclaim, cramming all the packaging under my thin shirt as Zander's warm body presses up behind me.

"Doesn't look like nothing." He laughs and kisses my shoulder blade, reaching around me. "Come on, hand it over."

I groan in humiliation as I realize there's no way Zander will let this go. He's like a dog with a bone. Therefore, I muster up a bit of confidence, grab the small, pale pink device, and turn on my heel to face the music. "It's a vibrator that Phoebe gave me after I told her I'd never had an orgasm before you."

Zander fights back a smile and looks dreadfully adorable as he does it. "I thought we weren't telling people about our situation?"

"Phoebe isn't people. She's framily. And apparently an influencer for..." I turn around to find the box the vibrator came in. "Lelo Sona." I exhale heavily. "I really hate her sometimes."

Zander reaches out and grabs the device from me, turning the button on and filling the loo with a faint buzzing sound. His brows furrow as he looks up at me. "Have you never masturbated before, Ducky?"

My nostrils flare with annoyance. "I've tried...but never properly. And never with a toy."

The corners of Zander's lips turn down as he processes that information. "This thing waterproof?"

"Yes, why?"

"Oh, I'm sure you can guess," he responds and reaches over his head to pull his shirt off.

I watch in rapt fascination as he discards the rest of his clothes and reaches into the shower to turn the water on. He helps me out of my clothes, and the next thing I know, we're inside my tiny shower, and he's still playing with the stupid vibrator.

"Do you mind?" he asks, his eyes slowly drifting down my body.

I swallow slowly and glance down to see he is fully erect. "Help yourself."

His abs bulge with his silent laughter as he pulls me close to him under the stream of water. He bites his lip and turns the device on, lowering it to the area between my legs.

I jerk away, the vibrating shocking me for a brief second.

"Just relax," Zander murmurs before lowering his lips to mine and kissing me softly.

It has the desired effect as my body sags into his, my hands running up his firm pecs and folding around his neck as we stand in my shower and make out like a couple of teenagers. He feels hard and slippery, and I find myself wishing for more.

"What do you want, Daphney?" Zander asks between kisses, his lips moving down my neck and drifting along my shoulder.

"I want you to use that thing," I say with a sigh, my head leaning back against the glass.

He nibbles on my neck, and this time when the device touches my center, I don't flinch away from it. My body is ready and wanting. Zander stops kissing me as he stares downward and watches as he operates the toy with ease, playing with the different settings. Occasionally, he hits the perfect spot, a spot that has my hands gripping harshly onto his shoulders as my climax builds.

And then, just as I prepare to let go, he moves the device, leaving behind a wake of sad, wanting flesh. I bite my lip, my patience struggling as he continues to do this over and over. He finds a spot, I feel a build, and then he moves. It's maddening honestly.

Finally, my temper snaps, and I reach down and grab the device out of his hand.

"What's wrong?" he asks, his eyes gazing down at me in confusion as steam billows all around us.

"You keep moving," I state firmly, shocked at how confident my voice is at this moment.

"That's kind of the idea," he argues, his head tilting curiously at me.

I shake my head and wipe the water off my face. "No, I don't think it is. It feels like this." I glance around, trying to find a prop to demonstrate my point. My shampoo bottle has a large teal lid, so I untwist it and hold it upside down, so it's like a tiny shot glass.

Zander hits me with his crooked smile as I hold the vibrator between us. "Imagine this is a bottle of really expensive alcohol, okay?"

He huffs out a laugh. "Okay…"

"And you're the one pouring me a shot." I hold up the vibrator like I'm pouring liquid out of its tip and put the cap underneath. "The cap is my clit."

"Got it." Zander doesn't sound amused anymore, but he also doesn't sound irritated. He appears intrigued.

I pretend to pour out of my vibrator, moving it all over the place while my cap desperately chases after the wild stream of liquid that isn't holding still. The point I'm showing Zander is that every time he starts to hit my cap, he moves, and I miss out on valuable alcohol.

Zander closes his hand over my shampoo lid. "Ducky, are you saying you want to drive?"

"Yes, I believe I am," I reply, my body on edge from being teased mercilessly for the past few moments.

He laughs and shakes his head, moving to the opposite wall of the shower. His erection is throbbing between us as he glances down at my breasts covered in water. He grips his shaft in his hands and slowly begins to stroke himself as a heated look darkens his face. "Then just let me watch you, sweetheart."

I inhale sharply at the surprising term of endearment when his Boston accent, that I don't normally notice, becomes more prominent. The sight of him standing there stroking himself as he gazes at me is so erotic, I'm not sure I even need the vibrator anymore.

Then again, I hate to waste a nice present.

Eyes locked on Zander's cock, I flatten myself against the glass and prop one foot up on the small ledge in the shower. I press the vibrator to my clit and work my way through a couple of settings until I find the one I like. I move it around for a moment, searching the place that Zander passed over and over.

When I hit it, I gasp and hold it firmly in place, my eyes struggling to stay open to watch Zander as he begins pumping faster and faster in front of me.

"Oh, my God," I exclaim, my voice echoing loudly off the glass walls.

"That's it, sweetheart," Zander growls, his voice gruff. "Let yourself go. Show me how you come for yourself."

His empowering words tip me over the edge, and I feel like I'm free-falling as a tingling warmth erupts from my center, fanning out through my pelvis and into my limbs, all the way to the tips of my fingers and toes. I don't realize I'm groaning a loud, long note until I open my eyes and see Zander staring at me. His hand is still on his dick, his eyes hooded as he watches me with rapt fascination.

"You're incredible," he husks, his voice strained along with his awe-struck face.

I struggle to catch my breath, my eyes blinking in shock at his bizarre choice of compliment. He could have said anything else. He could have called me sexy or cracked a joke and teased me for coming so fast. But he didn't. He chose to describe me in a way that has very little to do with my appearance.

It's…unexpected.

Without pause, I drop to my knees in front of him and take his wet cock deep into my mouth.

"Daphney," he grunts, surprise evident in his tone as his hand touches the back of my head. "You don't have to."

But I want to. That's the thing. I want to harness this confidence, this power, this sexual awakening I'm feeling and never ever let it go. I grab Zander's hips and pump my lips over him, dragging my tongue firmly along the base of his shaft. The noises I'm eliciting from his body are exhilarating.

Never having an orgasm seems a little thing to fret about missing out on my entire life. But it's not just the orgasm that shifted something inside me these past couple of weeks. It's the orgasm and the jingle and living on my own and having a casual affair with someone.

All of this feels like I'm finally done overthinking everything. I'm taking my bloody life back at last. And I'm not letting anyone mess with it ever again.

25

Fishing for an Invite

Zander

"YOUR DAD CALLED YOU BUDDY BOY, DIDN'T HE?" DAPHNEY ASKS, her finger lazily tracing the edges of the tattoo on the inside of my bicep.

We're both in a postcoital fog, me naked and staring up at the twinkle lights on her walls. She, also naked and draped over the top of me as my hands sift gently through her blonde strands.

After the surprising bus confession a few days ago and our crazy shower the next day, I've used the remainder of this week to remind myself exactly what I'm doing with Daphney. She isn't my therapist. She isn't my teammate. She isn't someone I need to confess my innermost thoughts to help me through all the shit I'm dealing with in my fucked-up head.

She's my hot neighbor who lets me fuck her.

Yes, her moment in the shower was somewhat mind-boggling. I'm not even sure why exactly. It was like I watched her come out of her shell before my very eyes. I've watched many women come, but watching her make herself come was somehow sexier and more stunning than any other woman I've been with. And mostly because I know it's new for her. It was impressive to see her take charge like that.

But Daphney and I are just sex. We have rules in place to confirm that decision. So, after a few late-night booty calls the past couple of days that were very much two-sided, I thought we were back on track.

I guess I was wrong.

I pull my arm down to conceal my ink. "Yeah, he did."

Daphney flattens her palms along my chest and rests her chin on the back of her hands. She looks so sweet and innocent, her toes pointing up to the ceiling as she swings them casually. "When did you get the tattoo?" she asks, her eyes gazing up at me.

Kissing her senseless sounds like a lot more fun than the direction of this conversation. But I don't want to be a dick, so I begrudgingly reply, "I did it the night I found out he died before I flew out to be with my mom. Probably not the smartest decision of my life."

"I think it looks nice." Her lips purse as she grabs my elbow and holds my arm back up to inspect the tattoo again. "Those B's are the same as your hat."

"My dad was a huge Red Sox fan." I swallow a knot in my throat.

"And you?" She quirks a dark brow at me.

I shrug. "I'm more of a soccer lover, but I was a fan of my dad."

"That's really sweet." A tender look sweeps across her face, and that little dimple in her chin forms again. "Oh, by the way, I have a cookie container on the counter for you to take to your match tomorrow."

I glance down at her in shock. "You made me cookies again?"

She shrugs. "I put a bunch in the freezer from the first batch I made. It's not that big of a deal."

I school my features to look grateful, but knowing that this cookie will taste the same as the last one I had to gut down causes my stomach to churn. Shit, that cookie was awful. And Daphney looked so excited when she gave it to me. It's like she has no idea what an oatmeal raisin cookie is supposed to taste like.

I could maybe blame her nieces for screwing up the batch, but surely Daphney tasted them, right? Even the smell of the cookie is off. Like it was made with decade-old flour or something. I feel like this is part of a long con, but I don't want to call Daphney on it in case she actually thinks her cookies are good.

And hell, at least she's trying. My mom has obviously given up. And it's not because she doesn't know how international mail works. She's figuring out how to send me baseball cards, no problem.

My mood is shifting to a place I'd rather not visit, so I quickly reach down and grab Daphney's leg to roll us over. Sliding down her body, I place openmouthed kisses along her cleavage and growl with pleasure as her back arches, and she feeds more of herself to me. Her skin is so fucking soft. And her noises make me hard again even though it's only been five minutes since I last came.

"What are you doing on Sunday?" I murmur against her flesh, wrapping my lips around her hardened nipple.

She groans a sexy noise as her hands fork into my hair. Fuck I love when she does that.

"What?" she asks breathily as she wraps her long legs around my back.

"Sunday," I say, moving my mouth over to her other breast to pay it equal attention. "We're in Leicester tomorrow, so I'll be gone late, but I'm free later on Sunday."

She inhales sharply as I apply expert pressure with my teeth on her nipple. "I have Sunday dinner at Vaughn's."

"Skip it," I growl, my lips moving down her belly and kissing softly across her navel. It's crazy how much I've become addicted to the taste of her this week.

"I can't." She gasps and curls into my touch. "Vi gets cross at me when I skip."

I grumble my displeasure as I nibble her hip bones that jut out slightly. "Can I come?"

"To Sunday dinner?" She whimpers as I tease my thumb over her slit. "That doesn't seem like a neighbors-with-benefits kind of event."

I lock eyes with her as I roll onto my shoulder and push my middle finger deep inside her. Daphney sits up on her elbows, her eyes hooded as she lets out a soundless cry. I bite my lip and pump slowly in and out of her.

"It's been ages since I've had a real family dinner." My eyes struggle between staring up into her stunning eyes or watching what I'm doing to her body. "You don't think Vaughn would mind, do you? He's my manager after all."

Daphney groans, her head sagging backward with loss of control. "My brother Hayden might mind, and he'll obviously be there."

I laugh and still my finger inside her. "We're not going to tell them we're fucking. Just tell him you're being neighborly." I dip my head to kiss her soft belly. "It's not a lie."

She eyes me warily for a moment, her hips thrusting up and forcing my finger to move inside her. "Don't stop. You're right there."

Smiling, I ignore her request for me to continue stroking her G-spot and decide to roll my thumb over her clit instead. Her head falls back as she lets out a guttural moan. She likes that too. We've only been sleeping together for a week, and she's become really good at telling me what she likes.

"Can I come?" I ask again, pushing a second finger inside her and curling them upward.

Her entire body tenses, and I can tell she's on the precipice of another orgasm. God, she's so responsive. I could climax just watching her.

She grinds against my hand and nods feebly. "Fine, whatever. Come to Sunday dinner. Now finish what you've started, Soccer Boy, or I will make you pay."

With a victorious smile, I swap my finger out for my tongue and savor in the double victory of her orgasm and my scored invitation to Sunday dinner.

26

Sunday Funday

Zander

"**D**ON'T WEAR THE HAT," DAPHNEY STATES, HER EYES BLINKING nervously at me from the driver's seat of her car.

"Why not?" I ask, removing it and combing my fingers through it because I'm sure it looks like shit now.

"It's very American and way too casual." She stares at the gated entrance of Vaughn Harris's house in Chigwell with a look of dread.

"Should I have worn a suit?" I inquire, anxiety prickling my mood. "You said a button-down was good enough."

"It is. You look fine." She tears her gaze away from the house, and her eyes soften as she takes in my appearance. She combs her fingers through my hair that's getting really long because I'm in serious need of a cut. "You look great actually."

"Why are you so nervous then?" I ask, my tone crisp because if anyone should be nervous right now, it's me. I'm walking into the home of a man who may or may not be my birth father and hoping to extract a lock of hair like a total serial killer. Pretty sure I should be the one freaking out right now.

"I just should have thought about this more," she rushes out, wringing her hands in her lap. "I don't want my brother to think you and I are together. That would be very, very bad."

"Well, I don't want that either, but why exactly are you so worried about it?" I'm surprised that I feel slightly offended by her statement.

She exhales heavily and chews her lip. "Because it's too soon after all the drama from last year."

I frown at that odd reply. "What the hell does that mean? What drama?"

She swallows and turns her blazing blue eyes at me. When she looks straight at me like that, it often takes my breath away. I don't think Daphney has any clue how stunning she is.

"Well, I ended up taking my last boyfriend to court, and it cost my parents quite a bit of money."

"Come again?" I ask, my voice taking on a strange tone as my hands clench to fists on my lap. "Did he…did he hurt you?" I'm shocked at the rage billowing up inside me. The fact that any man could hurt someone as sweet and innocent as Daphney is making me see red.

"He didn't hurt me physically, but he did steal from me." She shakes her head like it's a memory she doesn't want to revisit.

I frown, waiting for her to continue.

"It's a long story and you don't need to hear all the gory details. Just please don't give my brother any impression that you and I are sleeping together, okay? None of that winking you did in front of my other brother that day I was giving Marisa her piano lesson."

"I winked at you?"

"Yes," she snaps. "And Theo called me afterward to ask if something was going on between us."

"What did you tell him?"

"That you're a manwhore flirt, and you'd probably wink at a streetlight."

"Ouch," I pout but can't help but laugh. She's sweet and savage. It's a strangely sexy combination.

"Sorry, but am I wrong?" She looks at me sheepishly.

I harrumph my disapproval. She makes me sound like a horndog who would hump any nearby leg. I like to think I have some standards. "Just keep your distance, and we should be fine," I grumble, annoyed that it seems like I'm the weak one when it comes to our attraction to each other.

She pats me on the arm and moves to get out of the car when a rush of dread shoots through me. I grab her hand and stare at our fingers interlocked together. I shouldn't be using her like this. I shouldn't have guilted her into inviting me today. She's way too nice to be taken advantage of like this. And I really shouldn't be going to these sorts of lengths to figure out if Vaughn Harris is my actual father. I turned my whole life upside down because of a stupid fucking letter that may be complete bullshit. What am I fucking doing?

My body is trembling when I feel Daphney's cool hand touch my cheek as she turns me to look at her. "Hey, calm down. I'm sorry I said that, okay? I don't see you like that. Not really. And I'm glad you're coming today. I'm sure it's hard for you to be here in London all alone so soon after losing your dad. But this will be good for you. It's healing to let people in. To find new connections. It's going to be great. The Harrises are very welcoming."

I swallow the knot in my throat. "I don't think I should be here."

And by *here*, I don't mean Vaughn Harris's house. I mean…here, here. Playing for his club, living in his son-in-law's apartment building, inviting myself to a family dinner. Having sex with a girl who has no idea who I even am. I'm making moves right now that I'll never be able to un-move.

"Of course, you should be here," Daphney says, offering me a soft smile that's so full of hope, it makes me ache inside. "We're not just neighbors with benefits. We're friends, right?"

I lick my lips and move in to kiss her. I didn't realize we'd become friends in all this, but the fact that she sees me like that makes me feel human again. I know I have Jude back in the States and Knight and Link here, but since losing my dad and well, basically my mom too, I have felt so inherently alone. And this girl right here, this neighbor I bumped into? She somehow seems to brighten up the dark spots inside me.

Our lips are just about to connect when a loud smack jerks us apart. Daphney gasps and we both swerve our eyes forward to see a small brown-haired little boy spread across the windshield. He opens his mouth and smushes his nose and tongue against the glass as he emits a horrific high-pitched squeal.

"Teddy!" a voice booms, and I look over to see it's Booker. He jogs down the driveway and opens the gate before grabbing the boy off the car. He waves at Daphney and me inside. "I've been looking for him for almost twenty minutes now. Thought I lost him forever!"

Daphney and I break apart and quickly hop out of the vehicle as Booker clutches Teddy to his chest and offers me a smile. "I heard you were crashing the family dinner today. I should have invited you weeks ago."

"Oh, it's okay," I reply, gripping the back of my neck. "This one yours?"

"I'm afraid so." Booker laughs and gives Daphney a quick kiss on the cheek. "Come on in, you guys. It's freezing out here."

Booker lowers Teddy to the ground, and the little dude instantly comes running toward me. He pulls his leg back, swinging his boot straight for my shin. I lift my foot just in time, and his entire body swings backward when he misses, and he totally yeets it and falls flat on his back.

He lets out a loud squeal, and horror rains down over me. "Shit, I'm sorry, little dude!" I exclaim, reaching down and picking him up to see if he's okay. It takes a second to realize he's not wailing in pain. He's actually laughing. He's laughing so hard, he can barely breathe. He stumbles over to me and wraps his arms around my leg. I look up at Booker and Daphney completely confused. "Is he okay?"

Booker nods and smiles. "He likes you. And that's saying a lot because Teddy hates everyone."

"Okay," I state, watching Booker and Daphney walk through the gated entrance and up the gravel drive. I point down at the kid still wrapped around my leg. "Should I just…? Okay, I guess I'm giving you a ride to the house."

"Giddyup!" Teddy bellows, and I shake my head, finally allowing myself to laugh at this super fucked-up moment.

Vaughn Harris's home is a large three-story mansion with stately pillars, and a bright yellow double-door entrance. A giant staircase greets us when we walk in the front door. Booker points upstairs and tells me this is where his sister and his brothers all grew up as kids and laughs when he remembers all the girls Tanner snuck in through the window.

Booker leads Daphney and me down the long-marbled hallway before turning left through a swinging door to enter the kitchen. Although, at first glance, I can tell it's a lot more than just a kitchen. It's one of those rooms where everything happens. And not just because it looks like mass chaos with people everywhere.

On the left is the kitchen with high-end appliances and a long countertop and barstools. On the right is a grand dining table in front of an entire wall of windows and doors that open out onto the large patio. The backyard is surrounded by a wooded area, and I spot a gate that leads into the forest. Looking around at everyone, I can tell there are more people than there are chairs. And the volume of the voices all talking at once is so deafening, I'm not sure I can hear my own thoughts.

Vaughn is in the kitchen next to a blonde woman in an apron who's screaming at a kid that's currently standing on the countertop. He spots me and gets a big smile on his face. "Zander! Booker told me you'd be joining us today. Come in, son!" He walks around the counter and greets Daphney, then me. His eyes lower to my leg, where Teddy is still very much attached. "Did you make a new friend?"

I shrug. "I skunked him outside, and apparently, he likes a challenge?"

Vaughn laughs and bends over to peel Teddy off my leg. He screams and kicks but then finally gives in. "My grandson wants to be a striker, don't you, lad?"

Teddy nods and eyes me. "What do you play?"

My brows lift. "I'm a defender."

"He's a sweeper," Vaughn states. "He protects your daddy when the midfielders muck it up."

"My daddy doesn't need protecting," Teddy exclaims, then wriggles out of his grandfather's arms and takes off toward the backyard where a couple of other kids are playing on the thin layer of snow that's just fallen on the grass.

"Teddy is loose!" Vaughn yells, and a woman with short blonde hair that I recognize as Booker's wife, Poppy, nods and rushes quickly out the door. Vaughn redirects his gaze to me. "Glad you could join us, Zander. Daphney has become a good friend of the family since she moved to Bethnal Green."

I look at the other side of the room to see Daphney holding her niece Rocky, who I met at the pub when I first arrived in London. Her brother Hayden is frowning at me, and I do my best to redirect my attention to Vaughn. The less I look at Daphney or her brother today, the better.

"Well, thank you for having me. I guess I've been feeling a bit homesick."

"Of course, you have," Vaughn nods thoughtfully and puts his arm around my shoulders. "Let me introduce you to everyone properly."

The Harris family is a fertile breed. First, I meet Camden, Tanner's twin brother. He's killing it as a striker for Arsenal, and I obviously already knew his wife, Indie, since she's the team doctor. But I hadn't met their two children. They have a daughter Bex, who's two, and their son, Porter, who's one. Porter has red hair just like his mother and seems to have a challenging spirit like his dad.

Then I met Booker and Poppy's other little boy, Oliver. He was the one on the countertop in the kitchen. Their twins are five years old and have been playing football since they were three.

After that, Vaughn drags me over to his daughter, Vi, who looks really busy at the stove. She's the mother of the little girl named Rocky who I met when Hayden gave me the keys to my apartment at Old George. Vi chats with me for a bit about all the work that Daphney does in the building. It felt like a bit of an overshare when she said Daphney saved her and Hayden's marriage by taking over the building maintenance.

She begins to ask me about how I'm adjusting to London when I'm turned around and being clapped on the back by my teammate, Roan DeWalt. I'd completely forgotten that his wife, Allie, is a cousin to the Harris Brothers. Apparently, her dad is Vaughn's brother and still lives in the States. Their little guy, Neo, is turning one soon.

A couple of unfamiliar faces that I'm introduced to next are Mac Logan, who was the former midfielder for Bethnal Green, and his wife, Freya. They look like a cartoon family with their trifecta of ginger hair, even down to their newborn little guy, Fergie. I heard a lot about Mac's career for the club when I first arrived at Bethnal Green. Mostly from Knight because they play the same position, and Knight idolized Mac. Mac says he's happily retired now, though.

Finally, I meet Gareth, the eldest of the Harris Brothers, and to say he's not intimidating would be a total lie.

"How are you adjusting to Premier League?" he asks, his eyes severe on mine as he offers me a chair at the table beside him.

I hesitate to take it, feeling a bit like I'm about to be interrogated. "It was a struggle at first, but I'm catching up, I think."

"America doesn't give enough attention to football...the real football I mean."

"Yeah, I came over here for a camp when I was younger, and it about killed me."

"I've been trying to expand my youth program called Kids Kickers into the States. Perhaps you have some contacts over there that you could introduce me to?" Gareth eyes me, and even though it's a question, it feels a bit more like a demand.

"Yeah, maybe," I reply hesitantly.

"And I'd love to have you volunteer at a camp. The kids would get a kick out of an American." Gareth smiles and nods.

"Sure, yeah, I can do that." I smile back politely.

Gareth eyes me again for a moment. "I'm sorry, but you look really familiar. How old are you?"

I swallow nervously. "Twenty-five."

He scoffs. "I'm way too much older than you to have gone to that camp with you then."

"Yeah," I croak, doing my best to ignore the eerie sensation that I think we kind of look alike. I clear my throat and change the subject. "Any regrets on retiring?"

"No." Gareth scoffs and waves over a chestnut-haired woman with a little boy on her hip. "My wife, Sloan, and I are busy enough managing our kids. Our daughter, Sophia, is twelve, and she has serious feet, so I'm coaching her team. We're traveling all over for her football schedule now. It's very time-consuming."

"Is that right?" I smile up at Sloan as I shake her hand when she offers it.

"He failed to mention he scared away the last coach of her team." Her American accent is obvious as she slides unamused eyes over to her husband. "The poor guy quit in the middle of their first game."

"Only because he didn't know what the fuck he was doing!" Gareth snaps.

"Uncle Gareth!" Rocky coos, pointing at his mouth. "Swear jar."

Gareth's jaw looks taut as he digs into his pocket and sticks a bill into the jar full of money.

Tanner appears beside me out of nowhere. "Most of the money in that jar is mine. I've got the dirtiest mouth of this family. Can you imagine that, Williams?"

"I can actually," I laugh heartily.

"Let me introduce you to my wife." Tanner grabs a dark-haired woman and swirls her around in his arms, giving her a playful squeeze that she whacks him on the chest for. "Williams, this is my wife, Dr. Belle Ryan, and our youngest daughter Alexandra." Tanner pauses to look out the window where an older girl is running with a smaller one.

"Our niece Sophia is playing with our other daughter Joey. Short for Josephine."

"It's nice to meet you." Belle reaches forward and shakes my hand. "Hope Tanner isn't being too hard on you."

I chuckle and shake my head. "No, it's Coach Zion we all call a sadist."

The room goes very quiet. I swallow a knot in my throat when I see that all eyes have focused on me.

"What did you just say?" Gareth asks, his voice deep and grave.

I look around nervously. "I um… said Coach Z is a sadist." I laugh awkwardly. "I mean…he certainly acts like it."

Out of nowhere, Tanner slams his hand to the table. "How dare you speak of Coach Zion like that."

All humor drains from my face because I've never seen Tanner Harris without a smile. "Seriously?"

"He's like family," Camden says, stepping forward with a glower.

"Okaaay," I reply. "I didn't say he was a bad coach. I just said—"

"We heard what you said," Vaughn cuts me off, eyeing me sternly like he's about to grab me by the shirt and toss me out the door.

My eyes search the space for Daphney who's abandoned me in my hour of need. This moment right here is why I shouldn't have pushed for an invite. I don't know this family. I don't know what sets them off or who they're loyal to. They don't even get my sense of humor. I'm sure Daphney would tell me I'm being way too American. This is what I get for having sex with Daphney instead of finishing *Bridget Jones's Diary!*

Suddenly, everyone erupts into laughter, the kids, the wives, hell, even the little baby that Belle is holding looks like she's pointing her finger at me and having a gay old time.

"We're taking the piss, mate," Gareth says into my ear, slapping my shoulder heartily. "The look on your face."

Daphney pops up out of nowhere, and she has tears in her eyes she's laughing so hard. "You'll learn to love the British sense of humor."

I drop my elbows on the table and rake my fingers through my hair, feeling like I just lost years off my life. "Fuck me."

A little blonde girl walks over to me with eyes narrowed. "It's twenty quid for your first offense." She pushes the glass jar in my direction. "Don't worry, it all goes to charity."

27

Mission Impossible

Zander

"SO, THIS IS IT?" LINK ASKS, HOLDING A BAGGIE OF HAIR UP IN front of his face at breakfast the next day. He's inspecting it like it's going to show him the DNA results by sight alone.

"Stop messing with it," I snap and snatch the bag out of his hand, tucking it back into my coat pocket. I run two hands through my hair and grab my cup of coffee. "I can't have another invalid result. This shit is stressing me out."

Knight eyes me thoughtfully. "So how was the dinner?"

"It was fine," I state, shrugging casually.

The truth is, it was great. The entire visit was fun and funny. Delicious and warm. It was a real family dinner, and honestly, it was something I'd never experienced before. My parents were older when they had me, so I didn't have any cousins my age running around. My grandparents passed when I was young. Obviously, I had no siblings. It was always just my parents and me. It was nice but quiet.

The Harris Sunday dinner was the exact opposite. Everyone spoke over top of everyone. There was always a kid crying, missing, or pooping. The swear jar got passed around like dessert. After dessert, there was football talk over the kitchen counter, and condiment bottles were used to signal positions on a field. The ladies drank wine outside while the kids played in the snow. Hayden inspected Daphney's car because it had been making strange noises.

And there was love. Lots and lots of love. Couples kissing, kids hugging aunts and uncles. Photos being taken constantly.

It was chaos.

Beautiful, completely original, and foreign to me…chaos.

I didn't even have to try that hard to use Vaughn's bathroom. One of the kids made a mess in the downstairs one, so Vaughn literally gave me directions to his bathroom upstairs. His hairbrush was sitting on the counter, like an offering from the universe.

I looked at myself in the mirror after I'd pulled some hair off and I wasn't even sure who was looking back. I'm not a guy who enjoys big family dinners. I don't look like the eldest Harris brother. But I also didn't think I looked like my own parents either. Honestly, I felt like I was staring at the reflection of a fucking stranger.

The sooner I get this damn DNA sample sent, the sooner I can get back to my fucking life.

"It was fine?" Knight repeats my blasé response with a look of mistrust all over his face. "Come on, man. Even I would say more than that after having a meal at the Harris childhood home."

"I enjoyed myself, alright," I snap, annoyance prickling in my veins. "And I'm afraid that was something I didn't even consider."

"What do you mean?" Link asks, blinking curiously over at me.

I look back and forth between my two friends. "I didn't expect to like them. I expected them to be a bunch of pompous, overconfident assholes. I figured I'd find out they're all too famous and successful and rich to relate to. I thought they'd be arrogant and rude."

"And they weren't?" Knight inquires even though it's clear he knows the answer.

"No." I exhale heavily. "They were the diametrical opposite. They were laid-back and cool. They teased me like they'd known me for years. I feel awful."

"Why?" Link asks, his brows furrowed.

"Because I have a family." I let go of my coffee mug as my hands turn to fists on the table. "And I feel like every smile I gave on Sunday was like me shitting on Dad's grave."

Knight reaches out and grabs my wrist. "What if you don't send the hair in?"

"What do you mean?"

He shrugs. "Maybe what you don't know won't hurt you."

I sit back and shake my head. "I can't come this far and not finish this race."

"This isn't a game, Zander," Knight replies, his voice serious. "This is your life."

"I know!" I turn to look out the window. "And if I don't send this in,

I'm never going to feel settled. I have to know. The anxiety over not know-ing will be worse than whatever the truth turns out to be."

"I agree," Link says, offering me a half-smile. "Information is power. Whatever you find out, we can deal with."

Knight exhales heavily, and I'm hoping I can interpret that as silent understanding.

28

Friends With Benefits

Daphney

"**W**OULD WE BE BREAKING SOME RULES IF YOU CAME TO A wedding with me in a couple of weeks? I looked and saw you have a match in Southampton on Saturday, but the wedding is actually Sunday evening." I eye Zander as we sit at The Serpentine Restaurant in Hyde Park.

This place is a favorite of Phoebe's and mine. It's a quaint little glass-walled building on lakefront property that gives you a break from the city. Zander's been acting stir-crazy the past few days, so I thought maybe showing him another part of London might help get him out of his funk.

"Whose wedding?" he asks, taking a sip of his beer and glancing over at the guitarist playing in the corner.

"It's actually the club lawyer, Santino Rossi. Hence, why the wedding is on a Sunday."

"Oh yeah, I met him when I first moved here," Zander replies, turning his baseball cap backward. He always looks so cute with it backward. "He stopped by with my lease agreement, remember? I see him around Tower Park occasionally too."

"Oh, of course." I nod and smile, realizing that Zander still hasn't said yes to coming with me. "Well, he's marrying Mac Logan's sister, Tilly? You met Mac and his wife, Freya, briefly at Vaughn's house Sunday, and they've asked me to sing at their wedding. Everyone I know there will be coupled up, so it'd be nice to have a friend with me. And I know we're not in a relationship but the whole, being exclusive rule kind of mucks up me finding another date."

"Who else would you bring?" Zander asks, his eyes narrowing with curiosity.

"I don't know." I shrug. "Maybe that Scottish midfielder Banner MacLeod?" I can't hide the smile on my face.

Zander shakes his head, a smirk lightening his eyes.

"He seemed keen. And I haven't been able to stop thinking about the seedy underbelly of Edinburgh he told me about at the pub," I deadpan.

"That's enough of that," Zander grumbles, and it makes me laugh.

"I could ask him or Finnegan. He hasn't been getting much pitch time, so he's probably due for a nice cuddle."

"Finney needs no cuddles. Finney needs an exorcism."

"That's rather harsh." I lift my glass of wine to my lips and take a sip. "If I didn't know any better, I'd say you're jealous." I wiggle my eyebrows playfully before silence descends between us. My smile falters. Maybe I took this joke too far. Maybe I sound like a girl who wants the guy she's sleeping with to be jealous.

The truth is, I wouldn't want anyone else to go with me. And based on the awkward look on Zander's face, I realize that he's probably getting ready to let me down gently. I'll be crushed. And the fact that I'll be crushed is probably a bad thing because this is supposed to be casual. I should have just asked Phoebe. I'm likely going to be co-parenting with her when I'm still single in my thirties anyway.

"Did you say you're singing?" Zander shoots me a crooked smile, and hope reignites in my belly.

"Yes," I groan and play nervously with my hair. "I wouldn't have even said yes, but it's a paying gig, and I like money."

Zander huffs out a laugh. "That's all you needed to say."

"Shut up." I tilt my head and narrow my eyes at him. "You'll come?"

"Yeah," he replies, leaning forward and shooting me a dirty look that shows me exactly where his mind is at. "I've wanted to see you sing again ever since that night at Old George."

"Then why didn't you stop me from making a fool of myself?"

"'Cause I liked watching you try to make me jealous." Zander turns his hat forward, pulling it low over his eyes.

"It clearly didn't work," I grumble dejectedly, feeling like a proper fool.

"Didn't it?" He pins me with a knowing look, and I open my mouth to reply but suddenly feel at a rare loss of words.

Zander reaches over and casually plucks a chip off my plate. "Am I your friend, Ducky?"

I roll my eyes. "You've somehow become less horrible since we first met, so it would appear we're leading into friendship territory."

He laughs and waggles his eyebrows. "Or all the good sex I'm giving you has improved your normally grumpy disposition toward me."

"Don't flatter yourself." I giggle, and Zander surprises me as he leans across the table for a kiss. It's intimate and tender and lingers longer than I expect it to, sending all sorts of flutters to my belly.

He pulls back and pops an olive into his mouth like he didn't just make me see stars. "I'm great at weddings, actually. I've got moves like Jagger."

"Oh, this I have to see," I croak after I've recovered from that mind-blowing public display of affection. I redirect my attention to my food, feeling much more relaxed than before. It felt like a big step asking Zander to come with me to this wedding. But I figured if he can ask me to a Harris Sunday dinner, then this isn't totally off the mark. I smile up at him and add, "It'll be nice not being the odd one out in the Harris bunch for once."

Zander's brows knit together. "The Harris family is all going to be there?"

I nod around a strawberry. "Of course. Santino's been the Bethnal Green club lawyer for over a decade, I think. He's really close to the family."

"They're close to everybody, aren't they?" Zander says, turning his gaze out toward the water with a peculiar look on his face.

"What is that supposed to mean?" My voice pitches up in curiosity.

"Nothing." He shakes his head and clears his throat. "Aren't you worried they'll suspect something is going on between us? It was your rule to keep our little arrangement a secret."

"I'll bring you to the wedding as a friend just like I brought you to Sunday dinner," I reply, feeling slightly defensive. "Just don't bust out any *Dirty Dancing* moves on me, and we should be just fine."

A slow smile spreads across his face as he rises out of his chair and leans across the table. "You want to see a preview of my dance moves?"

My brows lift as I deadpan, "A lap dance would be far worse than *Dirty Dancing*, I'm afraid."

"I'm not giving you a lap dance, Ducky," he says and grabs my hand to yank me up out of my chair. He pulls me close and murmurs into my ear, "Not now at least."

He then wraps one hand around my waist and holds my other out in a formal pose. I nearly burst with excitement when he moves us around the table in a proper four-count, drawing the eyes of everyone in the restaurant.

My jaw drops in fascination. "Are we?"

"Waltzing? Yes, darling," he purrs in a horrid British accent.

"Oh, my God." I laugh and glance down at our feet. "I'm…"

"Impressed? Amazed? Turned on?" He pulls me closer, and the heated look in his eyes hits me deep in my belly.

I swallow the lump in my throat. "Perhaps all of the above," I admit honestly.

His chest shakes with silent laughter as he continues moving with great ease to the music.

"You never cease to surprise me, Soccer Boy."

"I could say the same to you, sweetheart."

29

Fair-weather Fan

Daphney

"**D**APHNEY CLARKE, AS I LIVE AND BREATHE!" PHOEBE BELLOWS as she barges into Old George kitted out in red and white Arsenal football gear.

"Hiya," I call over to her as I pause wiping down the bar with disinfectant. "You better watch yourself in that kit around here. Especially with tonight's FA Cup match against Bethnal Green."

She ignores my warning and props her elbows on the bar. "Haven't seen you in ages."

I roll my eyes. "It's only been a couple of weeks."

"That's ages in a teen's years. And you know I'm still a child at heart." She playfully bats her eyes.

I sigh heavily, feeling a bit guilty for being so short in my text exchanges with her. Three jobs and a healthy sex life leave me knackered. "Let's plan a proper date next weekend. Maybe we can get our nails done? I have that wedding I'm singing in next Sunday, so I could use a little pampering."

"Sold!" Her face contorts into something akin to speculative. "So come on then. Out with it."

"Out with what?"

"I'm sure you're in love with him by now." She rolls her eyes playfully.

"I am not in love."

She exhales dramatically. "Are you still sleeping with him?"

"Yes, but we're not spending the night with each other." I shoot her a cocky smirk like I outsmarted her for once.

"Well, that's new." She nods. "Maybe there's hope for you yet."

I laugh and shake my head. "We're having fun, and that's it."

"Well, good. I'm happy for you then."

I glance down her body once more. "So, what's with the getup? You've never been a football fan."

Her eyes glitter with intrigue. "You know that guy who I hooked up with in your flat a few weeks ago?"

"Well, I don't know him. But I heard of him." I laugh to myself when I recall how angry Zander was when he thought it was someone I was sleeping with. God, he's cute when he's jealous.

"He works in marketing at Arsenal, and guess what I scored?" She reaches into her large handbag and holds up two tickets.

I frown over at them. "Is that for tonight's match?"

"Yep," she flicks her hand over the top of them.

"Jealous! You two will have a great time."

"I'm not going with him, you daft cow," she replies, adding a playful shimmy to her head. "I'm going with you."

I laugh and shake my head. "Nice try…but as you can see, I'm all booked up."

Phoebe narrows her eyes. "We'll see about that." She makes her way down the bar and back toward my boss's office.

"If you are going into Hubert's office to plead with him, it won't work," I call out, but she's rounded the corner and out of earshot now.

I shake my head again because no way will Phoebe convince him to let me off. We'll be swamped tonight because of the match. People love watching football at a pub.

Moments later, Phoebe reemerges with a victorious expression. "You're off in thirty." She reaches into her bag and chucks a green and white shirt at me.

"How did you manage that?" I inquire, holding out the brand-new Bethnal Green hooded jumper that she must have just bought on her way over here.

She does a twirl and a curtsey. "I am woman, hear me roar."

"You don't think Zander will think this is a bit desperate of me to come to one of his matches?" I ask Phoebe as we make our way through the con-courses at Emirates Stadium.

It's a huge structure that I've never actually visited before. We grab some food and drinks and stand at a small table in the refreshments area to have a beer and a snack before we take our seats. I keep getting nasty looks for being in the opposing team's kit, so I pull my faux fur coat tight around my chest, hoping to blend in a bit more.

"It's not like we're at Tower Park!" Phoebe exclaims before taking a large sip of her beer. "And besides, he can't begrudge you for free footy tickets to a FA Cup game. Now, hurry up and finish. The bloke at the ticket counter said our gate was just over there, and I'm dying to see our seats."

We glug down our drinks and toss them in the bin as we maneuver through the masses of people toward our section entrance. When we emerge out into the light, I take a moment to breathe it all in. We're dead center on the pitch, and the stands are nearly full to the brim. There really is nothing better than a packed football stadium. Even if it is Emirates.

I frown when I see that Phoebe is going down the steps, not up. "My God, these must be good seats," I say as I continue heading down. The longer we go, the farther my jaw falls to the floor. "Phoebe!"

"What?" Her black ponytail flicks me in the face as she whirls around to look back at me before heading into an aisle.

"We're in the front row," I bark, completely gobsmacked.

"Surprise!" She smiles victoriously and grabs my arm to drag me behind her.

We make our way to our seats, and I glance around at everyone seated around us. They all look like they have a lot more money than I do, and none of them are wearing green and white.

"Why did you make me wear this?" I grumble, tightening my jacket even further.

"Because you have to support your boyfriend!" Phoebe laughs and shimmies her chest at me.

I shoot her a murderous glower. "Zander Williams is not my boyfriend."

Suddenly, the music dies down in the stadium, and my eyes swerve over to the player tunnel where I see the players of Arsenal and Bethnal Green marching out with the refs and coaching staff. They're all holding the hands of little children who look to be about the same age as my nieces.

I spot Camden Harris first in a single file line with his team. His inked arm pokes out of his Arsenal kit, and he looks perfectly at ease out there—a seasoned player certainly nearing retirement age but not showing it on the pitch at all.

My eyes move past the Arsenal club toward the Bethnal Green line. I spot Booker and Tanner and Vaughn. It would have been nice to see a

Bethnal Green match when Camden, Tanner, and Booker were still all playing for the club. I think Gareth left for Man U before they all ever got a chance to play for their father, but watching them all play at the World Cup was a magical experience for not just me, but for all of England, so I can't really complain.

My eyes are drawn to the players right in front of me next, and I gasp when I see Zander's eyes are locked on me. My entire body shivers with apprehension as he tilts his head and mouths something I can't quite discern.

I assume it's something along the lines of, *"What the fuck are you doing here, you creepy stalker? Is there no way I can escape you?"*

I shoot him an apologetic look, my face heating with mortification as I hook my thumb over to Phoebe by way of explanation. I smile good-naturedly, and he smiles back, hopefully not intending to call his club lawyer as soon as the match is over and ask for a flat relocation. I mean, we are having sex with each other. Surely, me watching him play a little football isn't more uncomfortable for him than me taking over the vibrator in the shower.

The match begins, and I'm relieved when Zander is too focused on his position as sweeper in front of Booker at the net to give me looks that I can overthink until the cows come home.

Bethnal Green takes a shocking lead in the first half after a flurry of chances. Honestly, there was so much action on the Arsenal side of the pitch, I was worried that Zander and Booker might be feeling a bit useless.

Bethnal Green's single goal that's earned in the thirty-fourth minute is a team effort. Roan DeWalt takes a shot from the edge of the box that takes a wicked deflection off the toe of the Arsenal goalkeeper. Thankfully, the twenty-three-year-old striker, Billy Campbell, is in the box and takes full advantage of the rebound. He crushes it straight into the net to make the score one-nil.

Arsenal is a lot less tentative in the second half, giving Booker and Zander a run for their money. Between the two of them, I counted at least seven big saves. At one point, Zander makes a sprawling save on a rebound deflection from Booker. And finally, the Irishman, Lance Finnegan, who's been struggling in his position as a center-back for the whole game, manages to help them both out of a scramble.

Near the end of the second half, Camden Harris catches a break as he cuts in from the left flank and ends up one-on-one with Zander. He tricks him out with a stunning spin maneuver, delivering a crushing blow with his fierce right foot just missing the tips of Booker's gloves.

When the ball slaps the net, the Emirates Stadium erupts, and my eyes move instantly back to Zander, who's on his knees, shoving his hands through his hair and looking painfully distraught. He shakes his head and stands up, his eyes turn toward the sidelines where Vaughn and Tanner are embracing Camden after his goal, passing out congratulations.

I move my gaze back to Zander, and the expression on his face is confused. He might even be angry. And not just from getting burned, but he almost seems bothered that they're congratulating Camden after the play? Perhaps he doesn't understand how close the Harris family is. They may be opponents right now, but anyone who knows this family knows that they blindly support each other, no matter what kit they're wearing.

Zander turns his back on them, spits into the grass, and gets back into position. The score is tied in the eighty-eighth minute. Bethnal Green has a corner kick, and everyone is pushing up into the Arsenal box, including Zander. Booker looks all alone in the back half as he cheers on his team loudly. This is likely Bethnal Green's last chance to score.

The corner kick comes in, and Roan DeWalt leaps up to crush a header. The ball hits the crossbar and goes wide. As Roan comes down, a defender's elbow cracks him right on the side of his head, propelling him sideways. When Roan hits the ground, he isn't moving, and the entire stadium goes deathly quiet.

A ref signals to the medical team on Bethnal's side, and I see Indie's red hair pop out as she sprints out onto the pitch with a carrier of supplies. Another medical person and possibly a nurse join her as they hunch down to assess Roan's injury.

"Concussion, I'm betting," I state, my hands on my cheeks with anxiety. If I was Roan's wife, Allie, I would be a nervous wreck right now. Headers are scary business, which is why they take head injuries so seriously in the league.

"Who will kick the penalty shot I wonder?" Phoebe asks, her voice hollow with worry.

"The other striker, Billy Campbell, I'm sure," I answer distractedly as I notice movement on the sidelines. I glance down and see Booker jogging over to Coach Zion to discuss something. He's pointing out to the pitch, and Coach Z doesn't look like he likes what Booker is saying. Vaughn and

Tanner come over to join the discussion, and they seem to be much more on board with whatever plan Booker has.

When Roan finally stands up, the entire stadium cheers in relief. Even the Arsenal fans. No one ever likes to see an injury on the pitch. The medics assist Roan to the sidelines as the ref sets about resuming the match.

Bethnal Green now has a penalty kick that could win the game if they can manage to get it past the Arsenal keeper who has been on fire today. I watch in curiosity as Booker jogs over to Zander, puts his hand on his shoulder, and points at the net. Zander looks confused and glances over at Coach Zion and Vaughn, who are both nodding back at him.

Finally, looking rather dazed, Booker and Zander part ways as Zander jogs over to the penalty spot and positions himself to take the kick.

"Are they having Zander take the kick?" I ask, gripping Phoebe's arm tightly as my eyes feel permanently glued to the pitch.

"You're hurting me!" Phoebe exclaims, peeling my fingers off her.

"Oh, my God, he's taking the kick!" I glance down at the sideline like maybe he's just holding the position for someone else. But there's no one else.

"Well, clearly Roan isn't up for it," Phoebe offers, and I shake my head in confusion.

"I know, but…Zander's so new!" I tear my eyes away from the pitch to look at Phoebe. My entire body tingles with anticipation. "This is mental!"

"I expect they know what they're doing," Phoebe replies and clutches my arm as we both refocus on the pitch.

The ref blows his whistle, and Zander pauses for a moment, exhaling a heavy breath before doing a slow jog up that quickly shifts into a sprint. He does a unique little hopping move right before he kicks with his right boot and delivers a sweetheart of a strike up to the top of the net.

Goal, Bethnal Green.

I don't even realize I'm screaming until Phoebe swirls me around to face her. I finally gasp for air and then start screaming again as I thrust my hand up into the air. The entire team is swarming Zander. Even Vaughn Harris jogs out onto the pitch to congratulate his sweeper. Eventually, I realize that Phoebe and I are the only ones properly losing our minds in our section, so I calm myself down and enjoy the view of Zander running back to his position on the other end of the pitch. The final seconds run out, and it's a Bethnal Green victory, two to one.

30

Fair-weather Fan Continued

Daphney

MY VOICE IS HOARSE BY THE TIME PHOEBE AND I MAKE OUR WAY out of the stadium. I was in a daze as Phoebe stood in the stands for ages talking to the bloke who gave us the tickets. I've never experienced a football game this close in my life, and it's an experience I will take to my bloody grave.

We finally make it outside when I hear a voice call out my name. "Daphney, is that you?"

I look off into the distance and spot the blonde hair of my sister-in-law, Vi, running toward me. "What are you doing here?" she asks, embracing me in a hug. "Were you at the match? Where were you sitting?"

I shake off the stupor I'm still feeling from that match and clear my hoarse throat to reply, "We had first row seats that Phoebe scored."

"I know a bloke." Phoebe laughs and flicks her hair over her shoulder.

"Oh my God, I would have loved to have joined you guys," Vi nearly growls as she ushers Phoebe and me over to where Poppy, Belle, and Allie are standing by a chain-link fence. "We were high up in a suite because that's what Camden booked us, and no one can hear me screaming from up there."

"Oh, don't you worry. They heard this one," Phoebe says, grabbing hold of my arm and pointing at me. "You should have heard her bellowing like a banshee at every play. Especially at the end when Zander took that shot."

"How is Roan doing?" I ask, turning my focus to Allie because it had to be scary seeing him lying on the pitch like that.

"He's doing okay," she replies with a sad smile. "Indie called and told me he's on concussion protocol, again, but they think he'll be cleared in a week. I just want to get him home and into bed. Is it awful of me to be ready for him to retire already?"

"Not awful," Vi responds, wrapping her arm around Allie. "Reasonable."

Allie smiles gratefully and then glances at me to say, "Zander did a great job filling in for him on that kick, though."

"Complete genius," Poppy adds. "They had no idea what to expect from Zander, so it was an ace move."

Vi's blue eyes lock on me. "It's very nice of you to cheer on your *neighbor*, Daphney. I see you're even sporting his club colors."

My cheeks heat with embarrassment. "Just showing the family some support."

"Zander isn't a Harris last time I checked," Phoebe coos, and I have to refrain myself from smacking her arm.

Vi winks at me playfully. "Wearing green and white is very neighborly of you, Daphney."

"Shut up, both of you," I exclaim, hating how Vi always sees right through me. "Zander and I are just mates."

"Wish I had more mates who looked like that," Belle adds, and everyone starts to giggle at my expense.

"Oh, my God. I'm going to leave." I make a move to do so.

"Keep your shirt on," Vi whines and grabs my arm. "We're just winding you up."

I cross my arms and harrumph. "Where's my brother tonight?"

"Home watching the child," Vi laughs. "We're having a tequila sunrise ladies' night tonight. We're just waiting for Indie to come out of the changing rooms."

"There she is now!" Belle says and points over at the gated entrance where several players' cars are all parked. "Oi, hot stuff! Were you peeping on your husband in the changing rooms? They'll take away your medical license for that!"

Indie laughs and shakes her head, walking over to the chain-link fence. "Hush, you," Indie chirps, toying with her mess of red curls piled on top of her head. "I'm just going to wait until Camden comes out to tell him good game, and then I'm ready for a drink!"

As if on cue, the doors open again, and I swear everything turns to slow motion as several footballers all come strolling out. They're kitted out in various stages of posh and casual, but no less expensive with their fancy watches, trainers, and matching jogger sets.

I hear collective audible sighs from all of the females within eyesight. And let's face it, males too. Footballers in England aren't something you get to see close up every day, and after a gripping match like that, it's really reminded me how God-like they all are.

I'm instantly snapped out of my fawning when I spot Zander's Red Sox hat sticking out of the mix. I turn on my heel and eye Phoebe harshly. "Shit, he's going to think I'm out here waiting for him like a WAG."

"No, he's going to think you're out here waiting for him like a neighbor with benefits. A NeWB, if you will," Phoebe murmurs.

I can't help but smile. "You really are a cheeky cow."

"Hey, Ducky." Zander's familiar voice sends chills down my spine.

Inhaling sharply, I brace myself as I turn around to face him. I open my mouth to reply, but nothing comes out. I'm sort of stunned by his appearance. I've watched him play on the telly a couple of times now, but after seeing him on the pitch, up close and personal like that, I can't help but slip into a full-blown swoon.

Did he get taller? More muscular? And did his eyes always sparkle like that? It's like they've been electrified with light, and he's pointing them right at me, and I am fucking dazzled into silence.

He laughs as I struggle to find words and asks, "Why didn't you tell me you'd be here?"

I swallow the lump in my throat and tuck my hair behind my ears. "I didn't know until Phoebe came and sprung me from the pub. I have no clue how she got Hubert to let me off."

"That will be a secret between Hubie and me." Phoebe waggles her eyebrows playfully at Zander, and the immediate flash of my jealousy takes me off guard.

I roll my eyes and attempt to gain control of my emotions and then realize that Zander isn't even looking at her. He's looking at me. He bites his lip as his eyes move down my body, making everything inside me clench with desire. My God, when will I stop thinking about sex every time I'm around him?

"What are you doing now?" he inquires, his voice huskier than before.

"We're headed to Old George for a drink," Phoebe says, throwing her arm around me.

I bite my lip and wish I could ditch my best friend right now. Zander has that look in his eyes that makes it very clear he doesn't feel like being social. I like that look. I think I could look in the mirror and see the very same look on my face.

"Can I come?" Zander asks, surprising me.

"Yes," I husk, my voice sounding so obvious that I want to slap some sense into myself.

"We'll meet you there!" Phoebe calls back and grabs my arm, dragging me away from the one thing I want.

31

The Original Daphney

Zander

I'M SEATED AT A PICNIC TABLE IN THE BEER GARDEN OF OLD GEORGE. A smattering of my teammates is running around, celebrating tonight's big win while I sit here drinking my beer in silence and trying my hardest not to eye-fuck the shit out of Daphney.

Adrenaline is still roaring in my veins. That game, the foul, that penalty kick at the end. I just scored my first Premier League goal during an FA Cup match, and it feels fucking amazing. And the fact that Daphney was in the stands and saw the whole thing? *Fuck, I'm getting hard just thinking about it.*

Why do I like the fact that she was there so fucking much? I've had girls at my games before. I always have a couple of tickets at will call for whoever I'm sleeping with at the time. But I've never looked up into the stands for a girl. I've never cared to impress one or sought out encouragement from a chick. All I've cared about is fucking them afterward.

Which is one hundred percent what I want to do with Daphney too.

But I also want to just bask in this feeling with her. Tonight was literally the most incredible moment of my entire soccer career, and I'm sitting in a crowded bar staring at her like a stalker because all I want to do is go back to her place and celebrate in private.

This is the clearest my mind has felt since I arrived in London. I'm not thinking about the DNA results. I'm not obsessing over that jealous twinge I felt when I saw Vaughn and Tanner embrace Camden on the sidelines after he scored. I'm not thinking about my mom or my dad.

I'm just thinking about Daphney and how she's the best thing that could have happened to me here in London.

Phoebe snaps me out of my thoughts as she drops down onto the open bench beside me. She leans in close and yells over the live band, "You don't want to be here, do you?"

I tear my gaze away from Daphney at the bar and take a drink of my beer. "What makes you say that?"

"Because you're not talking to anyone," she exclaims and nudges me playfully. "You're not dancing. You're not celebrating your big victory with your teammates at the bar. You're just drinking your beer in the corner and staring at my best mate like you've seen her naked."

I lift my brows and shrug. No sense in lying to Phoebe since she already knows the situation.

"You know she's more than a piece of meat, right?" Phoebe says, pinning me with a serious look.

"I know."

"But do you really?" She narrows her eyes at me. "Do you know how talented she is?"

"You mean her music?" I side-eye Phoebe as she nods back at me before adding, "Of course. I hear her through the walls every day. She's awesome."

Phoebe pauses for a moment, tapping her long fingernail on her glass. "Do you ever hear her sing any of her own music?"

I frown as I glance back at Daphney, who's talking to some guy at the bar. "You mean the Tire Depot stuff?"

Phoebe shakes her head and laughs. "No, like her own original music. Not the stuff for the adverts."

I pause as I process this comment. "She said she only does commercial stuff."

"Now maybe." Phoebe licks her lips thoughtfully. "But she has nearly an entire album worth of original music she's recorded. At least a dozen songs. Really beautiful stuff. She's poetic—like Sara Bareilles meets Adele."

I clear my throat, feeling a little unnerved that I had no idea she possessed that kind of ability. I knew she was musical. She plays her instruments like they're not even there. And her voice is obviously stunning. But why does she only do cheesy commercial stuff then?

"Has she ever tried to do anything with her songs?"

"You should ask her that."

Phoebe takes a long drink, and I get the feeling she's trying to stir the pot, and I should leave this alone. But I'm actually kind of annoyed that Daphney would hide this part of herself from me. For what? Why is it a secret? I flat-out asked her if she wrote her own stuff before, and she very clearly said no. Why would she lie about it?

"Am I interrupting?" Daphney asks, taking a seat across from me and waggling her eyebrows.

My interest is piqued, so I can't stop the words that come from my mouth next. "Phoebe was just telling me about all these original songs you've recorded."

Daphney's face falls as she shifts her attention to Phoebe. "Why are you talking about that?"

"I didn't say anything bad." Phoebe holds her hands up. "I just said you're talented beyond Tire Depot."

Daphney shakes her head, pursing her lips as she takes a drink of her beer. "It's no big deal."

"Why did you tell me you only do commercials?" I ask, propping my elbows on the table and watching her reaction.

"Because I do," Daphney replies crisply, showing me that she's clearly not happy with the direction of this conversation. "I don't write my own music anymore. Just stuff that pays the bills."

Her nostrils flare as she hits me with a look like I should drop this subject. It reminds me of how my mom acted when I started pestering her about her time living in London. It puts me on edge.

"Why don't you do it anymore?" I pry further.

Daphney's blue eyes narrow. "It doesn't matter."

"Well, if it doesn't matter, you should play one of them here to-night." I hit her with a smile that she does not reciprocate. "The mic is open right now."

"Forget it," Daphney says, forcing a laugh.

"Come on, Daph," Phoebe coaxes, her voice almost tender as she looks at her with a soft smile. "I haven't heard one of your songs in ages. It would be so lovely to hear one again."

"Would you guys please stop?" Daphney stands up, backing away from the table. She shakes her head, then grabs her handbag off the table. "It's getting late. I'm going to head home."

She offers a weak wave and turns on her heel to walk out of the pub. I watch her, stunned into a rare silence because she's clearly upset. Something I haven't seen on Daphney since the moment I met her. I've seen her angry. I've seen her nervous. But this moment right here…she looked almost…broken.

"Mind telling me what that was about?" I ask, looking at Phoebe for answers I'm sure she has.

A sad look flits across her face. "I think I've already said too much."

32

Just Friends

Daphney

Y MIND IS RACING AS I STRIP OUT OF MY JEANS AND BETHNAL GREEN jumper and slip into silk shorts and a camisole. I throw on my robe and turn on some music to calm my nerves as I head into my loo to take off my makeup.

Damn Phoebe. This is all her fault. We were having such a laugh, and she had to go and ruin it by bringing up stuff she knows I hate talking about. And to bring it up in front of Zander of all people is just maddening.

There are things I didn't plan to discuss with Zander. My ex being one of them. It's been nice re-inventing myself here in London and feeling more independent. Maybe I'm a casual sex kind of girl like Phoebe now. I feel like I'm doing pretty well with Zander so far, so why does she have to muck it all up?

A light knock on my door has me freezing in front of my mirror. It's either Phoebe or Zander, and I'm not sure who I want it to be less. I quickly dry off my face and pad barefoot over to the door to look through the hole.

I sigh heavily as I see who's on the other side. "I'm not in the mood tonight, Zander."

I can hear Zander's huff of laughter muffled through the door. "I'm not here for sex, Ducky."

I roll my eyes and swing open the door. The momentum causes him to nearly fall in as he was bracing his hands on the door. "When are you not here for sex?" I cross my arms over my chest.

He barks out a wounded laugh, and I don't miss the way his eyes flash to my chest. He redirects his focus on me and holds a hand to his heart. "That cuts deep."

"You'll survive," I grumble.

He tilts his head and hits me with a soft smile. "I mean it. I don't know what that shit was down there, but I know you left upset, and I don't like to see you upset. It gives me flashbacks of the mouse incident, and no one wants to see you in that horrible mouse-catching getup again."

I fail to fight back the smile that spreads across my face. Damn him. "So, what do you want from me then?"

"I want to cheer you up," he says coyly, chucking me under my chin. "But you're going to have to let me inside to do that."

I exhale heavily and step back to allow the man entrance because... well...I'm weak, and Zander smells really good right now. "Do you want something to drink?"

"I'll have a water, thanks."

I retrieve a couple of bottles of water, and as I close the refrigerator, I spot the cookie I took out of the freezer earlier today. I had planned to give it to him tonight after he got back from his match and nearly forgot.

"To keep the tradition alive," I announce as I hold the cookie in front of his face.

"Oh," Zander exclaims with a bit more volume than seems necessary. "You really didn't have to."

"Of course I did," I reply with a huff as I sit down on the other side of the sofa. "You're on a winning streak, and you don't want to mess it up." His face looks a bit odd as I sit and wait for him to eat it. "Well, go on then."

"Aren't you going to have one with me?" he asks, his eyes looking somewhat nervous for some peculiar reason. Maybe it's just the dim lighting in here from my twinkle lights.

"No, I can't stand raisins." I scrunch my nose up and shake my head. "That one's all yours. Enjoy."

He nods and smiles as he takes a tentative bite. His lips purse together as he makes a noise in the back of his throat.

"Good?" I ask excitedly.

"Mm-hmm," he mumbles and then points at his mouth, indicating he can't talk since his mouth is full. After a long bit of chewing for such a small bite, he finally swallows and says, "Very kind of you," before he hurries to uncap his water and take a large drink. "Makes me thirsty."

"Well, you played an amazing game, so you deserve it."

He exhales and puts the rest of the cookie back into the container, then sets it on the arm of the sofa behind him. It's quiet for a moment, neither of us saying anything and both of us focusing on our water bottles far more than is necessary.

"Well, this is awkward," I say to break the tension.

"Why is it awkward?" He frowns back at me.

I huff out a laugh. "Maybe because we still have our clothes on?"

Zander smiles and shakes his head. "We could sit here naked if you'd like. I'm a giver like that."

He winks back at me, and it causes my insides to flutter. "Thanks, but I'll pass."

He wipes a few cookie crumbs off his thigh before asking, "Do you want to tell me what that was all about at Old George?"

My body tenses with embarrassment because I wish I wouldn't have gotten so upset earlier. It was childish and stupid and not the direction I wanted tonight to go.

It's infuriating that my past is trying to overshadow my present. Especially because, as it turns out, I like my present circumstances! I have a cute footballer stretched out on my sofa. He's sexy and big and brawny, and he's looking at me with concern and offering me some form of comfort. What do I have to be upset about, really?

I shrug. "You basically know already."

"I do?"

"Well, I told you before about my ex that stole from me," I begin because I'd rather tell Zander the full story than have him think I was being dramatic down at the pub.

"Yeah…" He watches me thoughtfully.

"Well, it was my music that he stole."

Zander blinks back at me, his face the picture of serious as he waits for me to continue.

"I started writing my own songs when I was sixteen. I had fourteen fully produced tracks by the time I was twenty. I'd recorded them all in my sound booth back home. Just an acoustic album. Nothing fancy or professional. But I had these wild dreams of selling my stuff to a record company and hearing them performed by like Florence + The Machine or Tove Lo turning it into an ethereal pop song or even something really moody and haunting by Birdy."

"That sounds amazing," Zander says, his eyes alight with so much genuine excitement, it kind of breaks my heart to know I'm going to let him down with what comes next.

"Well, I was twenty-three and performing a few of my songs at local pubs. I really hate being on stage, and that will never change, but it's the best way to get noticed if you want to sell your music to a label."

"Okay…"

"Then I met Rex," I state flatly, leaving no room for interpretation. "Or Rex the Hex as Phoebe and I refer to him now. He was at a pub where I was performing, said he loved my music, and we just hit it off. Honestly, I fell head over heels for him. I think it was the first bloke I really dated that felt like a proper grown-up relationship. He even said he had friends in the music industry he could share my tracks with, so I felt like I'd really hit the jackpot with him.

"After we got a bit more serious, I gave him the files so he could send them to his friend, but it was months of nothing, and then finally Rex told me they weren't interested. I was gutted but not really surprised. Honestly, I think my music is all pretty shit. I wrote most of it when I was still a teenager, and they need some serious work. I think my Tire Depot jingle has much more long-term potential." I laugh, hoping to lighten the mood, but Zander is not laughing with me.

"I don't know if you're qualified to judge your own work, are you?" he asks, pinning me with a serious expression.

"What do you mean?"

He shrugs as he stretches his arm out over the back of the sofa. "We're always our own worst critics, aren't we? You shouldn't get to judge your own music skills the same way I don't get to judge my own soccer skills. We need unbiased parties."

"Right, well, that's beside the point," I reply, rolling my eyes at Zander's sweet optimism. "About a year after I'd given Rex my songs, Phoebe comes running into my dad's office where I was working at the time squealing about one of my tracks being on Spotify. I had no idea what she was going on about. I'd never uploaded any of my tracks to any site, but sure enough, there was my song."

"He uploaded your shit without asking?" Zander asks, his jaw taut with realization. "That's total bullshit."

"Not only that, but he had been collecting royalties on them for months. It wasn't a huge sum of money, but it was my work, and he clearly had no intention of giving me that money. When I'd discovered what he'd done, I demanded he take them down. I tried to issue takedowns on Spotify, but I discovered that he didn't just steal my work…he had filed copyrights for all of my songs. He claimed rights to my creations."

"Holy fucking shit," Zander replies, his nostrils flaring as his hands form fists on his lap. "What did you do?"

"I had to hire an intellectual property lawyer and take him to court. It cost a fortune, and I had no money for that. My parents paid for everything, but we had to do something. It was every song I'd ever made out there under his bloody name."

"Fuck, what a piece of shit." He shakes his head adamantly, and I feel my blood pressure rising as I relive it all again through Zander's reaction.

"Thankfully, I won the case and got my rights back, but he still hasn't paid me any of what he's supposed to. The lawyer says I'll have to take him to collections court. It's a nightmare. Meanwhile, I'm killing myself with all these jobs to pay my parents back because they didn't ask for any of this."

"Well, neither did you, Daphney," Zander snaps, his brows creased.

"I know, but I shouldn't have been so stupid." I shake my head, feeling disgusted by myself. "I was young and naïve, and I thought I was in love. Rex made me feel so good about my talent. He encouraged me to create more songs, and it felt nice to have someone take my music seriously. Could I have been any more desperate?"

"You're weren't desperate. You were hopeful," Zander responds, sliding closer to me. He rests his hand on my thigh and squeezes it gently. "You're an artist with a dream, and you were taken advantage of. That's not your fault."

I inhale a cleansing breath. "And the worst part is, I was in love with him. I was in love with him, and he was stealing from me the entire time. Do you know how much that messes with me still? To find out that someone you care about is just using you? It's sick."

Zander's hand stills on my leg, and an unusual expression flicks across his face. He looks down at his hand on my leg as he says, "I'm sorry that happened to you."

The change in his mood is obvious, so I grab his hand and dip my head to capture his eyes with mine. "I hope you know I'm not talking about you, okay? I went into this knowing you and I are just about sex and nothing more. That's honestly what I appreciate about our situation. There are no secrets here. What you see is what you get."

"Right." Zander huffs as the muscle in his jaw tics. He clears his throat and looks into my eyes with a sheepish smile. "Well, I'm just really sorry that happened to you. It makes perfect sense why you ditched out at the pub."

I purse my lips thoughtfully. "Phoebe wants me to get over it and play my music again. I haven't even so much as hummed any of my tracks since this mess happened. They feel tainted somehow. Ruined by all his ugliness."

"You know that's stupid, right?" Zander snaps, his eyes severe on mine.

"Fuck off." I let go of his hand and frown back at him.

"I'm sorry, but it is," he says, stretching his arm around me and eyeing me sternly. "They're your words, your notes, your heart and soul. No one can ruin that for you just like no one can ruin soccer for me. We only ruin it for ourselves." He pauses for a moment and gets a serious look in his eye before he adds, "When I first came here, I told you I was struggling on the pitch. I couldn't keep up; I couldn't find my stride. And look what happened for me tonight. I played the best game of my life, and that wasn't because of superior coaching or extra training. It was because I finally got out of my own fucking way." His glossy hazel eyes flick back and forth between mine when he states, "Don't let him take more from you than he already has. Get out of your own way, Daphney."

His words have such an instant effect on me, I can't help but lean forward and press my lips to his. It's a tender touch, as I hold his face, relishing in his light scruff as my tongue gently sweeps between his lips, asking for more. His hands flatten against my back as he pulls me closer and sucks on my lower lip, a deep growl vibrating in his chest.

I reach down to grab the hem of his shirt and feel the loss of him as he pulls away, breathless with eyes hooded. He struggles for a moment before finally saying, "I didn't come here for that tonight."

"I know," I reply with a smile and move in to kiss him again.

"Seriously." He pulls back, shaking his head firmly. "I came here to be a friend, Daphney. Please, let me."

I frown back at him, confused, frustrated, and a little touched. Biting my lip, I nod slowly and back off, pulling my robe tightly around my chest. "Okay."

Zander smiles softly as he reaches over and rubs his thumb along my jaw. His eyes dip to my lips, and I swear I see regret in his eyes as he leans in and kisses my cheek gently. He lingers for a moment before pulling back and stretching his arms. "Let's watch a chick flick or something. You have any popcorn in this joint?"

The laughter that bubbles up my throat relaxes my entire body. "I think I can scrounge up some snacks."

"Great," he says, grabbing the remote off the coffee table. "You look for the snacks, and I'll find us a movie."

"Okay then," I reply, the giddiness in my voice painfully obvious as I slip off the sofa and make my way into the kitchen.

Zander Williams continues to surprise me, and if I don't watch it, he's going to burrow his way into my heart whether I like it or not.

33

Envelopes and Flowers

Zander

THERE'S A KNOT IN MY STOMACH WHEN I LOAD THE BUS EARLY Saturday morning for our match in Southampton. I spot Link and Knight in the back and make my way over to them.

"You look exhausted," Link says, hitting my fist with his as I toss my backpack into the open seat by the window.

"Thanks," I mumble, shaking my head and sitting in the aisle seat directly across from them. "I slept like shit last night."

"Why?" Knight asks, leaning back from his row. "Are you anxious about today? You killed it last week. You should still be riding that high."

I hesitate for a moment before reaching into my bag and pulling out a large envelope. "I got this in the mail yesterday."

"Shit," Link curses, staring at the envelope in my hands. He pitches his voice low as he whispers, "Are those the DNA results?"

I nod slowly. "Yeah, and I haven't opened them yet."

"Why not?" Link inquires.

"Because I don't want to fuck up my game today," I reply honestly.

The truth is, I've been playing really well the past few weeks. In matches, in training. I'm laser-focused and killing it. And when I'm not doing the plethora of soccer-related things I have to do, I'm with Daphney. This past week after she confided in me about her ex, we started hanging out more. The other night, I even sat in the pub and read until she was done with work. We're developing a real friendship. I can't say the friendship is better than the sex, because the sex is fucking exceptional, but it's been freeing to spend time with someone who isn't completely focused on soccer. Daphney is a much-needed break from the real world, which is why I was so annoyed when the envelope showed up in my mailbox. It popped this really nice bubble I've been living in.

I lick my lips and add, "I might wait until Monday to open it. I'm going to this wedding with Daphney on Sunday, and the whole Harris crew will be there. If it turns out to be a match, there's no way I'll be able to act normal around them."

"That's probably wise," Knight says, watching me carefully. "You'll have a lot to deal with if it's a match."

"But it's probably not going to be…so all this waiting will be for nothing." I force a smile I don't altogether feel as I shove the envelope back into my bag and attempt to push it out of my thoughts.

There is no need to freak out. The contents of this envelope are only going to tell me whether or not my parents lied to me my entire life. Just another Saturday, right?

I pull my hood up to avoid the prying eyes of my two teammates. Now is not the time to be thinking about this. I have a match to focus on.

Daphney

"He sent me flowers for Valentine's Day," I whisper quietly into my mobile as I lean across the sink in my loo to apply my mascara.

"What?" Phoebe squeals excitedly. "Valentine's Day was nearly a week ago. Why the bloody hell am I finding out about this now?"

I bite my lip nervously. "Because I wanted to see how the rest of the week was going to go before I told you."

"And?" Phoebe barks, clearly impatient for my next words.

"Well, it was an extraordinarily ordinary week."

"What does that mean?"

I pause my makeup application to focus on everything I'm about to unload on my best friend. I'm due at the venue in an hour for Santino and Tilly's wedding, and I still don't know what dress I'm wearing, but this sort of girl talk must be prioritized.

"It means we hung out," I state, turning on my heel and leaning against the counter in nothing but my bra and knickers. "Like, we didn't just have sex like normal. I mean, we did. My God, he did this thing with me the other night, and I swear I peed the bed."

"Been there," Phoebe laughs. "Only I really did wee the bed."

"Shut up."

"Well, there was some liquid substance. No telling what it was, and I certainly wasn't about to investigate."

I laugh at that very on-brand response from Phoebe. "But besides the shagging, we spent a lot of time together, lounging around my flat. I worked on some tracks for Commercial Notes, and he laid on my bed doing sudoku puzzles. Pretty much if we were both home, we were together. It was very strange."

"A footballer doing sudoku is what's strange. I need to see photographic evidence."

"I snapped a cheeky picture of him actually. I'll send it to you." I cover my mouth and giggle along with Phoebe.

"So, does this mean I was right, and Daphney Clarke still isn't capable of casual sex after all?"

I tsk softly. "You might be right."

"Oh, bugger."

"I know."

"You fancy him as more than a shag then?"

"I do…" I hesitate before I add the last bit. "I think I'm falling for him, Pheebs."

"Fuck me," she harrumphs, leaving no room for interpretation.

"And I'm sure he's not falling for me, so obviously I will be taking that fun fact to my grave."

"I'll kill you before I ever let you say it first."

"Thanks for that."

She pauses for a moment before asking, "Do you think he's developing feelings too?"

"I don't know." I sigh. "He had a tough match yesterday and wanted to be alone last night. It kind of stung after the week we spent together, but he assured me he'd be good as new for the wedding tonight. I'm trying not to read into it too much. Footballer or not, I won't wait around forever for him to figure out his feelings for me."

"Bravo, mate."

I nod firmly at my reflection in the mirror. After the whole Rex debacle, I thought coming to London would make me feel stronger and more independent. I thought I could reinvent myself and find a new path in life. But in reality, I'm going down the same path again. This time, the only difference is that it's the path I'm choosing regardless of what any man might think. It feels good.

"I like Zander, and if it turns into something more? Great. If it doesn't, I won't let him crush me like I did Rex."

"Good. Now…what are you wearing to this wedding today? You need to look gorgeous to bag this footballer."

"The bride needs to look gorgeous," I correct. "I need to look invisible, which is why I didn't go out and buy anything fancy."

"You should check your wardrobe," Phoebe sing-songs. "I might have popped something in there when you were working last night."

"A dress?" I exclaim, padding over to my armoire and yanking open the doors. "Oh, my God, it's perfect."

"Thank me later."

I smile into the mobile. "I owe you big time…for more than just the dress."

She scoffs. "You checked my breasts for lumps. I'd say we're even."

34

The Look of Love

Zander

W HEN I WAS A KID, MY MOM USED TO BEG ME TO CURL UP IN BED
with her and watch girlie movies. Princess movies, teen romances,
makeover flicks, dance films, a few musicals. I acted like I hated
it. I'd roll my eyes and stalk into her room like she was asking me to give
up my soul.

Confession: I fucking loved it.

We'd pig out on movie snacks, and she'd play with my hair. The sto-
rylines of these films always made me feel warm and gooey inside. And I
appreciated the fact that I always knew how they would end. Happily ever
after is wicked cheesy, but there's a lot of comfort in no surprises.

In all of those films, there was always this moment my mom called
"the look of love" moment. It's when the two main characters have been
denying their feelings for each other for the entire movie and then usually at some formal event, a charity, a ball, a school dance when we're all
on the edge of our seats, the girl walks down a giant staircase wearing a
beautiful dress. The guy looks up and sees her…boom—the look of love.

I always expected I'd experience that feeling when I was older. When
I was done with soccer and able to focus on anything other than my er-
ratic and often stressful career. I did not expect to see it while sitting at a
stranger's wedding in The Shard, London.

Daphney had to be at The Shard early for a sound check, so she lined
up Booker and Poppy to give me a ride because she didn't trust me to find
it on my own. I felt kind of childish crawling into a taxi with them, but to
be fair, Daphney wasn't wrong. It's still a struggle for me to find my way
around in London. My life here has consisted of only going places I can
run or walk to or ride in the team bus somewhere.

I'm glad I at least did that London bus tour with Daphney, or I'd be ashamed of how little I've seen of the city so far. I guess that's what happens when you start sleeping with your hot neighbor, who's also wicked cool. Not much time for other things.

The Shard is a cool glassy pyramid type of building right along the River Thames. Booker, Poppy, and I make our way up to the sixty-seventh floor and are ushered into a small room with maybe seventy-five white, cloth-covered chairs. Giant glittery gold chandeliers are hanging from the ceiling, but the room could be empty, and it'd still be stunning because of the view. On the left of the room are floor-to-ceiling windows with sweeping sights of London. The sun is just starting to set, and I'm not ashamed to admit it took my breath away.

I say hello to the entire Harris clan, and my body starts to sweat as they fold me into their seating section. I didn't play well yesterday, at all. Booker was flustered by my lack of focus, and Finney even had to save my ass at one point. There's nothing I hate more than making Finney look good. Coach Zion took me out before the half and told me to "get my head out of my arse."

I watched the rest of the game from the sidelines, feeling like a complete waste of space. Miraculously, we still won, so I can only hope I didn't fuck up my chances for starting in next week's FA Cup quarterfinal.

The sad fact is, just knowing that those DNA results are sitting in my apartment right now along with that stupid letter my mom wrote all those years ago, all while I'm sandwiched between Booker and Gareth Harris with Vaughn Harris at the end of the row situated at a wedding of one of their close family friends, is a real mind fuck.

How did I find myself not just playing alongside these people on the field but entrenched in their social lives as well? Maybe I've taken this all a bit too far? Maybe I should have never sent that hair of Vaughn's in and gone down this path because now it feels too late to turn back.

My thoughts are distracted when Tanner's wife, Belle, and Camden's wife, Indie, twirl around from their seats directly in front of me.

"What's the deal with you and Daphney?" Belle asks, her dark eyes pinning me in my seat. "This is the second time she's brought you around. It must mean something."

"We're just friends," I reply, holding my hands up because now I have an entirely different reason to sweat.

"That's how Booker and Poppy started," Indie chirps. "Look how that turned out."

"Oi," Booker whines, his gaze snapping away from his wife sitting right beside him. "Leave my teammate alone."

"Never," Belle exclaims in a shrieky whisper. "She came to your match last weekend. That must mean something, right?"

"Her friend had free tickets," I respond honestly.

"How convenient." Indie waggles her eyebrows. "Do you two hang out a lot?"

"I guess. We're friends and neighbors. It's convenient."

"Convenient for…" She licks her lips and cups her hand to her mouth as she spells out, "S-E-X."

Gareth leans forward beside me. "There are no children at this wedding, so why are we spelling the naughty words?"

"No one's talking to you, Gareth," Belle snaps and puts her hand in his face.

Gareth sits back, shaking his head and laughing as he turns to whisper something in his wife, Sloan's, ear. I can't help but laugh myself because Belle checked him with such a sisterly snipe, I'm shocked they're just in-laws. Gareth is easily the scariest of all the Harris Brothers, and Belle didn't even bat an eye. This family is truly an odd bunch.

"It was also very *convenient* for Belle to fake date Tanner when they got caught naked on a London street corner," Indie adds with a giggle.

Belle's eyes go wide. "I was not the naked one! That was just Tanner. And if we're spilling all the family secrets, let's tell Zander about you snogging Camden in the hospital when he was your *patient*."

"You encouraged it!" Indie hisses, and the two face forward and begin to quietly argue.

I briefly wonder if I started this fight when suddenly, a pianist begins playing processional music on the grand piano in the front. I frown when I see it's not Daphney but some old lady. I've been looking all over for Daphney, and I still haven't spotted her. Where is she sitting?

Everyone's gazes move to the aisle as Santino Rossi, the team lawyer, makes a couple of trips to the front row in a classic black tux. He's ushering his parents and grandparents, and the bride's parents and grandparents to their seats, taking a moment to give them lingering hugs. I haven't spoken much to Santino since that day he stopped at my apartment with the lease agreement when I first came to London. I see him in passing at the club, but he always seems a bit awkward around me, so I give him a wide berth. He's a quirky kind of guy.

He joins Mac Logan at the altar, who's also wearing a tux and a giant smile as he claps Santino on the back before wiping a tear out of his eye.

Next, Mac's wife, Freya, proceeds down the aisle, but she's not alone. She's pulling something behind her that I can't quite see until she gets to our row.

Mac and Freya's ginger-haired little baby, kitted out in a tiny tux, lays on top of a mountain of white satin fabric in the wagon. The kid can't be more than a month or two old, but his eyes are wide and fixed on the gold chandeliers above him. Freya wheels the wagon over to someone sitting off to the side and takes her place opposite Mac at the front of the makeshift altar. There's still no sign of Daphney as the pianist begins playing the instrumental version of "A Thousand Years" by Christina Perri.

Everyone rises to their feet as the bride appears at the back of the room. She makes her way down in her long white dress, her light red hair pinned back under a long veil. I look back at Santino, and the guy looks awestruck. My mom would certainly appreciate this "look of love" moment.

The ceremony begins, and we all take our seats. Daphney still hasn't appeared, so I peek at my phone to make sure she hasn't texted, and there's nothing. I'm so distracted, I barely hear them recite their own vows to each other.

Finally, the officiant of the wedding announces that Santino and Tilly will light a unity candle. That's when I finally spot Daphney. She was seated behind a giant pillar this whole time.

My eyes travel down her long black dress that hugs her curves to perfection. The straps sag off her shoulders in a goddess way, and her blonde hair is curled and pinned loosely off to one side. She looks fucking stunning.

Our eyes connect briefly as she shoots me a soft smile and bends to retrieve an acoustic guitar sitting in a stand next to the piano. After she positions the strap over her neck, she adjusts the mic slightly before strumming a light, springy intro to a song I recognize instantly as "The Book of Love." This isn't the Peter Gabriel cover that I'm familiar with. It's the Magnetic Fields cover with a unique guitar accompaniment.

When she steps forward and begins singing, all air escapes my lungs. Her face is poised and emotionless, her fingers quick and confident over the guitar strings. Her voice reverberates clearly through the speakers, and the tone takes my breath away. When she gets to the longer, drawn-out licks of the song, her voice breaks with purpose and pain. Like a raspy cry. It's a perfect mix of raw and effortless emotion. It's utterly haunting.

My palms begin to sweat as I watch her sing the melody with all her heart for this couple who have chosen to share their lives together. I quickly glance down the rows around me, noticing how all the Harris Brothers and even Vi are holding the hands of their significant others. They're all sharing in the sentiment behind the song that waxes lyrical about a book of love that's full of rules and instructions, but deep down, all that matters is the moments when you read to each other or sing to each other. It's talking about the quiet moments of love between a couple, not what we all think love is supposed to look like.

When Daphney finishes, I realize the entire room was as entranced by her as I was. We were all captivated, including the bride and groom. She offers a soft smile to Santino and Tilly before sitting back down in her secluded seat. As soon as she's out of sight, I instantly feel the loss of her. I wish I could talk to her right now. Tell her how incredible she sounded. The entire time they exchange the rings, I find myself stir-crazy in my seat, feeling trapped in with the last people in the world I want to be with right now. I don't want to be here with this family. I want to be sitting with Daphney.

Finally, the service ends, and we're ushered out of the room and down a flight of stairs into a larger reception room. It's covered with white and green floral arrangements and another sweeping view that I couldn't give a shit about. My eyes scan the space, and when I see Daphney standing at the bar with a champagne flute in her hand talking to the bartender, I ditch the Harris group and make a beeline right for her.

"Of course you look good in a suit," she says, but I ignore the compliment as I take the glass from her and set it on the bar. I lace my fingers through hers and pull her through a few tables into a small hallway where the bathrooms are.

"What's the matter?" she asks, her brows furrowed as I clutch her shoulders and position her against the wall.

My answer is to grab her face and crush my lips to hers.

She whimpers in surprise but must not mind what's happening because her hands reach up and comb through the hair on the back of my head. I arch her chin up to deepen our kiss. Our tongues dance as my hands map the back of her neck and the feminine muscle that lines her shoulders. She squeezes me tightly to her, and the sensation of her nails scoring over my scalp travels all the way to my gut as that feeling of breathlessness rushes through me again.

I feel frantic and on edge right now. I'm kissing the life out of her because I'm certain words could never express how much I love hearing her sing. She's got such a gift, such an innocent beauty to her entire being. It's all overwhelming.

When I finally pull away from her, we're both dazed, and I can feel her pulse racing, just like mine. I drag my thumb over her lower lip and pin her with a serious look. "You have to take back your songs, Daphney."

"What?" she asks, her eyes dancing between mine in confusion.

"You're too special to let your music go. I mean it. No matter what happens, please don't let this side of you go. You're more than commercial jingles. Do you hear me?"

Her lips twitch like she wants to argue, but when she sees the sincerity on my face, she nods and bites her lip. "Okay."

"Okay?" I repeat for confirmation.

"Yes." She laughs and gives me a light shove. "You're acting mental."

I lean in and press a chaste kiss to her lips. "You look fucking beautiful, too." I turn to walk her back out to the party and freeze midstride when I come face-to-face with her brother Hayden.

"Everything alright here?" Hayden asks, his eyes narrowing on me first and then moving to Daphney behind me. His gaze dips down to our hands interlocked together.

Daphney clears her throat and wraps her other hand around my elbow. "We're brilliant. Cheers, Hayden!" She pushes past her brother and attempts to drag me behind her.

I shoot Hayden an apologetic smile as I call over my shoulder, "Cheers means thanks."

The reception is a casual buffet-style, and there are no seating arrangements, so Daphney and I grab some food and find an empty table with a view.

"So is your brother going to kill me?" I inquire, eating some sort of chicken on a stick.

Daphney shrugs, her long black lashes framing her gorgeous blue eyes in a way that makes it hard to focus on what comes out of her mouth. She plays with her salad and murmurs, "Probably."

Fear niggles inside me, and apparently, it shows on my face because

Daphney starts laughing. "Would you relax? I'm an adult. What's he going to do?"

"He could evict me." I take a drink of my beer, realizing how much it would suck not to live in the same building as Daphney anymore. I've become pretty addicted to her, as it turns out.

"He's not going to evict you. I'm sure your contract with the club didn't include…no dating any neighbors." She rolls her eyes and takes a bite of her salad.

"He could corner me later tonight and ask me what my intentions are." I watch her for a moment as she finishes chewing and dabs at her lips.

"What are your intentions?" she asks, as she lifts her stunning blue eyes to mine. There's a vulnerability in them that feels like a sharp punch to the gut. "This past week has felt quite a bit different than the casual sex arrangement we originally concocted, don't you think?"

I set my drink down and place my elbows on the table to lean in closer to her. "What do you want this to be?" I ask honestly because if there's one thing I've learned this week, it's that I don't want to lose Daphney.

She bites her lip nervously, and that little dimple on her chin emerges. "I asked you first."

I smile because that dimple means she answered my question without even saying a word. And the fact that I'm not terrified of what she's thinking is a new and different experience for me. Maybe it's time I try something new. I resume eating my kabob and mumble around a bite, "Fine."

She frowns at the food in my hand. "Fine, what?"

"Fine, I'll be with you." I look at her as I take another bite.

Her brows knit together in the middle with an angry sort of expression. "What the bloody hell does that mean?"

"I'll be in a relationship with you." I lick my lips and waggle my eyebrows at her.

"Are you joking right now?" Daphney snaps, sitting back in her chair and crossing her arms. "After all those rules and weeks of doing what we're doing, you think you can just change things like that?"

I set my chicken down and wipe my hands on my napkin. "Yeah. Why not? I like you."

"He likes me." She laughs and shakes her head, looking off into the distance with an exasperated growl as she takes a sip of her champagne before adding, "What makes you think I even want to be in a relationship with you?"

She looks like she either wants to claw my face off or kiss me. And I'm seriously banking on the latter. I reach over and turn her to face me. "Do you like me?"

Her lips purse together as her eyes drop to my lips. "I don't like you right now."

"Liar," I whisper before pressing a soft kiss to her lips. When I pull back, the corners of her mouth twitch into a smile that she's trying and failing to hide. God, she's so fucking cute when she pretends to be mad. "We have something good here, and you know it, Ducky. Just trust me."

The heated look in her eyes is all the answer I need, but we're yanked out of our little heart-to-heart by a voice in the distance.

"Daphney, you sounded absolutely beautiful," Tilly says in a strong Scottish accent as Daphney stands up to accept a hug from the bride. "I think I cried the whole time you sang."

"She did." Santino chuckles and leans in to hug Daphney as well. "My nonna even said you sounded like an angel, and she does not pass out compliments easily."

"Oh, it's no problem," Daphney replies, waving off their praise like usual. "I was thrilled to be a part of your special day. Tilly, I'm not sure you've met Zander."

"I have heard so much about you from Santino," Tilly states, reaching out to shake my hand. "You're a dead-brilliant sweeper for Bethnal Green. Well done."

I laugh and wince slightly. "Could have done better yesterday."

"Everyone has an off day," Santino says, shaking my hand next. "It's good to see you again, Zander."

"You too, Santino. Congratulations."

"Thank you." Santino glances over at Tilly as she continues chatting with Daphney. "I can honestly say I never thought this day would come."

"Probably true for most grooms, eh?" I chortle and elbow him playfully.

He turns his attention back to me and stares intently at my face. "You seem to be fitting in well with...*everyone*." His laugh is awkward, and my brows furrow at his odd choice of phrasing.

"I guess you could say that." I shrug and watch him speculatively. "You hooked me up with a pretty good neighbor." Daphney glances over at me briefly, and I shoot her a wink.

Santino watches me for a moment before saying, "Well, I'm glad you're settling into Bethnal Green okay. I wasn't so sure when you first arrived. But now I feel pretty good."

"Why weren't you sure?" I ask, my eyes narrowing on him curiously.

His face falls briefly before he quickly plasters on a smile. "Oh, just… the American in London thing. You know."

I clock the tense look in Santino's eyes, but our focus is diverted when the DJ calls the bride and groom out to the dance floor for their first dance. Santino and Tilly hurry away, and I try to shake off the odd exchange as Daphney and I watch them drift across the dance floor.

Santino said a lot of odd things to me in a short amount of time, but the ones I can't help but replay are, *"I never thought this day would come."*

Do any men see the women they fall for coming? I certainly didn't picture myself at a wedding with Daphney when I first hit on her at Old George. I didn't see myself developing real feelings for her either. But now, she's become a regular fixture in my life over here. The thought of losing her is something I cannot even fathom. And if being her boyfriend is how I can keep hold of her, then I will be the best boyfriend I can be.

"Okay, lovebirds. It's time to get this party started!" Vi exclaims, shuffling over to our table at the end of the song. She grabs Daphney's hand. "Come on, we need some young blood out there to show the old buggers how to dance properly!"

"How perfect," Daphney squeals and reaches back to drag me along behind her. "Zander is a self-proclaimed excellent dancer. Moves like Jagger, isn't it?"

I glare at Daphney's sarcastic tone as we join Santino, Tilly, Mac, and Freya on the dance floor. Feeling fancy, I spin both Daphney and Vi around a few times before Hayden walks toward me with a somber look on his face.

"I'm trusting you with my sister, Zander." He narrows his eyes at me and reaches out for Vi's hand as he pulls her close and begins spinning her away. "But not my wife."

We exchange a look over the shoulders of our partners that leaves no room for interpretation. Something along the lines of, *"Break my sister's heart, and I'll break your bloody neck."*

Message received, I think to myself as I spin Daphney away from me for a moment.

The dance floor fills up quickly when all four of the Harris Brothers with their wives join in. Everyone is animatedly busting a move in their own unique way, and I find myself having a genuinely good time. It's easy with Daphney in my arms.

I pull her in close and murmur in her ear, "So, are we official then? Are you going to start calling me your boyfriend now?" I sing the last bit at the end like the mature adult I am.

Daphney glares up at me. "That depends. Are you going to call me your girlfriend?"

I purse my lips together and nod. "But I prefer sweetheart." We stop moving as I cup her face and press my lips to her forehead. I linger for a moment, breathing in the scent of her and finding myself amazed that I could ever be this happy with a woman.

A soft sigh escapes her lips as she lays her head on my chest. "Don't break my heart, Zander."

Her words hit me like a ton of bricks when I realize that being in a relationship with her isn't just fun and games. It's a responsibility that I want to be good enough for. My dad cherished my mom. They were each other's person. I want to build that with Daphney.

Everyone begins cheering around us when the music shifts to the infamous *Dirty Dancing* song, "Time of My Life." I look at Daphney with a giant smile.

"It's destiny," I say, gripping her hips to mine as I begin to lead her in a salsa step. "This movie was one of my mom's favorites. And now I don't have to behave myself because we're not hiding our relationship from people."

"You absolutely have to behave yourself," she states, staring down at our hips swiveling together.

"Why? They're not." I point over at Gareth, Camden, Tanner, and Booker, who are all in the process of trying to do the big lift at the end of *Dirty Dancing*. The one when Baby runs into Johnny's arms, and he deadlifts her over his head. Their wives want nothing to do with it, so Tanner is trying to lift Camden, and Booker is trying to get Gareth to lift him, and they are all failing miserably. Finally, they bring in Mac because he's apparently the strongest, and if Tanner and Camden both stand on either side of him and Gareth braces Mac on his back, they can all lift Booker up together. Their wives are all standing at the edge of the dance floor, cringing and laughing along with Santino and Tilly.

They're just about to make their move as Booker begins a slow jog toward Mac's outstretched hands when Vaughn barrels between them and stops Booker in his tracks. He shakes his finger at Booker and Camden, telling them to stop acting like idiots before they injure themselves and sabotage their season. He then looks at Mac, Gareth, and Tanner like they should know better.

Tanner apparently takes that as an opening for him to attempt to deadlift Gareth since they aren't still professional athletes. The two collapse onto the ground in a heap after a massive failed attempt. Booker and Camden help them up, and the four of them are gesticulating wildly as they try to figure out where they went wrong and gear up for another attempt. Tanner even begins stretching.

"Do you trust me?" I murmur into Daphney's ear before spinning her out and away from me.

"What?" she asks, as her eyes blink curiously back at me.

I nod and slowly walk backward, giving us more space. "Do you trust me?"

"To do that?" She points at the guys who are still dusting themselves off. "Absolutely not."

"Come on, Ducky. It's my party trick."

"It's not mine," she exclaims, propping her hands on her hips. "No way. If professional footballers can't manage it, then I certainly can't either."

"Just trust me," I state it again and hold my hands out to her, nodding.

She bites her lip and wrings her hands in front of her, but I can see the uncertainty slowly melt away. She looks at me with that spark of confidence in her eye that I noticed the first time we met.

"Don't make me regret this, Soccer Boy," she says, slipping off her heels and tossing them to the side. The girls notice that we're gearing up for something big, and they begin catcalling out to the two of us.

The music crescendos up to the big finish at the end just as she runs straight at me and launches herself into my arms. I grip her hips and push her straight up. Her legs are bent at first as she holds my arms and squeals nervously. But then she relaxes and straightens her legs and hands out and holds the pose for a couple of seconds. The entire wedding erupts, cheering us on from the tables and the dance floor before she collapses and falls into my arms.

She laughs into my neck as her hands hold tight to my shoulders. Her euphoria is infectious as I grip her waist and brush the hair away from her face.

"I can't believe we did that," she squeals before turning around to embrace the females coming over to congratulate us.

"I can't either actually," I reply with a laugh. I've only ever done that once, and it was with my best friend's little sister at a college, and there was a lot of alcohol involved. Nice to know I still got it.

The guys all clamor around and begin firing questions at me about the technique and how I pulled it off. It's a bizarre feeling because once again, I'm surrounded by people who might not just be friends...they could very well be much, much more.

35

Marisa's Song

Daphney

KISSES OUTSIDE…
    in the taxi…
    on the stairs…
in the hallway.
Kisses outside of my door…
inside my door…
in my kitchen.
Kisses by my bed.

My skin tingles with endless kisses Zander places over every inch of my body as he slowly removes my clothes and brushes his lips upon all my newly exposed parts. When he removes his suit, I do the same. Relishing in the warm ripples of his muscles and his heartbeat thrumming wildly beneath his chest.

He lays me gently down on my bed, still kissing, always kissing. Kissing like he can't get enough of me, and I can't get enough of him.

Zander moves to grab a condom, and I grip my legs around his hips and hold him to me. "I'm on the pill," I say, staring up at him.

He frowns down at me, a halo of golden light surrounding him and making this moment seem even more like an out-of-body experience. "Are you sure?"

I nod. "I trust you."

His eyes dip to my lips, and we're kissing again. Soft, sweet, tender kisses as his erection brushes over my bare center. I reach down and position it between my legs, desperate to connect us on a deeper level.

Zander stops kissing me long enough to gaze into my eyes as he pushes every single inch inside me. I inhale, my breath suspended in my chest as I allow our eyes to remain locked on one another. I'm certain I've never felt this close to a man in my life.

Zander and I may have started off casual, but I know him, and he knows me on a deep, credulous level. It is that trust that makes this moment more special and more real.

I thought I'd been in love before. I thought I knew what love was and could identify it immediately.

I was dead wrong.

I stroke my hands up and down Zander's spine as he moves inside me slowly, lyrically, like he's taking note of every sensation and committing it to memory. His lips pepper kisses on my breasts and my neck as I brand this night into my heart as well. This night when I sang a song to a man I was falling for. This night when I opened my heart up to someone, and he accepted it in his own unique way. This night when I felt inspired to take my life back and create my own destiny.

The words are on the tip of my tongue, but I hold them back. It's too soon. I don't want to scare him away. It's good enough to think them for now as he moves inside me, pushing me closer and closer to climax with each ragged breath that dances between us.

Orgasms aren't just tied to good sex. They're tied to feelings and emotions. They're tied to your mind and the connection you feel with someone. Zander wasn't someone I thought would inspire this in me. It just goes to show you that destiny is the true driver of life.

"I want you to come in me, Zander," I husk, my voice ragged as he sucks on my nipples. Heat is building in my center already as I struggle to hold off my climax.

"Sweetheart," Zander murmurs against my flesh before his eyes snap to mine. The look of sheer vulnerability in them is breathtaking. "Are you sure?"

"Yes," I cry, my hips swiveling up to meet his thrusts. "I'm so close, Zander. Come with me."

"You feel too good," he grunts, his face looking tortured for a moment as his head hangs above me, shaking side to side. "I don't think I can stop."

"I don't want you to."

"Daphney." He says my name like a plea, looking down at our bodies.

"Zander," I state, tipping his chin up to lock eyes with me. "Look at me."

His eyes are devastating as he connects with my gaze. My lips part as I expel a silent cry, and both of our bodies freeze as we climax together in perfect harmony, my release milking his drop for drop. It's the most erotic, soul-changing experience I've ever had, and I immediately commit it to memory to hold onto forever.

Finally, Zander collapses on top of me. Our bodies are slick with sweat as they rise and fall in unison, struggling to catch our lost breaths. He softens slightly between my legs, and it's a heady sensation to feel his release drip out of me.

"Fuck, let me get you a washcloth," Zander says, pulling out of me and leaving me naked and bereft on the bed without him.

He's got that adorable, crooked smile when he returns, his cock still showing signs of life as he lowers the cloth and wipes gently between my legs. It's tender and sweet.

He smiles and shakes his head. "I've never done that with anyone before."

"Me neither," I giggle, feeling embarrassed and exhilarated all at the same time.

He finishes and holds the cloth up. "Where should I put this?"

"There's a wash bin in the loo."

He retreats to the bathroom, and as he's in there cleaning himself up, a euphoria tingles in my body. Feeling inspired, I pad over to my guitar and grab it off its stand, bringing it back to the bed with me. I sit cross-legged at the foot, holding it in front of my naked breasts. The lacquered wood is cool against my nipples as I begin to play a few chords to a song I haven't touched in quite some time.

I lose myself for a moment as I familiarize my mind with the melody. I look up when I see Zander walking back toward the bed. His eyes are focused on me as he sits down and props himself up against the headboard, covering himself with the sheet.

"Don't stop, please," he urges, his eyes glistening in the dark.

I smile softly and continue, taking in a deep breath before I say, "This is Marisa's song."

His eyebrows lift. "Your sister?"

I nod thoughtfully. "It's called 'Face in the Breeze.'"

Emotions course through my veins as I begin the first verse.

Was that you just now
Touching my face in the breeze?
Did you hear my call
As I was down on my knees?
It felt just like
The times we fight
But I know you want for me
To be happy

Was that you just now
Touching my face in the breeze?
If you could see me now
Would you like what you see?
Sometimes I fear
I'll never know
But I know you want for me
To be happy

Breezes feel so sweet
But they can pack a sting
Like in a storm

Every now and then
It's a salty breeze
And it burns.

All I wish, is to know
If you're happy?

All I wish, is to know
Are you happy?

I strum the last line and look up, shocked to see tears falling down Zander's face. I gasp and swing my guitar off my body and place it on the bed before crawling over to him. "Are you okay?" I ask, wrapping my hands around his arm.

He nods, his body trembling beneath the sheet. "I'm fine."

"You're not fine. What is it?" I drag my thumb along his tearstained cheeks. "Is it your dad?"

He expels a garbled noise and shakes his head. "Yeah, I guess so."

I inwardly chastise myself for selecting that song of all my songs. So stupid of me when it hasn't been that long since he lost his father. "I'm sorry, I shouldn't have played that one."

"No, Daphney. It was beautiful," he says, grabbing my hands and gripping them between us. "I actually…" He clears his throat harshly. "It made me think about my dad a lot." He wipes away the tears in his eyes but more dampen his cheeks. "This is a weird thing to say, but…I never cried after he died."

I frown, staring at him in the dark. "What?"

He inhales a deep breath. "I was too busy planning the funeral and taking care of my mom. And then I was playing soccer in Seattle still, and fuck, I don't know. Somewhere in dealing with all that shit, I just… blocked out the pain."

I swallow the knot in my throat as his tormented face tears through me. "I know how you feel."

"You do?" Zander asks, his voice guttural as he gazes at me with questions I'm not entirely sure I have the answers to.

But maybe it's not answers he needs. Maybe he just needs understanding.

I steel myself before I continue, "As the youngest of my family, I was so protected when Marisa died that I was literally shielded from so much of the pain everyone was going through in the aftermath. It was like they couldn't trust that I could handle Theo's PTSD or Hayden's thoughts of suicide because he couldn't stop blaming himself for Marisa's death. My mum and my dad surrounded me with quietness, and it made me crazy because I wanted to sit in the pain. Wallow in it. I wanted to talk about her, remember her. Acknowledge the loss of her. It's been ten years, and they still try not to bring up Marisa's name around me because they don't want to upset me."

"It sounds like they love you," Zander says, his voice wobbly.

"I know they do," I reply honestly. "And I respect that they are grieving in their own unique way. But I also needed to grieve in my own way. Phoebe and I talk about Marisa a lot. Sometimes it's sad, but usually, it's funny. Talking about her helps preserve my memories. I want her to still be a part of my life." I lace my fingers through Zander's and ask, "Can you tell me more about him?"

"About my dad?" Zander croaks, his voice rising in surprise.

I nod slowly. "Yeah, why not?"

"I'm too emotional to talk." He scrubs his hands over his face and shakes his head with disgust.

"That's okay." I press myself up beside him and lean my head on his shoulder. "Marisa hated fish but loved to fish in my parents' pond. She could never do it without one of my brothers there to take the fish off the hook."

Zander's chest vibrates with a soft laugh before he inhales a deep, trembling breath. "My dad was a terrible soccer player."

"Really?" I giggle and look up at him. "Where did you get it then?"

His brows knit together as he blinks up at the ceiling. "I'm not sure, but his lack of skill never stopped him from dribbling a ball around with me. I honestly think him being so terrible gave me wicked confidence."

"That's sweet." I smile and continue watching him as I ask, "What was he good at?"

"He was a sudoku puzzle master," Zander says with a playful lilt to his tone that makes my heart happy.

"So, that's where your hobby comes from." I tighten my grip around his arm and glance at the puzzle book he left on my end table earlier this week.

Zander smiles and nods. "He made me download this app where we could race each other on the same puzzles. We'd do it a lot when I was on the road for soccer."

"Who would win?"

"Mostly him." Zander laughs. "Once in a while, I'd beat him, and then he would tell me it was because he didn't have his glasses on, or my mom was distracting him."

"Competitive bloke then?"

"Oh, yes…and proud. Crazy proud."

"Proud of what?" I ask, staring at our hands interlocked together and cherishing the intimacy of this moment.

"He was proud of me." Zander's voice cracks, and I look up to see his face bending with a pained smile. "I never doubted his pride in me. Or his love."

My eyes well with tears as I watch him unpack that realization fully. "Your dad sounds lovely."

"He was." The muscle in Zander's jaw tics. "I miss him every day."

I kiss Zander's shoulder, remaining silent as I watch him because I don't think he's talking to me right now.

"He was so easy to love. And he was just one of those good guys who was selfless in all things."

I nod and see flashes of my sister. She was easy to love too. Warm and bright. Silly and forgiving. I idolized her and am to a point now where I'm grateful to have had the time I did have with her. I hope someday Zander can feel that way about his father, too.

Zander tucks his fingers under my chin and raises my face to look at him. "Thank you for tonight."

"For making you cry?" I reply with a laugh. "Oh, anytime."

He shakes his head. "Not just for tonight…just…thank you for being the one thing I can count on right now."

My brows puzzle over that bizarre response. I open my mouth to ask what he means, but he leans forward and presses a tender kiss to my lips. I taste the salt of his tears as he pulls away and murmurs, "Now can we please go to sleep? After unloading all that baggage, I just want to fall asleep with you in my arms."

"Of course," I respond as we shift down into the bed, situating the covers over top of us.

I lay across Zander's chest, and he kisses the top of my head and exhales a sigh that feels like it weighs a million pounds. I look up at him and say, "You should definitely talk about him more."

Zander nods, his eyes already closed as he mumbles, "I will."

I relish in the feel of his heartbeat beneath my palm and am shocked when only moments later, he's sound asleep.

36

Better On My Own

Zander

I WAKE TO THE SOUND OF DISTANT KNOCKING AND AM DISORIENTED FOR a moment before realizing that I'm not in my own bed. I'm in Daphney's bed, currently wrapped around her like she's my own life-sized teddy bear. Well, this is certainly new for me.

Gently, I remove my arm from her naked waist and pull the cover up over her shoulder before rolling onto my back. Jesus, what was that last night? Did I fucking cry in front of my new girlfriend on night one? *Girlfriend*…that's new for me as well.

Not that I've never had a girlfriend, but it's been a while. A long while. I turn my head and watch the slow rise and fall of Daphney's shoulders and can't help but smile. She's everything I never realized I needed. She's comforting and funny, heartfelt and challenging. It was easy to fall for her. I could use a little easy in my life.

In the background, my eyes catch sight of her guitar, and a wave of sadness hits me all over again. Listening to Daphney sing last night broke that dam inside me that I've been fighting with for the better part of a year. She looked like an angel with her guitar in front of her naked body. And her voice melted away all the hard parts of me that have calcified since my dad passed away.

I was finally able to grieve him last night. Miss him. My eyes sting with tears again, and I wipe away the dampness in them. For fuck's sake, what is my deal? I've gone the past year unable to shed a single tear over the loss of him, and one song from Daphney has unearthed a fucking spigot inside my body. I need to get my shit together.

The knocking sound from earlier resumes, and I hear the familiar voice of Link call out, "Come on, dude, the coffee is getting cold."

"I'll call his phone," Knight's voice murmurs a bit more quietly.

I cringe at how loud they sound out there. These walls really are paper thin. Thankfully, Daphney isn't moving a muscle. She must be exhausted after I basically had an emotional meltdown in front of her and then begged her to cuddle with me. She probably slept like shit worrying about the psychopath in her bed.

I quietly shift out of bed and slip my boxers on before grabbing my keys and vibrating phone off the counter. I pad barefoot out into the hallway and open Daphney's door to find both Knight and Link standing in front of mine. Their eyes swerve over to me, and they open their mouths to say something, but I press my finger over my lips. "Shut up. She's still sleeping," I whisper as I close her door behind me.

"You spent the night?" Link whisper-shouts.

I roll my eyes and gesture for them to follow me into my place. I unlock the door and stand back to let them in. "You still have to keep your voices down. You can hear a pin drop through these walls."

Link points at the wall that separates Daphney's and my apartment. "Why were you sleeping over? I thought you said one of your rules was no sleepovers."

"It's none of your business," I snap, my jaw taut with irritation because I have enough to unpack in my fucking head, I don't need to worry about Link's and Knight's opinion about my relationship status with Daphney. I stand in front of my dining room table and cross my arms over my chest. "What are you guys doing here?"

"We thought you might need moral support when you open the envelope," Knight says as he sets down the coffee carrier on the kitchen counter. "We brought coffee."

I laugh and rub the sleep out of my eyes. "You think coffee is going to lessen the sting of what's in that envelope?"

Knight shrugs and pins me with a look. "I don't think anything will, man."

I chew my lip nervously and grab the envelope on the table behind me. It feels heavier than it ever has before. I tap it on the palm of my hand. "I think I've decided not to open it."

"What?" Link asks, walking over to me. "You're joking, right?"

I shrug and shake my head. "I don't think I want to know the truth."

"You said you did," Knight offers, his eyes narrowing on me in challenge.

"Well, that was before…"

"Before what?" Link asks.

"Before…I don't know. Before I made a life here maybe? I just feel differently now." I drop the envelope back on the table and stride over to my dresser. I throw on a white T-shirt and turn to look at my two friends. "I don't think I need to know."

Knight hits me with a look. "I think you do."

"You were team ignorance is bliss before," I retort. "What's changed?"

Knight's eyes look grave on me. "You need closure, man. Your head wasn't in the game on Saturday. This is why."

I roll my eyes. "Don't spit out more sports psychobabble on me."

"It's not sport psychology. It's just common sense," Knight snaps, his nostrils flaring with irritation. "That envelope is going to haunt you the same way that letter haunts you."

I hesitate with how to respond next because deep down, I know Knight's right. This envelope is like a forbidden fruit. You have to know how it tastes because it's staring right back at you. Only I have a feeling I'm not going to like how any of this tastes.

But then I think about my dad, and losing him, and the fact that I didn't shed a fucking tear until last night with Daphney. I know why that is. I was suppressing my grief because I was focusing on the fact that my dad may have lied to me my entire life. But after pouring my heart out to Daphney, maybe I'm okay now. Maybe Daphney fixed me.

I shake my head at my two teammates, who are staring at me like I've got two heads. "Stop looking at me like that!" I snap as my frustration with the pressure they're putting on me builds. "You guys don't know how hard this is."

"Yes, we do," Link interjects, tucking his hair behind his ears and grabbing the envelope off the table. "We've watched you struggle with this since day one. Just finish the job you set out to do. You didn't use Daphney to score an invite to that Harris family dinner for nothing, right?"

"You don't know what you're talking about." My voice cracks because hearing him throw my own words back in my face is like a dagger through my fucking gut.

"Seriously!" Link exclaims, slamming the envelope against my chest. "This is your answer. This is why you took her on a double-decker bus tour—to get close enough to grab a DNA sample of Vaughn. Now you have to open this shit and deal with it, or you'll feel like you're living a lie the rest of your life."

"I already feel like I'm living a lie," I shout, my voice ringing in my ears as I slam the envelope back down on the table. "I don't even know who the fuck I am anymore. I feel like I'm lying to everybody. My mom, my manager, my teammates, my girlfriend. Hell, I even feel like I'm lying to my own father!"

"What girlfriend?" Link asks, his face contorting with confusion.

I rake my hands through my hair and look up at the ceiling, my head spinning. I don't want to talk about this with these guys. I know they mean well, but I should never have opened up about all this to them in the first place. I made the mistake of opening up to Jude in Seattle, and he's the one that got me into this fucking mess. Now I've doubled down on that mistake with these guys. Maybe telling Daphney about my dad was a mistake last night too. I'm better on my own. I always have been.

"Look, thanks for coming over, but I'm not dealing with this in front of you guys."

"Why not? We're your friends," Link barks, his voice the most serious I've ever heard.

"If you're my friends, then you will respect the fact that I need you to fucking leave." I stalk over to the door and open it up.

"You're kicking us out?" Link laughs, his face the picture of stunned.

I shake my head slowly. "Thank you for the support, but I got it from here."

Link looks over at Knight to see if he's going to argue. Knight gestures to the door.

"So much for teammates," Link scoffs once before storming past me.

When Knight reaches me at the door, I can barely make eye contact with him as he pauses directly in front of me. "It gets lonely on an island of self-loathing, my friend. Just don't forget you're the one who pushed us away."

When I close the door behind Knight, I feel sick and dirty about the mess of my life. I go from dreaming about my father, who was a good man, to questioning everything about him in the blink of an eye. And the fucker is too busy being dead to even be here to answer the millions of questions I have for him. I'm fucking lost, and I don't know what to do.

I stomp into my shower in hopes that I can wash some of this stink away and find some clarity. As the water rushes over me, I know only one person can take this pain inside me away.

Daphney.

I dress quickly and shove my phone in my pocket, damn near aching to see her again as I make my way down the hall. My brows furrow when I go to turn her doorknob and find it's locked. I thump on the door and call out her name, but there's no reply. I wiggle the doorknob again, but it won't budge.

"Daphney, are you in there?" I call through the wood and press my ear to the door to listen for the shower.

I'm met with silence, so I frown and pull my phone out of my pocket to call her. As I pull her name up, I see a text message from her.

Daphney: I thought I could trust you...I was wrong.

My stomach roils at those ominous words. What the fuck happened? What does she mean she doesn't trust me? Chills crawl over my entire body as it dawns on me. *She heard everything we said.*

"We all heard you!" the voice of Miss Kitchems calls up the stairs.

"Fuck!" I exclaim out loud and whirl around to kick the damn mouse house in the hallway. It breaks into several pieces, mirroring the swirling vortex of my insides.

"Heard that too," Miss Kitchems calls up again.

I cover my eyes, my mind a foggy mess of horror and guilt. So, so much guilt. She heard what Link said about me using her. She heard everything. I was going to tell her about all of this. I wanted to tell her. I should have told her last night.

Fucking hell! This can't be unfixable. Surely, she will understand once I explain it all to her.

I rush downstairs barefoot to see that her car is gone. Where did she go? I press call on my phone, listening to the line trill over and over again.

I thought I could trust you...I was wrong.

This is really fucking bad. And sadly, it's only the cherry on top of the shit sundae that is my life.

37

Give the Game Away

Zander

"**S**ANTINO?" I CROAK INTO THE PHONE LINE, MY FINGERS CLUTCHING tightly to the team lawyer's business card that's been sitting in my kitchen drawer since he stopped by my apartment after I arrived in London.

"Yes?" he answers, his voice ragged like he's just woken up.

"This is Zander Williams. I'm sorry to call you so soon after your wedding, but the club office said you were taking calls from players." I exhale heavily, forcing myself to loosen the grip on my phone before I break it.

It's been two days of unanswered calls from Daphney. Two days of her not showing up at her apartment and not working at Old George. And two days of me sitting in a misery of my own making. I've called in sick for training yesterday and today, and there's no way I'll be able to face the team tomorrow if I don't pull the trigger on this plan I came up with.

"It's totally fine you called, Zander. I'm not out of the country or anything. What can I do for you?" Santino asks, his voice crisp and professional.

I suck in a deep breath and say what I called to say. "I need to be transferred to a new team when the window opens up this summer," I state, my voice sounding robotic after how many times I practiced saying it out loud. "Preferably a club in London. Just not Bethnal Green or Arsenal. I don't have an agent. I just need a contract. I'll even go down to Championship League or the league below that. I don't care. I just want to stay in London and keep playing soccer."

I sigh heavily at the sound of my plan out loud. It probably sounds nuts to Santino, but if I can get away from the Harris family and forget all about that DNA shit and whether or not our hands look the fucking same, then maybe I can find a way to repair my relationship with Daphney.

I'm met with a long-drawn-out silence when finally, Santino replies, "So, your mum told you then."

My head jerks back. What the fuck does my mom have to do with any of this? Why would he know anything about my mom?

Licking my lips, I decide to play along. "Yeah, she told me."

He inhales sharply. "Look, Zander. I think we can deal with this quietly, okay? We can come up with a plan that makes everyone happy. And we can craft a story that the press will believe. We don't even have to tell Vaughn about this if you don't want to. That's up to you."

Chills erupt up my spine. "How do you know about Vaughn?"

"From when your mum called me," Santino says it like it should be obvious.

"When did she call you exactly?" I ask, my voice hollow.

"Well, probably about seven or eight months ago now." He scoffs, and I hear him rustling some papers. "I have a crisis management company that might be able to help us with this."

"What all did my mom say on this call?" I grind out through clenched teeth.

Santino exhales heavily. "Didn't she tell you all this?"

"No, Santino. My mom hasn't told me shit," I snap, my tone cutting. "I'm hoping you can enlighten me."

Santino stammers for a moment. "Then h-h-how do you know?"

I hesitate with how to respond to that because the truth is, I know nothing because I still can't bring myself to open up that damn DNA envelope. And Knight was right. The fucking thing is haunting me. It's why I want to get as far away from Bethnal Green as I can.

My jaw is taut when I reply with the truth because frankly, I've run out of lies to tell. "I found a letter my mom wrote to Vaughn Harris when she was pregnant with me telling him that I'm his son. I've known since the day I was recruited to Bethnal Green."

"Jesus Christ," Santino expels a breath.

"My question to you is, if you've spoken to my mom, how is it possible you haven't said anything to anyone yet?"

"Your mum made me sign a nondisclosure agreement," he replies tersely. "And I'm a lawyer, so I take those things seriously."

"What did she want when she called you seven months ago? And please don't lie to me. I'm done with the fucking lies."

Santino hesitates on the other end of the line.

"Just tell me," I state firmly.

His voice is grave when he responds, "She wanted me to find a way to kill your contract with the club because she was scared you'd figure out you were the son of Vaughn Harris."

My stomach roils at his response, and I have to bend over and brace myself on my knees. It's even worse than I imagined. I don't know what I imagined, honestly. My brain is a pile of mush these days, and my emotions are fried. But my mom trying to ruin my career over all of this hadn't even entered my mind.

Also…now it's out there. The confirmation I have been avoiding with all my might. Vaughn Harris is my father.

My voice is tight when I choke out, "I see."

"Zander, look. I'm in Bath with Tilly, but I can grab a train and be back in London in a couple of hours. Let's set up a meeting."

I shake my head even though I know he can't see it. "I don't need a meeting with you. I need a meeting with somebody else."

"What do you mean? I'm the one who should deal with this."

"You're wrong," I reply through clenched teeth. "My mom is who should be dealing with this."

38

Bar's Closed

Daphney

"**W**HY IS ZANDER WILLIAMS TEXTING ME ASKING WHERE YOU'RE at?" my brother Hayden growls into my mobile as I wrap silverware at Old George before we open.

"Because I haven't been to my flat in a couple of days," I reply crisply.

"Where have you been staying?"

"Phoebe's."

"What's going on?"

"Nothing, Hayden."

"Bullshit," he snaps. "Zander's texts don't seem like nothing. He says you won't take his calls, and he's been looking for you."

"I'll handle it."

"What did he do?" Hayden asks ominously. "Just tell me."

"No."

He scoffs into the line. "Why do the losers always find you, Daphney?"

"Because I'm easy prey, okay, Hayden?" I snap, my voice cracking as fresh pain rips through me for the fiftieth time today. "Because I'm a magnet for arseholes. Because I'm not good enough to find someone who can care about me in any meaningful way. Is that an answer you're looking for?"

"Daphney." Hayden's voice is pained but not as much as mine.

"Don't worry about me, Hayden. I'm fine. I'll talk to you later." I hang up, frustrated that I answered in the first place, but I wanted to make sure it wasn't something I needed to take care of at the building since I haven't been over there for a few days. Heaven forbid I let one of my responsibilities go while I'm wallowing in yet another relationship disaster. It's like déjà fucking vu all over again.

I woke up after that wedding feeling like the cat that got the cream. I swear I was even smiling in my sleep, for heaven's sake. I dreamed of Zander while he held me in his arms. My heart was so bloody full, I was making us coffee and thinking I could do this with him for the rest of my life.

Then I heard him next door talking to his teammates. I didn't think anything of it. I figured he'd be back because his suit was still on the floor of my flat.

Then I heard my name. And I heard Zander try to tell Link he didn't know what he was talking about. And then Link said something about the double-decker bus tour, and I felt sick to my stomach.

It was like I was listening to the voice of a complete stranger.

My mobile pings with a text notification, and I feel a small sense of relief when I see it's Phoebe and not another text from Zander since I've been ignoring him for three days straight.

Phoebe: Got out late from my audiobook session. Be there in twenty.

Me: You don't have to come here.

Phoebe: The fuck I don't. If that wanker tries to stop by while you're working, he's going to have to go through me first. See you soon. xx

My chin wobbles at the overprotectiveness of my best friend. I hate that she's had to pick me up off the floor the past few days. I hate that I've shed countless tears after so many countless kisses. I hate that I feel like my old self again who falls easily and blindly.

I hate Zander fucking Williams.

I lift a rack of the plastic outdoor pint glasses and carry them to the beer garden bar to restock the supply for tonight. I just need to focus on putting one foot in front of the other. Focus on my work. Focus on the task at hand.

I can see my breath in the cold as I walk behind the bar to begin transferring the glasses when a deep voice nearly startles me half to death.

"Hey, Ducky."

I gasp and almost drop the mug in my hand when I look up to see Zander sitting at the end of the bar. He's wearing his Red Sox hat faced forward and pulled low with his brown hair sprawling out from beneath it. He's also wearing just a hooded jumper even though it's freezing out here.

"Zander, what the bloody hell are you doing back here?" I ask through clenched teeth.

"Waiting for you." He licks his lips and props his hands on the bar.

"How did you get back here? We're not even open yet."

"I scaled the fence." He holds his arm up and reveals a tear in his jumper. "Caught my sweatshirt on a nail in the ivy."

"Well, that was pointless because I don't want to see you." I pick up the rack of pint glasses and move to go back inside.

Zander sprints around me and braces his hands on either side, blocking me in. "I need to explain," he says, and I can't help but note the dark circles under his eyes.

"You don't need to explain," I state firmly as I slam the glasses down on the bar and zip my coat up to my chin like it'll somehow protect me from him. "I heard everything perfectly clearly. Like you said, the walls are paper thin."

He hesitates for a moment, so I make a move to leave again, and his hand reaches out to touch my waist to stop me. The warmth of his palm may as well have been a hot branding iron through my coat. It hurts so bloody much.

"Don't touch me," I snap, my jaw tight as I back away from him. "Don't touch me. Don't talk to me. Just leave me alone, okay? I understand the bit. You needed me to get to Vaughn Harris. I don't know the particulars, but I heard enough."

"You get what I was doing, right?" he asks, his voice hoarse, his eyes wide and red-rimmed. "I was trying to figure out if Vaughn Harris is my fucking father."

"Oh, I got that." I laugh and shake my head, crossing my arms tightly over my chest. "So, you flirted with me, and took me on a bus tour, and made nice with me, slept with me even...all to score an invite to a Harris Sunday dinner so you could extract DNA from Vaughn Harris. Did I get everything?"

Zander blinks back at me. "Yes."

"Great, then there's nothing more that needs to be said. You accomplished your mission. Well done, you." My stomach lurches at being so close to him again and hating him this much. It's an awful, awful feeling.

"This isn't over between us, Daphney," Zander says, his voice raw. "We can get past this."

"No, we can't!" I laugh back at him. "This isn't something I can get past."

He dips his head so he can hit me with a lethal glare. "You don't think what I'm dealing with is maybe a slightly bigger deal than me not telling you about this?"

"Oh no, I do." I nod thoughtfully. "Good luck deciding if you're going to open that envelope. Sounds like a real nail-biter."

Zander's nostrils flare. "I'm glad you think my life's such a fucking joke."

"I don't think your life is a joke," I exclaim, my tone acidic as I step into his space. "In fact, I thought the *father* you described to me sounded very real. I loved the stories you told me about him. I could almost picture him, you described him so perfectly. But now I can't be sure who you were actually describing."

"That's…my dad, Jerry," Zander sputters, his emotions all over his face.

"So, did Jerry really die? Or is he alive and well?" My words are cruel and hurtful, but the pain inside me is louder than my empathy.

"Yes. Fuck, who the fuck do you think I am, Daphney?" Zander cries, his voice garbled with emotion that I cannot sympathize with right now because I'm too hurt.

"I don't know who you are, Zander! I thought that I was with a guy who would tell me about a very, very big thing happening in his life. Like questioning who his real father is. I know his teammates knew. They knew far more than I did. Guess that's football for you, eh? Never mind that I let you make love to me. Why on earth would I deserve to know about a possible genetic link to the manager of your football club? Too minor of a detail to share with a girlfriend, clearly."

"You were my girlfriend for less than twenty-four hours!" Zander hollers, the veins on his neck bulging angrily.

"And there it is," I bite, my voice shrieking at the end. "The truth of your feelings. I told you things. I opened up to you about my sister, my family, my ex. We had been more than just casual sex for weeks now and screw you for tricking me into feeling like I was safe in that."

Tears slip down his cheeks as he yanks his hat off, giving me a full daylight view of the devastating pain in his eyes. He looks broken and hollow, and a part of me wants to comfort him. To forgive him. But I've come too far in my life to let another man manipulate and use me again. I deserve better.

"What do you want from me, Daphney?" he cries, his voice weak. "I'm sorry, okay? I should have told you. I was going to tell you. I just… couldn't find the words."

"You couldn't find the words, and I can't find forgiveness." My chin wobbles, and tears sting my eyes as that painful reality sinks in. I was so stupid to think Zander was different. I was so silly to believe that he could be better than the other men in my life. That he could even be the one. My God, I'm a fool. He's standing in front of me asking what I want from him, and it should be glaringly obvious after everything we've shared the past several weeks.

This moment right here has to be goodbye. If I let him back into my life for even a minute longer, I will not recover when it inevitably all ends. And I refuse to let another man ruin my life.

My voice is determined when I step forward and hit him with the hard truth of it all. "The last guy blindsided me when I discovered he was using me for my music. Now you used me for my connection to the Harris family, and I was blindsided all over again. It's clear that I'm the common denominator in both these scenarios." My voice breaks at the painful realization that it's not just Zander I can't trust. It's me. It's me that I can't depend on. I thought I knew Zander. I thought he cared for me. I was wrong and naïve. So, so naïve. I shake off that pain and add with finality, "I can't trust my heart. And I can't trust you."

I make a move to walk past him, and his voice is pleading when he says, "Daphney, please. Don't walk away from this."

I inhale sharply and pin him with a look that reflects the self-awareness in my soul. "I may not need to hire a lawyer to get you out of my life, but I promise that I will forget you ever existed, Zander Williams."

39

Next Plane to London

Zander

"You're here," Link says, as he walks into the locker room to find me changing into my practice gear.

"Where else would I be?" I grumble, tying my shoelaces with a healthy dose of anger that I've let replace my pain since that epic fight with Daphney yesterday.

Link sits down beside me as Knight walks in next. He stops in front of me and glares, his face expressing zero emotion. "You missed three trainings."

I shrug. "Had shit to deal with."

"So did you do it?" Link asks, his eyes wide with worry. "Did you read the results?"

I shake my head. "I'm going to do what I should have done in the first place."

"What's that?" Link inquires.

"I'm going to get the truth from my mother." I glance up at Knight whose brows flicker curiously. "She's on a flight right now and should be here by the time we're done with practice."

Knight lowers himself onto the bench across from me. "And then what?"

"And then, we'll see." I lower my foot to the ground and sit back in my cubby. "The only thing I do know is I won't be playing for this club anymore."

"What?" Knight and Link both ask in unison.

I nod seriously. "I can't do it, no matter what the truth is. Too much shit has gone down."

"What do you mean?" Link asks, his jaw dropped in horror.

I shrug. "Daphney knows I used her to get to Vaughn. She heard our entire fucking conversation through the wall."

"Shit. I'm so sorry, Z." Link tucks his hair behind his ears. "I should have never said anything."

I shake my head firmly. "It's not your fault. It's my fault. This entire fucked-up mess is all my fault. I've been lying to everyone around me, including you guys. I told you Daphney and I were just casual, and even that was a damn lie. I knew I was in love with her the minute I looked up into the stands and saw her at that Arsenal game in a Bethnal Green fucking sweatshirt. I knew it, and I still wasn't honest with her. I wasn't even honest with myself. My dad would be ashamed of me. And those were words I never thought I'd say."

I stand and make a move to head out of the locker room, but Knight reaches up and grabs my arm, turning me around to look at him. "So that's it. You're just going to cut and run?"

I nod slowly. "I'll finish out the season and transfer when the window opens up. I need a fresh start."

"And your mom?"

I exhale heavily. "She has a lot to answer for. And I'm going to try to listen because honestly, the apple clearly doesn't fall far from the tree."

"Don't be so hard on yourself," Knight says, his jaw taut. "You weren't alone in this crazy plan. We were there at the start, and we'll be there at the finish."

I nod and squeeze Knight's arm gratefully before walking out of the locker room. When I turn the corner to head to the practice field, a voice calls out to me, "Zander!"

I tense and force myself to play it cool when I turn on my heel to face Vaughn. He closes the distance between us, his steely-blue eyes severe on me. "Missed three days of training, son. How are you?"

"Food poisoning, but I'm fine now," I reply gruffly. What's another lie at this point?

"You look a little rough still." He eyes me seriously, his face bending with sympathy. "This wouldn't have anything to do with what's going on between you and Daphney, would it?"

"What?" I jerk back in confusion. "How do you—?"

"Hayden mentioned something to me," Vaughn says, sighing heavily. "Do you want to talk about it?"

"Absolutely not," I snap, my tone bordering on disrespectful.

What is it with this fucking family? Why is everyone in each other's business all the damn time? Daphney's not even a member of the Harris family, and they still have to get involved in her fucking life? And why the hell did Daphney's brother have to tell Daddy Harris shit that has nothing to do with him? This is why I need to get away from this family.

Vaughn watches me carefully for a moment before reaching out to touch my shoulder. "You know, son…"

"I really should go warm up," I state in a hurry, cutting him off because the last thing I need is paternal vibes coming from this man right now. "I'll be good for Saturday, I swear."

Vaughn nods slowly, silently dismissing me. My cleats clack on the concrete as I make my way out onto the field and hope that Coach Zion has an extra dose of sadism for me today. I sure as fuck need it.

My muscles are jelly as I trudge home in the cold London air. A text from my mom after practice said she was in a cab and on her way to Old George, where I told her to meet me. I wanted to have this conversation in public because I need my mom to keep it together long enough to give me answers. And frankly, I'm not ready to invite her into my apartment. My life here in London feels like something she doesn't deserve to be a part of yet, especially if a lot of what Santino said turns out to be true. I know that it's possible Daphney will be there. A part of me wants her to be, and a part of me doesn't.

I don't know where I stand with her, honestly. It's clear she wants nothing to do with me, but now I sort of wonder if I'm better off without her. At first, I wanted to stay in London so I could slowly win back her trust, but deep down, I'm disappointed in her too. The fact that she can't extend me even a modicum of grace through a very hard ordeal cuts me deep. It was so easy for her to throw me away after one mistake. Maybe Vaughn Harris would have chosen to throw me away as well if my mother ever sent him that letter.

When my mom confirms what I already know to be true today, what will the rest of the Harris family even think? Odds are they aren't going to take kindly to a guy who infiltrated their group under the guise of a friend and teammate, only to be duping them the entire fucking time. I sure as fuck wouldn't welcome that guy with open arms.

I handled this entire scenario so fucking wrong. And Daphney was my one saving grace. My safe space. She was the one person in my life I could count on and now…she's dumped me without a second thought.

As I step into the familiar pub of Old George, my eyes instantly go to the bar in search of her. I can't help it. It's a fucking habit of the heart that will take some time to break.

Hubert looks up from what he's doing and offers me a slight wave. Even he looks like he hates me. My eyes scan the rest of the pub, and in the corner, I spot her…the woman who gave birth to me.

"Hey, buddy!" my mom croaks as she rises out of her chair and waves at me.

She looks smaller than I remember. Her short brown hair is still the same blunt bob cut it has been for the better part of a decade, but her frame seems to have shrunk since I last saw her. And she looks like she's aged several years.

"Hey, Mom," I say, walking over to her and hunching down to give her a hug.

She trembles in my arms, and I hear her choking back a cry. "I can't believe I'm here in London. I haven't been here since before you were born."

We part, and I offer her a half-smile. "I can't believe it either." I remove my backpack and gesture for her to sit back down. "Can I get you a drink?" I ask, struggling to make eye contact. "I have to order it at the bar."

"Um, I'll do a coffee if they have that here."

I nod and retreat to the bar to get two cups of coffee and a small jug of cream for my mom. My hands are trembling when I walk back over with them, feeling her eyes on me the entire time.

"Is it possible you've grown since Christmas?" She laughs, but it's weak.

I push the mug and cream in front of her. "They train me pretty hard over here."

"Clearly," she says, staring at my arms. "Your coat barely fits you anymore."

"It fits okay," I reply, staring down at my coffee.

She makes a little sing-songy noise in her throat. "Are you going to tell me why I'm here? I was worried you were injured, but you seem okay to me."

I shake my head and force myself to look into her eyes. They're a lovely shade of brown. My dad's were green. I always thought my hazel eyes were a combination of the two of them. I guess that thought would be wrong.

Steeling myself, I begin to have the conversation I should have had with her ages ago. "Mom, I need you to tell me why you called the club lawyer, Santino Rossi, seven months ago."

My mom's hands begin to shake as she pours the cream into her coffee. She rubs her lips together and glances up from what she's doing. "What?"

I exhale heavily. "I need to know every detail of the conversation you had with Santino Rossi when I signed with Bethnal Green."

"H-H-How do you know about that conversation?" she asks, her voice ragged.

My eyes sting when I croak out the next two words. "Mom, please."

Tears begin to fill her eyes, and her head jerks back and forth. "I didn't want you to come here."

"Why not?"

"Because it's too far away from home."

"Mom." I pin her with a serious look. "Cut the shit for once in my life, please."

She scoffs at my choice of words. "Well, it seems like you already know, so why don't you tell me?"

I rub my lips together and silently calm my nerves. "I need to hear it from you."

"This was what I was afraid would happen," she sputters, errant tears spilling down her cheeks. "I knew you would come here, and somehow, you'd figure it out. I didn't know how. I just knew if you were here, next to him…the truth would come out."

"The truth being?" I tee my mother up, once again.

She turns her head to the side, her lips twitching as she struggles to find the words.

"Mom, why is this so hard for you to say?"

"Because I never wanted you to know that Jerry wasn't your real father."

And there it is.

The truth…at last.

It hurts a million times more than I ever thought it would.

My eyes sting with unshed tears. "Why didn't you want me to know?"

"Because Jerry was your father from the moment you were born. He was your father even before you were born. He came with me to my ultrasound appointments. He put together your baby crib. He hung wallpaper in the nursery for me. He was everything a father should be."

I swallow the painful knot in my throat as I ask, "Who is my real father?"

She inhales through her nose and answers, "Vaughn Harris."

I close my eyes as I let those two words that have rolled over and over in my mind for the better part of a year wash through me. I've spent the past two months in London telling myself it couldn't be him. I watched him with his kids and grandkids and said, if he was my father, I would know it. I would feel it. He would feel it. We'd have an instinctual connection that defies logic.

I researched him and his kids online for nearly a year, feeling like it was way too fucking obvious that a family that plays professional soccer is my actual family. There's no damn way. And for me to be recruited to his club of all the clubs in the world? Life can't be that funny. Life can't be that on the nose.

Yet here I sit, faced with the truth I've been denying for months now.

My voice is thick when I ask, "Is it true you tried to sabotage my contract with Bethnal Green?"

My mother's chin wobbles. "Yes, but only because I was trying to honor your father's wishes. We never planned on telling you."

"Why not? Did you think I couldn't handle it? Did you think I'd love Dad less?"

"I suppose so." She leans forward and pins me with wide, watery eyes. "Vaughn Harris was a professional footballer. He was the type of father that kids without fathers dreamed of having. Jerry was a simple man. Wonderful and sweet, but he always feared that someday he would disappoint you and you'd seek out your birth father if you knew the truth. It would have crushed him, Zander."

That thought has my hands turning into fists on the table. "I would have never done that."

"You can't possibly know that," she tuts, wrapping her hands around her cup of coffee. "Kids do crazy things when they're hormonal teenagers. The fear of losing you was too much for Jerry. It's why he never wanted us to have any more kids. He didn't want to give you any cause to doubt his paternity."

My reality bends with her words, and I blink rapidly, trying to picture my father with these fears. Even in my angriest moments as a kid, there was never a moment when I fantasized about different parents. My parents weren't perfect, but they were mine, and I loved them. The fact that my dad lived his entire life doubting my love for him is soul-crushing.

"I wish he was alive for me to tell him that his fear was unnecessary," I cry, tears streaming down my face as my hands clench into clammy fists. "He was the best, Mom."

"I know," she blubbers, wiping her runny nose on the back of her hand. "He was a wonderful father and husband. I didn't believe in fate until I met him. Not many men would want to marry a four-month pregnant woman. But your father was all in."

"How did you even know Vaughn Harris?" I ask, feeling guilty for being curious about that.

The corners of my mom's lips twitch. "His wife, Vilma, was my best friend in college. After she passed away, I'd check in on Vaughn from time to time, but he was very troubled. He was raising five kids on his own and didn't have any nanny or family help. I worried about him. Then one night, I bumped into him, and I suppose we were both missing Vilma and found comfort in each other. I hated myself for betraying my best friend, though. She'd been gone for six years, but it was still unforgivable of me."

I stare back at my mom, feeling like I'm stuck in a nightmare I can't wake up from. "Don't you see, Mom? Now I'm not sure I can forgive you."

"Don't say that." A soft sob escapes her lips. "Don't you dare say that." She takes a napkin and shakily dabs at the tears in her eyes. "Do you forgive your father?"

I wince at that word because it feels tainted now. Like it doesn't quite fit. Yet I feel myself nodding. "Of course, I forgive him. I love him."

"You love him, but you don't love me?"

"You tried to ruin my career, Mom," I state again firmly, the reality of that like an open wound that will never heal. "And you had so many chances to tell me the truth before I came here. Once Dad was gone, it didn't need to be a secret anymore. I wanted you to tell me. I even delayed my transfer to give you more time to find the strength to be honest with me."

"I didn't know you knew," she exclaims, her voice garbled with confusion. "How long have you known the truth?"

My lips thin. "I found a letter you wrote to Vaughn Harris when I was searching for photos for Dad's funeral."

"Oh, my God." She covers her face with her hands. "What have I done?"

I pull apart her wrists, forcing her to look at me through all of this. "Did you ever send Vaughn a letter? Does he know I even exist?"

She shakes her head through more tears, and every single one of them feels like acid being dumped on my heart. This is too much. Watching her cry is fucking painful. She's a mess just like she was after Dad died, and I let her pain trump mine then. But not this time.

I push back and stand from my chair. "I need time to process this."

"Zander, don't leave." She reaches out and grabs my hand, her palms slick with sweat. "You can't just leave me here."

"I've booked you a room in Shoreditch. I'll call an Uber to take you there. Your flight leaves tomorrow morning."

"So, that's it? That's all you have to say to me?" Her red eyes look up at me, and I fear they too will haunt me in the dead of night, just like that fucking letter.

"I need space to come to terms with the fact that you lied to me my entire life. And for once, I'm putting my needs above yours."

She drops her face in her hands and begins quietly sobbing. It's a horrible, pitiful sight. But it's one I didn't cause. Knowing that, I lean in and kiss her on the cheek before walking out and not looking back.

40

Soccer Boy Save

Daphney

MY HEART IS IN MY THROAT AS I WATCH ZANDER LEAVE OLD GEORGE from my concealed place in the back room. The look of devastation all over his face was clear. And as the woman at the table begins crying into her hands, I know without a doubt, it's his mum. He's brought her here to confirm what he's already figured out.

That Vaughn Harris is his real father.

Guilt has been plaguing me ever since our fight out in the beer garden. I shouldn't have asked Zander if his dad had passed away. It was a cruel, low blow, and it cheapened the memories of the man who raised him. I hate myself for stooping to that level.

And after watching this exchange between him and his mother and seeing the pain in his eyes as he listened to her speak, my entire body aches to take this pain away for him. It takes every muscle in my body to stop myself from running after Zander to comfort him after what must have been the hardest conversation of his life.

But that's not what Zander and I are to each other anymore. I can't love someone I can't trust. And it's terrifying to me that I didn't see that Zander was just like Rex. Clearly, I become blind when my heart gets involved too deeply.

Guilt propels my feet as I approach the woman crying. "Are you Zander's mum?" I ask, and she looks up at me, her face red and puffy as snot dribbles out of her nose.

She nods and croaks, "Yes, I'm Jane."

"I'm Zander's neighbor, Daphney."

"Oh, hello," she offers weakly and takes my hand, but it's as if I'm shaking the hand of a corpse.

"Can I get you anything?" I inquire, taking the seat that Zander just vacated. "Tea?"

She shakes her head and barks out a wet laugh. "A time machine if you have it." Her American accent is just like Zander's, and it makes me miss him.

"How long are you staying for?" I ask, hating that I care because Zander doesn't deserve it.

Jane rolls her eyes. "I leave tomorrow, apparently."

"So soon?"

She shrugs. "My son is very upset with me."

I nod slowly, my heart breaking for the woman in front of me. The fact that Zander flew his mother out here to talk to him means that he loves her enough to have this conversation face-to-face. That has to mean something, right? Zander doesn't deserve my help here, but I can't help myself.

"I know you and Zander are figuring some things out, but I know that it's gutted him not to have you close as he's been playing in the Premier League this season."

"Oh, Zander doesn't care if I watch or don't watch his games," she huffs, waving me off as she swipes away the dampness on her cheeks. "Soccer was always his father's thing."

"He cares," I state it simply, making eye contact with her again. "And in a couple of days, it's the FA Cup quarterfinal being hosted at Tower Park, his team's facility. It's a very big game in the world of English footba...I mean soccer. I think it would go a long way for you to surprise him at that game."

"I wouldn't even know how to get tickets," she croaks, staring at me with desperation all over her face. "And Zander is too mad at me to even invite me, I'm sure."

I reach across the table and cup her hand. "I can help."

41

Football Over Bullshit

Zander

MY BODY IS ON AUTOPILOT AS I DRESS FOR TODAY'S MATCH IN complete silence, only half listening to Link as he rattles on and on to me about how good Manchester City strikers are.

I already know how good they are. I've been watching game footage of them all week, not just with the team but on my own as well. I know those strikers better than they know themselves. I know their tells, and today will not be the day I let my emotions get the best of me. Today, it's *football over bullshit.*

My mother is back in Boston, Daphney still hasn't come back to her apartment, Link and Knight are giving me space, and I'm avoiding the Harris family like the fucking plague.

Knight claps me on the back, offering me silent support as Coach Zion hushes the entire locker room to announce Vaughn for his typical manager speech that's become a regular occurrence on Cup game days. Vaughn probably gives a good speech. Today is a big day, and big days require big speeches. But I don't need to hear it, not from him. I only need to hear the voice in my head that says…*don't fuck this up, Zander.*

Our hands go in, and I'm silent as the team chants, "I am thine, thou art mine."

On autopilot, I touch the saying at the top of the door as we make our way out of the locker room and file into the tunnel. There are kids there, waiting to be escorted out onto the field. The little girl assigned to me grabs my hand and yanks me down to her level.

"Are you from America?" Her British accent is sweet, and I hate that her blue eyes remind me of Daphney.

I nod and clench my teeth as I attempt to maintain my composure.

"Can you say something funny?" She blinks up at me, and a piece of my armor falls to the ground.

With a huff, I repeat, "Say something funny," giving a little extra lilt to my Boston accent for effect. "How was that?"

She giggles, and then we're moving in a single file line out onto the field. The sun glistens off the pristine grass as the fans chant the Bethnal Green fight song at a roaring level.

I look up to see that the stadium is packed, the sun is bright, and the air is cool. A pit forms in my stomach as I drink this moment in because I've grown attached to Tower Park in the short time I've been here. I love the fans and the atmosphere. Bethnal Green feels like home and in a few months' time, I will be long gone. Santino and I are scheduled to talk about my future on Monday, and I can honestly say I'm going to miss this.

We line up down the field, and I force myself not to look up because I don't need to see the Harris family sitting in the front row like they usually do, screaming their heads off for Booker, Tanner, and Vaughn.

The truth is, I'm jealous of them. I'm jealous of their comradery and bond. I'm jealous of the unfailing support they give to each other. But most of all, I'm jealous of their innocence. I know they lost their mom when they were all young, but at least they knew who their mother and father were. At least they never doubted that.

As we stretch out on the pitch and wait for the match to start, I feel a firm tap on my shoulder. I whirl around and come face-to-face with Booker Harris.

"Hey, man, you good?" he asks, adjusting the straps on his keeper gloves.

I bend over and stretch out my hamstrings. "Yeah, I'm good."

"You've been quiet at training the past couple of days." I look up and see he's watching me with a serious look on his face.

"Has my performance suffered?" I snap, my tone overly defensive.

"No," Booker volleys, his head tilting in challenge. "You've been killing it on the pitch. I'm just checking in with you. I heard about you and Daphney."

"Not you too," I growl and stand to face him toe-to-toe. "I don't need another Harris pushing in on my life, okay?"

Booker cocks his head to the side and refuses to back down. "Well, just bloody well fix it because Daphney is like family to us. If you need a Harris shakedown to get your head on straight, that can be arranged."

"Family?" I snap, my rage boiling over as I clench my fists and use every muscle in my body not to freak the fuck out on him right now. "Don't you talk to me about Daphney or *family*. Got it?"

Booker huffs out a laugh of disgust, his brows furrowed as he backs away. "Sorry for bloody well caring."

He turns around and takes his spot back by the net while I look forward to focus on what I came here to do.

Daphney

This was a stupid idea, I think to myself as I sit in the nosebleed section of Tower Park field with Jane Williams beside me, waiting for the players to come onto the pitch.

Originally, I thought I wouldn't have to come to the game, but Jane wasn't comfortable coming to the match alone, and I can't say I blame her. This is her first time at a FA Cup match. And her son isn't currently speaking to her. The woman is holding on by a very thin thread, and I dare say, she's in good company.

I've been a nervous wreck ever since I helped Jane change her flight home and extend her hotel stay for a few more nights. I kept waiting for Zander to figure out what I'd done and show up at Old George to scream at me for interfering in his life. It was a stupid, stupid thing to do. Phoebe told me it was stupid about forty-seven times in forty-seven minutes. I know it's stupid!

Especially because the entire Harris crew is in attendance down toward the first row. This is a quarterfinal game, so everyone is here for support. It's hard to make them all out, but I'm pretty sure I spot Gareth and his wife, Sloan. Poppy and Allie, plus Belle, Vi, and Hayden. I think even Camden managed to attend since Arsenal was knocked out of the tournament by Bethnal Green a couple of weeks back. I even spot Mac and Freya's red hair from up here, and they look like they're sitting with Santino and Tilly. Honestly, it's no wonder I struggled to find decent tickets today. The Harris family has booked out most of the stadium.

I kept my hood up throughout the concourse on the off chance I ran into one of them. If Zander finds out that I dragged his mum here and potentially exposed her to the whole Harris crew, he will hate the ground

I walk on. Which maybe wouldn't be a bad thing because no matter how hard it was seeing him hurting the other day, I still haven't forgotten what he did to me.

I'm not here for Zander today. I'm here for his mum.

Jane looked so sad and alone that day at Old George. I couldn't let her stubborn arse of a son send her home without even the tiniest bit of closure. Maybe if Jane can connect with Zander after the game and he sees she put forth a bit of effort, he'll find it in his heart to forgive her.

"Is there no one that comes around with alcohol?" Jane asks, pulling her coat tight over her Bethnal Green kit that I helped her pick out in the shops outside. "My nerves are shot."

"No alcohol in the stands, I'm afraid."

She scoffs and adjusts her matching Bethnal Green stocking cap. "Yet another reason I never attended any soccer games when I lived here years ago. That and…I don't really care much for soccer."

My brows lift. "Really? All those years Zander played, you never warmed to the game?"

She wrinkles her nose and shakes her head. "Not the game, no. But I was always very proud of Zander, of course. Cried every time I saw him come onto the field. He just looks so grown-up in his uniform, and no matter how many times I see him, I can't help but marvel at the fact that I created that little man."

A smile spreads across my face. "He is pretty special," I state, feeling a pain slice through me at that remark.

Her chin trembles. "I just hope he can forgive me."

"He will," I say, reaching around and rubbing her back affectionately. "He's had a couple of days to cool off, now."

Jane licks her lips and nods. "You know, I went to Vaughn Harris's house to tell him I was pregnant."

My lips part in shock. "You did?"

"I never got around to telling Zander that part."

"What happened?" I can't help but ask. Despite myself, I still care about him.

"A little blonde girl who couldn't be more than ten years old answered the door. She was the spitting image of her mother, and it took my breath away. Vilma and I were very close when we were in college, but once she met Vaughn and started having kids, we lost touch. I didn't know her kids like I should have.

"But this little blondie was holding the hand of her little brother, and two other blonde boys were sitting on the stairs behind her. They all had tears in their eyes, so I bent over to ask her what was wrong. It was then that I heard shouting farther in the house. It was Vaughn fighting with his eldest son. Had to be oldest because the boy's voice was cracking as they bellowed at each other, and I think Vaughn's eldest would have been a young teen at that time. The little girl looked up at me and wiped away her tears and said in the most grown-up voice I'd ever heard, 'It's just Daddy and Gareth having a discussion. I'm handling it.'"

Jane shakes her head in amazement. "Such a tiny little thing but she spoke with such fierce confidence, I didn't dare question her." Jane sighs heavily. "It was clear at that moment that Vaughn's plate was overflowing, and since I was due to start my new job in Boston in just a couple of weeks, I didn't want to be yet another burden for that little girl to handle. Though I'm sure she would have been up for the challenge."

"Vi definitely would have been up for it," I say, my eyes glistening with tears. I've gotten to know my sister-in-law a lot throughout her marriage to Hayden, and fierce, momma-bear confidence describes her still to this day.

"Do you know Vi?" Jane asks, looking at me curiously.

I nod slowly. "She's married to my brother."

"Oh," Jane says, her eyes wide as she covers her mouth. "My God, I've said too much."

I reach out to grab Jane's hand. "You have my complete confidence, Jane. But I do hope you share that story with Zander someday. I think it'll mean a lot to him."

She nods and rubs her lips together. "If he ever speaks to me again."

"He will."

She eyes me thoughtfully for a moment. "You said you and Zander are just neighbors? Not something more?"

The question hits me right in the chest, and I do my best to school my features to remain calm and collected. "Just neighbors."

"Well, you're wonderful for going to all this trouble for me. I'm sure you feel like you've been plunked right into an episode of Maury Povich."

She laughs, and I almost feel bad when I reply, "I have no idea who Maury Povich is."

"Oh." Jane chuckles and rolls her eyes. "It's a vile talk show that's nearly entirely all about paternity tests. Awful joke I just made."

I smile and give her a light nudge. "It's good to joke in times of stress."

Suddenly, the stadium begins chanting the Bethnal Green fight song. I join in because you can't work at Old George for a year and not learn this bloody chant. Jane watches in awe as the crowd all rise to their feet, hollering at deafening levels down to the pitch. I point at the tunnel, and her focus zeroes in on the players making their way out, escorting their smiling youth mascots. Jane's eyes go wide when she spots Zander. It isn't long before she's wiping away the tears running down her cheeks.

"Jerry would have loved this," she yells over the fans, her face twisting in pain as she looks up to the sky and pulls in a deep breath.

A wobbly smile lifts my face, and I finally allow myself to glance down at Zander. My heart breaks at the beautiful sight of him all polished and brand new in his clean kit and holding a little girl's hand. If we were still together, would I have come today? Would he have wanted me to?

The hate I've had for him the past few days has shifted into something different. A melancholy has settled over me as I've empathized with the agony in his mum's story. I can even understand a bit why Zander felt desperate to seek out his own answers. I think I could even forgive him for using me to get to the Harris family, eventually.

But the problem is, he didn't just use me. He disappointed me. I thought we were something real, something special. I thought we were connecting on a level that superseded all of that. He clearly thought otherwise, and I'm humiliated that I let my heart run away without noticing that he was lying to me the whole time.

I suppose it's better to find out the truth now than when we're months down the road, and I've given my whole heart to him. Zander has enough to work through in his life. His mum, his career, his involvement with the Harris family. I don't need to be a part of that story.

Zander

A sweeper lives in two worlds.

The first is where they are a defensive player only. They are charged with the task of "sweeping up" the ball off the opponents who have encroached the defensive line from a failure in the system. It is their job to prevent a center forward from challenging the keeper. A sweeper must be safe and smart. They cannot afford to make any mistakes because they are literally standing in front of their own net. Mistakes here can be fatal.

In the other world, a sweeper is also an attacker. They must read the game and anticipate the moves of the other players to shift into the positions of greatest need. They have the ability to control the entire pace of the game, when to pass, when to keep, when to punt, or what play to set up next. A sweeper's decision in the backfield has a ripple effect that can result in a goal on the front field.

In many ways, it is the sweeper's game.

And as I play my ass off, feeling the euphoric effects of every save, every pass, every punt, every chant from the stadium, I can't help but feel as though my own life mirrors that of a sweeper.

Do I play it safe in my position and live the life that my parents set up for me? Or do I take a risk and lay my cards on the table to see what the chain of reaction will be?

And why is this all on me? Why do I have to be the one to decide all of this? I didn't ask for this. I didn't ask to find that letter. I didn't ask to be recruited to Vaughn Harris's team. Not really.

A sweeper is supposed to be a leader, but how am I to lead when the one man who taught me how to lead is fucking gone?

I'm playing the game of my fucking life today, but for who? What do seven saves and a launched pass up to Roan DeWalt from the back half of the field for him to drive in an epic goal mean anymore? Who is even watching?

Is my dad watching? Does he regret dying without telling me the truth? Is he heartbroken I discovered the truth on my own? How do I fucking know when he's not here to ask?

Booker rushes over to me to celebrate my pass, but I brush him off, my face stony serious as I refuse the bro fives and fake hugs.

"Zander, that was a brilliant pass!" he exclaims, his face twisted in confusion at my lack of enthusiasm as we walk back toward our end of the pitch.

I say nothing in response as I get back into position.

"You best get your attitude in check, mate," Booker seethes from behind me, but I don't look back. I don't give him a response because the truth is, if I blink for even a fucking second right now, I might fall apart.

The game continues, and I feel as though I'm watching myself play from the stands. It doesn't even feel like me. I'm faster than I've ever been before. My touches are quicker. I'm burning strikers left and right, and my movements feel as if I've entered into another dimension of my abilities that I've never tapped into before.

I scramble with a Man City striker and manage to achieve possession. I dribble the ball quickly up the field, bypassing Knight, who's open in the midfield, and push beyond.

I'm in the final third of the pitch, and both Roan and Billy are flanked on the sides, moving to shake off their defenders. There are opportunities for me to pass. I can give it to them and get back to my position on defense. I can play it safe.

But I don't want to be safe. I am in command of this field right now, and I want this shot.

I launch a long, left-footed bomber down the grass toward the left side of the goal post. The keeper is out of position and lays out in a diving leap with his hands stretched to the max. It sails in just out of his reach, and the stadium roars to life as it hits the net to bump Bethnal Green's lead by two.

I turn around and jog back to my position, ignoring my teammates who swarm me for celebrations. Knight approaches and attempts to put an arm around me, but I shake him off. He knows why but the rest of my team is looking at me like I'm a freak show. I do my best to block those looks from my mind so I can stay focused and on task.

Tanner Harris calls out to me from the sidelines. I give him a quick glance to ensure I'm not missing a call. When I see that he too is attempting to congratulate me on the score, my focus snaps back to the game at hand. No time for celebrations.

Three minutes are left in the game, and the Man City's strikers are fucking over me. They've been taking cheap shots, tugging on my jersey, and cursing up a storm every time I come at them. I can't blame them. I'm like a demon, possessed.

I steal the ball from their star striker, and I'm just about to pass it out to my center-back when the other striker takes a diving shot right at my feet. His cleat catches the inside of my calf, forcing my ankle to roll. I hear a faint pop as I crash on top of him to the ground.

The crowd is thundering as I roll onto my back, clutching my leg to my chest. Booker rushes over, and I shake him off, hopping up onto my feet and trying to walk it off. The ref is giving the striker a yellow card as he too lays on the ground writhing in pain. *That's karma for you, asshole*, I think as I attempt to shake off the bone-chilling ache that throbs through my left ankle. I've had injuries like this before. They're bad but not career-defining. I can walk this off. I'm okay.

Medics rush out to the field to help Man City's striker and I frown when I notice movement on the sidelines of my team. Tanner is talking to the fourth referee between the two team's benches. He makes a motion, and I assume he's about to substitute another player, but then his eyes lock on me as he waves me over.

I wave back at him and yell out, "I'm fine!"

"You're coming out," Tanner bellows back, his hand cupped around his bearded jaw. The assistant ref holds up my number, and I see Finney standing beside him, jumping up and down like a fucking bean to warm up.

I shake my head firmly. "I'm good. It's just tweaked."

I catch sight of Vaughn Harris as he walks over to stand by Tanner. He motions for me to exit the field, confirming what I thought was a sick fucking joke.

Seriously? One bad foul, and they're pulling me? I'm carrying this damn team right now! There are only two minutes left on the clock. I do high knees to show them I'm okay, but they don't seem to care. The main ref waves me over to begin the substitution.

Fiery rage sizzles in my belly as I stomp over to the sidelines where Finney, Tanner, and Vaughn are standing. Tanner steps forward first, reaching out his hand to me, but I slap it away.

"I said I was fucking fine," I roar, my teeth cracking from how hard I'm clenching them.

"Oi, watch the tone!" Tanner barks back.

Coach Zion steps into my space next and puts a hand on my chest. "You played a hell of a game. Go let Indie check your ankle and take a rest. You earned it, lad." He reaches his hand out to me, and I stare at it, refusing yet another congratulations.

It's poor sportsmanship not to slap the hand of your coach after coming off the field, but this is complete bullshit. I earned the right to finish this fucking game.

My shoulder hits Coach Z's as I move past him, and then I find myself face-to-face with Vaughn Harris himself.

"Lose the attitude, Zander. We need you well for the next game, and we're up two-nil. This is for your own good." His eyes are glacial on me as his nostrils flare. He's trying to put me in my place.

I won't have it.

"You can't possibly know what's good for me." I point back to the pitch and jut my face into Vaughn's. "Being out there was good for me. I only had two damn minutes left."

"And with an attitude like this, you'll be lucky to play two minutes in next week's game if you don't watch yourself," Vaughn thunders, the rage in his tone clear as day.

I growl and throw my hands out to the side to argue when an arm wraps tightly around my waist. "Chill out, Zander. Just chill out. It's not worth it."

I whirl around on my heel to see it's Booker. "Get back on the fucking pitch," I bite, yanking my arm out of his grasp.

"You played brilliantly," Booker says, turning me around to face him. He dips his eyes and clutches my arms tightly as he pins me with a look. "Don't let your headspace ruin this moment."

"Get out of my fucking life!" I shout and yank my arms free to shove him away from me.

Booker stumbles backward, looking stunned as he nearly falls on his ass. Suddenly, I'm swarmed by Tanner and a couple of sideline players. They hold me back like I'm a murderer about to rip Booker's fucking head off. Maybe I am.

The crowd audibly gasps behind us at the scene I'm causing. I glance back to see the entire Harris crew gaping at me like I'm a rabid dog in need of being shot.

Indie walks over, her voice gentle as she says, "Zander, let me look at that ankle."

"My ankle is fine," I roar because she's another fucking Harris.

I can't get away from them. They're all here looking at me, watching me like I'm a freak show, and it's too much. I walk over to the sidelines and kick a caddy of water bottles, launching them every which way before storming down the sidelines to the tunnel that gets me the fuck out of here.

I don't care if I just ruined my career. At least now my outsides match my insides.

My cleats clack along the concrete tunnel ground when the voice of Vaughn Harris calls out to me. "Give me one good reason not to suspend you right now, Zander Williams," he shouts, his voice uncharacteristically venomous.

I turn on my heel, my eyes slits as I stare at his silhouette walking toward me in the dark tunnel. "It must be nice," I growl, my tone lethal.

"What?" he asks, stopping in front of me and standing beneath a dim light that casts ominous shadows over his face. He looks like the villain right now. But the reality is, I'm the villain of this story.

"Oblivion must be nice," I retort and spit on the ground between us.

Vaughn looks at it as though I spit in his face. "What are you talking about?"

"I'm talking about the fact that you guys don't have a fucking clue," I exclaim, my voice echoing down the long, empty tunnel.

"Who?" Vaughn barks, his brows furrowed in confusion. "Me and Coach Zion?"

"No, not you and Coach Zion," I snap. "You…the Harrises. All of you. You live in your perfect fucking bubble with no idea whose lives you've completely fucked."

"Zander, you're not making any sense," Vaughn says, shaking his head. He pins me with a grave look when he adds, "You're being completely unprofessional. This isn't college football. This is Premier League. We took a chance on you. We trusted that you could rise to this challenge, and now you're blowing it over a girl. What would your father think if he saw you walk off the pitch just now?"

It's like a cold slap to the face that I didn't expect and the sting of it takes a few seconds before it explodes over my entire body.

"Why don't you ask my mom?" I say back, my tone low and deadly. "You two know each other very well, I hear."

Vaughn's face falls. "Your mum?"

I nod slowly. "Jane Woods was her name back when you two met."

Vaughn shakes his head, blinking rapidly as he processes this new bit of information. "Jane Woods was Vilma's friend."

"And your fuck buddy for one night about twenty-five years ago," I add, wincing at that thought. "Must have been some night if it resulted in me." I hold my hands out wide, like a sacrificial lamb, begging for slaughter.

Vaughn's face morphs into horror as realization sets in. "Zander, what are you saying?"

I huff out a noise, my body radiating with disgust. "I'm saying that even though my dad never shared my blood, somehow I still know he was twice the father you ever could have been to me."

I turn on my heel and walk away, refusing to walk Vaughn through this mind fuck because no one walked me through it. He can fall in this mess just like I did.

42

My Only Friend

Zander

MY HANDS SHAKE AS I TEAR OPEN THE ENVELOPE THAT ARRIVED IN the mail over a week ago now. I inhale deeply, prepared to read the results that I already knew to be true. At the top of the sheet of paper are the words: **Confirmed paternal match.**

And there it is.

I set it down on the table next to the letter, staring at the two pieces of paper that have turned my whole world upside down. I should have opened this days ago. I should have come to terms with this reality before I stepped foot on that pitch today. Now, I've trashed my career and any chance I had of a meaningful relationship with Vaughn Harris.

And that's the real issue here. I actually want to know him. I've spent the past few days a raging pile of anger because I was lying to myself about that. But I don't just want to know him because he was a pro footballer and could replace my own dad. My dad is untouchable. He was a fucking legend without even trying.

But I look at that Harris family, and I can't help but want to be inside of them. The times Daphney brought me around them, there was a feeling inside me that I was fighting so hard to ignore. A feeling of belonging. That only-child syndrome I fight so hard to deny lives inside me and makes me feel like I was cheated out of a life that could have enriched my own, not eclipsed. And that kills me because it's like I'm spitting on the grave of my father, whose biggest fear was me caring more about them than him.

But the truth is, the day my dad died, I didn't just lose him. I lost my mom too. And ever since that day, I have felt so fucking alone with information that I should not have tried to deal with on my own. That was why it was so easy for me to fall for Daphney. I was craving a connection with someone who was honest with me. She was overly honest. So honest that I didn't even realize when it shifted from friends with benefits to heartfelt intimacy. She filled up all the empty spaces in my heart. I was able to latch on to something real that I could count on. She helped me remember that I was more than just this secret. My life was more than the lie my parents crafted.

And I lost her now too.

More guilt plagues me when I recall how horrible I was to Booker and Tanner and Vaughn. They wanted the best for me, and I pushed them away. It's weird to care about people who had nothing to do with my life, but genetics are a strange and undeniable science. There is a connection there that feels important to me.

My thoughts are distracted when I hear voices whispering out in the hallway. Frowning, I walk over and yank the door open, expecting Link and Knight to come in guns blazing. They've been texting me since the match ended, and stopping by like this is pretty much their style. I fucking love them for it.

But it's not them.

It's my mom.

She's dressed in a Bethnal Green jersey that has my number on it, and she's clutching a plastic container in her hands.

"Mom?" I croak, my heart permanently lodged in my throat because even though she was here a few days ago, she doesn't exist in this world for me.

"Congrats on the win," she says, her voice shaking as she shoves the tub of cookies into my hands.

"What are you doing here? How? When?" I ask, my eyes blinking rapidly.

She looks off to the side nervously and murmurs something unintelligible. I step through the doorway to see who my mom is talking to. The air whooshes out of my lungs when I see who it is.

Daphney struggles to smile at me. "I'm sorry, I was just leaving." She points at her door, but I notice she's in green and white too.

"Were you two…together?" I inquire, unable to compute this image in my head.

My mom answers, her voice more stable than I've heard in a long time. "Yes, Daphney took me to the game today. You played so amazing, buddy! I couldn't believe how good you were!"

My head jerks back, and I turn my eyes back to Daphney. "You took my mom to the game?"

She nods and holds her hands up. "Yes, and I'm sorry for interfering. It was completely out of line, but I talked to your mum at Old George, and she really wanted to see you play, so I just helped her out." She shoots a wobbly smile over at my mom and blinks nervously back at me. "But I know you two have a lot to talk about, so I'll leave you to it."

She makes a move toward the stairs, and my voice is raw with emotion when I call out, "Please stay."

She turns on her heel to look back at me. Her shoulders drop with such profound sadness, I feel it in my soul.

I shrug and struggle to say the next words. "You're basically my only friend." My eyes burn at that painful realization that I've irrevocably ruined the only relationship I care about right now.

Daphney lets out an audible gasp before closing the distance between us and wrapping her arms around my neck.

I stand frozen in shock with cookies in one hand while my other hand is seemingly stuck to my side. Daphney trembles against me, and that sensation snaps me out of my disbelief as I wrap my arms around her waist and squeeze her to me. We hold each other for a long moment, our bodies reuniting after what feels like years apart, when in reality, it was only days.

"I knew you weren't just neighbors," my mom tuts quietly under her breath, but not quietly enough.

Daphney and I both expel a nervous laugh as we pull apart and look at each other before separating. My hand grabs hers like a lifeline as I pull her close to me and look at my mom. "Should we have some cookies?" I offer her a half-smile, and my mom's eyes well with tears as she nods eagerly.

Daphney

I make a pot of tea as Zander awkwardly shows his mum around his flat. It's obviously a struggle for him, but I think he took her attendance at today's game and the fact that she stuck around in London after their talk as an olive branch. I'm glad he's giving her a second chance because it's obvious she loves him.

Zander points out various sights outside of the windows to her, just like I did when I first showed him around nearly eight weeks ago now. Time is a funny thing, isn't it? Three days ago, I hated the ground Zander walked on. But a few minutes ago, I didn't care about our fight or how much he hurt me. I just let it all go so I could be here for him. We may not be each other's person, but it doesn't mean I can stop being his friend.

I bring the tea over to the table where Zander and his mother are sitting. He's showing her the letter she wrote so many years ago and the DNA results that he's apparently now opened. It's strange that I wasn't a part of all of this, but when I see the look in his eyes as he gazes at the pieces of paper, I can understand that it wasn't an easy thing for him to deal with.

His mum shares the story she shared with me at Tower Park. It seems to bring Zander some small mark of peace, which means a lot because when I watched him storm off the pitch after that substitution, I knew he was in a dark place. His mum didn't see it, but I did.

"I'm a bit embarrassed to say it now, but I was actually in love with Vaughn Harris when we were together," Jane says, sipping her cup of tea.

"What?" Zander asks, his eyes laser-focused on his mum.

She shrugs. "I had feelings for Vaughn even when he was married to Vilma. I never would have acted on them. But…Vaughn was a professional footballer who swept Vilma off her feet. He flew a bunch of us girls on a private jet to watch one of his matches at Manchester United. Everyone was smitten over Vaughn. He was a charmer."

Zander shakes his head and huffs. "Wouldn't your feelings have motivated you even more to be honest with him about me then?"

"Not at all," Jane replies, taking a sip of her tea. "My mom always said to find someone who loves you more than you love him. Vaughn was never going to love anyone the way he loved Vilma. They were soul mates. And your father was mine."

She leans forward and grabs Zander's hand. "And as much as I know this secret hurt you, I don't regret raising you with your dad. He was so fulfilled by you. You may not have shared blood, but he gave you his heart and soul completely."

"I know that, Mom," Zander croaks, tears sliding down his cheeks. He wipes them away quickly. "And I hope you know that whatever happens between the Harris family and me, Dad will always be my dad. No one will replace him. And no one can replace you."

Jane blubbers softly as she stands up and drags her son out of his chair for a hug. She's about half the size of him, so it's an awkward angle, but it's beautiful and honest and raw. And as much as I feel like a voyeur in this intimate moment and I should look away, it's a privilege to watch this kind of healing happen between a mother and her son.

43

Call Me Vaughn

Zander

ANOTHER KNOCK HITS MY DOOR JUST AS DAPHNEY, MY MOM, AND I begin opening our takeout bags from Old George. It's dark out, and apparently playing in a FA Cup quarterfinal and having a heart-to-heart with your mother who lied to you for your whole life can really work up an appetite. I frown and remove the ice pack from my ankle that's just starting to show signs of injury. Nothing career-altering. I'll just need it well-taped for the rest of the season. I head over to see who could be coming by this time of night. It was only a few hours ago that I felt bone-chillingly alone. Now I can't get any peace and quiet. I open the door, and the hits just keep on coming.

"Hiya, Zander," Vaughn Harris says as he stands on my doorstep with his hands on his hips. "I was wondering if we could talk."

My brows lift as I see Vaughn glance past me to the people inside. Might as well rip it off like a Band-Aid at this point.

I step back and gesture inside. "Vaughn, you remember my mother, Jane?"

Vaughn's eyes turn to saucers as his gaze snaps back and forth from me to my mom at the table. You can see the whites of my mother's eyes as she sits there, frozen with a french fry in her hand. Or a chip, as Daphney would call it.

"Hungry?" I ask, closing the door and laughing to myself because this has been a day of all days.

"Um…no. I can come back later if you prefer," Vaughn responds, looking awkward.

"Well, my mom already knows that I dropped the bomb on you today, plus I have a DNA test on the table if you'd like to look at it. And considering I don't know if I still play for your club anymore, I'd rather just get this all out in the open now, so I know where I stand with you."

The level of chill I am right now is unbelievable. I don't know if it's still the adrenaline from today's match or if I've just completely run out of emotions to have at this point. But it is what it is.

Vaughn's brows furrow as he pins me with a sincere look. "Of course you still play for Bethnal Green. Why would you say that?"

I shrug. "My behavior today was pretty shitty," I reply honestly. My dad always said it's better to admit bad behavior than try to cover it up.

"Well, I gather that you've been dealing with a lot since you arrived in London," Vaughn says, gripping the back of his neck. I wince at the motion because it's something I do a lot too. "I spoke with Santino, and he gave me a bit more of the story than you did."

I huff out a laugh. "It's been a weird couple of months."

"How do you have DNA results?" Vaughn asks, blinking back at me curiously. "Santino didn't say anything about that."

"I stole some hair off your brush when Daphney brought me to your house a few weeks ago." I say it like I'm ordering a burger and fries. God, life is fucking weird today.

"I see." Vaughn frowns as he processes that information.

"Daphney had no idea what I was doing that day," I state, by way of defending her. "She was as blindsided by all of this as you were."

"It's not really something anyone can be prepared for, is it?" Daphney offers me a soft smile that hits me right in the chest. I've only known her for two months, but it's like she's always been there. How is that possible?

"No, it's not." Vaughn laughs, scrubbing his nails over the whiskers on his chin. He turns his focus to my mother. "Jane…how could you never tell me?"

My mom's chin wobbles, and she shrugs, looking small and sad. "You had your hands full, Vaughn. And I was leaving for America. The timing was awful."

"I know, but…" He looks back at me again, his eyes raking over every one of my features like he's seeing me for the first time. His voice is hoarse when he says, "You play so much like Gareth. How could I have missed it?"

His words are candid, and for some odd reason, they bring me a sense of relief. A part of me wondered if Vaughn might deny the connection out of fear of scandal. The Harris family makes headlines very easily, and if something like this gets leaked, it's certain to cause a stir. But just because he's here in my apartment, openly talking about this, doesn't mean he's ready to acknowledge it to everyone. I know from my past conversations with Booker that it took a long time for the Harris family to become what they are today. A commotion like me might rock the boat too much.

"I feel like I've missed so much," Vaughn states, looking at me with red-rimmed eyes. "But it sounds like you had a great father?"

"He did," my mom says, standing up with a fierce look in her eyes.

"I did," I confirm, my chin rising with pride. "My dad was one of a kind."

Vaughn nods slowly. "I'd love to hear more about him and you if you're willing to share. I think he and your mum raised a tremendous son."

Hearing those words on Vaughn's lips causes my eyes to burn. It's almost like getting my dad's approval through Vaughn's mouth. It's tripping me out. Maybe this won't be as hard as I thought it would be. Maybe this can be okay.

I shake away the emotions clogging up my mind and ask, "Can I get you a beer, Vaughn?"

He laughs and shakes his head. "I better take two."

A couple of hours later, I'm standing at the door, hugging Vaughn Harris. It's fucking weird. It doesn't feel like my dad, but it doesn't feel like a stranger either. It feels…like something new. He and my mom are leaving together. He's offered to give her a ride to her hotel, and I have a feeling the two of them have a lot more to talk about.

"So, you're sure it's okay if I tell the rest of the family tomorrow then?" Vaughn asks, his eyes looking hopeful. "I know this is all happening really fast, but secrets in our family never last very long."

I laugh and nod slowly. "Yeah, I'm good with it."

"Good, good." Vaughn nods thoughtfully. "And then you'll join us for our Sunday dinner around six. I'll be sure to tell everyone early enough to give them time to adjust to the news, but I'm sure they're going to have questions for you."

I inhale a cleansing breath. This is what I knew would be coming. Telling Vaughn was easy. It was the heat of the moment, and I didn't have time to overthink my words or the setting. The rest of the family will be another experience altogether. A part of me wishes I could be there to see their reactions, so I know what Vi and the brothers really think of all this. But deep down, they deserve to have their own family moment, the same way I did with my mom.

"I'll be there at six," I say and note the relief in Vaughn's face.

He turns his focus to my mom. "Jane, you would be very welcome to join us as well if you like."

"I don't believe Zander needs me for this." My mom offers a polite smile to Vaughn as she reaches out to rub my arm. "Plus, I've got to get back to Boston for work soon. But I plan to stick around long enough to hear all about it. I'm just happy Zander knows what he wants because it's a lot to take in."

I nod firmly, letting her words fall over me. This is what I want. Which is another fucking weird thing. I finally know what I want. There's no guidebook to how to deal with this, only what feels right. I'm just grateful that what feels right to Vaughn aligns with what feels right to me. I'm done with the secrets. I want to go to Sunday dinner tomorrow with the truth all out in the open. I'm ready for it.

I hug my mom goodbye and hold her tight for a moment. She's been through a lot this week. I think if she had her way, I'd still be in the dark about all of this. She's protective of my dad and of me. I'm sure her history with Vaughn makes it difficult for her to accept all of this easily, but it's not up to her. She'll come around to all of this in her own time. And the fact that she's staying in town for a bit means she cares. And that's worth more to me than she'll ever know.

I close the door and press my forehead to it for a moment, feeling my body sag with relief, grateful to be done with all of that for now.

When I turn around, I find Daphney in my kitchen. She tosses a rag into the sink and offers me a soft smile that has my heart nearly bursting out of my chest.

Exhaling heavily, I move toward her to do the one thing I've been dying to do since the moment she stepped into my apartment with my mom. I cup her face and lean in to kiss her.

"Zander, no," she states, pulling back and covering her lips.

"No?" My eyes search her face for answers.

She chews her lip nervously as tension grows between us. "You can't kiss me."

I huff out an incredulous laugh as my hands drop from her face. "Why not?"

"Because…we're not together," she says it quickly like it's the most obvious thing in the world.

I grip the back of my neck and point at the door behind me. "You went to a soccer game with my mom. You showed up here with her after. You were beside me all evening. What do you mean we're not together? You're standing right in front of me, Daphney."

She shoots me a guilty look that I fucking hate. "I can understand how my involvement in all this confused you." She tucks her hair behind her ears and avoids eye contact. "But I only wanted you to find peace with your mum. And I guess I got caught up in all that today. Emotions were high, and I was just so happy to see you guys talking." Her eyes lift to mine when she adds, "But I haven't forgotten that you used me to figure all of this out."

"I made a mistake," I state firmly, my hands turning to fists at my sides. "But that's all it was. A mistake. We're bigger than that, surely. You wouldn't have cared about my mom if you didn't care about me still."

"Zander, I do care about you." Her face is resigned, her body language closed off. She's at complete odds with the girl who hugged me and gave me life only a few hours ago. "Against my better judgment, I care. But I cannot ignore the fact that you used me."

"So, that's it?" I snap, my tone acidic as frustration courses through my veins. "You're done with me?"

"You knew I was messed up about my ex, and you still didn't come clean about everything." She shrugs like that's all there is to it, but that's not all there is to it. There's so much more to it that my mind and my heart are currently battling over who gets to speak first.

Swallowing the knot in my throat, I step closer to Daphney, so she's forced to look into my eyes. "I am not your ex. I actually feel remorse for lying to you. I'm not a sociopath who fucking stole from you and doubled down in court. I struggled to let you in, but that's in the past now. I want you all in. Don't let your past trauma ruin that."

"It's not just about Rex." Her brows knit together in the middle as she looks up at me.

"Then what is it?" I exclaim, jamming my hands through my hair. "Tell me so I can fix it and kiss you."

Her face bends with emotion as her eyes search mine. "You can't fix it, Zander. It just is what it is. You and I aren't on the same page, and that's how I know this has to be over."

"That's really what you see?" I huff, backing up and tossing my hands out to put myself on display. "I've texted you and called you and looked for you for a week. I had the biggest game of my life to prepare for, and there wasn't a goddamn minute when I wasn't thinking of you. I scaled a fence at Old George just so I could beg for your forgiveness. That doesn't put me on your fucking page?"

"Look, I'm not saying you don't have regrets. I know you do." She lowers her gaze to nervously fiddle with the strings on her hoodie. "And I know you're grateful that I helped bring you and your mum together. But I don't want you to use that gesture I made to turn this into more than it is. That's not what I want."

"What do you want?" I croak, my voice guttural as my eyes begin to burn. Holy shit, I can't figure her out.

Daphney opens her mouth to respond, but nothing comes out, and that fucking dimple in her chin that I used to love appears, taunting me with a million unanswered questions. Her eyes cast downward, and her voice is resigned when she finally says, "I think it was a mistake for us to turn our neighbors-with-benefits situation into something more. It's better to end this now before we get to the point of no return. This way, we can stay friends."

"Friends?" A disgruntled laugh rips up my throat as an ache blooms through my chest at that horrible fucking label. "So that's where you want me?"

She nods woodenly. "I think it's what's best for both of us."

"It's best for you," I hiss and then step back because my body is starting to break down. The events of the past twenty-four hours are finally taking their toll. I spent the past year forcing myself not to feel the loss of my father, and now I feel everything all at once, and it's too damn much. I'm tired of feeling. And I'm tired of fighting for someone who has no desire to fight for me.

I turn on my heel and open the door for Daphney to leave, avoiding eye contact as she walks past me because if she looks at me, I'll crumple. I'll tell her that she's a disappointment because she doesn't see me for who I really am. But if she can't see me now, in my weakest moment, maybe she never will.

When she steps out into the hallway and makes her way over to her place, I close my door and can't help but think the final score in the Zander/Daphney relationship match is Zander: two, Daphney: two. And no one ever wins with a tie.

44

Another Harris Brother

Zander

I t's Sunday evening when I slide out of the black cab in front of the gated entrance of Vaughn Harris's house in Chigwell. I gaze down the driveway at the bright yellow double door entrance. This is the Harris childhood home. I've been here before, but I'm seeing it through different eyes now that everything is out in the open. I hope I know what I've gotten myself into.

"Just call when you want us to come back and get you," Link says, resting his hand on my shoulder as he stands solemnly beside me. "I mean it, we're just going to be at a pub a mile away. It won't take us long to get back. I'll fucking run it if we can't get a cab quick enough."

"Or if you want us to come in with you, we will," Knight offers, leaning against the open car door. He hits me with another one of his iconic serious looks. "The Harrises have each other to lean on, and you're going in alone. I don't like that."

I laugh and shake my head. "It's not like they're strangers."

"I know," Knight says and glowers back at me. "I still don't like it."

I glance between my two friends. Brothers from another mother, teammates, and so much more. These guys didn't hesitate when I called and asked them to meet me for breakfast this morning. And after how shitty I'd been treating them the past week, hell, the past several weeks as I've dealt poorly with all this family shit, I'm not sure I deserve their friendship. But I'll be damn sure I'm going to do everything in my power to be worthy of it now.

My phone pings with a notification, and I glance down to see it's from Daphney. Shaking my head, I slide it back into my jeans.

"Was that her?" Link inquires, pinning me with a curious look.

I nod and roll my eyes. "Yes, but I'm not going to open it."

"Now you're ghosting her?" Link asks, his brow furrowed.

"She made her decision last night," I state, feeling my jaw muscle shift with agitation. "Hell, she made her decision last week. I was just too stupid to realize it. She's not in love with me, and that's that."

Knight hits me with a flat look.

"Look, you weren't there, you don't know." I wince when I think about how she looked at me like I was nothing more than a buddy she was helping out. It was soul-crushing.

"Okay," he says, shifting off the cab to walk over to me. "Let's just deal with one drama at a time today, okay?"

"Something new and different for me," I reply with a laugh.

Knight shocks me by yanking me in for a hug. He slaps my back, then pulls back to stab a finger in my chest. "You got this."

"Fuck yes, he does." Link throws an arm around each of us and smiles. "We'd make a really sexy thruple, you guys."

Knight and I both laugh and shove Link away.

"What?" he exclaims, looking offended.

"Get out of here." I give him a playful kick in the ass as he slides back into the cab. "I'll call you guys later."

I wave them off and turn to make my way up the long gravel lane to the front entrance feeling like a kid walking in on my first day of school, hoping the kids all like me.

"Zander," Vaughn says as he opens the door and walks out onto the front step with a smile. He pulls me into a hug and sighs. "I'm so happy you're here."

"Thanks for having me," I respond, offering him a polite smile as we pull apart. I had no idea when I was just a footballer for his club that this guy was such a hugger. It will take some getting used to.

"Everyone's waiting in the kitchen." He gestures behind him. "Please come in."

I follow him down the long marble hallway, my stomach a swirling vortex of fireworks. It's really fucking weird to be nervous to see people you've already met before. But now that the truth is out, all our perspectives have changed. Like it or not, this will be weird.

Vaughn pushes open the door to the kitchen, and I swear it's like a cheesy movie moment when the record scratches and everyone in the room freezes to gawk at me. Vaughn remains silent as he steps to the side, leaving me standing in the doorway, all on my own.

I open my mouth to break the silence when Tanner blurts out, "Well this is awkward as fuck."

"Tanner," Vi exclaims, coming out from behind the kitchen counter. She points at the jar on the table.

"The kids are all out in the woods. Surely the swear jar rule doesn't apply when no kids are around." Tanner turns his attention back to me. "What I meant to say was…welcome, Zander."

I huff out a nervous laugh. "Thanks…but you're right…this is awkward."

"Well, come in," Vi says, shuffling over to me. "I have tea on the table, and I think we should all sit down and have a proper chat."

I nod gratefully and take the seat Vi points at in the middle of the long table. She sits down beside me, and I glance outside, wondering where everyone else is.

"Where is everyone?" I ask, glancing up at Vaughn, who takes the chair directly across from me.

"Hayden and the girls are all outside with the children," he replies, splaying his hands on the table in front of him. "A few years back, Booker and the boys built a playhouse deeper into the woods out back, and since it's not horribly cold today, we thought it'd be good for them to be out there to give us all a bit of privacy to talk."

"I see," I say, discreetly wiping my sweaty palms off on my jeans before taking the cup of tea Vi has just poured me.

My gaze moves around the table to silently gauge everyone's current mood. Gareth lowers himself to the left of Vaughn and has a very stoic look on his face that I can't quite read. Camden is by Gareth and sporting an easy grin, like this is just a normal Sunday. Tanner is at the end of the table by Cam and more focused on the bowl of nuts in front of him than the fact that he has a new half brother in the room. Vi seems nice and welcoming beside me, her smile genuine, but I can see the stress behind her eyes.

Booker finally joins us on the other side of Vaughn, and his mood is markedly more withdrawn than everyone else. I came in today knowing that I have a lot to atone for with him.

I swallow the knot in my throat and direct my attention to him. "Booker, I'd like to apologize to you first if it's okay."

Booker's eyes snap up to mine before looking around the table nervously. "Me? What for?"

"My behavior to you yesterday was shitty." I pause and dig into the pocket of my jeans for some money. I stick a bill in the swear jar as I continue, "I was rude and dismissive. You didn't deserve any of that. And I'm really sorry for pushing you on the sidelines like I did. That was completely out of line."

Booker's nose wrinkles as he waves me off. "It was nothing."

"I've given Tanner at least three black eyes," Camden interjects with a laugh. "The last one was just a few years ago."

"It was a cheap shot." Tanner harrumphs, touching his cheekbone like it still hurts.

Camden rolls his eyes. "He had it coming."

"Worth it." A lopsided smile spreads across Tanner's face.

I nod and smile, grateful for the olive branch they're offering me, but this is just the beginning of my apology tour. "Well, I appreciate that, but I'd like to apologize to all of you for not being honest from the jump," I say, my hands turning to fists beside my teacup. "I knew there was a possible connection here before I was even transferred to Bethnal Green, and it was deceitful of me to walk amongst you all without sharing that information."

"It can't have been an easy thing to open up about," Gareth says, his voice deep as his eyes stare directly into mine. "Not sure how I would have handled it."

"We're a forgiving family," Vaughn interjects, his face sincere. "We've all been through a lot after losing Vilma when the kids were so young. I didn't handle it well and needed all of my kids to forgive me for one thing or another."

They all nod in agreement, but I still feel a vibe from Booker that's not at all forgiving.

"So, you're our brother," Vi proclaims with a laugh, covering her mouth nervously.

"Half brother, yeah," I correct, feeling weird saying it out loud at last.

She smiles, and her eyes blink rapidly. "Why the bloody hell couldn't you have been a sister?"

She throws her hands upward like she's cursing the gods above, and everyone breaks into genuine laughter at the table, including me. It feels good. It's broken the ice that was melting way too slowly beneath our feet.

"I'm afraid I didn't get much say in the matter," I reply with a shrug. "I just find it incredible that I grew up loving soccer without any knowledge of any of you."

"Football," Vi adds with a wink.

"It's in our blood," Camden states, watching me thoughtfully as Tanner nods in agreement.

Vi touches my arm to bring my attention back to her. "Is it true your mum and our mum were close when they were in college?"

I nod slowly. "Yeah, that's what she said. I don't know a lot about their friendship, but she was at Vaughn and your mom's wedding."

"Wow," Vi gasps with a wobbly smile.

"And the funeral," I offer, and then curse myself when the mood in the room shifts instantly. I say the only thing that comes to mind next. "I lost my dad a little over a year ago, so I know a bit about how that feels."

Vi nods, and her eyes bend with emotion before she quietly asks, "Do you think your mum would like to have a chat with me sometime?" She offers me a shaky smile. "We were all so young when our mum passed, which means we're painfully desperate for stories about her."

Vi's voice cracks at the end and tears fill her eyes. I feel a bit stunned by that unexpected request, and I glance around the table to see all four of the brothers' eyes locked on me as they await my answer. It's then that I realize that I too can give something to this family. Or at least my mother can.

"I'm sure she'd love to share stories about your mom," I respond with a smile. "She said that she was on a private jet that Vaughn booked for your mom to come to one of his matches at Man U just after they'd met."

"Really?" Vi says with a garbled laugh and turns her attention to her dad.

"My God, I'd completely forgotten I did that," Vaughn replies, his face awestruck with red-rimmed eyes.

"She's heading back to Boston soon, but maybe we can do a dinner before she leaves," I offer, and Vi's returning smile is heartwarming.

Camden clears his throat. "How weird is all of this for you?"

"Crazy weird," I rush out, and he nods. "And I want you all to know that I don't expect anything from any of you. I'm honestly just grateful I don't have to live with this secret anymore. It was eating me alive."

They all give me looks of sympathetic understanding.

"Well, I'd certainly like to have a relationship with you," Vi states and smiles sincerely at me. "Dad says you and Daphney are close, and she is my sister-in-law, so it seems natural for us to get to know each other."

My body tenses at the mention of Daphney's name. "Daphney and I are just friends." The words feel foreign and wrong on my tongue even though I've said it around this group countless times. The only problem now is, it's true. But also, not true because I don't know how I can be friends with someone I've fallen in love with.

I want to take the words I said to Vi back and spill my guts about the whole fucked-up situation, but this isn't the time nor place nor people, for that matter. I've got Link and Knight for that.

"That might be for the best," Gareth says firmly, and Vi frowns over at her brother, who's looking at me with a dubious expression. He narrows his eyes at me in warning. "Things could get awkward for you around here if you ever broke her heart."

My chest aches, and I wonder briefly if any of them would ever consider that it's Daphney who's the heartbreaker. They know her and Hayden better than they know me, so I guess I can understand where their loyalties lie. "I can understand that."

"Don't listen to Gareth," Vi scoffs, waving her brother off as she shoots me a reassuring smile. "All four of my brothers have mucked things up with their relationships more times than I can count. Then they all come running to me for advice, and I have to find a way to fix the mess they've made. It's a very common brother/sister dynamic that you'll become well aware of in due time, I'm sure. If you and Daphney have something between you two, don't you dare let these prats scare you off her. She's a wonderful person."

I force a smile that I'm sure looks pained. I appreciate that Vi is talking to me like I'm part of the family already, but the truth is, her words about Daphney cut me deep. Daphney *is* a wonderful person. And the fact that we were over before we even started is something I'm not sure I'll ever be able to get over. Living next door to her will be hell, especially because the very last thing I want to be is her friend.

I refocus my attention on everyone else at the table. Vi has made it very clear she wants a relationship with me, but I'd like to know where everyone else's head is at.

I steel myself before asking, "So, what about the rest of you?" I cough softly as my voice gets caught in my throat. "Where do I stand with all of you?"

"I want you here as much as you're comfortable," Vaughn says, pinning me with a serious look. "I do not want to replace your father in any way, but I do want to get to know you, Zander. I want to hear about your upbringing and cheer on your future. I want to be a part of your life in whatever way feels right for us."

I nod slowly at Vaughn, and an image of my dad washes over me. I can't imagine how he'd feel about all of this. Would he be hurt? Jealous? Disappointed?

Then I remember the kind of man he was at his core. The kind of man who wanted to raise another man's baby without hesitation. The kind of man who supported my soccer aspirations even though soccer was never his thing. The kind of man who put together a damn highlight reel to get me a college scholarship. The kind of man who gave me the best example of being a father so that someday, I can be that to my own children.

My dad won't be hurt. He'll be happy for me. Maybe even proud that I had the courage to put myself out there like this. And I got it all from him.

"I'd like that very much," I reply to Vaughn because it's the truth. I'm not trying to replace my dad, but I'm not going to act like I wouldn't appreciate a connection with the man who is responsible for my existence.

"Teammate is just another word for family, isn't it?" Tanner says, sitting back and crossing his arms over his chest casually. "I'll take either label with you. What's another Harris brother to add in the mix?"

"He's a Williams," Vaughn corrects, and Tanner tips his head to me respectfully.

My brows twitch as I feel taken aback by his surprisingly poetic declaration. He certainly never sounds like that at Tower Park.

"My daughter Sophia is adopted," Gareth offers, folding his hands in front of him. "But I don't need to share DNA with her to know she's mine. I'm sure in time, I'm going to feel the same way with you."

A knot forms in my throat as Camden adds, "I say, let the fun begin. It'll be nice having another sibling to fuck about on the pitch since these two tossers are retired."

I laugh and shake my head. "I think I had your number at Emirates."

"Bollocks," Camden scoffs and waves me away. "One bad game doesn't a career make. I have a lot more years in me to embarrass you out there."

"I look forward to it," I respond, nodding fondly.

All eyes turn to Booker because he's the only one who hasn't made any clear indications on how he's feeling about all of this. Of all the brothers, I've felt the closest to him since coming to London. We did form a bromance, and we certainly had chemistry on the field. We protected the net together like brothers...because we were.

Booker shifts nervously in his seat and looks away to avoid eye contact with me. "Booker, I understand if you need time," I state, my voice thick in my throat. "You and I have become close since I joined the team, and I'm sure you feel betrayed that I didn't tell you about all of this."

Booker's jaw goes taut as he nods and stares at his hands. "I just…" He looks up, and I am shocked to see his eyes are full of tears. "I feel sort of cheated. Like we missed out on an entire lifetime with you."

Relief and sadness pummel me at his words because they aren't bad like I thought. In fact, they're good. Very, very good. My voice is hoarse when I reply, "Luckily, we're the young ones, so our lives are only just getting started, right?"

Booker half smiles and nods at me. "I guess I didn't know how bad I needed a sweeper in my life."

My returning smile is genuine. "I'm grateful to have a keeper."

"Oh, for the love of fuck all," Tanner scoffs, throwing his arms out wide. "If this is going to turn into a sappy made-for-TV movie, someone pass me a bucket because I'm going to be sick."

Booker rolls his eyes as Gareth turns a lethal glare to Tanner. "We've all had to put up with you and Camden licking each other—"

"Licking what?" I gasp, but my words go unheard.

"Bacon sandwich rule this and bacon sandwich rule that," Gareth continues. "They were roommates, and they married best friends and had bloody kids in unison. Honestly, Vi and I have had to share a sick bucket for years, watching the insane things these two do with each other. They cannot begrudge Booker the chance to have a little brother for the first time in his life."

"It was just a joke, mate." Tanner's nose wrinkles. "No need to get personal. And the bacon sandwich rule is a sacred Harris tradition. You lick it, it's yours. Zander, come here so I can lick you and claim you as my brother."

Gareth rolls his eyes and turns back to me. "I hope you're ready for this lot, Zander. We're…a lot."

I laugh and shake my head. "I think I can manage."

The score is tied thirteen all. It's the highest-scoring soccer game I've ever played in, but apparently, when you're kicking a ball around in the backyard of Vaughn Harris's house, and kids are involved, all bets are off.

The teams are divided up as follows:

Me, Booker, and Camden are on one team with Rocky, Teddy, Milo, and Bex.

Gareth, Tanner, and Hayden are on the other team, and their little ones consist of Sophia, Oliver, and Josephine.

Camden and Tanner are both holding their youngest ones in their arms as they play too, so technically, my team also has little Porter, and Gareth's team has Alexandra. Watching Camden and Tanner go at each other with kids in their arms doesn't look like the safest thing I've ever seen, but the moms are all sitting on the patio drinking tequila sunrises and laughing, so clearly, they are confident in their husband's abilities not to drop a child.

Thankfully, I have the best teammate and shadow ever...Teddy. Little dude won't leave me alone. But he's actually got some sweet feet for a five-year-old, so I'm using him to my full advantage.

When Cam and Tan get caught in a battle to steal the ball from each other and start knocking over kids like dominos in the grass, Gareth, Booker, and Hayden run in to save the day. I hang back with Teddy.

"Don't chase the pack," I state, touching my pointer to my temple. "Hang back. It'll break loose, and that's when we attack."

Teddy nods, his eyes wide and excited. As if on cue, the soccer ball flies toward me. "Cut to the net!" I yell to Teddy.

He does exactly as I say, and I send a left-footed pass right in front of him. He doesn't slow his pace a bit as he swings his right foot onto the ball, shoots, and scores!

His little fists thrust into the air as I knee slide over to him. "Yes, my dude! Great goal!" I hop back up on my feet and pick him up, holding him in a superman pose as I run in front of all the moms who hold their hands out to give him a high five.

We end our celebration tour with Booker, who's laughing and shaking his head as I set his kid back down on the grass. He ruffles Teddy's hair and says, "Nice one, Teddy Bear."

"Let's play again!" Teddy squeals and grabs my leg.

"Give Zander a break. Go terrorize your brother." Teddy's eyes alight with that prospect, and he takes off in pursuit of Oliver without looking back. Booker braces himself on his knees, working to catch his breath. "This game was more intense than yesterday's!"

"You can say that again," I reply, still heavily breathing myself.

I watch as everyone drifts away to their own prospective areas of the backyard. Gareth and Vaughn are discussing the potential of a yellow card on Tanner and Camden. The girls are pouring drinks for the guys while the kids still run around with endless amounts of energy. It's chaos but happy chaos.

"Do you guys play a game every Sunday?" I ask curiously.

"More and more as the kids are getting older." Booker stands and walks over to the table where Vi has just placed several bottles of water. He calls over his shoulder, "Do you want any?"

"Water? Yeah," I respond, jogging over to join him.

He half smiles at me. "I meant do you want any kids?" My eyes nearly bulge out of my head, causing Booker to laugh. He shoves me lightly. "Don't look so scared. You're good with them."

"Well, I'm pretty sure I need a partner to have kids, and that doesn't seem to be in the cards for me currently." I take a bottle of water off the table and unscrew the lid.

Booker eyes me thoughtfully. "Do I dare ask about Daphney? I know you wanted me to butt out yesterday, but you'll quickly learn the Harris family are slow learners."

I smile and sigh. "I wish I knew what to tell you."

"You're going to have to do better than that," Hayden's voice interjects from somewhere behind me. He bumps my shoulder as he reaches over to grab a water bottle.

The guy hasn't spoken a word to me since he joined us for dinner over an hour ago. He barely made eye contact with me this whole evening, and I kept expecting him to take me out during our friendly game of backyard soccer.

I clear my throat. "What do you mean?"

"I mean, I'm going to need more details about what happened between you two before I let you walk out of this house today." Hayden narrows his eyes on me. "All I know is that you texted me looking for her, and she won't tell me anything. Clearly, something's up because last time I saw you two together was at the wedding, and you guys were obsessed with each other." He exhales heavily and voices the next question in a slow, punctuated threat. "What did you do?"

I wince as images of Daphney singing, dancing, and laughing at that wedding flood my memory. It was honestly one of the best nights I've had since moving to London. Maybe one of the best nights of my life. It makes me wish I could go back and just be honest with her. Then again, would Daphney and I have become what we became if she knew the truth before we slept together?

I direct my gaze to Hayden and answer honestly, "I lied to her about all of this." I point at the Harris family all milling about the backyard without a care in the world. "About my supposed connection here. She thinks I was using her to get close to everyone, and I suppose I was, but that doesn't negate the fact that I fell in love with her along the way."

Hayden blinks back at me with an unreadable expression on his face. "Did you tell her that?"

I shrug. "She knows."

He takes a long drink and licks his lips slowly as he puts the cap back on his bottle. If he's shocked or pissed, he's hiding it well. With a resolute nod, he pats my shoulder before walking back to join the rest of the family. I watch him sit down next to Vi like I didn't just confess that I used his sister for my own personal gain.

"Should I be afraid?" I whisper to Booker, a pit forming in my stomach.

"Yes," Booker responds quickly.

45

It's 11:11...Make A Wish

Daphney

Phoebe: I don't understand how you don't want to drink with me. It's Saturday night!

Me: I don't want to leave my flat.

Phoebe: Alcohol is magically portable. I can even stuff a bottle of wine in my bra.

Me: I just want to be alone, Pheebs. I'm sorry.

Phoebe: You're wallowing.

Me: I'm working.

Phoebe: That's just grown-up talk for wallowing. You can't stay cooped up in the flat forever. Eventually, you will run into him.

Me: I know. I just don't want to go out tonight because I have another jingle to work on, and since Zander is in Watford for a football game, this is a good time for me to work before he gets back later tonight.

Phoebe: Has he still not replied to any of your "matey banter" texts?

Me: No, nothing. He hates me.

Phoebe: You broke his heart.

Me: He broke mine first. It's better this way.

Phoebe: For who exactly?

Me: It was never going to work out.

Phoebe: And why is that again?

There's a knock on my door, and instantly, I want to thump and hug my best friend because she never was one to respect boundaries. I march over to my door and swing it open. "Phoebe, I was being…" My voice trails off when I see it's not my persistent best friend on my doorstep. It's my brother.

"Hiya, Daph," Hayden says, walking in like he owns the place, which I guess he kind of does.

"Hayden, what are you doing here?" I ask, glancing at the clock to see it's after seven already.

"Just coming by to check on the building." He walks around my flat, inspecting the walls, the ceiling, my music equipment. He even annoyingly strums my guitar before sitting down on my sofa and spreading his arms out wide.

I cross my arms and hit him with a flat look. "Why are you really here?"

An awkward look flits across his face. "I have to take photos of the flat next door because I'm going to be looking for a new tenant soon. Zander said I could drop in sometime today while he was away at a football match."

Chills erupt over my entire body. "Zander is moving?"

Hayden nods slowly. "It would appear so."

I shakily lower myself onto the sofa beside my brother, struggling to get over the shock of this news. This past week has been worse than the first week we didn't speak. The first week, I was too angry to feel the loss of him. Now that I know we're over and can hear him coming and going through these stupidly thin walls, it's like emotional cutting every single day. This is exactly why you don't get involved with a neighbor. Him leaving shouldn't feel this devastating to me. I should be rejoicing. I should call up Phoebe and tell her it's time to drink after all.

But I'm not rejoicing. I'm crushed. "Do you know why he's moving?" I inquire, my voice sounding weak.

His brows lift. "I suspect it has something to do with you."

"What did I do?" I ask, feeling defensive because it wasn't me who lied in our relationship.

Hayden shrugs, adjusting the leather cuff around his wrist that he always wears. "I was hoping you could tell me. Zander was a little light on the details."

"So, you talked to him?"

He nods. "A bit. You know he came to Sunday dinner last week, right?"

I nod slowly. "How did it go? How did everyone take the news about his connection?" Nerves take flight in my belly as I wonder if it went badly and this is why he's moving.

"It went about as one would expect it to go. The Harris family is populating so much. What's another half brother to throw in the mix?" Hayden laughs and shakes his head. "The Harrises are good with dysfunctional, and nothing says dysfunctional like a secret love child no one knew about for twenty-five years."

I huff out a laugh at that very astute description my brother has given this whole situation. "But they were accepting of him?" I ask, holding my breath.

Hayden tilts his head at me. "Why do you care so much?"

"I don't." I turn my gaze forward and cross my arms over my chest.

"Yes, you do," Hayden says, poking his finger into my cheek. "Your face flushes bright red when you're lying just like Marisa's used to."

My wide eyes snap to Hayden's. "I haven't heard you say her name in a long time."

He shrugs, but I see the emotion in his eyes. "I saw 11:11 on the clock today, and it made me think of her."

A smile lifts my lips. When Hayden was struggling with depression and blaming himself for Marisa's death many years ago, the time 11:11 was a bit of a trigger for him. It took him to a very dark place, and it was me who told him that 11:11 was lucky and he should make a wish on it every time he sees it. It's kind of Hayden's thing now. He's such a different person today than he was back when he was struggling with addiction after Marisa's death. I don't give him enough credit for the work he puts in.

"I miss her," I state, feeling my chin tremble. "Sisters are good to talk boy stuff out with."

"Brothers aren't so bad either," Hayden says, frowning at me. "Seriously, Daphney, talk to me. Help me understand how what Zander did was so unforgivable."

"So you're on his side?" I retort.

"I didn't say that." He holds his hands up. "I'm always on your side, but if you're on the wrong side, as your big brother, it's my job to drag your arse over to the right side."

My teeth clench with anger that I'm having to rehash this whole nightmare again. I've been torturing myself with it for two weeks now, and I hate it. Now Zander gets to move out and be the martyr of this story. It's complete shit.

"Zander used me to get closer to the Harris family." I lay it all out there, no longer caring if Hayden will hate Zander for knowing the truth. If he can't even text me to tell me he's moving, he doesn't deserve my loyalty.

"I know." Hayden blinks blankly back at me.

My brows furrow because it appears he needs more to go on. "He didn't tell me about all the important stuff going on in his life."

"He didn't tell you about one thing," Hayden corrects.

"Wondering if Vaughn Harris is his birth father is a pretty significant life detail!" I exclaim, my head jutting forward defensively.

"What's really going on here, Daphney?" Hayden asks, his eyes piercing me with a knowing look. "Because my bullshit meter is pretty bloody good, and from what I can tell, the only bullshit I'm picking up on is coming from you."

"What?" I screech.

"Trust me, I tried to find the bullshit in Zander. A footballer living next door to my sister was going to be watched like a hawk. But from all of my run-ins with him, the only flaw I picked up on was his struggle to keep his eyes off you."

I roll my eyes to the ceiling. "So because he looked at me a lot, you have dubbed him worthy? That's the most ridiculous thing I've ever heard of."

"It's not that he looked at you, Daphney. It's *how* he looked at you. That bloke is in love with you."

"No, he's not," I spit back, anger flashing sharp and hot in my veins. "You don't know what you're talking about."

"You don't know what you're talking about," Hayden volleys back. "Daphney, if you're pushing him away because you don't love him back… great…I'm on your side. I will help him move out of this building myself to get him away from you. But if you're pushing him away because you're scared of giving him a second chance? My darling, I am living proof that second chances exist for a reason. I would literally not be alive if it wasn't for second chances."

My eyes fill with tears as a devastating pain breaks into Hayden's voice as he brings up a part of his past that we never ever talk about.

Hayden's past is dark and tortured, and there were years when he didn't exist in my world because he was too busy living in a hell of his own making. But now he's here, on my sofa, in my flat, as a father and a husband, and checking up on me like a proper big brother. I'm so lucky he's still here.

Hayden shakes away the haunted look in his eyes as he reaches forward and wipes a tear off my cheek. "You, Theo, Mum, Dad...even Leslie, you've all forgiven me for a lot of mistakes in my life. You can't tell me that what Zander did even comes close to what I did."

"No," I garble, my voice thick with emotion. "But Hayden, you don't understand. I'm in love with him, and it happened so fast and so easily. And it's bigger than I can handle. I'm terrified of it."

"But why?"

"Because I don't know if I can trust myself to choose the right person!" I cry, the emotions of the past two weeks spilling out of my eyes. "What if Zander is just like Rex?"

"He's not," Hayden scoffs, waving his hand dismissively. "Rex and all the blokes you've been with in the past were all a bunch of tossers."

"Thanks for that," I croak, wiping aggressively at my tears. God, big brothers can be such bullies.

Hayden levels me with an unamused look. "It's true. None of them had that thing...that spark. Tell me the minute you met Vi, you didn't know she was the one for me."

I huff knowingly at that idea. "You guys were perfect for each other."

"Because she had that spark," he says confidently. "And you and Zander have that."

I swallow the painful knot in my throat. "What if we don't work out? What if something else like this happens? What if he lies to me again? What if he doesn't love me, and I lose him?"

Hayden rests his hand on my shoulder and pins me with a sincere look. "Daphney, you can't let fear of losing love stop you from falling in love. Falling is the best part, especially when you've found a partner to pick you up. Vi still picks me up every bloody day. That's what great love is. You have to try for great love, no matter the risk."

Hayden's words are firm and unrelenting as they puncture holes in the protective shield I've been holding up ever since I heard Zander talking about me through the walls. The truth is, I wasn't crushed because he hid this part of him from me. I was crushed because I loved him and feared he didn't love me back. That fear caused me to push him away, and now that he's moving, I'm scared he's done pushing back. Do I even deserve a second chance after refusing to give him one?

46

Zander's Song

Zander

I'M SPENT BY THE TIME OUR BUS ARRIVES BACK AT TOWER PARK AFTER our match against Watford. It's dark, I'm hungry, and all I want is the comfort of my own bed.

Pain slices through me when I remember how empty my bed has felt all week. It's ridiculous how you can become addicted to the feel of someone beside you after one night. Seriously, how did Daphney swing that? How did she make me miss the feel of holding her body in my arms after one fucking night? My neighbor has bewitched me, and it's why I had to call Hayden to ask about breaking my lease agreement.

I can't sit in my apartment and listen to her work on her music through the walls every day and not feel my heart break with every note she plays. This week, I've been busy and distracted with my mom's departure and having a dinner with her and Vi before she left.

Next week, I'll be alone with my thoughts again and living next door to the first girl who ever broke my heart. It's too much for one person to handle. Moving somewhere else and getting a fresh start is what's best for everyone.

I say my goodbyes to Link and Knight, telling them good game as I make my trek back to my apartment. Sighing heavily, I trudge up the three flights, hating that I can still picture Daphney's ass on that first day when she showed me my place. Will I even be able to live in London if I'm not with her?

Fuck, I have it bad.

I roll my eyes when I'm standing in my hallway and see that bright pink mouse house set back up. Since I was gone today, I suppose she felt brave enough to reset the trap without getting seen by me. She's been doing a wicked job of avoiding me this week, which I guess is good. I don't want to see her any more than she wants to see me.

I change into my lounge clothes and flop onto my bed, gazing up at the lights pouring in from the street. They cast strange shadows on the walls that perfectly match my mood.

Suddenly, the strumming of Daphney's guitar fills my room. I sit up and frown, glancing at the clock to see it's after eleven. Daphney never plays this late. In fact, I assumed she was working at Old George tonight, but even if she wasn't, she still wouldn't be playing this late. She'd be too worried about upsetting all the other neighbors in the building. Maybe I'm the only neighbor who can ever hear her, and she's done being polite to me. Maybe this is her reigniting neighbor wars. If so, she's picked the wrong neighbor because I'm done playing games.

I jump out of my bed and stalk over to the thin sheetrock in my living room. I raise my fist to pound on the wall when her voice reverberates into my space, causing me to pause.

It's the tune of "Hey There Delilah," but she's changed the lyrics into something I've never heard before.

Hey, hiya there neighbor
When you moved in next door to me
You seemed a pretty mystery
But instead, you brought some history
In your bags.
I should have assumed a big snag
There always is.

Hey, hiya there neighbor
You're painfully awfully noisy
Don't you ever hear your alarm clock ring
Surely you know that it annoys me
Just wake up.
Or I might just blow up.
Like I do.

But then, you read Bridget Jones.
And I was cursed.
By your smile.

But then, you read Bridget Jones.
And I was cursed.
By your eyes.

Hey, hiya there neighbor
Turns out your noises don't bother me
Because your kiss has freed me
From an awful past history
That was a drag.
How did you know just how to act?
To bring me back?

Hey, hiya there neighbor
When you told me you were a dancer
I had no idea I was looking for
Someone to take a chancer
On me.
You seemed to know instinctually
You were what I need

But then, you read Bridget Jones.
And I was cursed.
By your smile.
But then, you read Bridget Jones.
And I was cursed.
By your eyes.

The biggest thing I've come to find
Is that my heart just isn't mine.
It was yours the moment that you read that book.
Soccer Boy, I want you to know
That I'm so sorry for all I've done.
I want you to forgive me.
Cuz I forgive you.

Hey, hiya there neighbor
Turns out I'm kinda in love with you
Is it possible that you could love me too

Or have I tarnished everything today?
Because I let my fears get in my way.
I'm so sorry.

Zander, I love you.
Could you try to love me too?
Zander, I want you to stay.
Could you stay a little while?
Could you stay a little while?

Like a dream, I hear Daphney singing a song about me. About her. About us. Her voice is pure and honest, and I follow it out of my apartment, hearing it in the hallway, and outside her door that's propped open, like she's expecting me. I walk into her place and find her sitting in the tub with her guitar in front of her. She's in her silk pajamas, and her hair is in a messy bun on top of her head.

She's never looked more beautiful.

The final note echoes off the tile walls, and her wobbly smile finds mine. My entire body trembles from the multiple proclamations in her lyrics. She's not just saying all the things I've been wanting to hear for the past week. She's singing them.

"You're going to wake the neighbors," I say with a weak laugh because I'm an idiot and can't come up with anything more meaningful at this moment.

"Was only trying to wake one neighbor." She moves to get out of the tub, and I quickly offer her my hand. She takes it, and the sensation of our skin touching is equal parts heavenly and painful as she steps down onto the tile floor.

She looks so small as she stands barefoot and vulnerable in her bathroom. Her guitar is clutched tightly in front of her like she needs to hold it for protection.

"Did you hear the whole thing?" she asks, her blue eyes glowing magically in the vanity light.

I nod slowly, my eyes searching hers. "It was beautiful."

"I started it weeks ago when I went back to my parents' to work on that jingle." She laughs dryly. "I changed a few lines tonight because... well, a lot has changed from then to now."

I swallow the knot in my throat. "Has it?"

"Yes, which is why I pushed you away." Her chin trembles as she looks to the side, avoiding my eyes as she struggles to say the next part. "You were just supposed to be fun, Zander. I was just coming off a horrible relationship, and you were going to be a fun distraction from my stressful and somewhat disappointing life. I wasn't supposed to connect with you and care about you and your mum and your cookie addiction. You weren't supposed to read *Bridget* bloody *Jones!*"

My face contorts in a confused laugh. "I'm sorry?"

"Don't be sorry." She sniffs and shakes her head, her eyes blazing into mine. "I'm besotted with you. Your playfulness and surprising tenderness have been the best surprise of my life. I pushed you away because I was terrified that I could be hurt again like before, but I've only now realized that before doesn't matter. No man has ever made me feel the way you make me feel. Orgasms included." She expels a garbled laugh and adds, "And I'd rather live in fear loving you than live safely not loving you."

It's as if she's taking the words right out of my mouth. And hearing her say all the things she sang before means so much to me. But she's still not all the way there yet.

"I don't want you to be afraid, Daphney," I state, reaching out to grab her chin so she's forced to look at me. I need to see her face when she answers this question. "What scares you so much about me?"

"That you don't love me back." She shrugs helplessly. "I guess I just can't imagine you care that much when you hid such a huge part of your life from me."

My brows furrow at the evident pain on her face. She doesn't get it. She doesn't get that it was because I love her that I hid this from her. I inhale a deep breath and move closer to her, my body hovering over hers, aching to wrap itself around her but knowing she needs to hear these words first.

"Daphney, the reason I didn't tell you was because since the day you and I started, you have been my safe place. My ally." My voice cracks at the end because the truth of those words is heavy and real. "At a time I didn't know where I belonged in this world, you made me feel at home. Your place, my place, the damn hallway with the mouse house. If you were there, I was home. And I didn't want to taint the one good thing in my life that I could depend on. That was you, Ducky. You and your music and your horrible fucking cookies."

"What?" Her face shifts from emotional processing to confused annoyance in the blink of an eye. "My cookies?"

"They were awful. They tasted like playdough and bad feelings," I reply softly, my nose wrinkling with disgust.

"Do you honestly think this is the time for jokes?" Her tone is scolding as she drops the guitar to her side. "I just sang a song begging you to forgive me, and you're making jokes."

"I'm not joking," I state seriously, feeling my stomach roil just from talking about them. "I mean it, Ducky. You can never make those cookies again. I love you, but those cookies taste like prison food and regret."

She huffs out a noise of indignation, and then her dazzling blue eyes snap to me. "Wait...did you just say you love me?"

"Hell yes, I did," I reply, taking a step closer to devour the sweet, shocking innocence stricken all over her face. She's so blind, but I will make it my life's mission to make her see this.

"Surely you're just having a laugh?" she rasps, her breath quickening as she props her guitar on the wall with shaky hands. She turns to gaze back up at me with nearly manic eyes.

"Does it look like I'm laughing?" I stare unblinking at her because I need her to see this, to accept it, and to let it wash over both of us so we're clean and new again. "I love you, Ducky."

Her chin trembles as she sputters, "Why the bloody hell didn't you say this to me before?" The hollows of her cheeks suck in as her brows pinch together in her classic punishing glower. She goes from sad to emotional to angry in like three seconds. It's an impressive emotional range. Right now, she's giving me warring neighbor vibes like when we first butted heads, and I'm here for all of it.

"Sweetheart," my voice is a plea as I cradle her face in my hands so she can see the sincerity in my eyes. "I knew I loved you the moment I looked up into the stands at Emirates Stadium and saw you standing there in my team colors. I've never wanted someone wearing my jersey more in my fucking life. I'm sorry I didn't say it sooner. I guess I was scared too, but after hearing your song, I know for certain that I love you. I'm not *in* love with you because that indicates I could fall *out* of love with you. And this love I have for you feels like a forever kind of love. Like the kind of love my dad had for my mom. The kind of love he must have had to raise me and claim me as his own his whole life without hesitation. I love you, Daphney. I love you."

My voice breaks on the end, and I gasp for breath, realizing I forgot to breathe during all of that. But it's stuff that's been circulating in my head for the past two weeks, and it feels so damn good to get it out.

Daphney inhales a shaky breath as her eyes well with tears. She reaches up and cups my hands over her cheeks. Her smile and tears are infectious, and I can't help but mirror them as she says three little words to me. "Please don't move."

I laugh and press my forehead to hers to inhale the sweet scent of her that I've missed more than I ever thought possible. "Those weren't the three words I was expecting."

"No?" she croaks, biting her lip nervously. "Then don't move and maybe I'll get to them."

I pull back and shake my head at her. "You're very bossy when you're groveling, you know."

"I'm a girl who knows what I want." She shrugs cutely, and then her face grows serious as her eyes lock with mine. "I love you, Zander."

Hearing the words spoken out loud sends a rush of adrenaline through my body stronger than anything I've ever felt in soccer as I crush my lips to hers. I don't bother asking for consent with this kiss. The second she gave me her love, her lips became mine. *She is mine.*

My hands map her neck, back, and hips, pulling her close and committing all the curves of her body to memory. She tastes soft and sweet, and I can't help but marvel at the fact that I barely made it two weeks without her. Deep in my gut, I know there will never be another girl I want to kiss as much as this one in my arms. That thought would have scared me a year ago. Now, I welcome it. I welcome someone permanent in my life. Someone I want to fight for and who is willing to fight for me. That song, her voice. Those are some of the best fighting words I could ever imagine coming from her lips, and it fills my heart with relief to have this feeling in my heart reciprocated at last.

Daphney skates her fingers into my hair and gives my strands a light tug. *God, I missed her hands in my hair.* Her tongue teases my bottom lip as I bite down on hers. I want to consume this woman. I want to take her to bed and never leave it. I want to whisper that I love her over every inch of her flesh until she's so fucking spent, she can't find the words to tell me to stop.

"Wait, I have one question," she gasps, using my hair to pull my lips off her neck. "Are my cookies really that bad?"

"God, yes." I sigh, and my lips are back to feasting on her flesh. "Did you seriously never try them?"

"No, they smelled awful."

My body shakes with silent laughter as I pick her up and carry her to bed, feeling better than I have in a very long time.

47

Dream Weaver

Daphney

THE TWINKLE LIGHTS CAST A GOLDEN HUE ON OUR BODIES AS WE LAY on my bed, facing each other in a mess of rumpled sheets and naked limbs. Zander's lips are still caressing my neck and shoulders, his hands sculpting over my bottom in a way that makes it obvious he is in no way ready for bed. How does he have the stamina for this? He played a Premier League football game today. Honestly, the man is superhuman.

"So, how are you feeling about everything?" I ask, forcing his lips away from my breasts so I can look into his beautiful hazel eyes.

He blinks sleepily. "Big fan of makeup sex."

I smirk and narrow my eyes. "I mean about the Harrises. Hayden came by earlier today and told me a little bit about last Sunday."

Zander's brow quirks. "Is Hayden who I have to thank for this epic makeup sex? That's going to be an awkward thank-you card."

I roll my eyes and pinch Zander's side. He tenses, and his muscles bunch in a really delicious way that makes me not at all ready for bed either. "Come on, I want to know. You've been dodging my texts all week."

"I was giving you a taste of your own ghosting medicine," Zander says, and a look of sadness flits across his eyes.

I stroke his cheek and try to soothe that pain on his face. "I promise no more ghosting ever. No matter how bad we fight, neither of us ghost each other."

"Deal." Zander presses his forehead to mine. "I missed the shit out of you, Ducky."

I inhale his manly scent. "I missed you more."

"Impossible." His eyes look vulnerable in the darkness as he adds, "You know I'm going to screw up again, though, right? I'm no relationship expert, but no one is perfect." He pauses for a moment before continuing,

"I guess I need to know that I can screw up once in a while and not have you doubt me again."

"I won't doubt you," I say, stilling my hand in his hair, and hating the insecure look on his face. "I doubted me. I doubted that I was strong enough to survive this if we don't work out."

"Well, that's an easy problem to fix. We just won't break up." He gives my side a cheeky squeeze and bites his lip teasingly.

"That would be helpful," I reply coyly, my body arching into his. "But mostly, Hayden made me realize that love is worth the risk. And I feel even safer knowing you love me too."

"I do love you," Zander says, pressing his lips to mine. "I'm sorry you couldn't see that more clearly." He goes silent for a moment as my fingers play with his hair. "I think I struggled to open up to you about everything because I wasn't certain I even wanted to know the truth. And since you were already so connected to the Harris family, if I told you…there was no way to take it back."

I nod thoughtfully because it's an answer I can completely empathize with. "Are you glad it's all out in the open now? No regrets?"

"No regrets." Zander exhales heavily. "If I didn't at least try to have a relationship with them, I would always wonder. And everyone has taken the news surprisingly well. Even the grandkids know, and they're sort of like…who cares, let's play soccer. It's funny."

"That's incredible." I smile back at Zander. "I would have loved to have been there to watch it all unfold."

"I think it was good I did it on my own." Zander's eyes look hopeful in the darkness as he gazes back at me. "But I'd love if you came with me tomorrow to Sunday dinner."

"I wouldn't miss it." I lean in and kiss him again because it's impossible not to. "I think you're very brave."

"I think you're very brave," Zander murmurs, nuzzling my neck. "Going to a soccer match with my mom last week without telling me. I'd swear you have balls of steel if I hadn't just been down there a few minutes ago and gave it a full inspection."

"Don't be vile," I say, laughing and shoving him away. He pulls me in closer, and it feels so delicious, it's hard to stay focused. "Your mum was nice. I liked meeting her, even under less than stellar circumstances."

"Well, you certainly made a good impression," Zander remarks, tucking his face into my neck and inhaling deeply. "Now I'll have to do the same with your parents."

"Oh?" I ask, my brows furrowed as I stare down at Zander, who's burrowing into my neck too much to see if he's having me on. "You want to meet my parents?"

"Well yeah." He peppers kisses along my shoulder like he didn't just say the sweetest thing in the world. "I mean, I clearly already won over your brother. Now I just better hit the rest of the Clarke family with my dazzling charm so you can never get rid of me."

My heart positively sings with all this future talk. I know Zander said he loved me but asking to meet my parents is another matter altogether.

"I could probably arrange something," I squeak out, trying to sound aloof.

"Maybe you can bring them to one of my games," he says, rubbing small circles on my hips. "I want you at more of my games. And if that means I must attend your music gigs, that's a price I'm very happy to pay."

"What music gigs?" I bark, gripping his hair to force him to look at me.

He winces at the tight tug on his strands, but the smile on his face is undeniable. "Well, you're not going to be able to sell your music to a record company if you don't start playing it again."

"And what makes you think I even want to sell my music anymore?" I narrow my eyes on him.

"Come on, sweetheart," he murmurs as he pulls me in close for a soft, sultry kiss. "You've got a hit song about me just waiting to be discovered. Plus, after all you did to help me with my mom, it's my turn to help your dreams come true."

48

FA Cup Champions

Zander
A Few Months Later

ROAN BOOTS A GOAL INTO THE NET JUST AS THE REFEREE WAS ABOUT to blow his whistle to send the game into extra time. I drop to my knees in awe, looking up at the scoreboard in disbelief. Bethnal Green one, Chelsea zero. I can't believe we just fucking won.

My eyes swerve to the stands for Daphney, but I'm immediately distracted when something pummels me in the back.

"We fucking did it!" Booker cries as he crushes me into a tackle hug on the ground. "We just won the fucking Cup!" Booker laughs at me from his position on the ground as he grabs my face in his gloved hands and pulls my head close to plant a sloppy kiss on my forehead. "We did it, bruv!"

The nickname of bruv is British slang for brother, and it's what all four of the Harris Brothers have taken to calling me the past couple of months. I hear it at every Sunday dinner, on the pitch, on the various double dates Daphney and I have gone on with the siblings and their spouses. It's even been picked up by the media now that the truth of my connection to the family has been released to the public.

It feels good.

Vaughn let me decide if we were going to tell the press about my relation to him. He said if I never wanted anyone to know, he would understand. But I knew hiding it put us at risk of them finding out anyways. Then it would look as though I was a dirty little secret and the headlines would be ugly.

And really, why did I care if the press knew or not? Just because I share DNA with Vaughn Harris doesn't make my dad less of my dad. The fact that I'm related to the Harris family just means my inner circle has grown. And after a couple of months, I realized that the Harrises have this uncanny way of bringing people into their world with very little effort. They feel like that old friend from childhood that you never talk to but when you run into each other, it's like no time has passed. It's weird, but comforting. It was that comfort that gave me the courage to release a statement.

The media accepted the news far more positively than I ever expected. Jude had given me horror stories of the British newspapers but it seems like since the Harris Brothers have all settled down and started families, the press is much kinder to them. I guess I was gifted that kindness by default and I will do my best to not take it for granted.

Booker takes off down the field to celebrate with the rest of the team as I stand back up and jog over to the sidelines. My eyes find Daphney's. She's sitting next to my mother who flew out yesterday to catch the final. Both of their arms are raised as they cheer me on and as I make a beeline toward them, I'm shoved off to the side by yet another brother.

"Fucking aces of a game, bruv!" Tanner yells, following his shove up with an aggressive hug. "Jesus Christ, I have a stiffy that could cut glass!"

He gestures lewdly to his groin as I laugh and shake my head. "Good luck with that."

He waggles his eyebrows playfully and jogs onto the field, allowing me to continue my pursuit of the woman in the front row. My eyeline is impeded by Vaughn Harris next. He has tears in his eyes as he holds his arms out wide to me.

I embrace him happily, knowing this is a big day for him. He's been saying at nearly every Sunday dinner that if we win the FA Cup, he's finally going to retire, and he means it this time. I'm sure this is an emotional moment for him, knowing that his life is about to change.

"Your dad would have been so proud," Vaughn says, cupping the back of my head.

A knot lodges in my throat as I point up to the sky. "He's watching."

Vaughn releases me, giving me one more proud, fatherly look before I move through the back bench with my mind on a very different goal.

I jump over the barriers blocking off the stands and pull myself up over the gate in front of the front row. When my eyes lift, I see Daphney situated in the middle of the entire Harris horde and my mom sitting right beside her. They both have tears in their eyes as I push through the people all pressing in close for the spectacle.

I make it to Daphney and she's staring at me in complete confusion as I reach behind my head and pull my jersey off. The crowd around us cheers loudly as I stand there shirtless, sweating, and breathless, but I block out all the noise as I move past Daphney.

"For Dad," I say, handing my jersey to Mom, whose face crumples with emotion.

She nods as she reaches out to yank me into her sobbing body. We hold each other for a long time, both of us imagining Dad here in the stands cheering louder than even Vi Harris, who has serious pipes on her. Dad's spirit is here, though. I'm certain of it.

Mom pulls back to wipe the tears off her face and releases me. She pulls my jersey up to her cheek and closes her eyes.

Without pause, I turn on my heel next and grab a surprised Daphney. I plant my lips so firmly that her squeal of surprise gives me a little stiffy too. The crowd loses their mind around us as I dip her in dramatic fashion. Her joyous laughter against my lips is the thing that dreams are made of.

I whip her back onto her feet, cupping her face in my hands as I say the three words I could say to her forever. "I love you."

She smiles and presses her forehead to mine. "I love you."

I struggle to let her go and head back down onto the field. I should be out there with my team. I should be celebrating this win with my brothers and my coach. But honestly, I don't think I would have been here without Daphney. She opened my heart up after I spent over a year with it closed off. She taught me to be vulnerable and honest. She challenged me in ways no woman has ever challenged me, and she pushed me to be a better man. I want to be the best man I can be for her. I found the one whom my soul loves, and I want to marry this girl. She is my family.

And if these past few months have taught me anything, it's that family isn't about genetics, or DNA, or even the people who raised you—family is about who you love and who loves you.

Family over bullshit.

49

Final Score

Daphney

"**W**E'RE LITERALLY TAKING A BATH IN BATH." ZANDER CHUCKLES, pulling me back against his chest as I step into the giant soaker tub.

I snuggle into his arms as bubbles pop and fizz around our bodies. Zander's season is finally over, and he surprised me with this gorgeous little period retreat in Bath. We hopped on a train yesterday, spent the entire day in bed today, and are finally thinking about cleaning ourselves up to check out the historical village. That is, if we can be bothered to put on some clothes when we're done here. I dare say, laying in a tub with this man as his lips tease the shell of my ear every time he talks sounds better than a dinner out.

This place is apparently where Santino and Tilly went on their honeymoon. Zander got all the details from Santino after they had their big meeting last week to determine if he would stay at Bethnal Green or go play for another club.

Zander has spent the last couple of months trying to decide if leaving the club would be a good idea after all. Not because of issues with Vaughn, Tanner, and Booker, but because he wondered if he might have a better experience getting to know them away from the football pitch.

However, Bethnal Green seems to be in a bit of transition. Shortly after Vaughn made his long-awaited retirement announcement, Coach Zion shocked everyone by accepting an offer at another club leaving two very large vacancies at Bethnal Green.

I don't think anyone was surprised when Tanner Harris was offered the head coaching position. Now we're all awaiting an announcement for who will be the new manager. It'll have to be a strong person to handle the personality of Tanner.

Regardless, that still left Zander in the position of playing for his family, and he wasn't sure that was a wise move. He doesn't know a family like the Harrises, who literally do everything together. Last weekend, they all attended Sophia's footy tournament. There were so many people taking photos, I actually felt bad for the girls playing their arses off on the pitch. The Harrises are in no way inconspicuous. I could see why Zander might want a little space from them since he grew up in a small family and isn't used to being a part of such a ruckus.

However, Booker Harris can be very convincing and he's apparently a master at grand gestures. He made it very well known that he wanted Zander to stay at Bethnal Green. In fact, he came up with a whole presentation at Tower Park that involved all the Harris grandchildren. It was like a weird little sporty variety show where all the children marched up and presented their memorized line that included a reason for why Zander must stay at Bethnal Green.

It ended with Booker's twins fighting and one of them hurting their wrist enough to go to the hospital for an X-ray, but Zander got the message: Bethnal Green one, other football club nil.

The true deciding factor, however, was more than likely the incredible extended contract offer that Santino and Tanner presented to Zander. Apparently, there had been interest from other clubs for Zander, and Bethnal Green wanted to ensure he would be very happy wearing green and white for the foreseeable future.

I thought I had a good idea of what footballers made. *I was wrong.*

"We'll have to take more little trips like this now that you've decided to stay at Bethnal Green, and we don't have to worry about you getting transferred to a club far, far away anytime soon."

"I was never going to a club far away," Zander growls into my ear and reaches under the water to punish one of my unsuspecting nipples.

I squeal and shove his hand off me, my body heating with arousal at that little point of pressure. My God, I've lost count of how many times we've had sex in that adorable little four-poster bed. When will I get enough?

"Don't you discipline me," I say, my hands dipping under the water to slide underneath his muscular legs that are propped up on either side of me. "I'm still cross at you for trying to move out of our building."

"Well, you weren't speaking to me," Zander argues, and even

though we're teasing each other, I can hear the pain in his voice. "I wasn't exactly thinking rationally."

He had to have been in a very dark place to call Santino and request a team transfer and then ask my brother to break his lease agreement. All this while he was having an incredible season with Bethnal Green. I hate that I put Zander through all of that pain by not just forgiving him right away, but I guess we had to have some bumps in the road to find ourselves on the right path in the end.

Honestly, the past few months of going to Sunday dinners at Vaughn's house with Zander feels as if he was always a part of that family. He fits in so easily with everyone, and they've wasted no time bringing him into different portions of their lives. He's even volunteering at several of Gareth's youth football camps this summer. If it weren't for Zander's American accent, I'd have thought he really did grow up with the Harris Brothers.

My brothers have even become rather matey with Zander. It helped that he came home to Essex with me a month ago for my niece Marisa's birthday and gave both her and Rocky tickets to see *The Lion King*. The bonus present was that it would be Zander and me taking the girls to the musical in the West End, giving Mummy and Daddy a proper night off. It was a genius idea on Zander's part. If ever there was a way to win over my two brothers, that was it.

My ovaries practically did the salsa when I saw Zander holding the hands of my little nieces as we walked into the theater. He was wearing a suit, and the girls were wearing matching dresses that my sister-in-law Leslie made. I hate to be "that girl," but it was impossible not to imagine having babies with the man after I saw him wipe away a tear during the "Circle of Life." My niece Marisa caught him crying, and they argued about whether it was dust or not.

Ovaries, uterus, vagina…all my lady parts were dancing.

Zander sighs a contented sigh in my ear before saying, "I was thinking it might be fun to do a quick trip to Boston before the preseason training starts."

"Oh?"

"Yeah, you can manage the time off now that you're not working at Old George anymore, right?" His arms appear from beneath the bubbles as he wraps them around my shoulders and kisses my temple.

I purse my lips together. "I still do have to work, you know. Those jingles don't sell themselves."

"Oh, I know," Zander says, smoothing bubbles up over my chest, just grazing the swells of my breasts. "But you've sold two jingles in the past two months. Surely, you deserve to be rewarded for your hard work."

"What do you think this trip is?" I ask, gesturing to our quaint little getaway.

Zander huffs a displeased noise in my ear. "A train ride for a weekend getaway isn't a real getaway."

"Well then, let's go home if this means so little to you." I make a move to get out of the tub, and Zander growls into my ear as he tightens his grip on me.

"First of all…I love when you call our place home so you're not even arguing with me very well right now."

I roll my eyes.

"Second of all, is it really that awful of a request for me to want to take you back to Boston and show you off a bit?"

"No, it's not awful," I reply, biting my lip excitedly.

The truth is, I'd love to go home with him, but I still feel a bit weird letting him pay for me. Zander makes a lot more money than I do, and since quitting Old George to focus more on my music, I feel the pressure to be successful. It's why I keep saying yes to the jingle projects. It gives me a safety net while I book some gigs at various pubs that do *not* pay well, at all.

Trying to sell my music is not an easy career path. But I'd be lying if I didn't admit that it's brought me back to life in so many ways. Last weekend, I played at a club in Soho, and Zander, my brothers, their wives, and the entire Harris crew were out in the audience, cheering me on. It was thrilling, and the club was packed. I may not have been discovered by any big record company, but I was reclaiming my music to the universe, just as Zander encouraged me to. That alone was worth more than any record deal. Nearly.

"So, what would we do in Boston?" I ask, tucking away my pride because when your boyfriend wants to take you to the home he grew up in, you just have to say yes.

"Well, the first thing I want to do is show you around Boston

College so we can have sex on the field I got my first big break on." His voice sounds boyish, naughty, and sexy all at the same time.

"Oh, how exciting," I exclaim, my voice rising in pitch. "So, I can be one of the many girls you shagged when you were there being a footy manwhore. Do I get my own patch of grass or do you use the same patch for everyone?"

"Sweetheart," Zander says, biting my earlobe. "I only bring marriage material girls on my sacred Boston College soccer field."

Water sloshes onto the tile floor as I swirl around to face him. I stare up into his eyes, my brows in a deep scowl to see if he's winding me up. "Are you saying I'm marriage material, Soccer Boy?"

His eyes grow tender as he reaches out and wipes a splotch of bubbles off my cheek. "Isn't it obvious, Duckmeister?"

I roll my eyes and smile. "I can never tell when you're serious or just having a go."

He brings his finger to my chin and touches my dimple that I'm certain is on full display. "You know damn well I'm being serious."

I inhale a sharp breath, my naked body erupting in goose bumps over his as I gaze into those beautiful hazel eyes. *Damn him, he is serious.*

I swallow down the gleeful knot in my throat as I calmly reply, "So that's where our relationship is at now? We're going to start talking about marriage?"

He shrugs. "First I thought you could move in with me, officially."

My jaw drops. "Move in with you? We've only been together four months."

"We're at each other's place all the time as it is," he points out. "And I'm traveling enough with soccer that you'll still have plenty of alone time to sit in my bathtub and practice your music to get the good acoustics. And there's plenty of room at my place for your music equipment."

I bite my lip nervously. "You're serious about this?"

He nods slowly. "Plus, you're my favorite alarm clock ever."

I shake my head and pin him with a knowing look. The prat still snoozes his alarm a million times. If I didn't wake up happy next to him every day, it really would be quite irritating.

"I guess I could be your roommate with benefits instead of your neighbor." I roll my eyes, like this conversation is such a bother when in fact, my heart is practically bursting with excitement.

Zander shakes his head and laughs. "Careful now, if you want to label us, I'll go ahead and put a ring on your finger and see how you like that label."

I press my head to Zander's chest and refrain from squealing like a silly little girl. Although, I dare say the final score of the relationship between Daphney Clarke and Zander Williams will be a hard one to call. I guess that makes us both winners.

(All Amy Daws books are available in Kindle Unlimited)

ACKNOWLEDGMENTS

Write a secret Harris Brother, I said! Your readers will flip out, I said! It'll be fun, I said. Was it fun? Was it? That's still up for debate, I think. (insert exhausted emoji here) This book very likely gave me PTSD, but in the end, I really am proud of it, which is a lot, coming from me!

And there is no way I could have finally typed The End without my team of helpers that were with me through every painful minute along the way. Julia, Jennifer, Beth, Ashley, Kathryn, Megan, Jessica, and Franci… you women saved me with this book! I've learned that communication is how I get through moments when I'm struggling, and I deeply needed you all at various stages throughout this story to push my fat ass up this mountain. I cannot, absolutely *cannot* thank you all enough for helping make this book what it is today. And of course I must praise my British eyes, Teresa and Lynsey! I appreciate my friendship with you guys even more than your British prowesses!

Thanks to Jenny Sims for editing and Julia Griffis and Lydia Rella for proofing and Champagne formatting for making this book look pretty.

Praise must go out to my readers too because honestly, throughout writing this book, I wondered how they heck any of you have continued to show up for me book after book after book. Seriously, I don't see the appeal because I'm a self-deprecating mess with low self-esteem, but thank you for allowing me to continue to pretend to be a writer!

To my hubby and my Lolo…thanks for tolerating my episodes of distress, self-doubt, anxiety, and all the negative emotions that come when you pour your heart into something difficult. Lolo, your hugs always got me through the darkest moments.

And finally, to my special six angel babies in heaven…you're still at the top of my prayers. Thank you for giving me the emotional strength to get through a story like this and for inspiring me to be on this crazy journey as an author.